TAKEN SHE SLEPT

A pulse-pounding Detective April Fisher crime thriller

C.J. GRAYSON

Detective April Fisher Thrillers Book 1

Joffe Books, London
www.joffebooks.com

Cover art by Nick Castle

ISBN: 978-1-83526-219-1

CHAPTER 1

She slowly opened her tired, heavy eyes, her pupils adjusting to the sliver of blinding light bursting through the crack in the closed curtain. Immediately she registered the pain in her head, and she knew why. The faded drumming in her temples increased as she moved her head, realising the tablets she'd taken before she went to sleep hadn't worked as well as she'd hoped.

She dropped her head back on the pillow, brought both palms up to rest on her face, and closed her eyes again for a moment. With an incredible effort, she rolled over gently — her naked, fragile body felt like it had been hit by a freight train — and reached out of the covers, picking up her phone off the bedside table.

It was still early. Just before 6 a.m.

She checked for text messages. There was one from a random number ending in 344. She smiled after reading the words several times, but, being honest, she couldn't remember his face very clearly, although big, bushy, slug-like eyebrows were familiar in her foggy memory, sitting above his deep, dark, alluring brown eyes. She remembered his smell too — scents of wood and aromatic aromas on his throat and neck which she could still taste on her lips and

1

tongue. The thought of it released a phantom smell as if he lay beside her.

Was he still there?

With wide eyes, she cautiously tilted her focus across the bed, finding it fortunately empty, thank God. She sighed in relief she was alone, and sat up slowly, dropping her head into her hands.

Why did she do this to herself?

She wasn't a teenager anymore. Nevertheless, it didn't stop her saying yes to DS Matthew Phillips when he suggested going out after their shift ended last night with the others, did it? Only a couple, she had agreed.

With a heavy sigh, she pulled the covers off her legs and swung them onto the soft carpet, soles sinking into the fluff. She slouched for a moment, staring at the half-open door to her en suite, wishing the pain in her head would go sooner rather than later. She played the night over in her mind like an incomplete, fuzzy film.

DS Phillips had said he was going to Last Orders, a family-run pub that had been their local for as long as she remembered. He said the usual crowd were going, like they did every Wednesday night, and she didn't take much persuading, agreeing to have just one drink before going home. By 9.30 p.m. and five drinks later, someone had suggested calling a taxi and heading into the city. PC Alex Clegg had proposed the daft idea, not needing to be in work until 3 p.m. the following day.

DS Phillips had enjoyed Fisher's company so much he'd persuaded her to join them. But drinking wasn't her strong point; it never had been. Generally, she knew when to stop and take herself home, but something was different last night. She'd let herself go more than usual. Maybe it was the stress of the latest case — Elaine Freeman, the thirty-nine-year-old care worker who'd been found dead on the bank of the River Irwell in Drinkwater Park.

The first bar was the Alchemist on New York Street. The bus stopped and they all got out, but Fisher stood outside, staring at the doors of the bar, feeling a flutter in her stomach. DS Phillips noticed and frowned in her direction.

'What's up, April?'

'I think I'm going to go home,' she'd replied.

Behind her, the taxi driver had quickly pulled away from the kerb to join the busy Manchester traffic with its late commuters and evening diners. Flashes of headlights split the incoming darkness; horns beeped every so often; lights spilled out of shop windows and bars, along with the faint music that filled the warm dusk.

'Too late now,' he had joked, the taxi now out of sight. 'Come on, stay for one. It'll be fun.'

DS Phillips smiled at her persuasively. He had worked with DS Fisher for several years now. Side by side, they'd seen a lot together, both starting as constables and working their way across to CID. They knew the city and knew the people. It was a game of chess they had learned over their years.

DS Fisher mulled it over in her fuzzy head and dropped her shoulders. 'Maybe just the one . . .'

He smiled and headed for the door.

DS Matthew Phillips was tall, clean-shaven, and had slicked-back hair. Looking at him, you might have thought he was in his early twenties, but once you spoke with him, you realised he was charismatic, confident, and a little charming, if geeky-looking. He'd just turned thirty-seven, putting him three years older than DS Fisher. He was engaged to a woman called Janice and they had a two-year-old boy called Dominic, who was named after one of Janice's uncles.

'Come on . . .' he had said, holding the door for her.

She curled her dark, short hair around her ear and smiled, showing her perfect white teeth, then followed him inside. They spotted their colleagues at the bar and went over, absorbing the loud music they couldn't seem to escape from, and joined in with their laughter and jokes.

It wasn't long before they moved on to the next place, which was louder and a little more modern: brighter lights, upbeat music, arguably a classier client list. Two heavyset doormen stood on either side of a double entrance glass door, both calm with their shoulders back. PC Alex Clegg claimed his friend was DJing, so had shown one of the doormen something on his phone as he entered. Whatever it was, one of the doorman had directed them to a special seating area upstairs which, thank God, was quieter and less populated than downstairs. A young blonde girl in her twenties wearing a black apron sauntered over, with eyes that glowed and a smile that made people go weak at the knees, to take their drink orders.

In that same place was the guy with the phone number ending in 344. She waited for her drink at the bar and felt something brush against her arm. She turned and a man apologised for accidentally getting too close. They got talking, and soon she found herself sitting alone with him, chatting about life. It wasn't long before he leaned in to kiss her, which took her by surprise. It had been months since she'd been on a date, even longer since she'd been in bed with someone. Her last relationship had been a flop. Although it had looked to be a promising one with a guy who seemed decent, it only lasted two months. She wanted to pull away from the kiss but she couldn't; months of isolation had yearned for it — to touch someone, feel someone close. His soft lips were something she couldn't deny, so she wrapped her arms around him, pulled him closer, and enjoyed the drunken, care-free moment.

They were in a taxi ten minutes later heading somewhere he'd directed the driver, but she couldn't hear where. Instead, she slumped on the back seat, her brain not quite comprehending the words due to too much alcohol clouding her ability. It wasn't long before they got out and . . .

She can't remember what happened after that.

She rubbed her face, picked up her phone from the bed, and read the message again. It was sent at 1.07 a.m.

What time had she got in?

Had he come back here, stayed for a while, and then left?

4

Was he still here somewhere? In the toilet? Downstairs?

Looking up from the phone, she searched for any evidence of him, any items not belonging to her. As far as she could tell, everything looked normal and as it should be, apart from the clothes she'd worn the night before, heaped near her closed bedroom door.

Her phone beeped. It was a text from DS Phillips asking how her head was. She replied with one word.

Sore.

She pressed Send.

He immediately replied.

Where did you go last night? I was worried. I called you at midnight but got no answer.

She frowned, wondering why she didn't answer his call.

Got in a taxi, went home. She hit Send.

The reply was quick: *Don't lie. I saw you walk out with the guy from the bar.*

She scrunched her face up and rubbed her eyes again, unsure how to reply. She did silly things like this when she drank too much. That was the exact reason she tried not to.

Another text came from DS Phillips: *Sorry. None of my business. Just looking out for you. See you at work.*

She smiled thinly before she put her phone on the small table, got up, her head still pounding, and made her way over to the en suite, her body feeling heavy and off-balance. Leaning in to turn on the shower she felt something knot in her stomach, making her grunt suddenly, the pain like a sudden jolt. She remained still until it passed.

The warm shower water felt good running down her skin, washing away the night before, the foggy moments of missing memory. Judging by the text from the guy with the number ending in 344, it was clear he'd enjoyed her company.

If only she could remember his name or an exact image of his face.

After she washed her hair, she stayed in there for a little while longer, before reaching up for the mixer handle to turn the shower—

5

'What the hell?' she whispered, scowling. Her eyes narrowed. 'What on earth?'

There was a black mark on her wrist which looked like a bruise. Where on earth had that come from? She turned the shower off and checked other parts of her body. A similar bruise was on the opposite wrist. She held the darkened mark, gave it a light squeeze with a thumb and finger, realising it was very tender. She focused on the rest of her body — her arms, her stomach, her shoulders, her legs, and thighs.

'What on earth . . .' she muttered.

There was bruising between her thighs, inches away from her vagina, inside of both legs. She stared wide-eyed at the marks, then vomited the drinks consumed from the night before, projecting onto the tiled wall within the shower enclosure.

She lowered to her knees, breathing slowly and deeply, contemplating what may have happened, watching the vomit seep down the wall, rancid aromas of sambuca, lager and bile filling the small enclosure.

She took a deep breath and stood up, rinsing her mouth out with shower water, then opened the glass door, picked up the towel, and stepped down onto the tiled floor. She turned to her left and saw her dull, grey reflection in the mirror. Her big brown eyes were lined with heavy, tired bags. Her soaked dark hair clung to her shoulders and the side of her exhausted, puffy face.

She didn't want to think about it, but she couldn't help it. Had she been raped? She couldn't have been that wasted, could she?

She dried herself quickly, determined to keep her emotions under control, and noticed her fingertips. They were red. Upon closer inspection, she was convinced it was someone's blood.

'What the hell happened last night?' she asked herself.

CHAPTER 2

DS April Fisher was sitting on the edge of her bed, unsure how she was feeling. The events of last night weighed heavily on her, the sense of being used and taken advantage of, but not knowing made it so much worse. She took a breath, picked up her phone from beside her, found his number, and pressed Call. It was answered on the second ring.

'April?' said DI James. '*This* is early.'

'Yeah, I'm sorry about that, boss.'

'It's fine, April. What's up?'

'I-I think I need to go and get checked out, sir,' she said, her words quiet and reserved, barely reaching his ear.

'Checked out? I don't understand, April,' he replied, a little concern creeping into this voice. 'What's happened?'

She closed her eyes and dipped her head. 'I went out last night with the work lot. It was only meant to be for a couple, but I . . .' She fell silent, slowly shaking her head. 'I got carried away, boss. Stayed out too late.'

He stayed silent and waited. DS Fisher didn't drink regularly, but when she did, having one too many wasn't exactly news to anyone.

'I-I can't remember really getting home. I-I've just showered and think something terrible has happened.'

'What is it? Please tell me what's up,' he asked softly.

'There's bruising on my wrists and my inner thighs, boss.' She paused a beat and stood up. 'I think I may have—'

'Go to the hospital, April. Go and get checked out. Let me make a phone call and get you seen to straight away. Do you need anyone to go with you?'

She considered the question, but decided she'd be okay doing it alone.

'Just let me know if you change your mind and I'll send someone along, okay?'

'You got it.'

'Take your time too. Don't be rushing back. I know we have ongoing cases, but you do what's right for you.'

'Appreciate that,' she said, before ending the call.

After her check-up, which had been painless and easy because of DI James's phone call to one of the doctors, she headed straight to work, walking into the Greater Manchester Police station only two hours later than usual. She wore her usual dark-blue jeans and a white T-shirt, mostly covered by her navy jacket which she always left open regardless of the weather. Fisher wasn't model good-looking, but there was something attractive about her — the way she carried herself, how she held her chin up and looked people in the eye. She smiled at Paul sitting behind the reception desk to her left as she walked through, swiped her key card to enter through the next door, and paced boldly down the brightly lit corridor towards the office as if everything was normal. Spotlights shone down on the freshly painted walls, and the scent of lavender hung in the air from multiple plug-in air fresheners dotted around that the DCI had insisted on.

If anything could be said about DS April Fisher, it was that she was resilient. Always had been.

She'd almost reached the office when a door opened close by. 'Hey!'

She paused and turned to the familiar voice of DI Thomas James, who stepped out of room 14 and edged the door closed.

'April.' He dashed over to her, his long, brushed-back hair bouncing as he moved. '*What* are you doing here?'

She frowned and tilted her head to one side. 'What does it look like? I'm working, boss.'

DI James sighed, gave a sad smile. 'How did it go?'

Fisher nodded twice. 'Good. They said they'll let me know. Now, if you'll excuse me, I'm already late for work.'

She was about to turn and start for the office when he took hold of her wrist to stop her. The tenderness sent a jolt up her arm, causing her to wince and quickly pull away.

'Shit! Sorry, April,' he said, realising what he'd done. 'Are you okay?'

She rubbed her wrists lightly, but didn't reply. 'I'm fine, Tom.'

'If you need to take some time off, you can, you know.'

'I'm fine, Tom. I-I can't remember getting home last night, and when I tried to open the door this morning, I couldn't find my keys, so I used a spare set I keep handy in the drawer. I then found my other keys on the gravel near the wall out the front. Glad they were still there, but I don't even know how I got in the house. It's all a blur, Tom.' The stiffness in her posture softened.

He placed a soft hand on her shoulder. 'Please, go home, April,' he said in a soft, soothing tone. 'Get some rest. Take a few days off.'

Taking a few days off to sit in an empty house was the last thing she wanted to do; it would only give her time to think about last night. She needed to put it behind her, move on, and solve the latest case. She didn't have time to wallow in self-pity.

She lifted her head an inch. 'Anyway, I don't know for sure that's what happened.'

DI James knew Fisher was stubborn enough to be awkward. If she believed strongly about something, she'd speak her mind, regardless of being an anomaly. She didn't feel the need to agree with the opinions of others. Some didn't like it and others were jealous. But on some level, she got respect for it, because an honest colleague was the type you wanted to be around, and someone you could count on.

'I need to tell you that DS Phillips is aware.'

'Sir, why? How does he know?'

'He cares for you and, as your supervisor, I feel it's important that he knows.'

She sighed heavily and broke eye contact, looking towards the office.

'You said the guy texted you last night?' he asked.

'Just after one o'clock, yeah.' She nodded.

'Give that number to Harry. He may be able to trace it.' DI James glanced down at his watch then focused back on her. 'We'll get PC Baan and PC Jackson to go to the bar, see if they can see him on the CCTV. Can you remember what he was wearing?'

She told him the man wore a red Oxford shirt and black jeans.

'Alright. I've already spoken to Liam about it. Give him a ring and let him know the finer details.' Liam worked at the council control room, monitoring the city's CCTV systems.

'We got a taxi . . .' she reminded him.

DI James nodded, remembering her story. 'We'll be able to trace the taxi.' He reached out and placed a palm on her small shoulder again. 'We'll find him.'

She half-smiled in reply.

'When the results come back from the hospital, please let me know, April.'

'You got it, boss.'

A moment of silence hung between them. 'Are you sure you don't want to go home?'

'I have work to do. We need to find the sonofabitch who killed Elaine Freeman.'

'That's true, but your well-being is more important to me right now. I think—'

'How long have you known me, Tom?'

DI James frowned, tilted his head in thought, and removed his palm from her shoulder. 'A while . . .'

'Long enough to know that it would do me no good at all sitting at home. I need to focus, Tom. I need to be here.'

He seemed to consider her words carefully.

'Fair enough. If there's anything you need, just let me know.' He stepped around her and made his way down the brightly lit corridor away from the office.

DI Thomas James had just turned forty. He stood over six feet tall and carried a few pounds more than he used to. If you said two years ago he'd feature on the front cover of a *Men's Health* magazine you wouldn't have questioned it. But things changed. His long-term girlfriend, Amy, whom he'd been with since his mid-twenties, had finally become sick of him working long hours, and subsequently, sick of being second best to his job and the gym. She'd given him plenty of ultimatums, demanding he changed his ways and put more time into her, but fitness and health was important to him. When Amy had left, it had affected him. He visited the gym less. He became vacant in himself, more withdrawn, less active, and lacked the enthusiasm that filled his personality. Everyone had noticed it within a few weeks but hadn't mentioned it — unsure if they could, given his position. After all, people were entitled to slip a little. He was, however, still good-looking. His piercing blue eyes, tanned skin, and chiselled jaw still earned him brownie points with the ladies, along with the shiny, brushed-back hair he hadn't had cut in over two years but maintained. It suited him, most people thought. The odd person suggested he looked stupid, one of whom had tried growing their own hair the previous year and failed miserably, so maybe there was an element of jealousy.

After DI James reached the end of the corridor and disappeared, DS Fisher continued through the frosted double doors and entered the office. Her second home. Recently it had felt very much like her first.

Idle conversations filled the air, computer keyboards tapped, chairs slid in and out. The room itself was a large rectangle, with the constables and sergeants located at one end and CID at the other. Non-CID constantly reminded

CID that they had the more luxurious half, with the more modern desks and comfier, newer chairs. Even the spotlights were different, apparently shining proudly in their white, superior brilliance.

Fisher walked through, smiling at some of the constables, one of them being Ashleigh Baan, a thirty-seven-year-old PC with short blonde hair and a curvy figure, whom she'd known for a long time and considered a very close friend.

'Morning, Ash,' she said, with a wave.

'Morning, boss,' she replied, with a smile. It was an inside joke between them after working side by side as constables before Fisher decided she wanted to work in CID. They spoke to each other daily; Fisher often listened to how Baan's long-term boyfriend had recently blown over two hundred pounds on silly bets. 'Men,' they'd say, shaking their heads in despair.

Fisher wouldn't know, not anymore. Her last relationship had lasted only two months. Was it that she didn't have time for men or was it that she didn't want to get too close, didn't want to give them the chance to leave her and break her heart again?

Or was it the miscarriage from the relationship before? Probably. After all, being with someone for four years then going through a six-month pregnancy with complications leading to a miscarriage would break most people. Chris couldn't take it anymore and left, adding further pain to her already fractured heart. So for now, she'd settle for being alone. If what had happened last night was any indication of what the world had to offer in the way of men, then she'd ride the train alone for a while until she was sure about the right one.

She reached her desk in the right-back corner of the room, and was greeted by a weary look from DS Matthew Phillips. His long brown coat hung on the back of his chair. Even in the height of summer it didn't deter him from wearing his knee-length brown jacket — it was almost his trademark, as if he took his role of detective too seriously, slotting into an old American noir detective film. He wasn't ugly, but there was something geeky about him, something that a certain type of woman would find attractive. His slightly bucked teeth when he smiled seemed to be the focal point of his face. And his laugh was sometimes a little over the top, which some barely tolerated.

His look was neither a smile nor a frown. It was a knowing look, a look which told DS Fisher that he'd be there for her whenever she needed him.

She smiled sadly at him, dropped her bag off her shoulder, placed it down on her desk in front of the keyboard and sixteen-inch monitor, and pulled out her chair.

'You okay?' he asked softly, placing his hands together.

She slid across, reached over with her left hand, and placed it on top of his. 'I'm fine, Matthew.' She drew her hand away and slid back across to her computer, indicating that was the end of that particular conversation. DS Phillips admired her ability to move on with things.

'Let me know if you need anything,' he said quietly before he returned to his own monitor.

In the square office space in the corner of the large room that CID primarily used, there were four desks. Two on the left hand side and two on the right hand side, facing away from each other. On both sides, there were two computers positioned a metre apart atop a long desk with a chair in front of each screen. For privacy, a blue board had been positioned between each monitor to offer privacy, but simply leaning back to peering sideways would deem the idea pointless. DS Fisher sat beside DS Phillips on the left, and behind them to the right, DC Arnold Peterson used one of the computers and the other was a spare now that. DI James had his own office now, somewhere to carry out his role more privately, so they didn't see him as frequently as they used to. They were a close-knit team, with years of experience and friendship between them. DC Peterson was the youngest at thirty-two, two years behind Fisher, and proved it with his occasional childish jokes and witty personality. It wasn't a bad thing, even though he often rubbed up DI James the wrong way; it seemed like he was used to it, and accepted the way Peterson was.

'What did I miss?' asked Fisher, referring to the morning brief. She typed in her password and pressed Enter. The screen transformed to her background image of Yoko — the yellow Labrador she used to have, but he was no longer fit and had to be put down last year — and opened her emails. Yesterday's morning brief focused on the current murder investigation of thirty-nine-year-old Elaine Freeman, who'd been found on the riverbank nearly two weeks ago, with both eyes and hands missing. The horrific blood-soaked scene spoke volumes of violence, a scene that would stay with the team for a long time.

'Nothing more than yesterday, April. Not yet anyway.' Phillips noticed Fisher glance his way, intrigued, and decided to expand. 'Pamela Boone was in with us too, going over some things.'

Pamela Boone was the senior forensic officer within the Greater Manchester Police. At sixty-two, she had over forty years of experience and usually worked by herself. If she needed assistance she would ask, but it was a rarity, obviously depending on her workload or the size of a crime scene.

'And what did she say?'

He finished typing and turned towards her. 'Can you remember Pam finding the footprint from what she thought was a walking boot?'

April nodded.

'Well, turns out it's from a steel-toed boot.' Phillips explained that Boone had sent the picture and measurements off to a digital specialist, who had come back after two days with a make and model of the shoe.

'What type?'

'A trainer safety shoe. Warrior. Size nine. From Arco.'

'Interesting.' Fisher turned away thinking what it could mean, what difference it would make. It could potentially mean the suspect was a tradesman or something similar. But it does mean they can now contact Arco and request the

14

recent sales of a size nine in that specific type of safety shoe. No doubt the list would be endless. But it was something to work with.

'Anything else?'

'We went over the scene again. Looked at the photos. Nothing you haven't seen before.'

When they got the call on Friday morning almost two weeks ago from the elderly lady walking her dog, Dispatch had described her as frantic. Mary, who'd had over twenty years' experience as a call handler, did her best to comfort the lady who said her name was Jackie, and had asked her to move away from the body but to stay close by as officers were en route. The body of Elaine Freeman was found on a grass bank of the River Irwell. Jackie had walked past at six in the morning, explaining she walked her dog Elly, a-ten-year-old Labrador she'd had since she was a puppy, every day, always going that route along the river and backing onto herself to return home. It had been ten minutes since she had turned down the footpath by the side of the shops on Littleton Road and noticed the body of Mrs Freeman a few minutes later. Jackie was hysterical, even by the time PC Baan and PC Jackson had arrived, which was a few moments before DS Fisher, DS Phillips, and the rest of the team had turned up.

They called for Pamela Boone immediately, who, after being there less than ten minutes, had determined her time of death — less than six hours before.

In the office, they had photos pinned up of Elaine Freeman, one of her severed wrist, another close-up of her face, clearly showing her missing eyes. The whole team, including DCI Andrew Baker, had been feeling the pressure on this one. Not only was it a horrific murder that had taken the city of Manchester by shock, but there were also many similarities with the murders of Kathy Walker the year before and Joan Ellison the year before that. In both cases, the victims had been found with missing eyes and missing hands.

Tomorrow would tally two full weeks that Elaine had been found. The Greater Manchester Police had nothing to go on apart from the footprints found at the scene. They were getting frustrated, as were the people of Manchester, who were living in fear that the same killer had now murdered their third victim and was still free to roam the streets. The media, especially the local paper, had been calling them the 'Hand-Eye Killer'.

Fisher and her team had concluded that there was a pattern. The MO was similar, as were the victim's appearances — all three victims having long dark hair, blue eyes, and a comparable height and build. It was hard to miss.

Fisher opened up yesterday's report to re-read before sending it on. She would have sent it last night if not for going for those *few* drinks. She shook her head, regretting that decision, and wondered what actually happened last night with the man in the red shirt. Her social life wasn't the greatest, but it wasn't something that bothered her. She spent much of her time at her parents' house and seeing her younger sister, Freya.

Her mother, Freda, had retired two years ago. For longer than April could remember she'd worked part time at a pottery shop in the city centre to keep herself busy while her father Mark was at work; he, like Fisher, was also in the force but had been retired for nine years. He hadn't drifted over to CID like Fisher had, although he'd had the chance and made his way up to inspector before calling it a day after ten years. He was very good at his job — well respected by his peers at all levels and offered promotions many times, but satisfied where he was.

Just before she hit the send button she heard footsteps behind her.

'April . . .'

She swivelled to see DI James standing there, who used a palm to smoothly brush back his long hair and place an A4 folder down on his desk with the other. 'DCI Baker needs to see you, April.'

'Right now?'

He nodded twice.

CHAPTER 3

PC Ashleigh Baan slowed the marked Astra and pulled over, stopping right outside the front of the Alchemist on New York Street.

'Are we okay parking here?' PC Jackson gazed around, unsure of the area.

Baan smiled. 'Of course. It's a loading bay anyway. Don't worry.'

'Why are we here?' he enquired, looking her way. It was the second time he'd asked, but she hadn't answered him.

'DI James needs a favour.' She turned to him and noticed something in his face. 'Don't worry, he's cleared it with Inspector Thorne.'

He nodded then pushed his lips out. Inspector Thorne was someone they didn't want to get on the wrong side of, that's for sure.

'What's the favour?'

She waited a second, her mouth open as if she was going to say something, then decided not to.

'Ashleigh?'

Moments of silence passed.

'We need to find someone,' she finally said. 'Need to track his movements. He was in here last night and got into a taxi. We need to ask them if we can see their CCTV.'

'Who is it?' He was clearly intrigued by what this some-one had done that warranted a favour from CID.

'The *who* is not important.' She returned her focus to the street through the front windscreen. 'It's the *woman* he walked out with that's important. And, potentially, *what* he did to her.'

'Speak English to me, please.'

'April Fisher was here last night, Adam. She went out with our lot. According to DS Phillips, she was talking to a guy before they disappeared and got into a taxi.'

'Then what happened?' He leaned forward a touch.

'April found bruising on her wrists and the inside of her thighs this morning. She woke up with a bad head, can't remember what happened or how she got home. She doesn't know for sure, but there's a possibility she was, you know . . .'

'Jesus.' He looked away, and shook his head in disgust.

'Yeah. So, we need to find out who he is. April went to the hospital earlier for a check-up . . .' She made several circles with her hand to indicate where the checks were made; PC Jackson was on her wavelength. 'So, she's waiting on results.'

'Okay,' he replied, finding a new lease of determination. 'Let's go, then.'

She took hold of his forearm gently. 'Keep this to your-self, Adam. DI James trusted me not to tell anyone.'

He nodded sincerely. 'Of course.'

They both opened their doors and stepped out into the hot summer air that felt warmer than yesterday; the air was stuffy and humid and both of them were suffering in their uniform. They crossed the road after a Salford Hire van passed, and made their way to the front of the large glass building.

'Ever been in?' PC Jackson asked, as he absorbed the size of the huge glass box, noticing it had at least six floors. The sun, coming from behind them, high in the sky, glistened off the windows and reflected down on the concrete below them.

'Once or twice.' She was observing a rough-looking cou-ple stood at the nearest corner. The man, who was wearing jeans with holes at the knees, clocked Baan watching him then tapped the scruffy-looking female on the shoulder, and they both stared back.

Baan stopped and watched them wearily until they disappeared around the corner out of sight.

'What is it, Ash?' Jackson asked, pulling his attention away from the building, realising she'd fallen behind, frowning at something.

'Nothing. Come on.' She passed him, reached the door, and pulled it open.

The inside was air-conditioned and cool. Inside they found a woman, probably in her early forties, restocking the bar. She heard their approaching footsteps and peered up.

'Can I help you?' She met them with a smile, but after noticing their uniform, it faded and was replaced by a cautious frown.

'We hope so.' Baan took the lead, explaining they'd like to look at the CCTV from the previous night.

'Why?' the woman asked. The name badge pinned to her white shirt had the name Marni on it.

'It's a very important police matter.'

Marni considered this and nodded, then tipped her head towards their left, inviting them through the bar. Baan and Jackson stepped through the open hatch and followed Marni down a small corridor, equally as cool and dark as the bar, the only light coming from dim spots above which seemed to be in some form of eco mode. She knocked twice on the first door they came to, grabbed the handle, and waited.

'Come on in,' said a rough male voice through the closed door.

They entered a large square room. It was brighter in there, a little warmer too; natural warm light shone through the floor-to-ceiling windows, battling against the air-conditioning unit above the door, seemingly equalling each other out.

'George,' she said, as she crossed the wooden floor towards a wide, dark wooden desk at the far side. A thin man sat behind it, his face peeping over the top of a computer screen.

'Yeah?'

'Police are here. They want to see the cameras from last night.'

George eyed them curiously. 'What's this regarding?'

'They explained it was a police matter,' she told him, 'and they'd appreciate the cooperation.'

He thought about it for a moment. 'Come on in.'

Baan and Jackson moved forward, and Marni left the room and closed the door behind her, her quick footsteps disappearing down the hall. George stood, invited them to his side of the desk, and presented one of them his seat. PC Jackson, being the gentlemen he was, offered it to PC Baan. She slid herself into probably the most expensive office chair she'd ever sat on.

George leaned over, took hold of the mouse, and navigated to where the files were. A strong smell of Jean Paul Gaultier radiated from him; Baan recognised it as the familiar scent of an ex-boyfriend. The file George opened contained six hours of content. He scrolled to the time they needed — the same time DS Matthew Phillips informed them he'd watched them leave.

'There!' she said, pointing. 'There they are.' She looked up at PC Jackson. 'Guy was wearing a red shirt. And that's definitely April.' They studied it another minute, watching them go out of camera shot; it looked like they were heading for the exit. 'Have you got a camera out front?'

He nodded, bowed over her, and found the file with a click of the mouse. 'Here you go.'

They watched them get into a Skoda Octavia. The registration of the car was visible from the impressive camera quality. PC Jackson picked his notepad from his pocket to jot it down. Satisfied, PC Baan stood up, thanked George for his time, and left the room with PC Jackson trailing her. They thanked Marni behind the bar, who smiled, and both stepped out into the hot morning air.

Baan picked up her phone once she was in the car and made a call to the office, asking for a check on the reg. She ended the call and lowered her phone to her lap. Silence filled the car for a minute.

'You okay?' Jackson asked.

Baan smiled and curled a few short strands of blonde hair behind her ear. 'Yeah. I hope nothing happened to her. She's a good friend.' Baan started the engine. A moment later, her phone rang through the car's speaker.

'Belongs to Street Cars,' said the voice through the speaker when she answered.

'Street Cars?'

'Roger that. You need the address?'

'No, thanks. Appreciate you getting back.' She ended the call. 'Let's go see who was driving last night. Hopefully, they'll remember where they dropped April off.'

CHAPTER 4

DI James accompanied Fisher down the corridor to DCI Andrew Baker's office, which was only a minute from their office. DI James knocked twice, waited for a murmur of something inaudible inside, and opened the door. DCI Baker was sitting behind the desk positioned at the back of the room with Dr Julia Gaze. They both smiled towards Fisher and DI James, then Baker thanked the DI for bringing Fisher along.

DI James nodded and disappeared.

'Close the door please, April,' Baker said quietly.

Baker was a short, bald, plump man in his fifties with a round, clean-shaven face. His blue eyes were set almost too close together, making him look strange. He'd held the position of DCI for nearly ten years now. Originally born in Manchester, he moved to the Met in London in his late teens — something to do with his dad's job as an accountant. But after five years of the fast-paced London life, Baker's mother wanted to move back to Manchester, closer to friends and family. They moved back and his father settled for a lesser-paid job with a smaller firm. Baker had worked his way up the ranks, sticking by the book and looking out for his own. If there was one thing to be said about DCI Andrew

Baker, it was his honesty. He told you how it was and what he thought of you, whether you liked it or not.

DS Fisher stepped closer to the desk, wondering why the doctor was there.

'Hi, April,' said Dr Gaze. Her tone was soft and professional. 'Please take a seat.' She motioned to the empty chair with her hand. Julia Gaze, among a plethora of other things, was a part of the occupational health unit.

Fisher dropped into the seat and kept her focus on Dr Gaze, unsure why she was there. She crossed her right leg over her left, and placed her hands on her lap.

Dr Gaze started by asking how she was doing.

'I'm fine,' Fisher replied, forcing a smile.

The doctor tilted her head a fraction. 'You sure?'

Fisher smiled thinly. 'Absolutely sure. Why am I here?'

Before Dr Gaze could reply, DCI Baker said, 'What happened to you last night isn't an everyday thing, April. We want to make sure you're okay. And as you can see, we are here if you need to talk or if there's anything on your mind.'

Dr Gaze nodded towards Baker in agreement, then looked at Fisher.

'I don't know for sure what actually happened to me, so until I get any results back from my check-up earlier, we should just act like everything is normal.'

Baker smiled thinly, admiring her resilience.

Fisher waited. Finding the bruises on her wrists and the insides of her thighs didn't necessarily mean she'd been raped. There was a high chance of it, sure, but she stayed positive regardless. She worked on facts, not assumptions.

'April . . .' Gaze said, this time softer, more personal, 'you don't need to hide your feelings. It's okay to feel somewhat angry and frustrated. Even a little empty.'

Fisher considered her words with a nod. 'I'm fine, thank you, Dr Gaze.'

It wasn't the first time Fisher had seen Dr Gaze. Five years ago, on a night out in the city with some friends, she was attacked down an alley on her way home. The man, who the police later found the same night due to several phone calls of a man matching his description mistreating other women, was in his late forties. In Fisher's statement, she told how Bryan Tollin had asked for a lighter when he stood at the opening of an alleyway she used to get home. She told him she didn't smoke and headed quickly down the alley to get away from him. Going the opposite way would have taken three times as long and been a clear indication she was scared of him, which, in her mind, would only encourage him. Before she reached the end of the alley, she felt his arms come from behind and she was pulled to the floor, followed by his frantic, desperate hands up her skirt. If it wasn't for the couple nearby who'd heard her shouting, she would have been raped. Three days later, Fisher knocked on the couple's door with flowers and chocolates to thank them for helping her.

'Listen, boss,' she said to Baker, 'I appreciate you calling me down here . . . but I'm fine. If the results come back and I've been raped, then it's my own stupid fault for getting too drunk and putting myself in that position. It's—'

'No, April!' Baker raised a chunky palm before slowly placing it on his desk beside a sheath of paperwork. 'It's not your fault at all.'

Fisher sighed, unsure what else to say. It was obvious the DCI and the doctor were expecting her to feel differently, but, knowing her, they should have known better.

'PC Baan and PC Jackson are looking into it,' Baker went on. 'I've just had word they've identified the taxi you travelled in. So we're finding out where you were dropped off and if the driver can offer any further information.' Baker finished with a firm, supportive nod.

Dr Gaze leaned forward a touch. 'April, you know where I am if you need to talk.'

'I know.' A long pause. 'Thanks, Julia.'

'Well, if you're happy to carry on, April. You're okay to go.'

Fisher stood, turned, and headed for the door in a resilient silence.

'April . . .'

She turned to the DCI's voice.

'We will find him.'

April smiled before she opened the door and left.

She bumped into DS Phillips on her way back to the office, carrying two coffees.

'Any biscuits with that?' she asked, knowing one of them was for her.

'There is, actually. You want some?' He turned.

'It's fine, I'll go. I'll meet you in the office.'

Fisher made her way down the main corridor and opened a door on the right, entering the large rectangular canteen. It had everything they needed, including a fridge, freezer, microwave, and plenty of cupboard storage. There was a table in the centre of the room capable of seating at least eight people, which rarely got that busy, due to people often going out for their lunches. The room was empty, but the smell of toast and coffee and washing-up liquid lingered in the air. She opened one of the top cupboards and grabbed a few biscuits, then returned to the office, receiving curious stares from colleagues dotted around the room, all peeking over their desks to look at the girl who may have been raped.

She sat down at her desk and pulled herself in. 'Thanks,' she said to Phillips for the coffee, then handed him a chocolate Hobnob, which he gratefully accepted and demolished within seconds.

There was an awkward silence. 'Is everything okay, April?'

She turned to him. 'Of course.'

'It's just, I'm here if—'

She stood up quickly and turned to face the room. 'Everyone, listen up please.'

Officers and detectives peered over the top of their monitors.

'You might have heard what happened to me last night. I've been to the hospital to be checked out. Waiting on results. In the meantime, I don't need — or want — your sympathetic stares. Okay? I'm a big girl. Thanks.'

She turned and sat down, a tinge of pink colouring her cheeks.

DS Phillips stared at her in amazement and smiled, returning his focus to his computer screen. He should have known better. Their first job was usually catching up on emails, which didn't normally take long. Often, some reports needed completing from the day before, reports which DI James and DCI Baker would be wanting to read.

DS Fisher noticed the time in the bottom corner of the screen. 'Right, come on. Time for our daily dose.'

The meeting room was a square-shaped hot box. The four windows positioned on the furthest side of the room were closed, the air humid and stagnant, making it uncomfortable to breathe. DCI Baker was standing at the front of the room with something between a scowl and frown on his face. He stood straight, something he often did to compensate for his lack of height. There was a whiteboard behind him with a projection coming from a hi-tech piece of equipment attached to the ceiling. He looked around the room. 'Any takers?'

DS Fisher raised her hand immediately. 'I'll do it.'

Baker smiled softly. 'You sure?'

Without a word, Fisher stood and marched to the front, taking the remote from him before she faced her colleagues. DCI Baker raised his eyebrows and took a seat at the nearest table, eyeing DI James in question, who shrugged lightly.

The screen behind her stated the date, followed by their most pressing issue: Elaine Freeman.

'Who killed this woman?' she asked, slowly scanning the room. No answers came back. 'Exactly. We don't know.' She gazed at the grey carpet for a moment before lifting her head. 'Why?'

Again, silence filled the room.

She looked at DC Arnold Peterson, seated over to the left, but he remained silent, unable to answer the question. It was a smaller meeting than usual with only five attending. Fisher could tell Baker was feeling the pressure with this case

— a reminder of what had happened the two previous years, sharing resemblances with the Hand-Eye Killer cases. Despite her troubles last night, she was doing her best to focus and make the most of the opportunity to lead the meeting — something she'd always do given the chance. DCI Baker had no doubt assumed, based on what *might* have happened to Fisher last night, she wasn't up for it. She made small circles near the front of the room, feeling the scrutiny of DI James, DS Phillips, DC Peterson, and DCI Baker.

'So,' she said suddenly, 'what do we know?'

'There's an obvious pattern, I think,' DS Phillips started.

'I agree. What is it, though?'

'They all resemble each other. Long dark hair. Similar physique. Large breasts.'

DI James nodded, and brushed a palm through his hair.

'What else?' she pressed.

'Well, the obvious,' added DI James. 'They all had their eyes taken out and both hands off with something Forensics believed to be razor-sharp.'

Baker, sitting to the left of the room, bowed his head. 'Correct. Now, I remember, and I'm sure you do too, the shitstorm this case caused not only last year but the year before. The media loved it, didn't they?' He paused. 'Is it a copycat? Someone trying to reignite the buzz the murders of Kathy Walker and Joan Ellison caused? Or is it the same person? Why the hands? Why the eyes? The killer's trying to tell us something. We need to find out what.'

Everyone silently agreed.

'Do we have the files on Kathy Walker and Joan Ellison handy?' asked DI James.

'They're on my desk,' Fisher replied. 'I've been through them a dozen times. But I'll go over them again. There must be something we're not seeing.' Outside the window, Fisher saw the sky was scattered with clouds but still bright, the sun rising from the east. She wandered over to the window while the others sat in thought, and stared out onto the car park, then across the road, observing the horizon, the shape of the buildings that made up the city of Manchester. 'I'll go through them once we get back to the office.' She turned to face them with determination. 'Is this meeting finished? We have work to do.'

'Yes,' said DCI Baker. 'Thank you for speaking this morning, April.' He looked towards DI James and DS Phillips. 'If anyone finds anything, call me. We need to start progressing in this case, otherwise we'll be out of a job, let me tell you.'

CHAPTER 5

He'd woken at six, got quietly out of bed, and made his way downstairs in his dressing gown. He'd made a coffee and toast, but had only managed half of it. His appetite was gone, although it didn't surprise him; it usually happened this time of year. Especially after what he'd done. He almost expected it now.

Now he was sitting on his one-seater chair by the window in the living room, reading the paper he'd just bought from the local shop less than five minutes ago. He loved reading up on the local news and everything going on in Manchester, and paid particular attention to the discovery of the body belonging to Elaine Freeman.

The *poor* woman.

He smiled to himself and read the article several times, the report stating how the trail had gone cold, how the police had no further leads to indicate who the Hand-Eye Killer was, with an additional question: *Are they back?*

'Interesting,' he whispered. '*The Hand-Eye Killer.*'

'Cup of tea, dear?' a voice said from the door. He looked up to see his wife standing in the doorway, a trying smile plastered on her tired-looking face. He stiffened a little and lowered the paper.

'Yes, please.'

As she vanished into the hallway, he peered out the window to his right. The sunlight was shining through the glass, gently warming the silent, peaceful room. Just how he liked it.

In the coming days, the police will archive the murder of Elaine Freeman, and allocate their stretched resources elsewhere. It won't be long before she's an unfortunate statistic in the history of this great city.

Until next time . . .

CHAPTER 6

Tony Anderson arrived home just after 10.30 a.m. It had taken him almost two and a half hours to travel back from Darlington, unfortunately hitting some of the early commuters in the manic rush hour. He had received a call from his brother Peter on his way back, who asked him to swing by an electrical supplier to grab some parts, which added an additional twenty minutes to his journey.

It had been a successful trip for Tony. He would have been home last night if it wasn't for his Ford Focus being unable to start, leaving him stranded after the meeting with Patrick Seymour, who'd signed the paperwork and handed the contract back to Tony with a smile, happy to do business. By the time he'd tried starting the car for the umpteenth time, Patrick was gone and unreachable on his phone. He wondered if it had been a flat battery and tried flagging people down in case they had jump leads, but evening drivers weren't interested, probably assuming it was some madman intending to steal their car. With no breakdown cover, he gave up, deciding to find the nearest Travelodge, and would try again in the morning; maybe Patrick's phone would be on and he'd be able to help.

Once he was on his way after Patrick had aided him with jump leads and a miserable-looking face after being woken up at 7 a.m., he travelled back to Manchester, excited about the deal that he'd just signed.

It was true what they said.

There *was* promise in this one. Not like the dribs and drabs that had been coming in over the past few years for the firm but something with potential, something that would build their reputation and keep them thriving. His boss would be happy, that's the main thing. It was important for Tony too, a chance to make an impact in his first year. So far, he was already set to be their best performer.

He slowly pulled up onto his driveway and came to a halt, the tyres crunching on the stones below. He sighed. He always felt like this after a lengthy drive, but it didn't help that he hadn't slept all that great, despite the comfy bed at the hotel. He unbuckled his seat belt, pushed his door open, and climbed out.

He made his way around the passenger side, feeling the warmth of the morning sun on his neck, which made a change from last night's dull, North East weather. After the downpour during the night, road edges had filled, spilling onto the pavement, evidently too much for the town's drainage systems to handle.

Before he reached the passenger door, his phone rang. He plucked it out and answered it.

'Hey.'

'Morning, Tony.'

'Morning, Frank.'

His boss asked him how his three days away were.

'Really good, apart from the car not starting last night on my way home, but . . . the contracts are signed. I was about to ring you.' He went on to give further details, to which Frank listened intently.

'Great. Bring them with you tomorrow.'

Tony ended the call, put his phone in his pocket, and smiled, humming a tune as he shifted towards the front door. Frank Johnson was happy, and that meant Tony was happy.

It was looking up for Social Streams. They were a company that helped both established and starter businesses with their social footprint, guiding their products and services into new avenues. Social Streams were experts in their field, but for some reason, it hadn't taken off just yet. Many companies already had departments that dealt with their social media and didn't require additional help, but Tony had proved he was a genius with it, although he'd only been on board for less than a year. Phil, one of the few colleagues he got along with on his team, had called him an interactive wizard, finally settling on the nickname Interwhizz. Tony thought it was cheesy, but it nonetheless inflated his ego.

Hey, Interwhizz . . . can you help me with this . . .

Tony opened the black-painted front door and stepped into the familiar scent of his hallway, making him feel warm inside. Evidence of breakfast hung in the air — burnt toast and coffee. It was perfect. He placed the A4-sized contract on the small unit at the base of the stairs and lowered his bag onto the floor.

'Amanda?' he said.

The house was silent.

A few moments passed before she replied. 'Up here. Two minutes.'

Tony left his bag at the base of the stairs, made his way into their spacious kitchen, flicked on the kettle, and stared out the back window. Their neighbour, Jim, was in his own garden opposite, standing on a ladder with a chainsaw in his hand and safety glasses on his face, sawing away at a tree. Tony grinned, impressed at the guy in his late fifties still being so busy.

Tony watched him for a few moments, the way he impressively controlled the chainsaw, and listened to the constant drone of the spinning blade bleeding through the kitchen window. He made a cup of tea for himself and a coffee for Amanda.

'Morning,' he heard a frustrated voice say behind him.

He turned around to see Amanda stomp into the kitchen, breathing heavily through her nostrils. Abigail, their two-year-old daughter, was in her arms, her eyes and face puffy, indicating she'd been crying.

Tony placed his cup of tea down and went over, kissing them both on the cheek.

'What's up?' he asked softly, frowning at his wife.

'Glad you're back.' She let out another sigh. 'You can take her. I have a Zoom call soon. I really wish you were home last night.'

Tony smiled, wishing the same, and took Abigail from her. 'You know what cars can be like.'

She narrowed her eyes at him. 'Hmmmm.'

He frowned at her. '*Hmmmm*, what?'

'Nothing.'

She whisked away from him, and he decided to let it go. Arguing with her as soon as he got home was something he wanted to avoid.

'And I'm not sure it takes that long to drive back from Darlington,' she said as she left the kitchen.

Tony shook his head, not bothering to explain he'd gone to the electrical supplier for his brother Peter, and forced a smile for Abigail. 'Well, I hope you've missed your daddy.'

She leaned in to cuddle him. He sniffed her small neck, inhaling her familiar scent.

He turned and went over to the window again, watching Jim leaning precariously on the step ladder. 'Look at what the man's doing with that big chainsaw.' Tony echoed the annoying drone and had a vision of his neighbour falling, the chainsaw ripping his guts apart, then decided if that did happen, it wouldn't be suitable for Abigail to see and moved away from the window.

As he looked down, he noticed something on her forearm, near her wrist. A dark-brown mark. Like a bruise. 'What's this . . .' He gently took hold of her arm and inspected it. 'What happened here, Abi?'

She didn't understand the question.

His phone beeped with a text message, distracting him. He lowered her to the floor gently until she was stable, and grabbed the phone from his pocket. 'Just a second, sweetie,' he told her, unlocking his phone.

With her little red lion, she disappeared into the hall, her tiny legs like pin drops on the laminate, before taking a right into the dining room where her toys were. Whatever the mark on her arm was, he was sure Amanda would know — probably knocked it on something.

He read the text message, then checked the time on his watch. He'd forgotten about his appointment, but he'd still make it if he set off soon. He went up to speak with Amanda, leaving Abigail to play on her own in the dining room. He reached the top of the stairs and took a left, noticed the landing was darker than usual; their bedroom door was almost closed. Amanda was speaking on the phone, some of her words spilling through the small gap between the door and the doorframe. He stopped and turned his head to listen.

'I can't do it, I've already told you,' she said harshly.

He tilted his head to the side and held his breath, now only a few feet from their bedroom door, trying to listen.

'I can't do this to him,' she said. 'It isn't fair.'

He was about to enter the bedroom when he heard a loud bang and high-pitched scream from downstairs. It sent icy fingers crawling up his spine.

'Abigail,' he whispered, before he dashed down the stairs.

CHAPTER 7

Tony reached the bottom of the stairs in no time, his heart drumming through his chest, desperate to know what the loud noise was.

'Abi, where are you?'

He raced into the dining room and saw her. 'Abigail . . . God!'

Over to the left, a wooden unit, roughly four feet high, three feet wide, had tipped over onto her. Abigail's left forearm, hand, and part of her face — mainly her squashed nose and mouth — were visible. She was still screaming, her panic filling the room. Most of the books and DVDs had fallen out, scattered on the floor around her.

'Jesus, Abigail . . .' He dashed over, grabbed the top of the unit, and hauled it up off her.

'What was that noise?' Amanda shouted down.

Tony ignored her, bent down, and picked Abi up. 'Baby, are you okay?' he asked softly, as he pulled her close. Her crying worsened, her pain filling all corners of the room, spilling out into the hallway and around the house. 'Jesus, Abi . . .'

Blood came from her lip and trailed down her chin. The tears streaming from her eyes diluted it to make it appear worse. Her forearm had a thick, raised red mark where the edge of the unit had trapped her skin.

'Are you okay?'

She battled through the tears and nodded slowly, holding on tight to her dad as if she was never letting go.

Amanda stormed in with a scowl, then noticed the mess on the floor and the fallen unit on its side. 'Jesus . . .'

Tony glared at her, shaking his head. 'Yeah, Jesus.'

She raced over and placed a palm on Abi's head. 'Abi, baby, are you okay?'

Abi ignored her and tucked herself into Tony, weeping and sobbing, rubbing her watering eyes with the back of her small hands.

'God bless her,' Amanda gasped. 'What . . . what happened?'

Tony turned to face her. 'How do I know? I wasn't there, was I?'

Amanda rubbed the top of her head and sympathetically pushed her bottom lip out. 'Come to Mummy . . .'

Abi shook her head and tightened her grip around Tony.

'She's fine *here*, thanks,' he said. Then to Abi, 'You'll be okay. Just a scratch, isn't it?'

Amanda picked up on his tone, and rocked her weight onto one of her hips. 'What do you mean *she's fine here, thanks*?'

'I mean if you had done what you said you were going to do then this wouldn't have happened, would it?'

'What! Me?' Her mouth gaped open as she took a step back. 'What the hell do you mean by that?'

Tony swivelled with Abi, nodded at the empty wooden unit on its side, the contents sprinkled beside it on the carpet. 'You said you thought that unit was dangerous and she could try climbing it. *You* said you were going to move it.'

She slammed her hands on her hips. 'You're not blaming me for this? *You* also agreed it was dangerous. Why didn't *you* fucking move it?'

His eyes widened. 'Will you mind your language around her, please?'

'Oh, here we go. Fucking Super Dad to the rescue. If you're blaming me for that you can get stuffed.' She was about to continue the heated debate when the phone in her hand rang. She glared down and sighed loudly. Her cheeks flushed pink. It was the director from the Liverpool office. 'God's sake . . .' She glared at Tony. 'Listen, I *need* to take this. But this—' she made a circle with her finger, indicating what had happened — 'will be discussed straight after!'

Tony watched her storm out of the room. 'Arsehole,' he whispered, so Abi wouldn't hear.

He lowered Abi to the floor to take a closer look at her lip. The bleeding had stopped, but a trail of blood ran down her chin. The cut was only small but he could see her cheek and chin were starting to swell and bruise.

'You okay, Abi?'

She nodded slowly, and wiped more tears from her red, puffy eyes.

'Good.' He hugged her again.

It was true, Tony and Amanda had *both* mentioned the unit was unsafe, that there was a possibility of Abi climbing on it one day and it tipping over, but neither had done anything about it. What pissed Tony off was that Amanda had mentioned it again last night, told him that Abi had been playing near it yesterday and that she would remove the DVDs and her books and put the unit in the garage out the way just in case. But Tony knew it was his fault as much as hers, and that was why he was angry. He hadn't bothered to move it either.

He let go of Abi and she picked up her little red lion before dawdling out of the dining room. Tony spent the next few minutes picking up the books and DVDs, and piled them on the dining table until they decided what to do with the unit.

Tony was making Abi some food in the kitchen when Amanda entered. Abi was waiting patiently at the small circular kitchen table over to the left, looking at the television that was fixed to the wall near the back door.

'I'm sorry,' she said calmly. 'I shouldn't have acted like that before. I was angry. That's all.'

'Come here.' He opened his arms, inviting her for a hug. 'I'm sorry too,' he replied into her ear. 'I'm angry at myself. I didn't mean to take it out on you.'

'It's my fault, I—'

The kiss on her forehead silenced her for a moment. She leaned into him further and he sniffed her hair, faint extracts of coconut filling his nostrils.

'I'm sorry, Amanda. With my grandad ill, I'm struggling a little at the moment,' he admitted.

She nodded in understanding. 'How're your mum and dad?'

'Finding it tough as usual.'

His grandad, George, had been in a care home for the past three years, and was progressively getting worse. Occasionally he lashed out at the other residents, argued with the staff, and on multiple occasions had got people mixed up. Tony's dad, Derek, had gone in last week and he was calling him Andrew, Tony's uncle that had died eight years earlier.

'They going to see him?'

'They go most days. But you should hear the stories about the things he's done and what he's said to other people. They may have to move him again.'

Amanda pushed her bottom lip out, understanding his pain.

'Daddy!' they heard Abi say from the table. 'Un-geee . . .'

'You're ungeeee?' Tony asked with a smile, as he pulled away from Amanda.

'Love it when she says that.' Amanda grinned at her.

Tony pulled the spaghetti hoops from the microwave, stirred them, and poured them into a bowl. He buttered the toast, cut it into four and placed it down on the table. He stepped back and checked his watch.

'Listen, I'll need to go soon. A guy contacted me about the car. He wants to have a look at it today.'

For a moment, Amanda's eyebrows furrowed, then she remembered. 'Will you be long?'

He shrugged. 'I don't know really. The guy's just having a look.'

'Would it be okay if you took Abi with you? She won't be any harm, will she? It's just I have another meeting soon, and if she plays up, it'll be a nightmare.'

He nodded twice, placing a hand on her shoulder.

'Thanks!'

'I'll wait until she's finished eating, then we'll go.' He noted the time on his watch again. 'Plenty of time.'

They had listed the car for sale last week. The Ford Focus had done them well, but it wasn't big enough anymore. In hindsight, how they'd lasted this long with it had baffled them, especially when they went shopping or went out for the day with Abi and needed her pushchair. The Focus's boot wasn't exactly built for prams and weekly shops, and God knows whatever else.

A thought entered his mind from back when he was standing on the landing, listening to her conversation when she was in the bedroom. 'Who were you speaking to earlier?'

Her lips slightly parted. 'When?'

'I heard you say you couldn't do it, and that you'd already told them. And that you couldn't do this to him?'

She stared for a few moments, in thought. 'Oh, I was saying to my manager about one of the men in the office, that's all. He hasn't been pulling his weight and he suggested I have a stern word with him. He's been going through some family trouble, so I said I'd leave it for now.'

Tony nodded, then gazed over to Abi, who was using a yellow plastic spoon to stuff spaghetti hoops into her mouth, most of which had dropped down her chin, landing on the table next to her plate. He smiled at the mess.

Amanda lifted her wrist to glance at the time. 'What time you going to meet that guy, then?'

Tony frowned; they'd only just discussed it moments ago. There was something different about Amanda, Tony thought. He couldn't say what exactly, but she didn't seem her usual calm and collected self. Something was bothering her.

'Is everything okay? You seem . . . diff—'

'Yes, yes. It's fine.' She broke eye contact and fixed her attention out the back. Their neighbour, Jim, was still standing on the ladder, cutting the trees, and the sound of his chainsaw continued to rattle the air. 'Just got a lot on with work. You know how it is.'

Things had changed in her job; she had been given more responsibility. The director, Jerry, from the London office, and Charlie, the development manager from Liverpool, had been on her case, making sure she was keeping on top of things.

They trusted her to do a good job, and that's why she was now the area manager. Abi was at nursery four mornings of the week, but her 'terrible twos' had taken their toll. Amanda clearly loved her daughter, but when seven p.m. came, she couldn't wait to get her upstairs, tuck her in, and crack open a bottle of wine. Sit down and watch whatever rubbish was on the television. Her time to relax and unwind.

Tony spent his time differently.

He liked to get out after a long day, hated being cooped up in the house. It wasn't that he didn't enjoy Amanda's company, but watching her sink copious amounts of wine to deal with the pressure of her new role certainly wasn't his idea of fun. Numerous conversations had ended in arguments, him storming out, often going to one of his brothers' houses to cool off or finding a pub in which to stare at the bottom of a glass, mulling things over.

Tony had two brothers. The eldest brother, Michael who was six years older, had just turned forty. He was an accountant at a firm based in the centre of Manchester. He liked to catch up with him a few times a month, but most of the time they spoke on the phone or sent each other funny emails relating to being a parent. Michael had two children, aged four and ten, a boy and a girl. His missus, Emma, dealt with them while he hid away in his office — a perk of a hybrid role — pretending to work while the football was on. It wasn't a secret that Michael and Emma were going through some difficult times in their relationship, or that they'd struggled in the past.

His other brother, Peter, two years younger than Michael, at thirty-eight, spent his working week installing and servicing commercial electrical systems. From a young age, he'd dabbled with DIY, then decided to pursue electrics. He couldn't wait to start earning money.

'Fin . . .' Abi said, putting her spoon down on her plate with a bang, splattering more spaghetti sauce across the table. They noticed some on the tiled floor near the base of her chair.

'Aww, Abi . . .' Amanda sighed, shaking her head in amusement.

Tony smiled, grabbed a cloth and cleaning spray, and crouched down to wipe the floor.

It wasn't long before the kitchen was clean and Abi had a new T-shirt on. A red one with flowers on it, the one Amanda's parents had bought for her — the one Amanda always put her in when she saw them because it made them happy.

It wasn't that Tony disliked her parents. He loved them, as far as a son-in-law could, but sometimes they got too much. He needed his own space and his own time, and they had a tendency to interfere with things too much, not that he'd ever admitted his feelings with Amanda.

'Come on then, little one,' Tony said, patting Abi's head when she appeared at the door wearing a smile and holding her little red lion, tucked into her small chest. Amanda placed a hand on her tiny shoulder and looked at Tony.

'How long will you be?'

'Not long,' replied Tony. 'He wants to look at it, then I'll head back. Maybe forty-five minutes, an hour, depending on traffic.' He shrugged. 'I'll call when we're coming back.'

She leaned in to kiss him, holding it longer than usual. He smiled. 'That was nice.'

'I love you, Tony Anderson. I'm sorry about this morning.'

He smiled and tilted his head. 'I love you too . . . Amanda Anderson.' A moment of silence passed. 'You sure you're alright?'

'Yeah . . . now, go on. I'll see you soon.'

Amanda stood at the front door while Tony leaned into the back of the car and fastened Abi into her car seat. He angled his head; through the front windscreen he could see her standing on the step, arms folded. He looked at Abi, who seemed content and excited about their little car trip, holding on to George, the red lion she'd had since she was born. It went everywhere with her.

Tony climbed into the driver's seat, closed the door, and buckled his seat belt. He waved at Amanda, then started the engine and backed out, the tyres slowly crunching on the gravel.

Was Amanda okay, he thought to himself as he took one last look at her. There was something in her face that made him not so sure.

CHAPTER 8

As Tony pulled off his driveway and slowly made his way out of Meadow Close, his phone rang, the ringing sound coming through the car's speakers. He looked at the information screen, which informed him it was his brother Michael. He accepted the call, tapping the loudspeaker icon on the central console.

'Hi, Michael.'

'Hey, Tone. How you doing?'

Tony said he was good and told his brother what he was up to.

'You haven't had that car very long.'

'I know,' he said. 'Amanda fancied a new one.'

Tony heard Michael sigh through the phone.

'To be fair, it isn't big enough anymore,' added Tony, in agreement with Amanda's decision. 'You know what she's like, Michael.'

He *did* know what she was like, as did the rest of his family. It wasn't a secret that Amanda didn't hold back telling them how she felt. On previous occasions, mainly parties or birthdays when they all got together, it wasn't unusual for it to escalate into an argument about something trivial. Where people would usually keep their opinions to themselves, Amanda didn't care. She was honest and open, often leading to another blowout and several weeks of ignoring each other, eventually breaking the promise of never speaking to each other again.

'Been a while since we've spoken. How've you been?'

'It has, mate. We're good. Just busy, you know how it is. Been away to Darlington for a few days for a meeting. Just got back this morning.'

'North East?'

'Yeah, not far from Newcastle. How's Emma and the kids?'

Michael said they were good, that the kids were at school and Emma was working.

Tony drove on and took a left on Granby Road, then a right onto Lime Road. The heat inside the car was almost unbearable. He leaned forward, turned on the air con, the sound of it whirring through the vents.

'I was thinking,' Michael went on, 'as it's Mother's birthday next week, you fancy going for a meal? Bring Amanda and Abi.'

'Depends on the time, I guess. You know Amanda, everything's by the book.'

Amanda certainly did have a way about her, especially when it came to Abigail. The number of programmes she'd watched and books she'd read on 'perfect parenting' was laughable really. Most of the time it annoyed Tony, but he'd been used to it for over two years, so her strange ways of doing things had, unfortunately, become the norm in their relationship. It was partly his fault because he'd let it happen and let her have her way. If only he'd told her how he felt. He couldn't be bothered with it; life was easier when you played along. What was that saying — happy wife, happy life? Tony certainly agreed with that.

'I'll check the available times,' said Michael. 'Ring you tomorrow, okay? You have a word with the boss and let me know.'

They ended the call as the satnav told him to take a right. He edged the car around the bend, barely avoiding a

Ford Fiesta that had taken the corner too wide, almost clipping the front end of Tony's car.

'Idiot!' screamed Tony, hitting the dash with his palm in frustration.

He peered through the rear-view mirror and noticed Abi was sound asleep, clutching her little red lion softly into her neck. His phone beeped from the storage section between the seats. He carefully reached down and picked it up. It was a text message from Martin Forlan, the guy he was meeting. The text told Tony his house number. In a previous message, he'd said his address was Elmstead Avenue, but he hadn't, for some reason, mentioned the number, which Tony thought was weird. He placed his phone back down in the storage space and put both hands on the wheel.

During the next stretch of road, he thought about the house. The list of things Amanda had scribbled down somewhere, jobs for him to complete. It didn't need much work, but if Amanda had her way, she'd rip everything out and start again.

It was a nice area. The neighbours were pleasant. They'd only lived there for a year after moving over from the other side of the city. It was an upgrade and much bigger than their previous house. The mortgage payments were the biggest thing Tony had worried about, but Amanda had assured him things would be okay and would work themselves out.

And, so far, she'd been right.

Things were looking up. During his dip into unemployment, he'd done a few courses in business management and another course in media, using the money from the redundancy package the engineering firm had offered him for his twelve years' service. Not long after completing his course he was taken on as a business development manager for Social Streams. He enjoyed it, proving himself to be a key member. The opportunity to attend the business meeting in Darlington had been good for him, definitely something the others were hoping to do too, but Frank had only allocated one staff member and had chosen Tony to represent them.

As long as the boss was happy with his performance, the hell with the rest of them.

'You okay, sweetie?' he said, gazing at the rear-view mirror.

Abi was still asleep, still clutching her red lion. It came with her everywhere she went. The last time when they forgot it, they were out for a meal and she screamed the whole place down, which forced Tony to drive home to get it. It was ridiculous really. He focused back on the road, noticed the red lights ahead, and slowed down. The roads were busy this morning, but no busier than usual. It was Manchester, a city of over half a million people, so it was busy all the time whether it was day or night.

He took a right and drove on the same road for five minutes before taking another right. The satnav told him he was a minute away from Elmstead Avenue, directing him right again, then another right. The meeting had been arranged two days ago. Apparently, it was the only time the guy was available. That was fine with Tony. As long as he did the projects that were handed to him he could be flexible with his working hours, Frank had said.

When the dot on the central console told him he had reached his destination, he slowed and looked for Martin Forlan, who said he'd be waiting outside his house when he arrived. He followed the rows of houses and slowed down, approaching a house where a man was standing. A small terraced house just before Longport Avenue.

The man was dressed in a thin black jacket, smart trousers, and black shoes, and appeared to have just finished a phone call, slipping his phone into his trousers.

CHAPTER 9

Martin Forlan had waited twenty minutes outside the fifth house along the street. It wasn't his house but he needed somewhere where the occupiers were out. There were no cars on the driveway and no one had answered the door when he'd knocked several times. The first four houses he'd knocked on had all answered him, then listened to his bullshit about changing their energy suppliers before they closed the door, politely telling him they weren't interested.

The house was a decent-sized terrace that required some TLC. The red door needed a fresh coat of paint, as did the wooden window sills, and the driveway to the house was short, bullied by overgrown bushes on either side that were taller than he was, acting as a good shelter for his position and limiting the number of houses that could see him.

His phone rang, which he pulled out and answered.

'Hey.'

'Have you found somewhere yet?' the voice asked.

'Yeah. Found a good one. There's no one in. The bloody fifth house I've knocked on.'

'Does Tony know the number?'

'Just texted him moments ago.'

There was a pause. 'Are things in place?' the voice asked.

'Yeah. We'll take care of it,' Forlan replied confidently.

'Let me know when it's done.'

'Here he is — just turned into the road. I have to go. Speak soon.'

Martin Forlan hung up, placed his phone into his black trousers, and watched Tony Anderson approach in his blue Ford Focus.

He was ready.

CHAPTER 10

DI James had just finished a call when there was a knock at his open office door. He placed his phone down on his desk and looked up to see PC Ashleigh Baan and PC Adam Jackson standing there. Recently, he'd been given a new office to use. Baker wanted to separate him from Fisher and Phillips, although he often used his old desk behind them when they were working on cases together and brainstorming.

'Hey, please, come in,' he said, pointing to the chairs on the other side of his desk. 'Excuse the mess.'

There was no mess. The desk was immaculate, apart from an empty mug next to his keyboard and a neat pile of papers to his left. He was always known for his orderliness, the way he methodically went about his business. They could recall many times the DI reminding people about tidy desks and keeping things in order.

They edged the door shut, walked over, and dropped into the spare two chairs.

'We spoke to the taxi firm, got hold of the driver,' Baan said. 'The guy reckons he dropped her off at home. St Nicholas Road.'

DI James frowned. 'What about the guy in the red shirt? Did he get out with her?'

'Driver said he was dropped off first at Westerling Way. A mile and a half from her house.'

'He's sure?'

'Seemed pretty confident.'

DI James fell into silence, tipping his head back, wondering how Fisher had sustained the bruising on the insides of her thighs and her wrists if the man had got out before she did. 'Okay, thanks for checking that out for me. Tell Inspector Thorne I owe him one.'

They nodded, stood, and left, closing the door behind them. James also stood, then went to his window and looked out onto Chorley Road. A string of thoughts entered his head, almost like a checklist of the things on his mind. April Fisher. The murder of Elaine Freeman. The likelihood it's the same killer as Kathy Walker and Joan Ellison. Pressure from DCI Baker.

He returned to his desk, sat down, and pulled himself in. To his left, he grabbed the neat pile of papers, placed them down in front of him; the top sheet was the pathologist's report on Elaine Freeman. The interesting thing, he noted, which made Elaine's murder different to Kathy Walker and Joan Ellison, was that she never had anything in her bloodstream, whereas there were traces of Rohypnol present when the pathologists tested Kathy and Joan. The nature of the killings, the way the murderer had removed the eyes and cut the hands off, was the same. Elaine was found by the river. Kathy and Joan were also found by the same river, although not in identical places. The area had become somewhat famous for all the wrong reasons. Even house prices began to dip and the neighbours were constantly wary. The discovery of Elaine Freeman would only fan the flames, and the local people, who, for a while, had managed to put the shock of Kathy and Joan out of their minds, would be thinking the worse again.

'Has he changed his method, become more confident?' he asked himself out loud. The most pressing issue for DI James was finding whoever it was before anything else happened.

CHAPTER 11

Tony unbuckled his seat belt, left the keys in the ignition, and opened the door. The guy smiled and nodded in his direction.

'You must be Martin?' Tony said, closing his door quietly so he didn't wake Abigail. He extended a hand towards the man.

'That's me.' They shook hands firmly and exchanged a friendly grin. Martin was taller than Tony, but most people were. Tony was only five nine and seemed to have stopped growing back in year nine at school, when his childhood dream of playing basketball quickly disintegrated into ash.

'I see you made it all right?' Martin smiled, revealing his coffee-stained teeth.

'It wasn't far.'

'So,' he said loudly, pointing to the blue car behind Tony, 'this is the famous Focus.'

'Indeed it is. Please—' he motioned him forward with a hand — 'have a look.'

Martin, smartly dressed and wearing his sunglasses, stepped forward and studied the exterior paintwork first, before he moved around to the front of the car. 'Where've you driven from? Not too far, I hope — sorry I couldn't come to you.'

'It's no problem. It's only a few miles.'

Martin nodded, waiting for more, but Tony didn't elaborate. 'Cool. Can I have a look in the boot? I'll need to use it mainly for work and need to see what I could fit in there.'

Tony nodded. The keys were still in the ignition but the central locking was open. 'Sure.'

'Thanks.' Martin studied the side of the car and peered inside the boot. 'Think I'd fit a body in there?'

Tony frowned, eyeing him with a sudden caution.

Martin smiled and was close enough to pat his back. 'Sorry, man — bad joke!'

There was a black raincoat, a tackle box a similar size to a shoebox, a selection of rods, a set of golf clubs, and various carrier bags inside the boot.

'You do a lot of fishing?'

'Now and then. When I have time.'

'You play golf too?' Forlan asked, seeing the heads of the golf clubs in a carrier.

'When the missus lets me . . .'

They shared a knowing short laugh before Tony noticed the top of Abigail's head. Martin hadn't spotted her yet, or if he had, he hadn't mentioned her. He lowered to a crouch and angled forward, his head almost to the ground, and peered under the rear of the car to see the exhaust system and underside of the car. Tony gently closed the boot.

'What's the milage, mate?'

Tony pushed his lip out. 'Had it from new. Only nineteen thousand, near enough.'

Martin curled his lip. 'Almost new, then. You haven't driven it hardly anywhere.' He remained crouched down, looking at something Tony presumed had caught his attention.

'I work from home now, so only go out with family.' He watched Martin down on his knees, curious what he was looking at. 'What's caught your eye?'

'Have a look at this.'

Tony lowered to his knees to get closer, becoming aware of an approaching vehicle somewhere in front of the car. He heard the sound of footsteps, followed by a door closing and the sound of an engine turning over.

It was the Focus starting up, the exhaust near his face rumbling to life.

Tony frowned. 'Hey, what the—'

It all happened so fast. Tony jumped up, stared through the rear windscreen and saw someone sitting in the driver's seat. A large man with short dark hair.

'Hey, who's th—'

As Tony stepped towards the driver's door, Martin leaped up, grabbed both of his shoulders, and yanked him to the ground.

'Hey, what the f—' Tony shouted, crashing to the floor, his back colliding with the road.

The car then shot forward, the whirr of the engine and wheels spinning on the tarmac until it took a left onto Longport Avenue, then raced out of sight.

Tony attempted to get back to his feet, but Martin mounted him and punched him several times in the face; the hard blows to his nose and temples disorientated him.

It wasn't long before he lost consciousness and his world went black.

He opened his eyes and looked up at the cloudless bright-blue sky above him. His nose was full of blood and the throbbing pain in his forehead came in agonising waves. He slowly climbed to his feet, his head spinning, his vision a little blurry, and looked around frantically. The realisation of what had happened returned to him like a sickening sledgehammer.

Martin Forlan was nowhere to be seen.

His car was gone. Along with his daughter.

CHAPTER 12

Tony banged on the house where Martin Forlan had told him he lived, but no one answered. He even tried the handle, but was confronted by a neighbour, who informed him no one lived there. He searched the streets frantically for his missing car and daughter, but couldn't see them anywhere after covering the four closest streets to where he'd been attacked. He'd tried pulling out his phone, but remembered it was in the storage compartment between the two front seats so he couldn't make any calls. He knew by now it was long gone. Although struggling for breath, he screamed, completely lost for what to do next. He'd never been in this situation before. A parent's worst nightmare.

A couple of kids stopped their game of kerby down the road and glared at him. It wasn't long before their dad, a stumpy guy dressed in a white vest, blue tracksuit bottoms, and flip-flops, came out and noticed Tony in the middle of the road on Golborne Avenue, panting hard, hands on his hips.

'Dad, what's wrong with him?' one of the kids asked, who appeared around the age of eight or nine.

The dad placed a hand on his small shoulder. 'I don't know, Son. Go inside. Take your brother with you. Go.' He gently shoved his eldest son in the direction of the house and studied the man, wondering what to do.

The man slowly approached Tony with caution, and stopped a few metres from him. 'You okay, mister?'

Tony jumped a little, not hearing him approach, and turned to him with tears in his eyes. He shook his head dramatically. 'No. No. I'm not okay.' The man seemed unsure about Tony and backed away a few steps.

'What's wrong?'

'My car — my car's been stolen,' he said in between short, quick breaths. 'My daughter's inside.'

'Jesus. Just now?'

Tony nodded several times.

'Where did this happen?' the man asked, trying to remain calm.

Tony pointed down the street, stabbing the air as if his arm was a mechanical piston. 'Elmstead Avenue.' He explained the situation about meeting Martin Forlan and selling him his car. 'Do you know anyone called Martin Forlan?'

'No.' The man sighed, unable to help.

He asked where Martin had told Tony he lived, and they walked to Elmstead Avenue, to the house where Tony had first pulled up.

'I've tried the door,' said Tony. 'No one lives here.'

The man moved past him, trying the door for himself.

'Can I help you?' they heard a voice ask nearby.

Tony snapped his neck to the right, seeing the same elderly gent who'd confronted him before.

'I've told you no one lives here,' he protested, staring at him over the top of thick, square glasses.

The men, although living nearby, clearly didn't recognise each other. 'Did you see anything?' He pointed at Tony. 'This man was attacked. His car was stolen with his daughter inside. Did you see anything at all?'

'I've already told this madman I haven't. Now leave me alone.' He slammed the door closed, evidently not interested in anyone else's problems.

Tony stared at the door of the apparently empty property, unsure of what to do.

'Have you phoned the police yet?'

Tony sighed. 'My phone's in the car.'

'My God, you should have said.' He quickly pulled his phone out and called the police. 'It's ringing now.'

'*Hello,*' answered the calm operator. '*Which service do you require?*'

'The police, please,' the man said evenly. When he was patched through he said, 'I have a situation on Elmstead Avenue. I'm with a guy who's been attacked and his car's been stolen. His daughter was inside the car. She's gone.'

'What's your name?'

'My name is Andy Walker.'

'Okay, Mr Walker,' the calm female voice said. 'What's the name of the man you're with?'

'Hey, mate,' he said, getting Tony's attention. 'What's your name?'

'Tony — Tony Anderson,' he said, struggling with his breathing. It was all getting too much for him. 'Tell — tell them about Abi. Tell them about my daughter . . .'

Andy nodded several times and passed on the information while Tony kept glaring up and down the street for any indication or sign of the car.

'Okay, Mr Walker, can you ask Mr Anderson for his car registration?'

Tony told him. 'Thank you. We'll get units looking for it immediately.'

Andy nodded at Tony, who was watching him, to indicate a little progress was being made.

'Sit tight,' the operator went on. 'We have your location. Help is coming right now.'

The call went dead.

'Please, what's happening?' Tony was desperate.

'They're coming now.' Andy lowered his phone. 'Do you need to phone anyone else?'

Tony's eyes widened. 'Yes! My wife.'

Andy handed him the phone. Tony started to type, then stopped. 'Shit, she's got a new phone. I don't know the fucking number.'

'The police are coming now. They'll be able to contact her.'

'They will?'

Andy wasn't sure, but nodded anyway.

Tony was unsure of any phone numbers off the top of his head and returned the phone to him. He glared vacantly at the driveway where he first saw Martin Forlan, as if somehow he'd magically reappear with Abigail.

He knew one thing: his car and daughter could be miles away by now. It wasn't long before the sound of sirens filled the air and a police car pulled into the street.

CHAPTER 13

The marked Astra sped around the corner of Meltham Avenue and accelerated towards Tony and Andy, the sound of its diesel engine rattling through the air, along with the wailing siren and flashing blues. PC Jackson slowed the car and stopped at the side of the road where the men were standing. PC Baan opened the passenger door, climbed out, and weighed up the scene in her head.

'Andy Walker?' PC Jackson said, as he closed the door and stepped up onto the path.

'Yeah, that's me.' Andy raised his hand.

The PC stopped at Andy but focused on Tony behind him, seeing his swollen, bloody face.

'You okay, sir?' he asked Tony, stepping towards him.

'Obviously I'm not okay, I—'

Jackson raised a sudden palm. 'I need to ask you to calm down and—'

'How can I be calm?' he screamed, nostrils flared. 'My car's been stolen and my daughter's inside. Please do something!'

Jackson studied Tony for a moment before looking at Andy, who shrugged at the officers, unsure what to say. He'd only heard Tony shouting and couldn't confirm he'd actually seen the Focus being stolen or confirm his daughter was inside.

'Andy, can you tell me what you know?' Jackson asked.

Andy relayed what Tony had said. Jackson glanced his way every few seconds, but PC Baan watched him like a hawk.

Regardless of the situation, they had to gather all the facts before moving forward.

'Sir.' Baan stepped around the front of the bonnet and up onto the path, her movement slow and steady. 'We're here to help you. But we can only do that if everyone is calm.' She passed Andy and stopped before Tony.

'For fuck's sake, stop telling me to be calm. I am calm. My car has been stolen and my daughter was inside of it. She's been taken.' He grunted, throwing his hands to the top of his head. 'Mr Anderson, my name is PC Ashleigh Baan. You can call me Ashleigh. Is that okay?'

Tony nodded and wiped some blood off his cheek with the back of his hand. The cut to his temple was still wet, but the bleeding had slowed.

She looked into his eyes, then pointed to her right. 'This is PC Adam Jackson.'

Tony nodded again but didn't seem fully with it, as if the smaller details didn't matter to him.

PC Jackson turned to Baan. 'I'll speak with Andy over here. Can you have a word with Tony?'

It may have been a risky move taking his eyes off Tony, but, through his experience of working beside PC Baan, it always worked. She was the best communicator he'd ever worked with.

Baan smiled at him and took a step closer. If he lashed out at her, she'd position herself so she could step back quickly. 'Can you slowly talk us through it, please, Mr Anderson, so we can get a better understanding of what we're dealing with?'

Tony quickly explained about the Marketplace advert, then the call from Martin Forlan saying he was interested in the car. The only term was that he came to him because Martin didn't have a car. He said he'd only texted him a little earlier with the house number. At the time he thought it was weird, but hadn't given it much thought. He wanted to meet him, let him look around the car, and make a deal.

'Can you tell me the registration, please?' she said.

He did.

She used her radio to inform Dispatch of the current situation, including the car details so traffic police could start looking for it.

'They know the details. We should hear something soon, Tony.' Baan looked around. 'Where does he live?'

Tony spun around and pointed to the house behind him, stabbing the air in rage. 'There! He was standing there when I pulled up. I've tried knocking, but the old guy next door said no one lives there.'

Baan walked up the driveway and knocked for herself, leaving Tony with PC Jackson and Andy on the path.

'Thank you for helping Tony,' PC Jackson said to Andy, nodding.

'No problem at all.' Andy offered a sad smile, but didn't seem to know what else to say to Tony, who was clearly distraught. Andy smiled thinly at PC Jackson before he crossed the road and went around the corner out of sight.

After no answer, Baan made her way back to the path. 'So you didn't actually see the man come from the house? He was just standing in the driveway?'

'No, I didn't.' He gave another hefty sigh. 'But he told me this address and was standing at the end of the driveway. I had no reason not to believe him.'

PC Jackson felt a gentle breeze coming from behind and could smell cannabis somewhere in the air but kept his attention on Tony.

'Oh, not this guy again,' said a voice behind them.

Baan and Jackson turned to see an elderly gent charge down next door's driveway.

'Officers, please.' He jabbed a finger towards Tony. 'You need to get rid of him. He's been shouting and banging on doors. He threatened me.'

PC Baan glowered at Tony. 'Is this true, Mr Anderson — did you threaten him?'

Tony was flabbergasted, and threw his arms in the air. 'What?! I've done no such bloody thing.'

'He was shouting and banging on the door like a mad man,' the elderly gent went on, still poking the warm air in front of him.

'You old fool — I've been attacked.' He moved forward. 'Look at my face, for God's sake. My car's been stolen. My daughter's missing. The last thing I need is you talking shit. Now go inside and mind your own Goddamn business!'

'Please listen, Mr Anderson.' PC Jackson leaned forward, placing a palm on his right arm. 'We're here to help you sort this whole thing out.'

The old man made a circular motion beside his head with his finger, indicating Tony had a mental health issue. If it wasn't for PC Jackson holding him back, he'd have pounded down the driveway and probably belted the old man.

'Calm down.' Jackson held his arm tight.

Tony shoved his hand away and paced a few steps away from them to cool off.

'Go back inside, please, sir,' PC Baan said to the old man, who waved away the situation with a shake of the head and stepped inside, slowly closing the door.

'Have they found the car yet?' Tony asked Baan.

'Nothing yet.' Still, he peered down the street one way, then the other. 'They'll let us know when they find it.'

'I need to tell Amanda about this.'

Baan frowned.

'My wife,' Tony said to eliminate the confusion. 'She doesn't know anything about this. I can't remember her number off by heart.'

'What's her name?'

'Amanda Anderson.'

'Her full address?'

Tony told her.

'What phone provider is she with?'

'EE.'

'I'll make a call. We should be able to get her phone number.'

Tony nodded a thanks.

From behind, Tony heard the footsteps of two teenage boys walking on the opposite side of the street. PC Baan looked over.

'Looks like he's come out worse,' one of them said, then laughed. He was a tall, lanky type, wearing a full blue track-suit and Nike Air Max trainers. 'Go on, PC Plod, give him another whack, then.'

Jackson and Baan ignored him, keeping their focus on Tony.

'Go on, PC Plod,' the same lad said again, this time louder. 'Pigs!'

Jackson and Baan were used to continuous taunting from youths and thugs and ignored them.

'Piggy, piggy, oink, oink!' the other said. He was a smaller, fatter version, also wearing a tracksuit.

Tony span around. 'Get a job — go on, piss off!'

The teenagers came to a halt. 'Oh, big man, eh?' The taller one charged across the empty, quiet road towards Tony, swaying his arms as he moved.

PC Jackson immediately stepped down off the path in front of Tony, and raised a hand in front of him. 'Please keep moving. We are assisting this gentleman.'

PC Baan stepped over to her left and positioned herself in front of Tony.

'Well,' the smaller one said, 'keep this cheeky bastard quiet, then, or I'll make that face of his worse than it already is.'

Out of character, Tony snapped and shifted past Jackson with a raised fist, and connected to the side of the taller one's face, forcing the teenager to crash to the road with a thud.

'You fucker!' screamed the teenager, no doubt embar-rassed he was on the ground.

Then Tony went for the shorter one, who jumped back and threw up his fists.

'Come on, then!' Tony screamed.

PC Baan quickly grabbed her radio. 'Immediate back-up required. Elmstead Avenue. Potential fight and outnumbered.'

There was a crackle and a hiss.

'Roger that, officer. Sending immediate assistance,' replied a quick, efficient voice.

Before she had the chance to put the radio back into her belt, PC Jackson grabbed Tony and pulled him to one side, away from the youths. The taller one, with a cut to his cheek, clambered to his feet.

'Come on, then!' he shouted.

'Come on!' the other hissed, fists clenched.

Two of them were on their toes, bouncing around like boxers in a ring.

PC Jackson had managed to get Tony's arm in some kind of hold, which, judging by the expression on his face, caused him considerable pain. It was time for Baan's communication skills to come into play.

'Right!' she squealed. 'Listen to me: this ends now. Backup is coming. This man—' she pointed at Tony — 'is going to be arrested. Do you want to get arrested too, spend a few days in the nick?' Her voice was loud, clear, and filled with authority.

Across the road, several curtains twitched to see what the commotion was about.

The teenagers' expressions softened, and, after weighing the severity of the situation, they both decided to back off.

'Make sure he gets nicked!' the taller one said, stabbing a finger towards him. 'Can't go around hitting people like that.' He made a show of touching his face where Tony had punched him.

'We'll take care of it, I promise.' PC Baan then encouraged them to walk away.

'Mr Anderson.' PC Jackson grabbed a pair of cuffs from his belt and placed Tony's hands inside, then clicked them tight. 'Under the Crime and Disorder Act 1988, I'm arresting you for actual bodily harm.'

CHAPTER 14

Tony was taken to a small, hot, square room with no windows and walls that needed a fresh coat of paint. Light shone down from an ancient strip light onto the table located in the middle of it. It was the only object in the room; there was no shelving or picturesque imagery on the dull, magnolia-coloured walls. He occupied the single chair on one side of the table and the two chairs on the opposite side were empty, waiting for the PCs. The room had no air. A scent of stale coffee lingered as if spilled in the past and never properly cleaned up.

He felt himself getting more agitated as time went on. Precious time was being lost. So far, he had no idea if the police had located his stolen car. God only knew where Abigail was. But he was here because he should have controlled his emotions earlier, and couldn't blame the police for arresting him. He did, however, need PC Jackson and PC Baan on his side, and to make them understand exactly what was going on.

He put himself in the officers' shoes, thinking if he turned up to a guy with his face bloody and swollen, angry and agitated, claiming his car had been stolen with his daughter inside, but his phone was inside the car, so he couldn't prove he had arranged the meeting with Martin Forlan or that his daughter actually existed, or who he really was . . .

The door opened to his left, giving him a good view of the bright, busy corridor. PC Baan and PC Jackson entered, closed the door, and made their way to the table.

'Mr Anderson,' PC Jackson said, as he adjusted his position on the seat. 'Sorry we took so long.'

'Where's my car? Have the police found it?' He frantically switched his gaze towards both PCs.

'Nothing yet,' replied Baan, with a sad smile.

'Have you phoned my wife yet?'

Baan nodded. 'Yes. EE provided her number, but there's no answer, unfortunately.'

Tony sighed and shook his head several times. 'She needs to know.'

'I tried a dozen times, but, like I said, she didn't answer.'

Jackson leaned to his right, extended a hand, and pressed a button on the recording device. Tony watched him, wondering how much further time would be wasted. 'For the recording, can you tell us again exactly what happened this morning? Summarise it, please.'

A sigh escaped Tony's lips, and his shoulders dipped. Over the next three minutes, he explained what had happened, starting from the original message from Martin Forlan to blacking out after he'd been attacked.

PC Baan stood. 'I'll go see if there's been an update.'

'I understand your frustration, Tony,' said PC Jackson after she'd left. 'I don't have children myself so I won't pretend I understand what you're going through or how you're feeling. All I ask is that you give us the time to process this properly so we have a better chance of finding your daughter.' Tony nodded. 'The more we know, the better chance we have,' Jackson explained further.

'So what's happening now?' Tony glanced the closed door.

'PC Baan is checking with traffic control to see if there's a hit with your Ford Focus. We have camera systems around Manchester that are capable of locating vehicles.'

'I should be out there looking for my daughter. We're wasting—'

'And you would be if you hadn't punched a teenager in the face,' Jackson reminded him.

Tony shook his head several times, disappointed with himself, and looked down at the table. 'He deserved it.'

'I'm not arguing with that. Believe me, I've seen some of the finest examples of teenagers that our great city has to offer.' The PC smiled, but became serious again. 'Once we find the car, we'll take it from there. We've told our team about your situation, explaining what Abigail looks like and what she's wearing, but without a picture of her, we can't forward that on to our media and news outlets.'

Tony understood that. If only he'd grabbed his phone when he got out of the car to meet Martin Forlan,, then they'd be in a much better position.

The door opened to Tony's left. He glanced up to see PC Baan enter and take a seat at the table.

'Nothing yet on the car.' She settled into the chair and put her notepad on the table. 'We've alerted others to your missing daughter Abigail.' Baan looked him in the eye. 'We'll find her.'

CHAPTER 15

Baan and Jackson had updated Inspector Thorne on the situation so far, and he'd agreed with the idea of them both accompanying Tony home to locate his wife. Once there, they could get a photo of Abigail and get it out to the media.

Tony sat upright and stared out of the window as Baan navigated through the usual busy traffic, desperately searching for any signs of his daughter. Chances were she wouldn't be casually wandering the streets, but he didn't want to miss the opportunity if she were.

They pulled into Meadow Close fifteen minutes later, and Tony leaned forward from the back seat, pointing to the corner of the street. 'That's my house. There.'

It was a nice-looking semi. Well kept. The door was freshly painted black, matching the colour of the wooden window frames and fascia board under the guttering.

PC Baan slowed the car and pulled up on the kerb outside. They opened their doors, got out, and could feel a slight chill around them. The sun had disappeared behind a cluster of threatening grey clouds that had come from nowhere.

The PCs allowed Tony to lead, who stepped forward, patting his pockets, then stopped at the door, frozen with wide eyes. 'Shit — my keys. My keys were in the car.'

PC Jackson wasted no time in stepping around him, trying the door handle. It was locked, so he knocked several times. 'If she's in, she'll answer.'

Tony moved to the left, placed his palms on the living room window, and peered in. The living room was empty. He moved away. 'Ahhhh.'

'What?' Baan said, frowning at him.

Tony bent down, tipped over a plant pot and picked up a key. 'Bingo.'

He unlocked the door and went inside, smelling a faint scent of coffee in the air. Amanda loved her coffee. Ever since they'd met, she'd always had the best — and often most expensive — coffee machines. The ones where you can buy the beans and do it yourself. Tony didn't really like coffee but had to admit it smelled unbelievable.

'Amanda . . .' His panicked voice filled the house.

PC Jackson and PC Baan followed him inside, looked around, taking it all in.

'Amanda,' he said again, this time louder. The house was silent. Something to his right caught his eye, down on the floor, resting against the skirting board. 'What's that?' he whispered.

The PCs watched him lower to the floor and grab something.

'What the . . .'

'What is it, Mr Anderson?' PC Jackson asked, leaning to one side to get a better look.

He turned and frowned at the item in his hand. 'It's Amanda's phone. Why — why is it there?' He turned his head quickly and shouted, 'Amanda!'

Tony, Baan and Jackson listened, but there was no reply. 'I'll check upstairs,' Tony said, keeping a hold of the phone and taking the first step up the stairs. 'If she's working, she'll be in our bedroom and might have the door closed.'

Jackson nodded positively. 'I'll join you.'

As the two men climbed the stairs with a beat of urgency, PC Baan moved into the living room. It was a reasonable size, with two new-looking leather sofas, one against the wall to the right as he entered the door, and the other, perpendicular to it. The small space in the corner was occupied by a small waist-high table with a lamp and a paperback book next to it. She stepped further into the room and noticed a flat-screen TV fixed to the chimney breast, positioned just above the fireplace. Either side of that contained a symmetrical set of shelving with various photos and ornaments.

She backed into the hallway, swivelled right, and peered into the kitchen. She frowned and came to a halt, looking closely at the objects scattered on the floor.

'What on earth?'

She pulled out her truncheon and held it tight in her right hand.

'Hello?' she said, as she looked around, her eyes darting left and right. Most of the cupboards were open. Glasses and plates had been smashed, leaving a sea of broken pieces all over the tiled floor. Packets of food and loose fruit were scattered along the worktop and on the floor too. She took another step and then she found it.

'What the hell . . .'

* * *

PC Jackson followed Tony up the stairs until they reached the top and took a left. The door to the front bedroom was closed — a plausible excuse why she hadn't heard the knocks at the door.

'Amanda?' he said, cautiously opening the bedroom door in case he startled her. The scent of her sweet perfume lingered in the air. 'You in here?'

The bed was made perfectly. Everything was in its place. A slight hum filled the air but Tony couldn't place it. He stared and stayed quiet, trying to listen. A familiar sound, a noise which was only heard when Abigail wasn't playing with her toys or screaming the house down in one of her tantrums. Then he noticed the red laptop on the vanity unit, plugged into the mains socket close by. The screen was open.

He rounded the bed, leaned over, and picked it up. She was on a Zoom call, judging by the message on the screen: *Zoom meeting ended.*

'Where is she, Tony?' Jackson asked, a few paces behind him.

He turned and shrugged. 'I-I have no idea.'

'Hey . . .' They heard PC Baan's voice from downstairs. 'You two come and see this. Now!'

CHAPTER 16

PC Jackson and Tony dashed down the stairs, following PC Baan's voice into the kitchen. Tony came to a sudden halt and stared, taking in the blood on the floor. Not only was it on the tiles, but there were streaks down the side of the cupboards and across the white worktop.

'What the hell?' He tried to dash over, but Baan pulled him back.

'Wait, Tony!'

'What . . . ?' whispered Tony, eyeing the mess. 'A-Amanda!'

'Please stay back, Mr Anderson. We need to get Forensics here,' said Baan.

Jackson nodded, agreeing with Baan about preserving the scene for Forensics to collect anything important first. He studied the kitchen, assuming by the state of the place that something violent may have occurred. 'What happened here?' The question was directed at Tony, who was standing beside Baan near the kitchen door, speechless, with his mouth open.

'I-I don't know.' He slowly raised a palm to his forehead. 'How would I know? I've been out.'

'We need to call this in immediately, Adam.' Baan pulled her radio from her belt and stepped away from Tony, who was staring at the kitchen in a worried silence. She told Dispatch what they'd found and to send backup along with a team of forensic officers.

The operator asked if they required CID.

'Yes, please,' she replied before the crackle ended, then placed the radio back in her belt. 'Help is coming now,' she informed Jackson and Tony.

'What on earth is going on?' Tony asked no one in particular.

The stolen car.

His missing daughter.

The mess of the house.

The blood.

No sign of Amanda.

Tony backed sheepishly out into the hallway. Baan and Jackson watched him closely.

'Listen, Mr Anderson. Help is coming. Whatever's happened here, we will find out.' Jackson trailed him to the base of the stairs. 'Any idea where she might have gone?'

Tony didn't reply and stopped near the stairs, dropping his face into his hands. 'I don't understand. First Abigail, now Amanda . . .'

PC Jackson placed a hand on the outside of his shoulder for support. 'Help is coming, Tony. We'll fix this.'

Tony stared for a few moments, then leaned forward and opened a small drawer of the unit at the base of the stairs.

'What are you looking for?'

'Her passport.' Tony frowned as he picked up his own, but not hers. 'Amanda's isn't here. I don't understand.'

It was then they heard several hard knocks at the front door.

CHAPTER 17

DS Fisher and DS Phillips were standing at the door when Baan opened it. Although Phillips was standing on the small area of concrete before the house, he was still taller than Baan.

'Hey, you two.' Baan examined Fisher, trying to decipher how she was feeling by the look on her face. She'd known Fisher for years and had seen her through some tough times, and she needed to know more than anyone that she was okay.

Fisher smiled. 'I'm fine.'

Baan smiled, unsure whether to believe her or not, but decided not to push it. 'Is Pamela Boone on her way?'

'Just spoken with her. She's very close,' said Fisher. 'Can we get everyone outside for when she gets here?'

Baan nodded, turned, and shouted, 'Adam, can you and Mr Anderson come outside, please? Forensics are coming now.'

Baan stepped across the threshold, followed by Tony and PC Jackson. Behind Fisher, they heard a car engine approaching. They turned to see Boone in her white van. She closed her door and walked over with a small case in her right hand.

'Hey, Pam,' Fisher said.

'Is there anyone inside?' asked Pamela, sparing the small talk.

Baan shook her head and held the door open for her.

'Who's been in there?'

'Mr Anderson, PC Jackson, and myself.'

Boone nodded, eyeing them all. 'Before I enter, I'd like to take some fingerprints, please.'

Baan motioned Tony forward. 'If you wouldn't mind, Mr Anderson?'

Boone lowered the case she was carrying and opened the lid, revealing her forensic kit. It contained a number of items whose uses Tony could only wonder. She took his prints using a small portable scanner.

'Thank you,' she said, placing it neatly back into her case before closing the lid. There was no need taking Baan's and Jackson's prints as they were already in the system. 'If you wouldn't mind staying out here for now, guys, I'd appreciate it.' She directed her words at Baan, Jackson, and Tony, knowing Fisher and Phillips would want to come in and inspect the scene from a safe distance, making sure they didn't get in her way.

* * *

Boone entered the house and slowly made her way down the hall, studying every surface. She'd just turned fifty last week, and had celebrated it with her family by going for a meal in the city. It was an expensive affair but her husband, Harry, who earned plenty from his job as a solicitor, had paid for everyone. She had very short blonde hair which was often gelled and spiked — someone had once described her as quirky, although she didn't really know if that was a good thing or not, nor did she care. She enjoyed getting tattoos, even to this day, and enjoyed a cigarette; the wrinkles by her mouth and crow's feet lining her eyes were a testament to that.

'Any more in there?' Phillips asked, referring to the over-shoes she'd just slipped on. Overshoes would at least preserve anything going forward.

'Sure.' She pulled out a second pair, handed them over.

DS Fisher smiled at him, shook her head, and pulled a pair from her own pocket. One foot at a time, leaning against the wall, she pulled them on.

'What do we have?' Fisher asked, standing straight again.

PC Baan, from the doorstep, pointed towards the kitchen. 'Through there . . .'

The two DSs and the forensic officer went to the kitchen. Tony Anderson, PC Jackson, and PC Baan waited outside.

'What's the story?' Boone asked them, as she slowly entered the kitchen, absorbing the mess and the blood spatter.

'Tony was meeting a man who'd arranged to buy his car. He was attacked and knocked unconscious.' Fisher paused a beat. 'His daughter was in the car and unfortunately has been taken too.'

Boone sighed. 'And now the wife's missing too and the house is left like this?'

'Seems that way,' replied Fisher, entering the kitchen for the first time. She stopped near the door and swallowed the scene as a whole before cautiously moving further in. 'Mind that glass.' She pointed down to the tiled floor, mainly for DS Phillips's benefit.

'What are your first thoughts, Pam?' Phillips asked, watching her methodically move around the kitchen.

'There was definitely a struggle,' Boone replied, pondering the items that were out of place across the worktops. She took hold of the camera hanging around her neck and starting snapping photos.

'We'll leave you to it, Pam,' said Fisher, who backed away. 'We'll be outside speaking with Mr Anderson if you need us.' Fisher and Phillips left the kitchen, walked down the hall, and went back outside.

* * *

'Can we have a word, Mr Anderson?' Fisher asked, as she stepped down onto the gravel.

76

Tony was at the end of his driveway, speaking with Baan. PC Jackson was a few metres away with a phone pressed against his ear, chasing up on any developments regarding the whereabouts of Tony's car or his daughter. Tony nodded and took a few steps towards Fisher.

'Is there anyone you can contact in relation to your wife's whereabouts?'

Tony scowled and shrugged, indicating there'd be no point in it. 'Isn't it obvious something bad has happened to her?'

Fisher understood his frustration. 'Despite what the inside of your house looks like, we need to cover the basics. I won't lie to you and say your wife has decided to go for an innocent walk and while she's been out, your house has been broken into, because that's unlikely. But we do need to eliminate that from the investigation.'

A doubtful smile ran across his face. 'She wouldn't have gone anywhere without her phone, Detective. It's usually stuck in her hand.'

'It can't stop us trying though.' She curled a few strands of hair behind her ear and turned to Phillips. 'You got your notepad?'

He reached inside the internal pocket of his long brown coat and pulled out a small, A5-sized pad, followed by a black pen.

'Just before we make a list of people who know your wife,' noted Fisher, 'can you send me the most recent picture of her? Something we can use to send the media and get it out to the world?'

'All of my photos are on my phone!'

Fisher tilted her head in thought. 'What about Amanda's phone?'

'Ahhh, yes!' Tony enthusiastically removed her phone from his pocket scrolled through some recent photos, finding an image of the three of them, taken just last week in the garden. 'Will this do?' He turned the phone towards the detectives.

'That's perfect, thank you.'

Once Tony had forwarded the photo to Fisher, she emailed it to a contact at the station, reminding the receiver who the people in the photo were and the situation they were in. 'So, regardless of what's going on in there, can you tell me a list of her friends or anyone she usually spends time with?'

Tony rattled off a few names and DS Phillips jotted them down, nodding after he'd written each one.

'Do you have their numbers?'

'My wife will.'

Tony searched through his wife's phone and started calling people on the list, the first being her best friend Jane Alexander, who'd said she was expecting a call from Amanda at some point this morning but hadn't heard anything. Tony didn't want to waste time, but quickly informed her of the situation with Abi and the missing Amanda.

'*Oh my goodness, Tony,*' she said. '*Is there anything I can do?*'

'If you hear from her, please ring me as soon as possible — on her phone.'

Tony hung up and called the second name on the list that DS Phillips had noted. It rang out several times, reaching answerphone with each attempt.

'Who's the third?' pressed DS Fisher.

Tony scrolled down the list and found Erin Tullen.

'Who's that?' asked Fisher.

'She used to go to fitness classes with her. They often go out with Jane.' Tony held the phone against his ear and looked down at the gravel in concentration, wishing for it to be answered.

'*Hey, Amanda,*' Erin said, in a chirpy tone. '*How you doing?*'

'Hey, Erin, it's Tony. I'm sorry to bother you, but have you seen Amanda this morning?'

A beat of silence was heard.

'Erin?'

'*No, not today. I saw her on Tuesday but haven't seen her since. Sorry, Milo's being a pain in the arse.*'

Tony knew that was their dog.

'Have you spoken with her?'

'*Just by WhatsApp, not actually spoken to her. Is everything okay, Tony?*'

Tony explained again, sick of hearing the same story from his lips and wasting time.

'*That's awful. I-I don't know what to say,*' she replied.

'If you hear from her, please get in touch.'

'*Absolutely,*' she said, before the call ended.

Tony lowered the phone slowly and sighed heavily. Fisher noted his beaten body language and came up with a suggestion.

'I have an idea. For now, can you send a text message to all the contacts in her phone, mentioning that it's you and you're wondering if the recipients have seen Amanda or know where she is?'

Phillips angled her way and nodded, approving the idea. 'Smart thinking.'

Fisher tried to judge whether Tony approved. Texting everyone in her contacts with such a strange message would obviously lead to multiple confused replies, but, at the same time, it could result in finding Amanda. 'What do you think?'

Tony seemed to mull it over for a few moments before gradually nodding. 'I suppose it's the quickest way of getting the message out there. Yeah, let's do it.'

Fisher smiled appreciatively, watching him compose a cleverly worded message. Once he'd finished it, he showed it to her and Phillips for their approval.

'Perfect,' confirmed Fisher.

Tony held tight onto the phone in case a reply came quickly.

DS Fisher smiled. 'What does your wife do?'

'She's an area manager for a social care firm.' Tony watched Phillips jot it down. 'It's called Care Eazy.'

'How long has she worked there for?'

Tony thought for a moment. 'Six years, I think. She's recently been promoted.'

'Does she enjoy it?'

'She seems to,' Tony said, then added, 'It's more stressful though.'

Fisher narrowed her eyes. 'How so?'

'More responsibility. She gets pressure from above. She mentioned a manager from London is always on her case. Bloke called Jerry. And a guy from Liverpool called Charlie.'

'Do you know their surnames?'

'Not off the top of my head, but I could find them somewhere, I'm sure.' He frowned. 'I don't understand what this has to do with anything.'

'We're just trying to gather all the information we possibly can. Anything, however small, might help us. The more we know, the better chance we have of finding out what's happened.'

Tony contemplated the question for a short time. 'I can check her laptop for any emails from them?'

'Maybe she has a work planner on there and had planned something work-related which you weren't aware of?' DS Phillips wondered out loud.

Tony scowled in silence. 'I'll check her laptop, but I doubt that.'

'Where is it?'

'Up in our bedroom.'

DS Phillips walked across the driveway and opened the door, asking if Pamela Boone wouldn't mind going upstairs and retrieving the laptop.

'I have things to do here, you know, Matthew,' she said, after going up to collect it and returning downstairs to hand it over.

He smiled, knowing her humour. 'Crack on, then. Stop messing about.'

Boone closed the door on him, and he turned, giving the laptop to Tony once he'd put the latex gloves on that Fisher had handed him; she always carried a stash of spares because she'd been caught out by that before.

Just after Tony sat down on the step to make himself as comfortable as possible, he opened the laptop and logged on, then a text message came through on Amanda's phone.

'Who's this?' Tony said, pulling it from his pocket. The detectives watched him. 'It's from a Mark Applewhite. He says he hasn't seen her in over two years and sorry he couldn't help.'

Tony placed the phone down on the step beside him, expecting more texts to come through. Fisher was sitting beside him and Phillips was standing on the opposite side, just in front of the bay window. Tony opened her emails and started scrolling in frustration through various catalogue subscriptions and online clothing balances.

'Found anything?' Fisher asked to keep him focused, seeing the same emails and noticing his eyebrows knot in confusion.

'Erm . . .' He continued to scroll and saw an email from Gerry Thorpe with the subject 'Meeting'. He clicked on it and scrolled down, finding a signature with his mobile number. 'We could try calling him?'

'It won't do any harm,' Fisher agreed.

Tony made the call, explaining the situation. Gerry told him he didn't know her whereabouts and hadn't spoken with her today.

'Thanks for your time, Mr Thorpe.' Tony hung up, lowering the phone again.

'Tony, a bit of an odd question . . .' Phillips said. 'Is there anyone you can think of that your wife doesn't get along with? Someone who may want to cause her harm in any way?'

Tony frowned. 'I-I can't think of anyone, no. Sorry. Apart from her recent stress from work, she's generally a happy person. She sees her parents a few times a week and sees a couple of her friends regularly.'

'Her parents — what are their names?'

'Jack and Rachel. Their second name is Mulberry.'

'Do they get along with Amanda?'

'Yes, very well.' He smiled. 'Like I said, she sees them several times a week.'

'What about you, Tony?' Fisher asked, leaning in a little. 'Is there anyone you had a recent argument with, or anyone that may want to get back at you?'

Tony sighed heavily. 'No.' He exchanged glances between them. 'Can we please hurry up here? We should be out there looking for Amanda and Abigail.'

Amanda's phone started ringing on the step. The caller was named *Dad*.

'Oh, brilliant.' Tony answered it with a lack of enthusiasm.

'Tony, what's going on? I've just received a message from this phone?'

Tony, for the umpteenth time, explained.

'Are you being serious?'

'Very serious, Jack.'

'How can this happen?'

Her father's question was buttered with the patronising sarcasm. Tony didn't reply.

'Where are you?' Jack Mulberry asked.

'At home.'

'Who's there with you?'

'The police. And a forensic officer taking a sample of the blood.'

'We'll be straight over, Tony.'

Tony lowered the phone and dropped his gaze. 'This'll be fun.'

CHAPTER 18

'Sorry to bother you,' Pamela Boone said as she opened the front door and pulled her face mask down to her chin. Fisher, Phillips, and Tony all turned to her, as did Baan and Jackson, who were further down the drive. 'Does Mrs Anderson have a hairbrush or a toothbrush? I would appreciate a sample of her DNA.'

Tony stood and turned. 'Her toothbrush is in the bathroom. A purple one.' He squinted in thought. 'There's a hairbrush on her vanity unit in the bedroom.'

'Thank you. While I'm here, can I just take a swab of the inside of your cheek, please?'

'Why?'

She raised her arm. In her hand was something that resembled a cotton bud, but the end was purple and a different texture to cotton. 'Because I need to eliminate you from anything I find.'

Tony couldn't argue, so stepped forward and opened his mouth for Boone to run it inside either cheek.

'Thank you.' She slowly removed it and placed it into a small plastic bag.

'You need any assistance in there, Pam?' asked Fisher.

'I might do soon.'

'Let us know.'

Boone disappeared and closed the door once again.

Phillips looked at Fisher for a second, who nodded at him, then concentrated back on Tony. 'We have another question. Have you and Amanda fallen out?'

His eyes narrowed. 'Fallen out?'

'Yeah. Have you two argued this morning?'

He sniffed the warm air, and shook his head at Phillips. 'No. I mean, no more than usual. We had a heated discussion about when Abigail hurt herself in the dining room this morning.'

'What happened?' he pushed.

'We were upstairs, then heard a scream. Abigail had climbed up one of the units, pulled it over with her weight. I was angry because when I was away Amanda had mentioned making it more secure. She hadn't got around to it.'

It was hard to miss the frustration in his voice.

'Was Abigail okay?'

'A scratch on her arm and cut to her lip. It hit her in the face I think too, judging by the mark.' He fell silent, then a sudden thought entered his mind, and he addressed them all. 'Where is my daughter and where is my fucking car? Can we not be looking for it while Forensics are inside?'

Fisher turned to Baan and nodded, indicating for her to chase it up again. She made eye contact with Phillips for a brief moment. They both knew what the next question was going to be.

'While PC Baan is chasing that up to see if there are any updates, we have another question.'

Tony waited, his expression now telling the officers around him his patience was wearing thin.

'Has anything ever got violent between the two of you?'

Tony's neck almost snapped in reaction to the question. 'Violent? I'm not sure what you're asking. And I'm also not sure I like it. I've never touched my wife. Not in that way — *never* in that way.'

'What about Abigail?' Phillips added.

'Are you fucking kidding me?' Tony shouted and jumped up from the step again, this time doing small circles around the driveway's gravel. 'What are these questions?'

Fisher held up a gentle palm. 'It's just routine, Mr Anderson, nothing more.'

'I haven't been violent towards my wife, I haven't been violent towards my daughter. I went out to meet Martin Forlan — if that is his bloody name — this morning and he attacked me, took my car. My daughter was inside. I came back here to find no Amanda and blood . . . that's it. That's the story. And if you continue to ask stupid questions, I'm going to start wandering the fucking streets myself.' He let out a heavy sigh and dropped his head. 'Jesus,' he whispered.

The front door opened and Boone appeared, once again pulling her mask down to her chin so they could hear. 'April, you mind stepping inside?'

She nodded, pulled out some plastic overshoes from a pocket and slipped them on, followed by latex gloves. 'On my way.' She edged the door closed once she was inside. 'What have you found, Pam?'

'This way.'

Fisher trailed her into the kitchen, mindful of the glass on the floor.

'We've found something in one of the drawers.' She turned with wide eyes. 'It certainly might be useful. I've put it on the table. Here.'

Fisher nodded and considered the object on the table.

'Whoever put it there,' Pamela Boone said, turning to face Fisher, 'didn't want it to be found. It was right at the back of the drawer.'

Fisher nodded. 'Have you taken prints from it, Pam?'
'Yes.'
'What about a sample?'
Boone nodded at Fisher. 'Done that too.'
'Good.'
'Photo it, then bag it.'

Pamela Boone acknowledged her request, leaned forward, picked up the bloody knife, and carefully placed it into a clear plastic bag.

As Fisher left the kitchen, her phone rang in her pocket. She checked the caller, seeing a number from a Manchester landline that she'd hadn't saved.

'Hello?'

'Ms Fisher, it's Dr Shaam from the hospital. Are you able to speak for a moment?'

It was the doctor that assessed her earlier that morning before she went to work.

'Yeah,' she replied, readying herself.

'The results of the swab have come back and I'm happy to inform you there were no signs of semen found in your body. When I examined you this morning, I couldn't see any immediate signs of any genital injury in relation to the concerns we had. In my medical opinion, you weren't the subject of a sexual attack last night.'

Fisher smiled silently.

'Ms Fisher?'

'Hey, sorry,' she said. 'I'm just relieved. Thank you for the call, Doctor.'

'Have a nice day, Ms Fisher.'

She hung up the phone and placed it slowly back into her trousers, wondering about the bruising.

'I need to fucking stop drinking,' she whispered to herself.

CHAPTER 19

DS April Fisher decided not to mention to Tony that Boone had found a knife. Why would a knife, covered in blood, be hidden at the back of one of the drawers? Boone was right — it was likely hidden. Boone had already taken Tony's prints, so once she obtained any prints from the knife, she'd cross-reference them and find out if he'd handled it. With him living here, there was a good chance he'd used the knife when chopping food. If his prints were there, it wouldn't prove anything.

Fisher returned outside and joined Phillips and Tony.

'What was it?' asked Tony, his eyebrows raised. 'Please.'

Fisher gave a thin smile. 'The forensic wanted a second opinion on something, that's all.' To redirect the conversation, she angled over to PC Baan and PC Jackson. 'Any word about the car?'

'No, nothing.'

Fisher let out a tired sigh. 'It can't have just disappeared.'

'I know,' PC Jackson replied.

Fisher faced away from the house and peered up. The sun had crept out from behind a passing sheet of clouds, the day now brighter and much warmer.

'We need to start asking neighbours if they've seen anything.' Baan and Jackson immediately understood their task, turning and starting with the house next door.

* * *

The neighbour's house was similar in style to the Anderson's, only everything was on the opposite side. PC Baan led the way, knocking twice on the door. Either the occupant didn't want to answer or there was no one in.

The following two houses were also vacant, their empty drives implying the occupants were at work or elsewhere.

'The street is quiet, isn't it?' Jackson noted, as he walked up yet another empty driveway. The house looked neglected, the rendering weathered from years of it not being properly maintained. The outer finish was flaky, making way for the abandoned layers to show underneath. The windows and frames were still wood, whereas most of the houses in the street were PVC. Behind the glass of each window were old creamy-brown nets that once used to be white. It made PC Jackson wince a little. The red door was probably painted a decade ago; half the paint had gone, the other half crumbly, barely clinging to the wood.

'Ladies first.' Jackson stopped and motioned her forward with his hand.

'What a gentleman.' She approached the old tiled steps, unsure if they looked strong enough to hold any weight. She knocked three times and moved back so she was level with Jackson.

'Just coming,' said a muffled voice behind the door.

The door creaked open to reveal a plump woman in her seventies, wearing tight, discoloured leggings and a plain blue T-shirt a few sizes too small for her size. She smiled at them, exposing a mouthful of yellow teeth; several of them were missing.

'Hi, sorry to bother you,' said Baan. 'We were hoping to ask you a couple of questions — do you have a minute?'

She glanced down at her thin wristwatch, blinking to focus. 'I have four minutes. My programme starts in four minutes.'

Baan nodded. 'I'm PC Ashleigh Baan with Greater Manchester Police. This—' she motioned towards Jackson — 'is PC Adam Jackson. We were wondering if you'd seen anyone coming and going earlier today. Late morning, to be precise.'

'What time?'

'Between ten and twelve?'

The elderly woman edged forward, pulling her eyes away from them and directing her gaze the police car parked at Tony's house. 'Has this got something to do with them? Tony and Mandy?'

A thin smile found Jackson's lips. 'Amanda, you mean?'

'Is it Amanda? I'm not sure. We don't talk to them much. They haven't been here all that long. Not compared to us anyway.' There was a hint of pride and neighbourly right in her words as if she had more ownership of the quiet street because she'd been there longer.

'Can you remember seeing anything this morning that you thought was unusual?'

The elderly woman brought her hand up to scratch her chin. 'Tony came back around ten. I remember because I was upstairs in my bedroom and heard an engine outside. I looked out as he pulled up. Looked like he'd been away for work. He was gone two days. He left Tuesday morning.'

Jackson nodded, noticing her unusual attention to detail, and half smiled, finding it amusing that she didn't speak to them.

'Did you see him leave the house this morning?'

She thought hard. 'I didn't see him leave, but I heard his car around half eleven. I know the sound of that little blue engine, you see.'

Baan and Jackson nodded, waiting for more.

'I then looked out nearer twelve because I was putting the clothes on the radiator. We don't have a washing line, you see.' She sighed tiredly. 'Roger was meant to buy one last week but he hasn't, so . . .' They could hear the disappointment in her voice, and imagined what their relationship was like behind closed doors. She went on, 'So I assumed it was his car what I heard.'

'Okay.'

'What's happened? Why are you at their house?' She shuffled forward, seemingly ready for some gossip-worthy information.

'We're just enquiring about something, that's all.' Baan paused a moment. 'How well do you know them?'

'As I said, we don't talk much. The odd hello but apart from that, nothing. They don't get along though, everyone knows that. Probably that young child of theirs causing them trouble. I know myself what having kids is like. Bloody hell, I have three of them. The hardest job in the world, let me tell you.'

Baan said, 'How do you mean, they don't get along?'

'The arguments. The shouting. He often leaves the house, drives away late at night after they've argued. It isn't a secret around here. If I was Amanda, I'd have already left him for the things he's said to her.'

CHAPTER 20

While Baan and Jackson were knocking on neighbours' doors, DS Fisher stayed with Tony, who was still sitting on the step with his head bowed a little, fixating on the stones covering his driveway. Fisher was standing in front of the bay window close by, watching DS Phillips, who was positioned at the end of the driveway with his phone pressed against his head, speaking with PCs back at the station about any updates.

Amanda's parents, Jack and Rachel Mulberry, were on their way over, but no harm would come trying to get in touch with others in the meantime. Several messages had come through on Amanda's phone from some of her distant friends and ex colleagues apologising they couldn't help Tony and wished him good luck in finding her.

'Oh God, I need to tell my parents. I can't believe it.' Tony pulled Amanda's phone out frantically and found their number. 'Dad — Dad, it's me . . .' Tony said quickly into the phone.

'*Tony?*'

'Yeah, it's Tony. Listen . . .' He was lost for words for a moment. 'Have you seen Amanda today?'

'*No, Son. We . . . It's Tony calling,*' his dad said, his voice momentarily becoming quieter as if he was speaking to someone else. '*Sorry, Son. Mum was asking who was phoning. What was it you were saying?*'

'Have you seen Amanda today?'

'*No, we've been at home.*' There was concern in his voice. '*Why? What's happened?*'

Tony told him the events of the morning, from driving to meet Martin Forlan up until finding the blood in their kitchen.

'*Jesus. Have you phoned her?*' his father asked.

'Of course I've phoned her, but her phone is here, Dad. The place is a mess. I don't know where Abigail is. I-I don't know what to do, Dad . . .' Tears formed in his eyes and he looked down at the driveway, covering his face from DS Fisher and DS Phillips.

Fisher and Phillips stared at him; Tony was either one hell of an actor or he was genuine. Phillips wondered what he'd do in the same situation if his daughter was kidnapped, his car stolen, and he returned to a ransacked house to find blood and a missing wife. Would he act the same way as Tony had?

The knife that Pamela Boone found hidden in the kitchen drawer definitely threw a spanner in the works. If Tony had something to do with this, which was something they had to consider, then would he really be stupid enough to hide the knife where it could so easily be found? Maybe he'd panicked?

'*Hold on, Son. Let me get sorted and we'll be over,*' his father said, emotion creeping into his voice. '*Give us ten minutes. Hold on.*'

Tony ended the call, pushed the phone into his jeans pocket. He spent a moment rubbing his red eyes and let out a loud, tired breath. 'I'm sorry.'

'Don't apologise,' Fisher said softly. 'You've been through hell this morning, Tony.' She gave him a reassuring rub on the back, then concentrated on Phillips. 'Is there anyone else you can call? Perhaps a brother or sister?'

'Oh yeah. I have two brothers. Michael and Peter. I'll ring Peter first — Michael is usually busy.'

Fisher smiled, watching him retrieve the phone and find the number. She observed his expressions, the frantic eye movements, hypothetically wondering whether, if she were married herself and she went missing, would her husband be acting in a similar manner. She hadn't been on a date for nearly two months. The last one was a self-absorbed prick who only spoke about how many contracts he had landed, how highly his company praised him. Not once did he ask April about her own life or her work. He'd told her on more than one occasion he'd slept with a lot of women, oblivious that it was the biggest turn-off for a woman. Ever.

The previous date had been better. A guy called Aaron, who was a few years older than she was. He worked as a self-employed joiner. Really good-looking, tall, and physically fit, no doubt a six-pack under the gorgeous white Oxford shirt he was wearing. Throughout the meal, she couldn't take her eyes off his, the way the light-blue shades swallowed her up. And not forgetting the Australian accent he still possessed even though he'd lived in Manchester for nearly twenty years. He was a charmer, that's for sure; even the women at nearby tables stole sneaky glances at him, Fisher had noted. But Aaron had baggage. His wife had died last year in a car crash, leaving three daughters between the ages of fourteen and nineteen. With no kids of her own, it wasn't something she wanted to dive into right now.

Tony's brother Peter answered on the second ring. He sounded busy. A clatter of something was heard in the background, probably hand tools.

Tony asked if he had seen Amanda.

'*No, why?*' replied Peter.

He gave a summary.

'*Jesus Christ, Tony! Where are they?*'

'The police are here now. We're trying to work out what's happened.'

'*And they think it's* her *blood in the kitchen?*' Peter's voice was clearer now, the clatter of tools had stopped.

'We don't know.' Tony physically shrugged and took a breath.

'*I'll head over, mate,*' his brother said. '*Anything I can do to help.*'

Tony thanked him, hung up the phone, and placed it down beside him. He turned to Fisher. 'My brother Peter is coming too.'

They heard a vehicle approach and all looked to see a car pulling up behind the police cruiser. It was Amanda's parents. Tony caught a glimpse of Jack's scowl.

'Here we go,' whispered Tony.

CHAPTER 21

Jack Mulberry didn't wait for permission to walk up the driveway and ask Tony, 'Right, where is she?' His voice was abrupt and to the point. He was a tall man with broad, stocky shoulders. He had a serious, hard face that appeared bronzed from a recent holiday.

Slowly trailing him was his wife, Rachel, who appeared a little sheepish, no doubt given Jack's short fuse.

Tony stood. 'I have no idea, Jack.'

Jack sniffed loudly and glared around him, eyeing Fisher first then DS Phillips. 'Where is my daughter and granddaughter?'

'We're doing our best to find out. The house is currently occupied by our forensic tech.'

Jack frowned and pointed to the front door. 'Is Amanda or Abigail inside the house?'

Phillips shook his head, unsure what he meant.

'So why the fuck are you just standing there?' He took a few paces towards him. 'Why aren't you looking for them?'

DS Fisher moved away from the bay window, wanting to intervene before Jack got too close to Phillips. Although he was tall and thin, and appeared unthreatening, if pushed the wrong way, Phillips would react; she'd seen it before.

'I think the best thing we can do right now is calm down.'

Jack turned to Fisher quickly, the front of his shoes scooping up the stones. 'And you are?'

'My name is Detective Sergeant April Fisher from the Greater Manchester police.' She paused for a moment, raising her eyebrows. 'And you are?'

'Jack Mulberry.' He paused, as if that would mean something. 'I'm Amanda's father.'

'Well, Mr Mulberry, as you can see, we have a very sensitive situation. Regarding the fact why we're *just standing* here, we're waiting to have a look around Tony and Amanda's house after our forensic tech has finished, which won't be long at all. In the meantime, we have several units patrolling the streets in search for Tony's car, your daughter, Amanda, and your granddaughter, Abigail. And we have traffic police monitoring the roads around Manchester too.'

'So, you're a detective?' he asked, tilting his head.

'I am.'

'At least there are people with a little about them on this case, then.'

'Meaning what exactly, Mr Mulberry?'

He smiled. 'Meaning I don't want just anyone ordinary on this case. I want the best there is.' He eyed her up and down, deciding if she was ordinary or not.

Fisher ignored the patronising behaviour; instead she grinned at him. 'Well, I guess you're in safe hands then, sir . . . And you are?' Fisher said, focusing on Rachel, who stepped forward timidly with her hand outstretched.

'I'm Rachel. Amanda's mother.' She shared a smile with Fisher. Mrs Mulberry had short dark hair in the style of a bob. She wore a beige-coloured pencil skirt, brown flat shoes, and a black T-shirt. She wasn't slim, but possessed what some would call womanly curves. For someone her age, she was attractive. Fisher could see the resemblance in the photo of Amanda Tony had provided.

'Do we know anything yet, Detective?' she asked.

'We have teams looking for your son-in-law's car and searching the neighbourhood where you granddaughter was last seen. We have sent a photo of your daughter to our media team, who'll get it out to the press very soon.'

Rachel gently smiled by way of gratitude, obviously more understanding of the process and actions that had to be put in place to handle such a big task in a city the size of Manchester.

'We'll do our very best.'

'Okay,' said Jack, who slowly turned to face Tony. 'Tony, I think it's time you started being honest with the police. Don't you?'

CHAPTER 22

Tony tilted his head in response to Jack's comment, which aroused the curiosity of both Fisher and Phillips.

'What the hell is that supposed to mean?' Tony demanded, frowning hard at him.

Jack laughed as if a joke had been said. 'Oh, come on, Tony. Tell them about what happened years ago. About what you did.'

The frown on Tony's face deepened, but it was obvious to DS Fisher, who was standing a few feet from him, that he was thinking hard about it.

'I-I can't remember . . .' He exchanged glances between Fisher, Phillips, and Rachel, before settling back on Jack. 'When?'

Jack's shoulders deflated. 'Tony, don't play the innocent one here. Why would Amanda just disappear? Why would there be blood in your kitchen?'

DS Phillips was still at the end of the driveway and plucked out his phone. He typed a message to Pamela Boone, who was still inside: *Pam. Need the fingerprints from the knife processed ASAP.* He pressed Send and put his phone back into his pocket. Rachel Mulberry looked his way, but he offered a smile, then faced Tony again, interested to see where this was going.

'I know as much as you do, Jack. And listen . . . don't you dare come in here saying things like that.' This time, it was Tony who raised the volume, something which neither Fisher nor Phillips had heard yet. 'This is *my* wife that's missing. *My* daughter that was taken. *My* fucking car that was stolen. *My* face that was punched and kicked. So I'm not having *you* come into *my* fucking house insinuating things. Do you fucking hear me?' Tony waded forward a few steps.

'Wow, big and hard, eh? This is new, Tony.' He shook his head, smiling. 'Why not tell them about your birthday party? That night four years ago. I'm sure they'd love to know.'

Tony laughed out loud, theatrically waving the comment away. 'Why are you bringing that up? It's in the past and you know it was a one off.'

Jack shrugged, curling his bottom lip over his top. 'Just thought they'd want to know, Tony. The police usually need to know all the facts first. It helps them with their investigation.'

It didn't take a genius to work out the relationship between Tony and Jack wasn't very solid. Fisher and Phillips decided to let this unfold and find out why.

'What happened four years ago, Tony?' asked DS Fisher, seeing Jack faintly smile to her right.

Tony sighed and his body physically deflated. 'It's really nothing. I don't even know why we're—'

'Tell them, then, Tony. If it's nothing, tell them.' Jack nodded at him. 'Go on . . .'

Tony's eyes darkened, and DS Fisher waited a while, switching her focus between Jack and Tony, finally settling on the latter. 'Tony?'

'It's really nothing . . .'

They all stared at him with narrowed gazes.

'Fine.' Tony sniffed loudly, cleared the back of his throat, and placed his hands on his hips. 'We argued. Amanda ended up storming out, went to her parents' house for two days. A typical argument, really.'

'A typical argument?'

The surprising comment came from Rachel Mulberry. This time her voice appeared much more confident than earlier.

Tony concentrated on her and half nodded.

'A typical argument?' She sniffed. 'You seem to be forgetting the part where you came home drunk after losing a bet and started waving a knife around in the air, Tony.'

Her comment piqued the serious interest of both DS Fisher and DS Phillips.

'Jesus . . .' Tony sighed tiredly. 'Come on, you know that was a one-off. I'd had a bad day. Yes, I was a fool to lose that money, and I shouldn't have taken it out on Amanda. She just . . . She . . .'

'She what, Tony?' Jack angled his head slightly, obviously trying to get him to react in front of the detectives. Behind him, Rachel folded her arms, making no secret of her disapproval.

'She wound me up, that's what. If she'd have just left it, let me go to bed, then it wouldn't have happened.'

'You scared her to death, Son,' said Jack, in a serious tone.

Tony's mouth gaped open for a moment. 'Don't be ridiculous, Jack, come on. You know what she's like. You've said it yourself in the past. She overreacts to things. Things which mean nothing she makes a big song and dance out of.'

'I disagree with you, Tony. I've never said anything of the kind.'

'She knows how to wind me up, that's all. If she had just left it, then I wouldn't have reacted the way I did. I wouldn't have scared her.'

'Is that what happened this morning? Did you *scare* her again?' his father-in-law asked, slowly drawing the words out. Jack furiously shook his head, and before Tony could respond, clearly stuck for words, Jack added, 'Where is she, Tony? What have you done with her?'

Tony turned away and faced the house.

'I just find it strange she texted me last night saying she wanted to see me today,' Jack said. 'Wanted to speak to me about something important. She needed my advice. No doubt another one of your fuck-ups.'

DS Fisher watched Jack, wondering the meaning behind the words.

Tony seemed none the wiser about the text message and stayed quiet, trying not to rise to his father-in-law's needling.

Jack didn't get the reaction he was after, which infuriated him further, and he lunged forward, his finger stabbing the air. 'You listen, Son!'

DS Fisher stepped across towards him to cover Tony. Behind Jack, DS Phillips bolted forward, grabbing Jack's muscular shoulders to pull him back. Realising he wouldn't get to Tony without a fight, Jack settled on a hard stare towards his son-in-law. 'I'll find out what you've done. You can count on that.'

'I think it's best that you leave, sir,' suggested Phillips, his hand still firmly on Jack's meaty shoulders.

Jack promptly shrugged it away. 'Fine. We're leaving anyway. We're going to look for them. We'll be more helpful than you lot sitting here doing sweet FA all day.' He turned abruptly to Rachel. 'Come on, leave these to it. Let's go find our family.'

CHAPTER 23

Derek and Karen Anderson had been in the car less than a minute before she picked up her phone and rang her son Michael. He answered and said curtly, 'Mum, can I call you back?' She sighed, hung up the phone, placed it back down on her lap, and rolled her eyes.

Michael was always busy doing something or other. Not that his job as an accountant wasn't important, but she had the feeling he was happy living a solitary life, hiding in his home office away from the responsibility of their two children and unhappy wife. It wasn't a secret Emma didn't seem herself these days. With Michael working all the time, she was left with the job of both the mother and father, often taking their son to his football training and matches. It was hard-going, but she had to get on with it, had to do it for the children.

'He's always busy,' Karen said. She shook her head and looked out the window, watching the city of Manchester pass them by.

'He's probably working.' Derek had two hands on the wheel, his eyes straight ahead. They approached a round-about and he slowed the Zafira in good time before the junction, something the car behind didn't appreciate, the driver pounding the horn a few times. 'Jeez . . . some people are so bloody impatient.'

Karen and Derek had had numerous arguments about his driving, how he braked too early or often too quickly, or how he set off too slow and cornered like he had all the time in the world.

'Yes, he's probably busy,' she agreed. 'But he never seems to have time for us.' She looked his way, seeing the side of his jam jar glasses. 'When was the last time he came over to ours?'

Derek slowly angled the car around the roundabout before he answered. The window was open, which allowed a cool breeze to seep in from the west. The air freshener hanging from the mirror had only been opened yesterday, making the car smell new, almost making Karen sick.

Karen shrugged. 'I wish he'd try harder with us . . . with his own family.'

'You know,' Derek said, 'I read something the other day.'

She rolled her eyes. 'What?'

'That the family you make is more important than the family you come from.'

She frowned at him. 'Load of rubbish. He should be seeing us.'

Derek slammed a palm on the steering wheel, and the noise filled the car, taking Karen by surprise. 'God, will you let him be? He's busy working. He's busy with his family. He lives in a big house worth half a million pounds. If anything, I'm proud of him.'

'It's all for her though. All for show. If it was up to him, he'd just—'

'But it isn't, is it? It's up to both of them. As a couple. They are entitled to decide between them. Regardless—' he raised a finger — 'if he's happy with it, then what's the problem?'

No one said anything for a minute.

'I'm sorry, Karen. I . . .' He trailed off in thought. 'I'm frustrated about my dad, that's all. The care home called me earlier, saying he was acting up again. I may have to go in later to see him.'

'I know, Derek.' She placed a hand on his lap, patted it gently for a few moments, then pulled it away, resting it back on her own.

Derek took the next right, and slowly worked his way through the gears. 'I wonder where they've gone. It doesn't sound very good.'

Karen smiled. 'Whatever shit Tony has got himself into this time, we'll get him out of it. Just like we did it last time.' He looked at her. Their eyes met. 'If we have to, we'll do it again.'

Derek silently nodded before he returned his focus to the road. Within a few minutes, they pulled into Meadow Close.

CHAPTER 24

Four houses down from the Andersons', Mary Leatham was staring out of her bedroom window. She could see a marked Peugeot, a large white Volvo XC90 she didn't recognise, and the familiar brand-new red Mondeo which she knew belonged to Amanda's parents. She spent much of her time at the window, had a fascination with what other people were doing.

She hadn't seen the Volvo before, neither had she seen the police car. She removed the clothes from the radiator in their bedroom and decided to hang around to find out what was going on. Her plans for tomorrow consisted of meeting her friend Margaret, so a good gossip about whatever was happening four doors down over coffee and cake would be something to look forward to.

When the police car arrived almost an hour ago, she'd quickly dragged a single chair over and positioned it near the window to give her the perfect view. Tony Anderson stepped out from the back seat of the police car. Why on earth was he there? Where was his car? Where was his wife and child, she wondered. Then the Volvo had turned up shortly after. A smartly dressed woman stepped out of the driver's seat with dark-brown hair to her shoulders. Mary observed her elegant, professional movements, taking the street in with her eyes. The passenger door then opened to reveal a tall man dressed in a long brown coat, looking like a character from an eighties sitcom. She assumed they were both police.

A little while after, she watched two police constables — the ones who arrived there first with Tony — leave the house and start knocking on doors. The first house didn't answer, nor the second, but the third did. She heard a quiet conversation going on but, unfortunately, couldn't hear all the juicy details. It wasn't long before the police officers came back into view, obviously moving to the next house. Mary got excited and descended the stairs as quick as she could, and before she reached the bottom of the stairs, the knocks at the door echoed in her hallway. 'I'm just coming.' She opened the door.

'Sorry to bother you.' The female PC smiled. 'I'm PC Baan, and this is PC Jackson. We were hoping you could answer a couple of questions.'

Mary dipped her chin and raised a palm to her chest. 'What's happened — am I in trouble, officer?'

Baan smiled politely to reassure her she wasn't. 'No, nothing like that. We were just knocking on doors, hoping to speak to anyone who might have seen anything unusual this morning.'

'Oh . . .' Mary edged forward and lowered her hand by her side.

Baan half-turned and pointed at the Anderson house. 'Have you seen anything strange going on at that house?'

Mary frowned deeply and stepped down off her low, worn step, following Baan's finger, pretending she didn't know which house the PC was referring to. 'Tony Anderson's house?'

Baan nodded.

'No. Why? What's happened?'

'We aren't at liberty to give out any information just yet.' Baan remained professional. 'But we're asking the neighbours if they've seen anything unusual, including the last time they saw Amanda Anderson.'

106

'Amanda . . .' Mary exhaled a little. She looked away from them, down at the floor. 'I-I think I saw her yesterday around teatime. She went for a walk with Abigail. She was on her little red bike thing. Like a bike but had two back wheels.'

PC Jackson nodded. 'What time was that?'

Mary peered down at her watch as if it would help her think more accurately. 'Must have been around five.'

'When was the last time you saw Tony?' Baan this time.

'I saw him when he got out of your police car. God — what's happened?' Mary leaned against the doorframe with wide eyes, folding her arms, pretending to be the caring neighbour.

'As I've said, we aren't at liberty to discuss the details.'

A scowl ran across Mary's ageing face. 'Fair enough. Tony hasn't been there for a few days. He goes away on business sometimes. Has a good job, so Sheila says.' She pointed a finger at the house next to the Andersons, indicating the name of the neighbour.

'Does Sheila live next door to the Andersons? We haven't been able to talk to her yet,' said Baan.

'Sheila's out. Her car isn't there.' Mary didn't even have to check the driveway a few doors down. 'Works long days as a senior midwife.'

Both PCs nodded, absorbing the information.

'Okay.' Baan frowned in thought. 'How did Amanda seem when she walked past with Abigail yesterday?'

Mary considered the question. 'She seemed fine, I think.'

'Do you ever hear them argue?' Jackson asked.

Mary's eyes narrowed, not sure how to answer. Would her answer get either of them into any trouble? Finally, she said, 'Listen, I'm just a neighbour. I don't know what's going on and haven't seen anything weird.'

'So, I'll take that as a yes?' PC Baan pressed.

'I think everyone argues at some point, especially when they're married and have children. That's all me and Ronny argued over. Bloody kids. And money. Kids and money . . .' She trailed off, shaking her head.

PC Jackson and PC Baan thanked Mary for her time and turned, making their way to the gate and back onto the path.

Mary closed the door and threw a hand to her chest when she noticed Ronny standing behind her with a small shovel in his hand, covered in soil.

'God, Ronny. Don't do that.' She groaned and turned the key to lock the door. 'Scared the Jesus out of me there.'

'Who was that?' He pointed the tip of the dirty tool towards the door. He was dressed in his rags: an old brown T-shirt he'd had for probably longer than they were married, tucked into red shorts dotted with different-coloured dried paints from DIY projects over the years.

She moved past him down the hallway towards the kitchen. He followed her.

'It was the police, asking if we'd seen anything unusual this morning. They're at Tony Anderson's house right now. He arrived earlier in their car. God knows where his own car is. They wouldn't say much on the matter, but I have a feeling something bad has happened to Amanda, his wife.'

'What were they asking?' he said, leaning to one side, his hand on the worktop, taking a fraction of his weight off his bony, skinny legs.

'The last time I saw her. Told them I saw her last night walking Abigail.'

Ronny nodded, his long, thinning hair moving like a wave for a moment. He then nudged himself off the worktop and struggled across the kitchen towards the back door. 'Stick the kettle on, love. Cup of tea would be nice.'

'I'll bring it out,' she said. 'Biscuit?'

He replied with a smile, stepped down, and returned to his flower beds. When he was kneeling on the foam pad to take the strain off his bony knees, he thought hard, staring at the parts of the planter he'd already dug up. He then frowned, unsure of something himself. Had he seen something earlier when he was in his bedroom getting changed? Standing at the window? He shook his head, unable to remember clearly. At his age, he couldn't even remember what he had for dinner.

CHAPTER 25

DS Fisher had spoken to Pamela Boone on the doorstep. The senior forensic tech had told her she'd been through the living room and found nothing useful, so if they wanted to take a seat in there instead of sitting on the front door step, they were welcome to.

'Interesting man, your father-in-law,' commented DS Fisher, as she took a seat on the sofa to the right.

Tony pressed his lips together, but remained standing in the middle of the room, as if he was unsure what to do with himself. 'Let's just say we've had our differences in the past and haven't quite made up for them yet.' Instead of taking a seat, he drifted over to the window and peered out in a lost gaze. 'Do we know any more?' He slowly turned to them. 'Because I can't just sit here doing nothing.'

'We're doing everything we can, Mr Anderson,' said DS Phillips, who was standing in the doorway. 'I can assure you.'

'Traffic police must have located the car by now, surely?' He tilted his head, losing his faith in them.

'It would be logical to assume that, Tony, but we don't have cameras in every street, unfortunately. Please bear with us.'

He smiled thinly. The detectives were unsure if the smile was a sign of him willing to bear with them or a polite way of

109

losing his patience. Tony turned back to the bay window and leaned forward, placing his hands on the windowsill.

'You know . . . she loved them,' whispered Tony.

Phillips frowned at him. 'Loved who, Tony?'

'She dug them up. Did it all herself,' Tony added. 'All by herself.'

Fisher stood up with a quizzical look plastered on her face and padded over to Tony to see what he was staring at. 'Who did? Amanda?'

A nod from Tony.

'What did Amanda do, Tony?'

'The plants in the corner.' He pointed, lightly tapping the glass. 'She planted them all by herself. She'd even asked Abigail what colour she wanted.' He turned to her. 'I thought that was a sweet thing to do.'

Fisher gave a gradual understanding nod. 'Okay.' She looked to DS Phillips for a moment, unsure what was going on inside Tony's head.

Outside they heard a car engine.

'Look, they're here,' he said. 'My parents.'

Fisher watched a green Vauxhall Zafira approach the house, slow down, and eventually stop in front of next door's driveway. The man inside, who Fisher assumed to be Tony's father, looked confused. Fisher switched her attention to the woman in the passenger seat, noting she appeared nervous as she got out, a worried expression on her face and her body tense and robotic.

'We'll go outside, Tony. As we have Forensics here, it's better to keep the scene as clean as possible until our tech has been through the whole house.'

Tony nodded at Fisher in understanding, left the living room, and opened the front door, looking happy to get some more air. The detectives followed and Fisher stopped in the hallway, noticing Boone approaching from the kitchen.

'Everything okay?'

Boone nodded. Her forensic kit was clutched in her hand. 'I've covered the kitchen.'

'Find anything?' asked Fisher.

She paused a beat until Tony had stepped through the threshold and onto the driveway, then leaned in. 'Other than the knife, no. You're free to have a look for yourself, you two. I've taken photos and a video to study later so feel free to have a perusal.'

'I'll have a look,' Phillips said. 'April, have you got—'

Fisher pulled another pair of latex gloves from the pocket of her dark-blue suit jacket and handed them to him.

He smiled gratefully and snapped them on.

'Where you going next, Pam?'

'Upstairs. It's obvious to see something went on in the kitchen, but it may have started upstairs.'

'Let me know if you need any assistance. PC Baan and PC Jackson are still here, so just shout us up if you need to. I'll head outside with Tony. Might be interesting speaking with his parents, see what their take on all this is.'

With her free hand, Boone raised a hand and saluted Fisher before she slowly trailed up the stairs, her slim body rustling in her paper suit. Phillips angled left and sauntered towards the kitchen.

Fisher stepped outside, pulling the door closed but leaving it open an inch. She watched Tony's parents approach.

'God, Tony,' Karen cried, as she dashed towards him up the driveway. 'What's going on? Have they found them?' She embraced him and squeezed him tightly. Her hair was long and dark, her brown eyes sat above sunken semi-circles — a sign of tiredness or decades of smoking would be Fisher's guess.

'No — no, not yet, Mum,' he explained, his voice muffled because his face was pulled into her shoulder. She let him go. 'They have people at the station looking for Amanda and Abigail. They have people searching for the car too.'

Karen gave him another hug and made way for Derek, who shuffled forward and did the same, but the hug wasn't as tight or held for as long. When he moved back he placed a palm on the outside of his shoulder. 'You okay, Son?'

He nodded solemnly, doing his best to hold it together.

Fisher noticed his father walked with a slight hindrance. A limp of some sort. Maybe the ankle or knee, she couldn't be sure.

Derek and Karen looked at Fisher. 'Who do we have here, then?' Derek said.

Fisher stepped forward and held out her hand towards Derek. 'DS April Fisher, Greater Manchester Police.' She shook his hand firmly, which took him by surprise, judging by his expression. 'I'm Derek. This is my wife Karen.'

Karen smiled but kept her distance, deciding not to engage with a handshake.

'I hope you're doing your best to find my daughter-in-law and granddaughter?'

'Absolutely, sir. We have our best team on it.'

'So, can I ask . . . why are you not out there looking for them? Surely if you were helping, there'd be a greater chance of finding them?'

Fisher understood his point. He had every right to ask questions. It was expected and certainly didn't take her by surprise.

'Why are we out here — can we not go inside the house?' Karen asked, feeling a sudden chill. The sun had crept behind a grey blanket of clouds, dropping the temperature a few degrees.

'They're treating it as a crime scene, Mum,' explained Tony. 'There's blood in the kitchen.'

Karen suddenly threw both hands to her mouth. 'Blood?'

Fisher nodded. 'It's procedure, unfortunately.' Derek and Karen looked her way. 'Whether or not someone pricked their finger on a nail or something more sinister, with Abigail being taken and your son's car being stolen, *and* the condition of the house, we need to treat this very seriously. It won't take long. But we need to do it. If we want to find them, that's what must happen.'

Derek agreed with a nod. 'Makes sense.'

'How much blood?' Karen asked, scowling.

Tony shrugged. 'Enough to be concerned about.'

Derek leaned forward and grabbed his shoulder gently. Tony gave him a sad smile then noticed something on his wrist.

'What's that, Dad?'

'Gardening. Did it with the shears earlier.'

Tony took hold of his forearm to take a closer look. 'Looks nasty.'

'I'll survive. Look, we're not here about my arm, we're here about Amanda and Abigail.'

'Excuse me a second,' DS Fisher said to Tony and his parents before she turned, and made her way back inside.

* * *

Derek watched Fisher retreat to the house and step through the front door. The door then slowly closed until there was an inch gap.

'Tony,' he said, quietly but seriously.

'What, Dad?'

'What happened this morning?'

'You know what happened. I-I've told you.'

Derek leaned forward and grabbed his forearm, his grip tight enough to let Tony know he was being serious. 'Have you had your medication today?' he whispered.

Tony stared at his father for a few silent seconds before finally shaking his head. 'No, Dad.'

'God, Son . . .' Derek sighed and let go of his arm. He turned to Karen and shook his head, then focused on his son again. 'You know what you're like when you don't take your pills.'

CHAPTER 26

Tony broke eye contact with his dad and stared down at his feet.

'Whatever happened, we'll fix it, Tony,' said Derek, again placing a comforting hand on the outside of his shoulder.

Derek was going to say something when they heard a car approaching from behind them, so all turned to see Tony's brother, Peter, pull up in his small dark-blue work van, parking behind their car. The fancy gold writing stating Anderson Electrics gently glistened in the afternoon sun that had just broke through the disappearing sheet of clouds above.

'He's here,' Tony said, barely above a whisper.

'He told you he would be.' Karen smiled. 'That's the good thing about Peter. He actually turns up.'

Derek sighed and scowled at her. 'Would you give it a fucking rest, woman?'

'When Peter promises you something, you know he always follows it through.'

Derek shook his head at her. 'Just be quiet.'

Tony padded down the driveway, ignoring his parents, his trainers crunching on the stones until he reached the end, and waited.

'How you doing, Tone?' Peter said before he reached him.

Tony smiled and hugged him when he was close enough. 'I'm surviving.'

'Any word yet?' He looked around, confused. 'Who's here with you?'

Tony pointed behind Peter. 'There're police knocking on the neighbours' doors and there are some detectives and a forensic tech inside.'

Peter took a short breath and nodded.

'Sorry you had to come,' said Tony, peering at his brother's workwear. 'I know you're busy.'

His work trousers had multiple pockets on either side of his knees. One side was empty, but the other had a selection of screwdrivers and a pair of pliers peeking out the top. He also wore a loose-fitting green T-shirt with a logo of a spanner and his business name in a small, black, neat font. His hair was past the length of needing a cut, brushed to the side, but he was a handsome man. All the brothers were, even Michael.

'Fuck work. This is more important. I said I'd be here,' Peter told him, patting the side of his arm. 'Just tell me what I need to do.'

Close by, Karen gave Derek a told-you-so look, who did well to ignore it and watch his sons comfort each other.

Peter noticed the front door open and a woman appeared, wearing a dark-blue suit. She had dark, straight hair down to her shoulders and smiled as she approached. 'And who do we have here, then?'

'This is our other son, Peter,' Derek told Fisher.

Peter smiled politely, and checked his hands for dirt and debris before offering to shake hers. They were relatively clean, so he leaned forward.

She accepted it. 'Nice to meet you. Good to see some family support.'

'Whatever we need to do to help Tony find his family,' he replied with a nod, making eye contact with Tony and their parents, who agreed.

The front door opened again. DS Phillips appeared. 'DS Fisher?'

She turned. 'Yes?'

'A word, please.'

'Excuse me for a moment.' She made her way up the drive and went through the door, once again closing it.

Peter leaned in to Tony. 'Have you taken your pills today?'

Derek heard the question and edged a step closer. 'That's what *I* asked him . . .'

For the second time, Tony shook his head, knowing it would disappoint them all.

Peter clamped his eyes closed and sighed heavily. 'You know what happens when you don't take them . . .'

* * *

Fisher edged the door closed and looked to see Phillips waiting at the base of the stairs. 'What is it, Matthew?'

'We've found something interesting.'

'Where?'

'Upstairs, in the bathroom. Boone wants to show you.'

'Lead the way,' she said, trailing him up the stairs. She knew by his tone that whatever it was, it was very important to this case.

CHAPTER 27

'Jack, please,' Rachel Mulberry said to her husband. 'We can't keep driving around here for ever. We've been down this street four times now.'

They approached Meltham Avenue and he snapped his head left and right in desperation. 'We need to find them. Tony's bloody useless. And the police won't do a thing. You know what they're like.'

He was referring to Layla McPherson, the seventeen-year-old who mysteriously went missing. The Mulberrys had seen it on the news, along with the majority of Manchester and the rest of the country, but it was only when Amanda had started seeing Tony that they learned that Layla, at the time, was in a relationship with Tony, the same man their own daughter was seeing. Jack was sure after meeting Tony for the first time that he looked familiar, no doubt recognising his face from the news, appearing distraught, speaking about his missing lover at one of the news conferences.

Rachel didn't reply to him. She knew he could be like a broken record at times, and it was easier to say nothing. She'd learned when to pick her fights with him. Once he got something in his head, she couldn't change his tune. He was on repeat, playing the same song over and over; there was nothing she could do about it.

'I knew it . . .' he whispered.

She'd bitten her tongue for as long as she could and turned to him. 'Knew what?'

'That we couldn't trust him, Rach.'

He turned right then took a left onto Abberton Road, and searched the street frantically, his body rigid in the driver's seat, hands tightly gripped around the wheel.

She shook her head, rolled her eyes, and focused on the windscreen again.

'What?' he said, noticing her disapproval.

'Tony is fine.'

He tightened his lips.

'We need to go home. What if Amanda is there waiting for us? We can't keep driving around here, for God's sake.'

He slowed the car and pulled over to the kerb, pulling the handbrake and dropping his hands from the wheels to fall onto his lap.

'Jack . . .'

He looked tired, heavy bags sitting under his dark-brown eyes.

'If you believe what you think about Tony then why are we driving around these Goddamn streets? If you really believe he's caused this, then we're wasting our time. We need to go home.'

He sighed heavily and knew she was right. The sun had disappeared over Manchester, again replaced by a sheet of clouds, this time much darker, filled with rain.

'Okay.' He slowly raised his hands to the wheel and put the car in gear. 'Let's go home.'

Rachel grabbed his forearm gently. 'You need to be careful when we speak to the police, Jack.' He scowled her way. 'The last thing we want is to attract any attention. We don't want them looking into us . . .'

CHAPTER 28

Amanda's eyes gradually opened and she peered around the enclosed darkness, unsure where she was. Her head throbbed with a pain that ran across her temple, the same temple pressed against the cold, hard floor below her.

She strained as she moved, finding her efforts were restricted, and felt feeble as if her body wasn't her own. A dull ache pulsed in her chest and she felt progressive pains in both of her shoulders. She lay on her front, her stomach and chest pressed against the solid floor underneath her. Her arms were pinned behind, her wrists bound together with something much stronger than she was. Her nose felt sore and inflamed against the floor, so she adjusted her head to ease the weight off for a moment, feeling another strain in her neck. How long had she been in that position for? She recognised a slight taste of metal inside her mouth which she distinguished as blood.

She shivered suddenly, feeling so cold despite it being summer. As well as feeling vulnerable, she was confused and scared.

What the hell? she thought, and gazed around, hoping to understand where she was and more so the reason she was there. She attempted to open her mouth, but the gag wrapped tightly around her face made sure she couldn't. Her cheeks hurt, so instead she let out a moan.

In front of her, she could see the base of a wooden staircase that disappeared out of sight. The wood on each step was rotten and seemed structurally weak. She lifted her head to the right and saw an ancient row of cupboards against a brick wall.

None of it was familiar. Above the worktop, up in the corner, there was a small cone of dreary daylight coming in from a small window. It was the only light source in the room, which allowed her to see an old-fashioned refrigerator to the left of the worktop, the sort she hadn't seen in over a decade. She painfully panned the murky room, taking it all in, breathing light and quick, inhaling the scent of hanging dust and abandonment, which she too felt inside. Apart from the items to the right and the staircase in front of her, the space contained a few cardboard boxes.

Then she understood it was a basement.

A cold, unused basement.

Was it a house?

A factory?

A space below a shop?

Wherever it was, she was alone and neglected and cold.

The smell around her grew stronger: dusty concrete and decaying wood, along with the smell of the iron in her blood from her cut, swollen lip and bruised nose.

What happened? Amanda wondered. She closed her eyes, trying to think how she got here.

She remembered being at home in the bedroom, sitting on her bed, working on her laptop. Tony had just left with Abigail going to see the guy about buying the car, then she received a text message. She couldn't remember what the message said, but knew it had angered her. A moment after, she recollected urgent knocks at the door, so charged down the stairs to open it.

Then . . . nothing. Her mind was blank.

Who was at the door — why couldn't she remember?

CHAPTER 29

Fisher followed DS Phillips up the stairs until they joined Pamela Boone in the bathroom. The forensic tech was standing near the toilet, concentrating on something in her gloved hand, an item she'd evidently found in the cabinet fixed on the wall. Both of the mirrored doors were open, the contents momentarily hidden from Fisher from her position in the doorway.

'Hey, Pam,' said Fisher, panting a little. Boone gave her a nod then looked back down at the object in her hands. Fisher took a step closer, noticing the smell of lavender and various scented candles around them. 'What is it?'

Phillips stepped aside to let her in so she could see it clearly; he was already aware what Boone had found.

Boone turned to Fisher and showed her the small container. 'Venlafaxine.'

'Antidepressants,' Fisher noted without hesitation.

DS Phillips looked her way, but didn't comment on why the name was familiar to Fisher.

'Yeah.' Boone moved the pill bottle closer to her face to read the label clearer.

Fisher moved across to gain a better view of the contents of the little cupboard. Along with a selection of packaged soaps and cosmetic items like tweezers, nail clippers, and earbuds, were a variety of small, cylindrical prescribed pill containers, all with labels on.

Fisher narrowed her eyes, absorbing the unusual names; some of them she recognised.

'What are they?' Phillips asked Boone.

'Mainly antidepressants,' Boone replied. 'Some of them tackle anxiety or stress.'

Fisher craned her neck towards Phillips. 'Why is Tony Anderson on all these tablets?'

Boone offered a gentle shrug. 'It's not every day you see this many tablets prescribed to only one person. I think you guys better find out why.' She sighed. 'Whatever it is, this is serious, April.'

Fisher held out her left hand towards Boone. The forensic officer handed them over.

'Dated only last week too,' Fisher observed.

'Most of them are dated within a month, April,' Boone added.

'Is it the same doctor on all the pills?'

Boone nodded. 'Yes.'

'Well, we need to speak to—' she squinted at the tiny font — 'a Dr Alex Thirst.'

Phillips plucked his phone from his long brown coat, unlocked it, and typed the name on a note.

'Make a note of all of them please, Pamela. If there's anything else you find, please let us know. We're heading downstairs to speak to Tony.' Fisher paused a beat. 'We need to find out what's going on here.'

With that, they left the senior forensic officer by herself to continue looking through the cabinet and the rest of the bathroom. She'd already checked the bedroom drawers and wardrobes. Nothing seemed out of place or unusual. The tablets were the first thing they found they considered strange.

Fisher and Phillips descended the stairs, opened the front door, and stepped down onto the driveway. Tony, his brother Peter, and their parents, Derek and Karen, were still standing, discussing something quietly. Whatever they were talking about, they became silent and all looked in the direction of the detectives.

'Do we know anything yet, Detective?' asked Derek impatiently, placing a hand on his hip.

She slowly shook her head. 'No, not yet, sir.' She eyed Tony, wasting no time. 'Are you on any medication, Mr Anderson?'

Tony's eyes narrowed. 'Sorry?' He looked to Derek and Karen, then back to Fisher. 'Medication?'

Fisher nodded twice. 'Yes, we found a variety of tablets upstairs in your bathroom. I can see they are prescribed to you, Tony.' A silence filled the air around them. 'There seems to be a lot of them . . .'

Before he had the chance to comment, his father Derek limped forward. 'It's from his accident nine years ago.'

Fisher frowned his way. 'His accident?'

Derek nodded firmly. 'Yes.' He exchanged a reassuring glance with Tony, letting him know he'd tell Fisher about it. 'He was involved in a car accident. Nearly lost his life.'

Fisher switched to Tony. 'Is that true?'

Tony nodded. 'Yeah. I often feel anxious and nervous about the smallest things.' He broke eye contact for a second. 'I'm embarrassed about it.'

'Don't be ridiculous, Son.' Derek grabbed his shoulder and squeezed it. 'No need to feel embarrassed at all. It wasn't your fault.'

Tony gave his dad a thin smile, appreciating the support.

'What are the tablets for?' Phillips asked.

'They keep me calm and relaxed. I . . . I sometimes struggle to leave the house. Sometimes the thought of getting into a car worries me because of what happened. The pills keep me positive. They allow me to block out the bad thoughts and the worry I sometimes feel.'

'How often do you take them? There seems to be a lot of tablets up there.'

Tony narrowed his eyes on Phillips, and weighed up the intentions of the question. 'Daily. I take three tablets. Two for my anxiety and stress, and another to . . . well, the doctors said it would take away the nightmares and the visions.'

Fisher looked beyond him towards Derek and Karen, gauging their reactions to his words. They simply nodded in agreement, as if reliving the memory of that awful day. 'And do they — take away the visions?'

'Yeah. They help me.'

'What happens if you don't take them, Tony?'

'Then he doesn't feel himself, does he? I thought you guys were detectives?' said Peter from their right. His abrupt outburst caught the attention of not only Fisher and Phillips but Derek and Karen too.

Tony was hesitant with his answer. 'I feel agitated. I don't feel myself.'

'Have you taken them today?' asked Fisher, remembering some of the pills were unopened.

He nodded. 'I have. First thing this morning. I take them every morning.' He raised a hand to his swollen face where he'd been attacked earlier, and touched his tender cheek with his fingertips.

Fisher stared for a moment. 'Okay, Tony. Thanks.'

'So, what happens now?' said Derek. 'Are we any closer to finding our family?'

'What happens now is I'd like to ask Tony to come down to the station. I believe we can get some more information that could help us with finding Amanda and Abigail.'

Derek frowned. 'Hang on a minute. Tony has already been to the station — he's told you everything he knows.' He sighed, then turned to his wife. 'Tell them.'

She shrugged hopelessly. 'I don't know what more Tony can tell you, Detective.'

'It's a formality, Mr and Mrs Anderson. By asking Tony if he's willing to come back to the station to help us find his missing family doesn't imply anything. We can't go back into the house because our senior forensic officer hasn't finished.'

Derek huffed and puffed. 'Well, how long will that take?' He leaned forward and placed a hand on Tony's shoulder again. 'You can stay at ours while the police clear this up.'

'It would be better if he came with us, sir.' Fisher looked at Tony. 'Would that be okay?'

'Why do I feel you are treating my brother as a suspect here?' asked Peter, who suddenly folded his arms tightly.

Fisher had taken various courses on how to read people during her time in the force. One of the courses, which she believed she excelled in, was the ability to read people's body language. The folding of arms usually meant feeling discomfort and unease, or shyness or insecurity. It was strange Peter had folded them as soon as he'd asked that particular question.

'I can assure you, sir, we are not treating your brother that way. We have adequate seating arrangements down at the station where Tony can relax while the forensic officer is collecting evidence at the house, evidence which could help locate your sister-in-law and your niece. If he thinks of something during that time, he's close by to inform us. It'll make things easier and could speed things up. I'm sure you'll all agree on that?'

No one said a word, but no one looked convinced.

'Go with them, Son,' said Derek. 'Your mother and I will follow you over.'

CHAPTER 30

Four doors down from the Andersons' house, Ronny had drained his tea, placed his empty mug by his side, and slowly lowered himself back to his knees to continue with the gardening, trying to work out what to do with the remaining planters. He struggled to concentrate, his mind working overtime. Since the stroke last year, it had taken him months to get back on his feet and continue living his life like he used to. Unfortunately, the stroke had left him with confusion and visions of things that weren't there.

The sun had crept behind the cluster of clouds that had flown in from the east, the world now basked in a dull-grey blanket. The temperature had dropped, and a slight chill brushed his bare arms.

Ronny became still, unable to concentrate on where to position the remaining plants.

'You okay, Ronny?'

He snapped out of his gaze and looked to his left, seeing Mary standing at the back door, smiling at him. 'Yeah.'

'Time for a break?'

He considered the question and nodded, then slowly stood up, using the rigid side of the planter for support.

'Come on, I'll make you some tea. Time's getting on,' she said before disappearing into the kitchen.

He padded along the path, his ageing bones struggling, and went inside, seeing Mary standing near the cooker in the kitchen, her hands moving inside a mixing bowl. Beside it were various utensils, most of them covered in a white, sugary paste. There was a sweet smell lingering in the air, coming from the oven whirring away in the corner.

'What are you baking?' He took off his cap and wiped his brow.

'Can't you remember? We spoke about this ten minutes ago.'

He stared blankly at her.

'You'll just have to wait and see, then.' She smiled, watched him pad tiredly over to the table, pull out one of the chairs, and drop into it. 'How're the planters?'

He shook his head, shrugged in defeat. 'Think I've bought too many.'

She focused back down on the bowl she was cleaning. 'You'll find a place for them, I'm sure, Ronny.'

He nodded in hope, then the small smile disappeared from his face as he fell into silence.

'What's up, Ron?' She'd been with him long enough to know when he wasn't quite himself.

'I-I'm not sure about something,' he confessed.

'What, Ronny?' She stopped cleaning the bowl and faced him.

He frowned. 'Who knocked on the door before?'

'The police.'

'What did they want?'

'I've told you,' she said, sighing lightly. 'They were asking if we'd seen anything unusual this morning.' She turned back to the bowl. Then, after a beat of silence, looked back at him, noticing the frown still on his face. 'What's the matter? Something is bothering you.' She lowered the bowl and went to the table, taking a seat beside him.

'I think I saw something, Mary.'

'When?'

'I don't know. I can't remember. It feels like it was last week though.'

She nodded, understanding his mind now struggling to comprehend timescales. Something which had definitely became worse over the past year.

'What did you see?'

He squinted and lifted his chin, as if looking for the answer on the ceiling.

'It's okay, Ronny. Take your time.' She studied his confusion and watched the mechanical cogs turn in his mind.

'I-I was at the window,' he started, then looked down at the table. 'In our bedroom.' He clamped his eyes shut, trying to capture the memory more vividly. 'I remember a big white van, I think.'

'Then what, Ron?' she softly encouraged him. She knew getting frustrated with him would only close him down.

'It was parked at the Anderson house. Two men were beside it. One of them knocked on the door.'

Mary waited. 'Then what happened?'

'What?'

'Then what happened, Ronny? The two men, one of them knocked on their door.'

He pouted a little.

She sighed. 'You were at the window,' she reminded him. 'What happened after one of the men knocked at the Andersons' door?' She pointed in the general direction of their house, as if it would reignite his thoughts.

'Oh yeah.' He nodded, then fell into a deep frown, reliving the scene in his head. 'One of them grabbed Amanda, I think, and put her in the back of the van.'

She tilted her head and pressed her lips together. 'Ronny, why didn't you say anything earlier?'

'I-I wasn't sure if it was real or not.'

She smiled sadly at him, fully aware of his visions.

'Just moments before, I was sitting on the bed talking to my dad about the holiday we went on.'

Tears formed in her eyes. She reached forward and took hold of his hand, knowing his dad had passed away more than fifteen years earlier.

'I'm sorry, I—'

'Don't worry. You've told me now.'

She got up, went over to the worktop, and grabbed her phone.

'Who are you ringing?'

'The police,' she said, dialling 999.

CHAPTER 31

The detectives put Tony in a different room than he was in before, a way to make him feel at ease. The last thing they wanted to do was treat him like he was a suspect. DS Fisher opened the door, padded over with a coffee in her hand and a smile on her face, and placed it down on the small coffee table in front of him.

'Any word on the car or Abigail or Amanda?' He stood up, as if expecting news.

'I've just spoken to traffic police. Nothing has come up yet.'

He gave a couple of small nods, thinking hard. 'The longer it goes, the less chance we have of . . .' He trailed off.

'If your car appears on any of the main roads around this city, we'll see it. Don't worry about it.'

He smiled thinly, reaching forward and picking up the coffee. 'Thank you.'

The room had a television, a three-seater sofa, and a coffee table in the centre. Several windows lined the opposite wall to where the sofa was, and through the glass, he could see the sky heavy with grey clouds. The day had survived without rain so far, but you'd bet your mortgage rain would fall before the end of the day.

Fisher took a seat on the same sofa and casually rested her right hand on the arm of it.

'I would have brought you some biscuits if we'd had any,' she confessed apologetically.

They were alone in the room. Tony's parents had followed Tony down to the station but were asked to wait outside. After mild objection, they had no choice to oblige and wait in their car, telling Tony to ring from Amanda's phone if he needed them. Further texts had come through following the text he'd sent earlier. Still, no one had seen or heard from her.

'Tony, I need to ask more questions about the crash.'

He turned to her and waited.

'Firstly, tell me about the tablets, please.'

'What do you want to know?'

'How long have you been taking them?'

He squinted in thought. 'Ever since the accident.'

'How long is that?' She remembered his father, Derek, saying nine years but needed him to confirm it.

'Nine years ago.'

She paused. 'How did it happen?'

He shuffled a little as if getting his body comfortable. 'It was a winter's day. Sometime in December, I think. Before Christmas anyway. I'd been to see my mum and dad. The roads were so icy. The weather reports constantly said keep under twenty at all times. The last thing I remember is pulling up to a junction at the end of their road and turning, then I woke up three days later from a coma. My shoulder was fractured and I suffered a severe concussion. Apparently I'd come off the road and hit a wall.'

He leaned forward, grabbed the coffee, and took a long sip. There was a sadness in his eyes as if reliving the moment.

Fisher nodded slowly.

'The insurance gave me a new car, different type, but brand new. My mum and dad sorted everything out for me.'

Fisher smiled softly. 'That was nice of them.'

Before Fisher had the chance to say anything else, there was a knock at the door, then it opened. She looked up to see DS Phillips enter.

'April,' he said.

'Yeah?'

He nodded backward indicating he wanted to speak to her privately. She excused herself, and went out into the corridor so they could speak freely.

He kept his voice close to a whisper. 'Just been speaking to Dr Thirst — the guy who's prescribed him with the pills.'

She folded her arms. 'What did he say?'

'That Tony Anderson is under his care and has a history of psychiatric issues. He has done for years.'

CHAPTER 32

'Please,' DS Fisher said, 'take a seat.'

Tony's parents took a seat, pulled themselves in, and looked around, obviously not too keen on their surroundings. Karen couldn't hide the frown plastered on her face as she stared across the rectangular table towards Fisher.

Derek scowled. 'Can I ask why we're speaking in this room? I feel like a suspect of some sort.'

'I'm sorry, Mr and Mrs Anderson, it was the only room available,' Fisher explained. 'If it's okay, I'd like to ask you two a few questions.'

'Where's Tony?' retorted Derek.

'He's down the hall, watching television. He's fine.' DS Fisher was alone with them. She had mentioned to DS Phillips beforehand it would make them more likely to open up, giving them a subconscious feeling of power — two against one. The presence of Phillips would appear more threatening, which would only keep their guards up.

'I'm looking for more information about Tony, if that's okay?' She reached across the desk and opened the first page of a thin brown folder. 'How long has he been in psychiatric care for?'

Judging by the look on their faces, they seemed shocked by the question. Derek made a small 'O' with his mouth and Karen stayed deadpan silent, unsure how to answer.

Fisher waited before repeating herself.

'Around fifteen years,' admitted Derek.

'I thought you said he'd been on tablets for nine years?'

Derek sighed heavily and glanced towards Karen, who presented him a thin, defeated smile. He looked back at Fisher, who hadn't taken her eyes off him.

'I'm sorry, I didn't think it was relevant. You asked me about the tablets. I know he got some tablets after the crash because of the injury to his brain and because of the nightmares.'

'But he'd been in psychiatric care six years prior to that?' said Fisher, regarding both of them.

It was Karen's turn to nod. 'Yes.'

'Why? What happened to him?' she asked, watching them consider the question, imaginary mechanical cogs whirring in their brains.

'He struggled with depression in his teenage years. Tried to commit suicide when he was eighteen.'

Fisher listened carefully. 'What was the reason?'

'We don't know, not for definite.' Karen adjusted herself in the seat. 'He was always down about something. We think, at the time, it had something to do with a girlfriend but we're not sure. We asked him over and over.' She raised a palm to her mouth. 'It was awful, Detective. I remember going to his room because his music was blaring, and he was laid flat on his bed. He looked asleep, but he wouldn't wake up. Then we found the empty tablet wrappers under his desk. He'd taken nearly twenty-five co-dydramol tablets. We took him straight to the hospital.'

Fisher knew by their faces it was an awful time for them. Derek placed a palm on Karen's back and rubbed it gently, something he'd no doubt done over the years when they remembered or spoke about it.

'Tell me, what's the relationship like between Tony and Amanda?' asked Fisher.

'They are . . .' She paused for a moment, a tell-tale sign she was being careful. 'They are married. They seem happy enough though, I'd say.' She looked at her husband for support.

'Yeah, they are generally good,' added Derek. 'They have the odd argument, but don't we all? Karen and I have our fair share of disagreements, let me tell you.'

'When was the last time they argued?'

Karen pushed her bottom lip out in thought. 'Hard to say, really. Tony came over a few weeks back, saying how she was complaining that he wasn't spending enough time with her, or with Abigail. I thought it was nonsense because he does his very best for them. I can assure you of that. Tony is a great husband to Amanda; I wish Derek would treat me in the same way.'

Fisher took it all in.

'Guilty as charged, Detective,' said Derek. 'Us men try our best, but sometimes it isn't good enough.'

'Does Amanda do that frequently?'

'Complain?' wondered Karen.

'Yeah.'

'Not more than any other woman I know. You must know yourself when it's our time of the month — and I don't want to admit this in front of my own husband — but we tend to have a shorter fuse. Maybe take things the wrong way.'

'Give me an example.'

Karen sighed. 'I-I can't think of anything specific.'

'Speaking of Amanda, why aren't you out there looking for her?' Derek commented.

'Mr Anderson, we have informed our social media and newsroom about Amanda and Abigail, and passed on descriptions and photos of them. They'll feature on the news tonight, so the public will be made fully aware. Until then, we have officers searching the streets and determining when and where both Amanda and Abigail were last seen.'

Derek half smiled and glanced towards Karen. Her answer seemed to satisfy him for the time being. 'Is there anything else you'd like to know, Detective?'

'No, that will be all. Thank you for coming in.' She closed the file in front of her. 'I'm not one hundred percent sure if Forensics have finished at your son's house, but it might be a good idea for him to stay at your house tonight. To keep an eye on him, make sure he's okay. With Amanda and Abigail both missing, he will no doubt need the support from his family.'

Derek and Karen both agreed and stood, pushed their chairs in courteously, and headed for the door.

'I'll contact you guys tomorrow, if not sooner. We have your details,' Fisher said before they reached the door.

* * *

Derek and Karen stepped into the bright corridor. Brilliant white lights shone down, their reflection bouncing off the hard floor as they moved towards the room Tony was in.

Karen angled her gaze at her husband and kept her voice low. 'Derek, we need to stop protecting him.'

He scowled at her, then glanced behind to make sure no one was there. 'We'll do whatever we need to do, Karen.'

CHAPTER 33

Fisher was at her desk and drained the last of her coffee before she placed her empty mug down next to the keyboard. The time was just after 6 p.m. It had been a very long day for the police. Fisher had been chasing up with traffic police for any signs of Tony's blue Ford Focus, but no one had seen it anywhere.

'It's like it's vanished,' one of the digital techs had said to her less than an hour ago.

'Keep looking,' she'd encouraged before she hung up.

She'd spoken with the search teams who'd been driving around Manchester with Abigail and Amanda's photo at hand, but they hadn't located them just yet. It may have helped if Amanda had her phone with her, something the police could locate using the technology available to them. Tony had gone to his parents' house at least for the night, to give the police enough time to collect everything they needed to at the Anderson house. But other than the mess of the kitchen and the tablets in the bathroom, they hadn't found much at all.

Fisher had asked PC Baan and PC Jackson to gather any information from the neighbours, but nothing immediately important was reported. The PCs, however, had noted neighbours' comments on the relationship between Tony and Amanda as being a little rocky, hearing arguments and one of them unexpectedly leaving the house at strange times. Fisher had added the notes to the case file. She'd also been interested in speaking with the doctor who'd prescribed the pills to Tony. If the doctor had suggested certain pills, then it was obvious he knew Tony well, much better than the police did. Knowing he'd been taking them for fifteen years, she wanted to hear a professional opinion on it and know if Tony had improved over the years, or the issues were still present.

Nearby she heard the footsteps of DS Phillips, who sighed as he sat down and placed his phone on the desk.

'Is she alright?' asked Fisher, looking his way.

'She's fine, thanks, April.' Phillips pulled himself closer to the desk, picked up his phone, then placed it back on the desk. 'Janice is moaning because she made dinner a while ago and reminded me that I promised to be home for it. Another promise I've failed to keep, so she said.'

Fisher smiled sadly. 'It's a tough job sometimes, Matthew.'

It wasn't a secret that DS Phillips's fiancée, Janice, occasionally vented her frustration at the long hours he worked. He'd explained to her it was part and parcel of the job, and he couldn't just knock off at five and come straight home, especially when they were on to a potential lead or dealing with something important. Maybe it was the fact they now had Dominic, their two-year-old son. He understood it wasn't exactly anyone's idea of paradise when you're stuck at home on your own night after night.

'She'll come around, you'll see.' Fisher reached over, and placed a palm on his shoulder.

'Did you speak to Dr Thirst?' he asked, to change the subject.

'I did. Interesting chat.'

Phillips turned to her, waiting for the update.

'So, when Tony attempted to commit suicide, Dr Thirst worked with him for several months, trying to find out why he did it. Although Tony couldn't define the reason for definite, the doctor seems to think it was something to do with his girl-friend at the time, Layla McPherson, going missing.'

Phillips's eyes narrowed. 'She hasn't been found in all this time, has she?'

Fisher shook her head. 'Not as far as I know. The case is still open. A dead end, but still open.'

'Did Dr Thirst say if he'd got better over the years?'

'Well, that's what I found interesting. He said he had seen improvements in Tony, but still feels he needs the tablets to keep him right.' She curled her lip. 'I'm no doctor, but I think if someone has been on medication for that long, there must be a serious reason for it.'

Phillips turned back. 'End of the day, whatever the reason, it'll be doctor and patient confidentiality. So either way, we won't know the ins and outs.'

'April. Matthew.'

Fisher and Phillips turned to see PC Baan, who was panting slightly.

'What you still doing here?' She looked at her watch. 'You should have finished by now.'

'I know, but we've just had a phone call. I need to tell you about it.'

Fisher swivelled fully to face her. 'What's up, Ash?'

'An elderly woman four doors along from the Anderson house got in touch. She said her husband, Ronald, may have seen a van at their house earlier. Something about two men knocking on her door and taking Amanda with them.'

'The call just came in, you said?'

PC Baan nodded, her blonde fringe bouncing a little.

'Okay, thanks for telling us.' She turned to Phillips. 'You coming?'

He smiled, knowing he'd get earache no matter what time he got home. 'After you.'

* * *

It took them a little under fifteen minutes to get to Meadow Close; the traffic was lighter than usual. They spotted the occasional drunk on their route over, staggering along the paths — after-work drinkers, no doubt, or the ones who didn't work and spent their days in the pubs.

They stopped outside the house belonging to the woman who'd called earlier. Phillips noticed someone peering at them from one of the upstairs windows. Phillips looked up, and the shadow vanished.

They got out, closed their doors, and stepped up onto the path. Fisher gazed down at the Anderson house to their right. The curtains were open, leaving the house to sit in a lifeless, miserable existence. The cul-de-sac, apart from their footsteps, was silent. There wasn't a whisper anywhere.

Before they reached the door, Mary opened it and waved them in. They stepped inside, feeling the warmth from the radiators, despite it being summer.

'Please, come through,' Mary said, and led the way to the kitchen.

The house was as Fisher had expected: dated. Thin-framed, gold-tinted pictures hung against thick lining paper from the nineties; the carpet and rug looked expensive but showed heavy signs of wear, especially in the middle where people had previously walked, the colour faded and thinned.

A thin-framed man was seated at the table, and peered up with a faint smile on his face.

'Please, take a seat,' Mary said. 'Can I get you anything? Tea? Coffee?'

Fisher raised a gentle palm. 'I'm fine.' She looked at DS Phillips, who also gratefully declined, and lowered herself into a spare seat.

Fisher took the lead. 'Thanks for your call, Mr and Mrs Leatham. We app—'

'Please, call us Mary and Ronny.'

Fisher smiled. 'We hear you saw something that could be very important?'

Ronny blinked a few times and looked at the detectives. 'Yeah . . . I might have seen something earlier . . .' His voice was quiet and sheepish.

'Might have?' asked Fisher, resting her forearm on the table, unsure what he meant.

Phillips plucked a small notepad from his coat pocket along with a pen, then placed it down on the table, opening it on a clean, empty page.

'I was upstairs in our bedroom,' he started, then paused, closing his eyes.

Fisher made brief contact with Phillips, then returned to Ronny.

'It's okay, Ronny,' said Mary in encouragement. 'Take your time.'

He nodded, as if collecting his hazy thoughts.

'I was putting a few things away. I'd just had a conversation with my—'

'Tell them what you saw from the window, Ronny.'

Fisher frowned at Mary, confused why she'd interrupted him.

'I saw a van pull up at their house. Two men got out and knocked on their door. Amanda answered it.'

Phillips jotted some notes down.

'Then what happened?' pressed Fisher.

'She opened the door and the men went inside,' he said.

Mary, who was seated to his right, frowned at him. 'You didn't tell me that part.'

'I-I've just remembered about it.'

Mary sighed and looked away from him.

Fisher studied them both. It was clear he was struggling to recall the events very clearly, and Fisher made a mental note to ask Mary if Ronny had some form of dementia.

'And how long were the men inside?' asked Fisher.

He shook his head several times. 'I don't know. A few minutes. Maybe ten minutes.'

'And you stayed at the window until the men came out?'

He said he did.

'And what happened exactly?'

141

He scowled at Fisher. 'She didn't want to go with them. She tried to go back inside. But one of them was tall and looked strong. He picked her up and put her in the back, I think.'

They all absorbed the story for a moment.

'Could you describe the appearance of the two men?' asked Phillips. 'Have you seen them before?'

'No, I don't think so. I don't get out much though. I spend much of my time reading the paper and out in the garden. But they didn't look familiar to me.'

Fisher glanced at Mary, who confirmed his words. 'Yeah, he loves the garden. We occasionally go on little walks around the neighbourhood. But generally, he stays inside or in the garden, as he said.'

He leaned back, patted his thighs. 'My legs aren't what they used to be.'

'Can you remember what type of van it was?'

He shook his head. 'A big white one. I don't know cars or vans very well. I didn't get around to driving myself, so . . .' He trailed off, looking down at the table as if embarrassed about that fact.

Phillips jotted something down. 'Anything else unusual?'

'Not that I know.'

'Can I have a quick word with you, Detective?' Mary asked Fisher, who nodded, and indicated the direction of the hallway with a tip of her head.

Mary pulled the kitchen door closed, leaving her husband with Phillips in the kitchen. 'I'm very sorry we didn't call sooner. Ronny had a stroke last year and gets things mixed up. I know it sounds a little crazy but he has these visions sometimes and forgets things very easily. He even said he was talking to his father earlier.'

Fisher knew what was coming.

'And he died fifteen years ago.'

She nodded, aware that often strokes can spur on early dementia.

'Do you believe him?' asked Fisher, tilting her head.

She considered the question. 'Yeah, I believe him.'

'Good enough for me.'

CHAPTER 34

Fisher's head pounded when she woke up. It had been a rough night. She'd awoken several times because of the howling wind and heavy rain that had continually tapped at the windows. At 2 a.m., she'd sat up, sighed, and decided to get out of bed, padding over to the window and pulling back the curtain. On the dark street below, she watched the rain pound the roads and the path. Up above, despite it being in the middle of the night, the sky was filled with a dense sheet of thick, thunderous clouds, hiding the cluster of stars she often stared at when she couldn't sleep. The streams of water flowing down each side of the road had filled and was blocking the drains, the water now creating large puddles in various areas.

She raised her hand to the window, trying to touch the droplets of rain as they slipped down the other side of the glass.

The usual cars were parked down in the street, belonging to her neighbours. Pete, the guy next door, who'd lived there ever since she had, had just bought himself a Porsche Cayenne. Fisher wasn't overly interested in cars, so his excitement had quickly faded when he'd mentioned it to Fisher, who stared at him like he had three heads. It didn't impress her one bit. To her, a car was a means of getting from one place to another — as long as it was comfortable, worked, and kept the rain off her, that's all that mattered.

She had purchased the Volvo XC90 a year ago, a bargain considering it had only gone sixty thousand miles. The salesman, a guy in his fifties desperate for the commission, told her she'd be missing out on a fantastic deal if she decided to walk away. She wasn't all that fussed but liked the style and feel of it when she was inside. And it was white, her favourite colour, so was happy to pay the monthly instalments he'd calculated for her.

She pulled the curtain across, climbed back into bed, and succumbed to sleep until an hour later when she woke up again. Whether it was the excess noise that had kept waking her or the fact that things were on her mind, she didn't know. The recurring dream of leaving the club and getting into the taxi with the guy in the red shirt kept coming back to her. As the taxi pulled to a stop, every time he got out and opened her door, she woke up, not remembering where she was or what happened after. She was exhausted and couldn't stop thinking about what must have really happened. How did she get the marks on the insides of her thighs and on her wrists?

At 7 a.m., she finally got up, went to the en suite, and turned on the shower. She had received a text message from her sister Freya and one from her dad, but decided to read them later. She removed her underwear, threw them in her wash basket, and got inside the warmth of the falling water, pulling the door closed once inside. She thought about her family, how she should make more time for them. After all, they weren't getting any younger and wouldn't be around for ever. If there was one thing that working in the police had taught her, it was that life was short, and often shorter for others. She decided to stay in longer and sat down in the shower tray, watching the space around her fill with steam. She brought her knees up to her face and wrapped her hands together around her knees, thinking about the past. Good times with her parents and sister, various holidays they'd been on — anything to take her mind of recent cases.

Then the image of Amanda and Abigail came to her mind, their posed smiles on the photograph Tony Anderson had given the police yesterday. Where the hell were they?

It was bad enough a woman going missing, but a child . . .

Her first job of the day would be to chase down the whereabouts of the van that Mary and Ronny Leatham had told her about. She'd phoned Traffic Control last night, asking them to trace the white van, but without a registration plate, they'd be aimlessly searching for hundreds and hundreds of vans due to all the trades and commercials in Manchester.

Today, she promised herself they would make progress.

* * *

She walked into the office less than an hour later, dressed in her usual work attire. Dark-blue jeans, a white top, and a blue blazer. She'd dried her hair and brushed it back, but instead of straightening it so it hung down just above her shoulders, she had tied it in a short ponytail.

'Morning,' DS Phillips said to her, hearing her approach. He was already at his desk, sipping coffee, with his emails open on his computer screen.

'Hey, Matt.' She tiredly shrugged off her jacket, hung it on the back of her chair.

'Sleep well?'

'Worst in years, to be honest,' she said. 'The bastard rain kept waking me.' She sat down, edged herself in, and reached for her mouse.

'Tell me about it. Janice was up a lot too, complaining about the same thing. Funny thing was, Dominic actually slept all night. Bloody typical.'

'It didn't wake him?'

'He was dead to the world . . . for a change.' He smiled and focused back on his screen.

'What are you on with?' Fisher leaned over to see his screen.

Phillips raised a hand to cover his screen. 'Top-secret spy stuff. Below your paygrade, unfortunately.' They shared a smile and he lowered his hand. 'DI James wants me to speak with Forensics about the footprint found at the river where Elaine Freeman was.' He placed his cup down, angled towards her, and noticed she looked worse than he'd originally thought. He wondered if it was just a lack of sleep or something else. 'You okay?'

She closed her eyes and took a long breath before she swivelled his way. 'Matthew, I'm fine.'

He accepted her response and was wise enough to say no more. He cared for her, that was all.

'How we doing this morning?' a voice said behind them.

DI James had a folder tucked between his arm and hip. His hair was gelled back, his face clean-shaven and moody-looking. He was wearing a black jacket and white shirt, along with smart trousers and shoes.

'Where are you going — the ball with Cinderella?' Fisher mused, trying to lighten the mood.

'I scrub up well, don't I?' He smiled at her briefly before he resumed the frown. He explained a member of senior management was coming in.

'What for?' Fisher itched her chin with a fingertip.

'To see how we handle our reports, but I know they're looking for an update on what's been going on. They're making the rounds in Manchester throughout the stations, making sure we're all up to date with things.'

'They from headquarters?' asked Phillips.

DI James nodded at him. 'Yeah. Guy called Liam Watson. Heard of him?'

Both Fisher and Phillips shook their heads.

'Me neither. DCI Baker knows him — says he's a right clown. One of these guys who's never done the job himself and goes around telling people how we should be running things.'

Fisher knew the type, and rolled her eyes. 'Well, we'll be on our best behaviour if he comes in.'

Footsteps approached from the left.

'Morning, guys.' PC Ashleigh Baan stood there, dressed in her uniform, with an unusual shy expression on her face.

'Hey, Ash. You okay?' Fisher asked, turning fully towards her.

Baan nodded. 'How are things, April?'

DS Phillips and DI James looked at each other and left to give them time to speak alone.

Baan lowered herself into Phillips's chair. 'So, how are you?'

Fisher smiled. 'Listen, Ash, if this is about what happened the other night, I'm fine.'

'Look, I've known you long enough to know you don't like to dwell on things too much, but let me know if there's anything I can do, or if you just want to chat.'

'You'll be first person I speak to, Ashleigh. Thank you.'

As PC Baan slowly stood, Fisher squeezed her hand appreciatively, before she disappeared into the office.

* * *

In the control room at Manchester City Council Town Hall, Jessica Thorpe was still looking at the white van that DS Fisher was interested in. She'd made a note of the events that happened yesterday, the location of the Anderson house, and scribbled down the time DS Fisher was expecting the van to be seen on the CCTV system.

As you'd imagine, monitoring the CCTV in Manchester was pretty much hell.

The council itself had several buildings across Manchester and, in total, employed over twenty-six thousand people, including bin men, plumbers, electricians, and so on. But this building, located on Albert Square, was the oldest and most historic of all. It opened in 1877 and took nine years to build. Jessica had worked there since she'd left school at sixteen. She didn't have any real qualifications and was unsure what to do after leaving school, but her mother, who worked at the council at the time, managed to get her a job answering telephones at the front desk. After a few months and the continual boredom of dealing with the ridiculous calls that came in, she wanted to do something different. Luckily, there was an opening in the control room as an assistant.

The CCTV control room was huge, located in the corner of the ground floor. Through its main double door, there was a long walkway in between neat rows of desks on either side. The room was bright and airy, with plenty of light coming from the floor-to-ceiling windows that had been a challenge to install at the time. At the end of the room, there was a bank of sixteen monitors all fixed to the wall, all positioned neatly and equally spaced around a single, monstrous monitor located in the middle. An impressive control panel was positioned in front of it all, built into three large wooden desks, controlled mainly by just one person.

Today that person was Jessica.

Another eighteen people were working in the room alongside her, many of them sitting at individual desks, which remarkably had three monitors each. The employees searched for cars, people, or whatever else they needed to. Much of their work was a result of police requests.

Jessica shared the role of head controller with an Asian man called Tally, short for Talisham. He'd been doing it for nearly five years and knew the system inside out. Jessica had obtained her degree in IT, which both her mother and manager suggested would do her some good, and had applied for the role to work alongside Tally. She had a lot to learn, but her attitude and willingness to do so was unparalleled.

Jessica sat down at one of the spare computers and logged on. She searched the closest camera to Meadow Close and pressed Enter. The results showed a camera was located on the A5145, thirty yards down from Lime Road, the road that led to Granby Road and eventually Meadow Close. She entered the time that Fisher had suggested, being roughly 11.30 a.m.

The video streams were recorded in one-hour increments, and saved automatically in a folder, before a new feed started. They figured this was the easiest and most efficient way of going back.

Moments after, a white van came into view, approaching Lime Road, and took the left. She paused the screen and scrolled the time bar back a few seconds until the van's registration plate was closer and clearer.

She pulled her phone out, made a note of it, then continued to watch.

Eighteen minutes later, the van appeared, turning out of Lime Road, pulling onto the A5145, and taking a right.

'Jessica,' a voice said from her left.

She looked up to see Annie, one of the council apprentices. 'Yes, Annie?'

'Could I have some help with this over here, please?'

'Give me a minute, okay?'

The ginger-haired, shy-looking apprentice nodded, and disappeared back to her desk. Jessica paused the screen, the driver and passenger of the van visible. The driver looked to be in his fifties, and wore a cap. The passenger had a similar appearance but had short dark hair and looked at least fifteen years younger. She screenshotted the image, opened up her email, typed in DS Fisher's address, and included the reg plate: R34 WUG. She pressed Send.

She found Fisher's number and pressed Call.

'Hey, April.'

'Found anything?'

'Yup. Check your emails. It's the only white van on the road with two men inside of it within the hour.'

'Really?'

'I know. I couldn't believe it myself. Anyway, the info should be with you now.'

'Thank you.'

'Anytime. Good luck.' Jessica ended the call and headed to Annie's desk, where she was waiting for help.

CHAPTER 35

Fisher was studying the photo Jessica had sent over when she heard something behind her. She turned to see Tony Anderson and his parents approaching, accompanied by PC Baan, who'd collected them from reception.

'Morning,' Fisher said to all of them as she stood, and extended a hand to Tony. 'How are you, Mr Anderson?'

'I've been better.' He shook her hand. Dark semicircles pulled his eyes down. 'I didn't sleep much. Spent half the night driving around with my dad, but didn't see them.'

Fisher looked at Derek, who looked equally as exhausted, and smiled sadly.

Tony was wearing a black T-shirt, blue jeans, and white trainers. His hair was messy, and judging by a faint smell coming from him, Fisher guessed he hadn't showered.

'Please, take a seat,' she said, motioning to the empty chair that DS Phillips normally occupied. Tony dropped into it. Fisher sat in hers and smiled. Derek and Karen gazed around for a moment, but there were no spare chairs, so they remained standing in defeat and stared at Fisher. PC Baan smiled and walked away in the direction of her desk.

'Is there any news yet, Detective?' Derek Anderson asked, folding his arms, apparently annoyed he wasn't offered a seat.

'We've spoken with one of Tony's neighbours, who informed us a van pulled up at the house yesterday morning.' She looked at Tony. 'This happened just after you left. Two men got out, went to your door. Amanda answered and they went inside.'

His eyes widened. 'Two men? They went inside my house? Who were they? Who was the neighbour?'

'Mary Leatham. She lives four doors up from you.'

'She saw a van?' asked Derek.

'Well, no, her husband Ronny did.'

'According to Mr Leatham, the men left your house with Amanda and put her in the van, then drove away.'

Karen came close to Tony and placed a comforting hand on his shoulder and the other to her open mouth.

Derek probed, 'Who were the men?'

'Take a look,' she said as she turned to her computer. 'It isn't very clear, but I'm just about to check the registration on our system — it will bring up the owner's information.'

Fisher opened the two pictures of the van. One of the registration plate and the other of the two men sitting inside. It wasn't the clearest image, but they could see their basic features. The driver wore a cap covering most of his face and the passenger was slouched in his seat, looking very relaxed.

'Who are they?' said Derek, edging closer to the computer screen with a frown.

'The guy in the passenger seat looks familiar . . . I think,' said Karen, squinting.

'Does he?' asked Derek. 'Who is he?'

'I don't know . . . I'm not sure.'

'We have their registration,' added Fisher. 'I have a PC putting it through the system now.'

Before either Karen or Derek replied, they heard a voice behind them from across the office. 'April?'

Fisher leaned to her right, seeing PC Baan hurry towards her.

'April, there's been a report about a blue Ford Focus.'

'Is it mine?' asked Tony, peering up from his seated position.

PC Baan maintained her focus on Fisher. 'We found it in a small lake.'

'Is it Tony's car?' pressed Derek.

'We don't know. From the reports, the registration plates aren't visible. The divers are going in now to check it out and there's a tow truck on its way to pull it out.'

'Is it . . . is it mine?' Tony asked again.

Fisher thanked Baan with a nod and turned to Tony. 'If you wouldn't mind coming with us, maybe we can identify it in some way.'

'Is there anyone inside?' Tony asked Baan.

'We don't know, Mr Anderson. We'll know when we pull it out.'

Fisher took a breath, feeling mixed emotions. 'Right, come on, let's go. PC Baan, you come with me. Derek, you take Tony. Follow us over.'

Derek nodded at Tony, who seemed to be frozen to the chair in some kind of trance. 'Come on, Son. We need to see this.'

* * *

It had been reported by a woman in her fifties, who'd been walking her dog and had noticed the rear of the car sticking a few feet out of the water.

The operator who'd answered the call had asked her if she could see the registration plate. She told her the car was quite far under and only the rear windscreen was visible.

Karen and Derek, with Tony in the back, followed Fisher's white Volvo across the city. The car was in a small lake at the end of Millgate Lane, close to Millgate fields, Didsbury, a small town roughly five miles from Tony Anderson's house and over two miles from where Tony had been attacked and had last seen his daughter. It was roughly twenty miles from the station and took them a little over half an hour in the traffic — the longest and most anxious thirty minutes of Tony's life. He sat in the back with tears in his eyes.

Derek was agitated, Karen could tell. He kept turning the wheel erratically and staying too close to the rear of Fisher's Volvo.

'Derek . . . if she brakes, you'll—'

'Karen, I can fucking drive. Leave it.'

'Both of you just be quiet,' Tony's voice echoed behind them, sick of the petty bickering he'd heard since they left the station.

They immediately fell silent. Karen wanted to soothe Tony, but knew it was pointless. Nothing could be said to make the situation any better. Tony's thoughts bounced around his heavy head, wondering what the divers would find. Would Abigail be in the back of the car, her little body still strapped in her seat and—

He shook the thought away and filled his cheeks with air. Karen glanced behind and studied him with tears in her own eyes. They all needed to stay positive, although it seemed impossible considering the circumstances.

'Just up here.' Derek followed DS Fisher down a narrow lane, watching the Volvo rock side to side as it passed over the uneven ground until it eventually levelled out a moment later. Several police cars and a van were parked in front of where Fisher had slowed, seemingly deciding where the best place to stop was. She angled over onto a small area of grass beside the lake.

They'd never been here before. Never knew of its existence. Derek pulled on the handbrake, turned the engine off, slowly stepped out, and stared in amazement at what he was seeing. The rear of a Ford Focus was visible, poking out from the still, murky green water that surrounded it.

'Jesus,' he whispered.

Karen remained in the passenger seat, unable to move. There was silence all around them, but for the murmurs of police officers and the dull sounds of footsteps on the muddy ground from last night's rain.

Tony jumped out, slammed the door, and raced towards the lake, the sloppy mud almost pulling him to the ground as he navigated through it.

Fisher spotted him and pointed. 'Get him!'

PC Baan bolted around the front of Fisher's Volvo and managed to reach him before he got to the water, grabbing his forearm to prevent him from going in. 'Tony . . .'

'Abigail, Abigail!' he screamed, his frantic energy filling the air as he tried to shake PC Baan's grip, but she held him tightly.

A few nearby PCs from another station frowned at them, weighing up whether to intervene, but it seemed Baan had Tony under control for the time being.

'Please, Tony,' Baan said evenly. 'You *need* to stay calm.'

He understood her demand, but it didn't stop him trying to prise her hand away. 'I need to see — I need to see if it's my daughter. Let me go.'

'Tony, please . . .' DS Fisher said from behind as she approached them.

He turned her way and panted hard. She placed a hand on his shoulder. 'The divers are looking now. We need to wait. Okay?'

Tony reluctantly nodded and his shoulders dipped a little, enough for Baan to feel she could ease off and let go of his arm. In the water, there was movement on both sides of the car. The occasional splashes caused ripple effects that reached the edge of the lake. The divers' heads appeared a few moments later. Their faces were covered in large goggles and rubber hoods to keep dry in the water. One said something, and the other nodded twice, before they made their way to shallower waters and battled to their feet.

'What's going on?' Tony asked Fisher, who knew as much as he did.

Derek and Karen stood watching from behind, holding each other in anticipation. Tears fell from Karen's face, pulling down streaks of the mascara she'd put on earlier this morning.

Fisher peered at Baan. 'Would you mind waiting here with Tony while I go speak to the divers?'

Baan nodded as Fisher moved towards a few figures standing at the edge of the water, two of which she didn't recognise, dressed in police uniform. Another figure stood by in a wet suit, only a small amount of his face visible. Beyond the diver was another man with a goatee, dressed in smart trousers and a thin black fleece.

Fisher moved over to them, eyeing the lake and the back end of the car peeking out of the water. Across the lake, the sun shone down from above, splitting the thick trees to the left and casting dull shadows on the water. If it wasn't for the car and the devastating situation they were in, the lake itself would have been picturesque, the foreground of a perfect shot surrounded by high trees and bright-blue sky.

'Hey,' said Fisher, stopping near the officers. They all looked her way. 'DS April Fisher.' She extended a hand to both PCs first, then to the guy in the smart trousers. He had thick eyebrows along with his goatee, was probably somewhere in his late forties, and what was left of his receding hair was gelled to the side. He leaned forward and took her hand, giving it a firm squeeze. 'Nice to meet you, April. I'm DS Alex Maclean.'

She acknowledged him. 'Thanks for the call.' He nodded. Then she said, 'We'll need to get the car out of the water as soon as possible.'

'Already on it, DS Fisher. The tow truck is almost here.' He lifted a hand to see the time on his watch. 'Should be any minute now.'

The divers trudged out of the water, slopping towards Fisher and DS Maclean, soaking the ground as they moved. The first one pulled off his goggles and pulled the hood up off his head, revealing the face of a man in his late thirties with green eyes and a thin beard. He blinked several times, his eyes adjusting to the beating sun.

DS Maclean addressed one of the divers. 'What's happening, George?'

George waited for the other diver to become level with him, watched him pull his goggles and hood down, then faced the DS. 'There's no one in the seats but we've pulled the rear seats forward to check the boot. We can't get in properly but it feels like material. It could be clothing. It's possible there's someone in there.'

CHAPTER 36

Less than twenty minutes later, Fisher heard a rattling sound coming from the narrow track they'd driven down to get there. She turned, seeing a small but hefty-looking tow truck, powered by a low rumbling diesel engine and huge, thick wheels.

The line of vehicles, including Fisher's Volvo and Derek's Zafira, needed to be moved further down to allow the truck enough room to manoeuvre. The driver of the truck, a small chunky guy with a moustache, managed to turn the truck around in eight points so it was now facing away from the car, its powerful winch now ready to be lowered into the water. He'd left enough space for the car to be pulled onto the grass.

Fisher hadn't relayed the information back to Tony, Derek, or Karen about what the divers had thought they'd seen in the boot of the car. She needed to be sure before delivering such devastating news. While they'd waited, Fisher had asked the divers about the registration plate, a definitive way to know if it was Tony's car.

'The plates have been removed, Detective,' George had told her.

The driver had a brief chat with the team about next steps, before he climbed back into the seat of the truck and readied his controls, while the divers returned to the water, slowly battling through it until they reached the car. Between them, they manoeuvred a large fabric sling, roughly fifteen metres long, in through one of the rear windows, through the back of the car and out the opposite window, then joined the ends with a heavy-duty shackle that weighed so much it tested both their strengths.

The driver pressed a button, causing a loud whirring to break the silence of the worried onlookers, and the heavy-duty hook was lowered into the shallow water. George, the diver, swam back a few metres towards the truck, grabbed the hook, and with his colleague's help, attached it. Once secure, he waved at the driver. The winch started rattling again, this time louder, the mechanism pulling the wire taut, peeling the car off the bottom of the lake.

It took a painfully slow five minutes to pull the car onto the grass.

Tony made a dash for it but DS Fisher stepped in his path. 'Tony, please wait,' she begged. 'Let us check it out first. Please.'

He considered her words, nodded slowly, then turned away, padded over the damp grass to Karen and Derek, who offered him a sad smile and a caring hand on his shoulder.

DS Fisher and DS Maclean led the search, both equipped with latex gloves and rolled-up sleeves. Fisher was keen to see what was in the boot, so rounded the saturated car, mini waterfalls of lake water seeping through the crevices down onto the grass.

'I'll check the driver and passenger seat,' DS Maclean informed her. One of the PCs followed him, the other was behind Fisher.

Fisher reached for the boot handle and pulled it upwards with everything she had, surprised at how heavy it had become with the surplus water, and stared inside. The fabric the diver declared looked to be a black golf cart bag positioned on its side. It had wheels on the bottom of it and a handle on the top. Among the mess was a coat and an umbrella. She sighed in relief, seeing no small body of a child.

Which meant one thing. Abigail was still out there.

'What can you see?' Tony shouted from a few metres away, his agitated voice filling the silent air around them. She ignored his question, left the boot, and went to DS Maclean, who was leaning into the passenger seat, rustling through the contents of the passenger-side glovebox.

'Found anything back there?' he asked, sensing her watching him.

'No. You?'

He edged back out and straightened up. 'Maybe?'

Her attention fell on the object in his hands. A passport. He opened it up, scanned the name, then held it open and turned it to her.

Amanda Anderson.

'No wonder we couldn't find her passport at home,' said Fisher. 'It's been here all along.'

DS Maclean narrowed his eyes in thought and scratched his chin with his spare hand. 'Mean anything to this case?'

Fisher had briefly described what had happened with Tony Anderson and the disappearance of his wife and daughter. Finding the passport in the glovebox of the missing car certainly rang alarm bells, especially when they'd usually keep such important personal items secure at home.

'What's happening, DS Fisher?'

Fisher peered over to Derek Anderson, who seemed to be just as anxious as his son Tony, both watching the detectives carefully. Fisher thanked Maclean and excused herself, making her way over to the Andersons.

'Is it my car, Detective?' asked Tony.

Without the plates, the only thing that could determine if it was his car would be whatever was inside. And, judging by the conversation between Fisher and the other detective, Tony knew they'd found something.

'Tony,' she said, 'the good news is that there's no body inside the vehicle.' She paused a beat, then showed him the passport. 'But we found this in the glovebox.' She held it out for him to see and pulled it back when he attempted to grab it. 'I'm sorry, we need to check it for prints. We need to understand why her passport was in your glovebox.'

Karen didn't look happy. 'I'm sorry, Detective . . .' She took a step closer. 'But you aren't insinuating Tony had anything to do with this, are you? The car isn't just Tony's, you know. It's both of theirs.'

'I'm just explaining what's been found and that we'll need to check it for prints. If the person responsible for Amanda's whereabouts has touched this passport, we need to find out who it is. It could lead to where she is, and . . .' She paused. 'Maybe it could help us find Abigail too.'

Derek, Karen, and Tony all nodded in understanding. Tony stared longingly at the passport. Fisher understood — it was the closest thing to Amanda there was at the moment. He sighed heavily and turned away, his eyes filling up. Karen swivelled around and placed a comforting arm around him.

'If she isn't here, Tony, it means she's still out there,' she reassured him, trying to stay positive.

'I just don't know why her passport was in the car.'

She had no answer so instead held him for a while.

* * *

Tony watched the truck driver lift the Focus onto the bed of the truck. DS Fisher came over, informing them the car needed to be taken back to the station for analysis, mentioning Forensics would need to check the vehicle for any signs anyone had been in the car. At least they'd be able to get DNA from the guy Tony knew as Martin Forlan, the guy who'd attacked him yesterday morning and stolen his car.

'Would you be okay coming back to the station, Tony?' Fisher asked him, then noticed the reaction on his father's face.

'Don't you think he's been through enough, Detective?' Derek said sternly.

'Can't he just come home with us? He's been through hell,' added Karen, shaking her head at Fisher.

'We need to wrap things up.' Fisher's eyes flicked between them. 'I'm sure you can understand . . .'

Tony didn't understand, nor did his parents, but they accepted what she said and slowly turned, making their way back to the Zafira. Once the flatbed truck had vanished from view and the narrow road was clear, Derek turned around and headed back to the station.

* * *

Fisher and PC Baan followed them from a distance in the Volvo. They could see Tony in the rear of the car through the windscreen, his body slouched, but occasionally he moved suddenly as if they were having a debate about something. Whether it was heated or casual, neither Baan nor Fisher could be sure.

PC Baan angled towards her, and thought about the text from the CCTV control room Fisher had shown her. 'Did you tell them about the message?'

'No,' said Fisher. 'It will make for an interesting conversation with Tony, I'm sure. That's why we need him back at the station.'

Baan looked away to the bright-blue sky of Manchester. In the distance, dark-grey clouds were approaching; the day looked like it was taking a turn for the worse.

CHAPTER 37

Fisher sat at her desk with DI James, DS Phillips, and PC Baan. They watched the video twice.

'It's him, isn't it?' DS Phillips said, as he leaned over her shoulder, trying to see clearer.

'Certainly looks like him,' she agreed. 'And we can't argue about the registration matching his.'

The footage showed the Focus intact, the plates there, fixed to the car. When they'd been removed was anyone's guess at this point.

DI James stood up.

'What are you thinking, boss?' Phillips noticed his expression change suddenly.

The office had become warm over the morning due to the windows being closed. A rookie mistake in any office environment.

'Why he'd be driving that way, that's all.'

'Well,' said Fisher, standing, 'let's go and find out.'

The text that Fisher had received from Jessica at the town hall control room said she'd spotted the blue Focus, driving along a road yesterday morning close to where the car was found. Fisher had phoned Jessica on her way to the station, requesting more details. The Focus had been heading southbound on the A34 near Didsbury. It rang alarm bells. What reason did Tony have to be near Didsbury?

Jessica had sent a still shot of the best angle and emailed it immediately. Bingo.

Fisher's phone rang in her pocket before she reached the interrogation room. She paused in her stride and accepted the call.

'Hello.'

'April, I've run a check on the white van, registration plate Roger-three-four-Whiskey-Uniform-Golf. We have a match. It's registered to a guy called Rory Appleby. He lives in Little Bolton near the M602.'

'Okay, thank you.'

'I've recorded the address on file, but I can text you it over if you like?'

'Great. Thank you.'

'Any time, DS Fisher.'

She placed the phone back into her pocket and continued along the brightly lit corridor, passing the door to the interrogation room that the Andersons were occupying, and opened the next door, which led to a dark square-shaped room with a faint light above. She spotted DS Phillips and DI James in the darkness, watching Karen, Derek, and Tony through the one-way mirror.

'Hey, guys.' She closed the door and ambled over. 'How are they doing?'

DI James turned back and smiled, then faced the mirror again.

'They said anything useful?' Fisher probed, joining them at the tinted glass.

'Not really,' DS Phillips whispered. 'Derek assured Tony he thinks Amanda and Abigail will be found soon. It's the same support I'd give to my own son, to be honest.'

DI James said nothing, continued to watch them closely.

'What d'you think, boss?' asked Fisher. She could smell his aftershave — sweet and woody and manly.

'I don't know for sure.' He grinned. 'Go in, April. Do your thing. Ask him why he was driving near Didsbury.'

She nodded, turned away towards the door, but came to a swift halt. 'Ops have been in touch about the van. Registered to a Rory Appleby. Lives in Little Bolton. Any of you recognise the name?'

DS Phillips shook his head. 'Nope.'

'Not that I know of,' replied the DI. 'I'll get some of our team on that immediately.'

Fisher left the room, closed the door, and entered the interrogation room, where the air was nicely conditioned. She made her way around the opposite side of the desk, pulled out the chair, and dropped into it.

'What's going on, Detective?' insisted Derek. 'Why do we need to be here? My son's wife and daughter are still out there.' He pointed in the direction of where he thought outside was. 'This—' he pointed at the desk to indicate them being there — 'is wasting not only our time but yours.'

Fisher held his gaze for a few moments, then looked at Tony. 'Tony, where did you drive yesterday?'

His eyebrows met the centre of his forehead. 'Yesterday?'

'Yeah, you said you'd travelled back from Darlington on a business meeting?'

He gave two gradual nods. 'Yes?'

'Did you go straight home?'

'No, I went to drop something off for my brother. He was working. He phoned me, asking me to call at the electrical suppliers on my way back and drop something off. He'd said the customer was being a pain in the arse.'

'I see. Where was your brother working, Mr Anderson?'

'Erm, I can't exactly remember where . . .' Tony shifted his head, trying to think.

'Why the questions?' asked Derek, dropping the 'Detective' title now.

'Because Tony was seen on the A34 near Didsbury yesterday morning.' She lowered her right hand, pulled her phone from her pocket, and placed it on the table, then observed their confusion. 'See this?'

The three of them peered over at the screen. Derek squinted hard. Fisher noted by a flash of recognition that he knew what he was looking at.

'That's me,' said Tony.

'It is,' said Fisher. 'You were seen near Didsbury, very close to the lake where we've just located your car.' She flicked her attention between them. 'I just don't understand why Amanda's passport was in the glovebox.'

'Haven't we been over this, Detective?' Karen sighed. 'He said he doesn't know. Is that answer not good enough for you?' She finished with a shake of the head, and gave her son a poignant stare. 'Look at him. Hasn't he been through enough already?'

Derek and Karen glared at her.

'Tell me, does the name Rory Appleby mean anything to you?'

The answer hung in the cool air for a long time, until Tony said, 'No. Never heard of him.'

Fisher then directed the question at Derek and Karen.

Derek shook his head, but there was something on Karen's face that made Fisher believe the name was familiar to her in some way. 'Karen, does that name ring any bells?'

Her eyes narrowed. 'I'm not sure . . .'

Derek twisted towards her. 'Does it?'

After some time, she said it didn't and Fisher moved on. 'Okay, you guys are free to go.'

'Of course, we are!' scolded Karen, who stood up, hitting the chair with the hind of her knees, knocking it back across the floor. 'Tony has done nothing wrong.' She leaned over Tony to help him up, his body fragile as if he'd just finished a marathon. 'Come on, Son, let's get you home.'

Derek shuffled out slowly and got to his feet, the scowl on his face indicating he was suffering pain in his knee.

DS Phillips walked in moments after the Andersons had left. 'Interesting pause from Karen when you mentioned that name — think there's more to it?'

Fisher squinted, still sitting at the desk, mulling things over. 'I don't know yet. Maybe. Are you ready to go on a trip to Little Bolton to find out who this van belongs to?'

'After you, Detective.'

CHAPTER 38

Derek took a left when he joined Chorley Road and headed towards the city centre. The drive to their house would take less than ten minutes on a good run, but because of the time of day, it was closer to twenty-five.

Halfway to their house, Tony said, 'Can you drop me off at home, please, Dad?'

Derek craned his neck to the back of the car. 'Home?'

'You don't want to do that, Tony,' advised Karen. 'Come home with us. We'll make sure you're okay.'

'Mum, I'm in my thirties now. I'm sure I'll be fine.'

Derek didn't appreciate the tone he had used. 'We're only trying to be there for you, Son. I know it's hard what's happened — me and your mother are going through it too. All we're saying is that we think you'll be better off coming back to ours. That's all.' He studied him through the rear-view mirror.

Tony's head was bowed, as if he knew his father was watching him. 'I'd like to go home, please. I appreciate your help and support. But I need some space.'

Derek shot Karen a look of concern. She replied with a shrug, then looked back out the passenger window, switching her gaze to the passing people as they dawdled through the congestion.

167

'You sure, Son?'

'Yeah, Dad, I'm sure.'

Derek took the next right and headed for Meadow Close.

* * *

Tony gave a half-hearted wave at his parents as they drove away, watching them with tears in his eyes until they reached the end of the road and took a right. He sighed, opened the front door, and stood for a moment, absorbing the silence of the house. He missed the sounds of Abigail banging toys or crying somewhere. The annoying sounds of American women talking about something that didn't interest him on the television in the living room. He'd do anything to hear those sounds right now.

'Where the fuck are they?' he whispered to himself, before he clenched a fist and punched the wall to his left, his knuckles compressing the layer of plaster and subsequently bleeding from the blow. He wished he hadn't because it hurt like hell and his wrist ached.

He closed the door quickly, bent down to pick up the small selection of mail that the postman must have delivered earlier that morning, and strolled into the kitchen, the sound of his footsteps louder with echoes of loneliness. He turned on the cold water and held his hand underneath it for a while.

He watched his neighbour through the back window, could see the top of his head moving across the back fence, which reminded him he'd cut the trees down.

Then he froze still when he heard the sound, his body suddenly feeling ice cold. He slowly turned, peered down the hallway with wide eyes, unsure if he'd imagined it or not.

Bang.

Another sound.

He frowned, told himself he was imagining—

Bang. The sound was coming from above him.

There was someone upstairs.

Silently, he tip-toed across the kitchen floor and into the hallway. The sounds of footsteps above him were more prominent now. He stopped and listened. He could feel his heart pounding in his chest.

Was it just one person or more?

His eyes widened, the sound now louder.

They were coming down the stairs.

What the fuck? Tony mouthed silently, lowering at the knees, his body starting to shake. He waited and stared to his left, waiting for whoever it was to come into view. A thin man dressed in a black hoody stepped down into the hallway, half of his face partially visible, the other half blocked by the hood up over his head.

The man immediately noticed Tony to his right, and froze, glaring at him.

Both men stared at each other.

The intruder had something in his hand. A book. No, it wasn't a book. Tony recognised it as Amanda's diary.

'Who — who the fuck are you?' Tony's voice quavered in fear of this unknown man. 'Why have you got my wife's diary?'

The intruder didn't wait around to answer the question and darted for the door a few feet from him. Tony dashed over and crashed into him before he manage to open the door, and both men collided into the wall, then onto the floor with an orchestra of hefty blows.

Tony landed awkwardly on his side, his right hand somehow underneath the weight of his twisted body. 'Who the fuck . . .' Tony gasped, trying to hold on to him, but the wiry, thin man was quick and Tony couldn't get a good grip.

The man found his feet first, and when Tony stood up, the man grabbed the outside of his shoulder and leaned in quickly, headbutting Tony in the mouth, which knocked him on his arse. The pain was unlike anything Tony had ever felt. He blinked, tears streaming in his eyes and his mouth throbbed like it had been hit with a hammer. Blood poured down his chin from the deep cut caused by the blow.

'Fuck!' screamed Tony, as he slowly used the wall to help him find his feet. His head was pounding and his adrenaline sky high. The front door was wide open. He looked out, seeing the stranger sprinting down the street. There was no way he'd catch him.

He only had one thought.

Why would someone be so desperate for Amanda's diary?

CHAPTER 39

Little Bolton was a small place with only a few streets. Fisher slowed her white Volvo and squinted at the street sign up ahead.

'Here we are,' she said, as she guided the Volvo into the road. She checked the numbers on the right-hand side while DS Phillips eyed the numbers to the left.

It became apparent they didn't need to follow the numbers anymore when a large white van came into view, parked on the driveway of a semi-detached house. In front of the house was a marked police car, belonging to the PCs they could now see knocking at the door, reminding her that DI James said he would send assistance immediately while she was speaking with the Andersons back at the station.

Fisher stopped the car and they both got out.

'No one in?' Fisher asked PC Baan from the end of the driveway.

'No one's answering.'

For mid-summer, it was extremely quiet. Eerily quiet. No children were playing in the street or on front lawns, no elderly men sitting out on deck chairs reading the daily newspaper or sipping cups of tea. No music playing from any open windows.

Fisher and Phillips walked down the drive, both study-ing the potential access and egress from the house. The prop-erty was divided on either side with a five-foot fence that ran the length of the driveway. There was a path to the left they assumed led to the rear of the house. Fisher took a few paces left to get a better look. There was a closed gate. She returned to the front.

'Been knocking long?'

'Only a few minutes — got here when we could,' Baan said.

They had a rough idea of what the driver looked like from the CCTV they had seen and waited a few more min-utes until they heard someone say, 'Can I help you?'

The frail voice came from the right. A woman dressed in a knitted cardigan, with fraying thin hair and jam-jar glasses peered over the top of the fence, the top half of her head visible.

'Could you tell me where Rory Appleby is? We'd like to speak to him.'

'Oh, you've just missed him.'

'Where's he gone?'

'Away somewhere for the weekend with Jackie. They're always going away, those two.' There was bitterness in her voice, Fisher could hear it. 'Me and my Roger used to do that before he passed. Oh, we'd go all over, we did.' The neigh-bour slowly shook her head in reminiscence.

'Where's he gone?'

'I'm sorry, I don't know . . .'

'Any idea when he'll be back?'

'Do I look like his mother?' There was a silence between them. Then she realised she was being harsh, and added, 'They usually go away until the Sunday evening.'

Fisher nodded.

'Why do you want to speak to him?' the neighbour pried. 'I can't imagine Rory would be involved in anything that would warrant the police being here.'

'We're not at liberty to say.'

PC Jackson looked at the van closely, checking out the windows, leaning in with a cupped hand to block out the sun. He then tried opening the door.

'Hey, you can't do that! That's not your van.' The elderly lady shuffled down the drive stabbing a finger at PC Jackson. 'That's trespassing, is that.'

'Not when the van has been involved in a police matter,' Fisher chirped in.

'Really?' The old lady's eyes narrowed. 'What's happened?'

'As I said, I'm not at liberty to discuss any further.' Fisher turned and knocked on the door again.

The lady laughed. 'I've told you, he isn't in. He's away for the weekend. Whatever has happened, it probably wasn't him anyway.'

'What do you mean?' DS Phillips this time.

'He lends people his van all the time. His friends mainly, but sometimes others use it, people who need a cheap van for a few days. He advertises it online or something. Rarely uses it himself. Whatever's happened, he probably doesn't know anything about it.'

'Thanks for your time,' said Fisher, padding back towards the path, deciding not to waste any further time.

'What now?' PC Baan asked when they were back at their cars.

'We'll have it recovered. If it was involved in the disappearance of Amanda, then we have no choice. Forensics can have a good look at it to see what they find.'

Fisher's phone rang. 'Hello?'

'Detective Fisher, it's Derek Anderson. Tony's Dad.'

'How can I help you?'

'Tony's been attacked. Someone broke into his house.'

'Stay with him, we'll head straight over.'

CHAPTER 40

Before Tony called the police, he phoned his parents to tell them about the intruder. They nearly broke the land speed record and arrived less than ten minutes later.

'Jesus, Tony,' Karen said as they dashed up the driveway. When she saw the cut on his lip and the swelling on his face, she raised a hand to her mouth in disbelief. 'As if you haven't been through enough.'

Tony had decided to stay out the front to wait for the police. He also wasn't sure if the man was coming back or not and felt like he needed to guard the house. He knew there'd be no way of catching up with him, judging by the speed he'd shot off, but the last thing he wanted was to see him near his house again.

'Tony, that looks sore,' his mother added.

Tony smiled thinly, which caused him a little pain when his lip stretched, opening the cut further. He could feel it was wide and deep, and his nose throbbed. The gash had come from his lip colliding with his teeth from the hard head of the intruder.

'The bastard!' Derek shouted. 'Fucking bastard.' He glared at his son in disbelief. 'Who was he?'

Tony offered a shrug. 'I-I don't know, Dad. I can't work out how he got in. The door was locked when I got here.'

'What did he take?' Derek scowled.

Tony frowned. 'He took Amanda's diary.'

'From everything in your house, he took Amanda's diary?' Karen said, confused. Tony nodded. 'Why did he take her diary?'

Another tired shrug. 'He wasn't giving it up either.'

'But why did he need her diary?' his father asked.

He looked at Derek with wide eyes, clearly irritated. 'How do I know, Dad?'

'Okay, Son,' Derek said softly.

'Come on, let's get you inside,' Karen said, taking a hold of his arm.

'Mum, I'm not fucking five. I can walk myself.'

He went inside, and his parents exchanged a worried look between them before they followed him in.

Tony went straight upstairs to wipe his face and get rid of some of the blood. He pulled off his blood-soaked T-shirt and threw it in the wash basket, then went to the bedroom and grabbed another one from his wardrobe. The silence in their bedroom reminded him of Amanda not being there. He stood at the end of the bed and imagined her, head on the pillow, the covers pulled up to her chin, with gentle light coming from her phone as she scrolled through it.

He returned downstairs to find his parents in the kitchen, standing by the door, staring at the mess.

'Oh God, Tony.' Karen smiled sadly at him. It was the first time they'd seen the kitchen. She stepped forward. 'I need to clean this up.'

He held her back. 'Leave it, Mum. The police are coming soon. Whoever it was may have been in here. They might want to check for fingerprints or something.'

* * *

It wasn't long before they heard knocks at the door.

'I'll get it,' said Derek. He stood up and left Tony and Karen sitting on the sofa in the living room. They'd left the

kitchen how it was and stayed in one room in case the forensic tech returned.

Tony was seated next to Karen in silence. The detectives
entered, seeing Tony and the bag of frozen peas pressed against
his face.

'How are you feeling, Mr Anderson?' Phillips asked.

'Never been better.' Tony removed the peas and forced
a smile, then pressed them against his face again.

Fisher took a seat beside him. 'Let me take a look.' Tony
swivelled slightly so she could see easier. 'Nasty, that.'

Tony nodded in agreement.

'Talk us through it, please.'

He relayed the story from arriving home up to the part
when the man ran down the street away from the house with
Amanda's diary.

'Her diary?'

He nodded. 'I-I know. It's weird, isn't it?'

Fisher and Phillips absorbed the story, wondering why
her diary would be so important.

'What does she normally write in her diary?'

Tony tilted his head in thought, moving his fingers while
holding the bag in his hands, causing a quiet rustling sound.
'What she's been doing, I suppose. What she has planned
over the next few weeks. Work stuff. That type of thing. To
be honest, I don't know. It's her diary, so that's her business.'

Fisher bobbed her head and waited for more, but he
stayed silent.

DS Phillips was standing in the middle of the room and
took out a notepad. 'Can you describe the male who attacked
you?'

Tony did.

'His hood was up?'

'Yeah.'

Phillips finished writing and put his small notepad,
along with the pen, back into his pocket.

'This must be something to do with Amanda, Detective
Fisher,' Derek said.

She looked over, offered a sad smile. 'All we can do is attempt to trace the movements on local CCTV circuits.' She studied Tony. 'Do you need to see a doctor?'

Tony raised his free hand and used a finger to feel the tenderness in his lip. 'I'll be fine. It hurts, but nothing some painkillers won't sort out.'

'Have you received any more messages on Amanda's phone?' asked Fisher.

'I have, but nothing helpful.'

'Okay.'

There was a knock at the door. Tony jumped a little and lowered the bag of peas, no doubt apprehensive due to what happened earlier.

'Don't worry,' Phillips said, 'it'll be our forensic tech.' He answered the door and allowed Boone to enter.

'Thanks, Matthew,' she said, stepping inside.

Phillips gave a brief summary of what had happened earlier and they agreed on Boone having a quick look around but putting her main focus on the door handles and the drawer where Amanda kept her diary.

Once she was done, she gave the detectives the thumbs-up from the living room doorway. 'I'll be in touch when these come back.'

'Thank you, Pam,' Fisher said, watching her leave.

'We're heading off too, Tony,' said Fisher, standing. 'We'll be in touch with anything as soon as we know.'

'Thanks, Detective,' Derek said, offering a thin smile as they made their way to the front door and closed it behind them.

'You okay, Son?' Karen asked, leaning over to him.

He sighed heavily and nodded. 'I have to be. I just don't understand, Mum. I don't understand this at all.'

She gentle rubbed his back. 'I know, Son. We'll find them, I promise.' She and Derek exchanged glances.

CHAPTER 41

Jack Mulberry knocked back his third whiskey, sitting at the kitchen table of their spacious four-bedroom semi-detached house. Rachel sat across from him, sheepishly watching his mood worsen, worried about where this was going. She'd seen him on countless occasions lose his temper, most of the time due to the whiskey.

'They're fucking useless. All of them,' he said, matter-of-factly.

Rachel smiled lightly. Her patience was wearing thin. 'Jack, there's nothing—'

He slammed his palm down on the table, the sound of the slap echoing around them, which silenced her. 'Yes there is, Rachel. There's always something that can be done.'

She glowered. 'You want to drive around the streets looking for them? Fine, let's go, then.' She stood up quickly, knocking the chair back. 'Come on, Jack . . .'

He screwed his face up. 'Oh, here she goes . . .'

She snapped her neck in his direction. 'What is it you want me to fucking do, then? Please, tell me.' She waited, halfway between the table and the door to the hallway. When he didn't respond, she said, 'Well?'

His face softened. 'I'm sorry, honey. I-I'm just frustrated, that's all. Amanda and Abigail go missing, then the car is found with her passport in. I think something's going on here.'

She returned to the table, and sat down, pulling her chair in. She was tense and rigid. 'I know. It's shit. But what can we do?'

He reached for the bottle of whiskey.

'I think you've had enough . . .'

'Are you my mother?'

She frowned. 'Sorry?'

'Are you my boss?'

'What are you going on about now, for God's sake?'

'Are you the almighty God who controls how many fucking whiskeys I have?' His eyes grew dark.

She laughed, shook her head, and gave a heavy, familiar sigh. 'Three whiskeys and you're acting like this.' She stood. 'You're pathetic sometimes.'

She turned away from him and headed for the door.

'I'm sorry,' said Jack. When she didn't slow, he added, 'I'm just frustrated, Rachel. Please . . . don't walk away. Hey, take it away. I've had enough anyway. Here . . .'

Before she reached the door, she turned back to him, and after some thought, went over and grabbed the bottle and his empty glass and positioned them on the worktop to the right, out of his reach.

'Please,' he said. 'Sit.'

She settled in opposite and looked him in the eye. 'What, Jack?'

'I'm sorry about that, honey. I-I . . .' He trailed off.

'I know. The police are doing their best, I'm sure.'

He looked away for a moment.

'What is it?'

'It can't be a coincidence though, can it?'

She scowled. 'What can't, Jack?'

'Amanda's missing. Abigail has gone.'

'I don't understand . . .'

'Layla,' he explained.

She sighed deeply. 'We didn't know Layla McPherson and we definitely don't know what happened to her.'

'She was never found, Rachel.' His eyes narrowed. 'What if it happens again?'

'We . . . listen, we can't think like that. Layla went missing before any of us knew Tony. We've heard the story from Amanda. She said she didn't come home one night, and Tony never saw her again. Her body has never been found, even to this day. We can't just assume that Tony had something to do with it.'

'Come on,' he protested. 'The tablets he's on . . . the injury to his brain . . . he could be capable of anything. I knew—' he slapped the table lightly — 'that I couldn't trust him. I *knew* there was something off about him.'

Rachel had heard this countless times, the disappearance of Tony's ex-girlfriend, Layla McPherson. Tony, at the time, had been with her for nearly three years. They were both eighteen, and were, according to Amanda, truly in love. They rented a flat together on the outskirts of Manchester, but one night Layla never came home. Tony said he'd cooked them a romantic dinner and set the table with candles, the night before her birthday. While he had waited for her, there was someone at the door, which turned out to be a neighbour. Time had ticked on. When it got late, he'd phoned her numerous times until the phone battery died and all he could do was reach her voicemail. He was getting worried about her. According to the local news at the time, the reporter had mentioned strange happenings in Manchester, people going missing, and that people needed to stay vigilant, clearly expressing the fact that no one was safe.

Unfortunately, her body was never found.

To this day, it's still a mystery. Of course, a few people assumed the worst and suspected Tony. One of those people was Jack Mulberry. He'd always had his doubts about him.

'I'm going to find out what's happened — I don't care what I have to do,' he said, just above a whisper. 'You'll see . . .'

* * *

Across the other side of Manchester, Abigail was sitting on a small, uncomfortable sofa in silence. The room was small and musty, with a tiny window that only opened a crack. Warm air seeped in, but it was hard for her to breathe properly.

Her only company was her little red lion, which glared up at her, looking as lost as she felt.

When she woke, she'd searched the room, looking for a way out after realising she couldn't quite reach the door handle. She'd tried standing on her lion to get higher, but that didn't work. And apart from the old grey sofa up against one of the walls, nothing was in there.

She'd spent most of her time at the window, peering onto the street, watching people go by. On several occasions, she'd knocked on the window to get someone's attention, and when she did, the three teenagers walking by had looked up, smiled at her, and waved, obviously not understanding she was stuck in a place that wasn't her home.

It wasn't long before she was hungry again and said, 'Mummy.' Her tone was dull, and she spoke quietly, unsure when she'd eat again.

The door to her right opened.

She stiffened and pulled her teddy into her chest, holding it with all her strength.

'Here you go,' the tall man said as he walked in with a tray of more toast and a glass of juice, placing it next to her. It was all she'd eaten since she arrived. Toast and juice. At least it was something.

She smiled sadly and whispered, 'Mummy.'

The man stood up and studied her. 'You'll see Mummy soon, little one. I promise.'

CHAPTER 42

Just before 8 a.m., the man made his way through the garage to the roller door, unlocked it, and lifted it gently, trying not to disturb the neighbours too much.

It was surprisingly bright up above, the sky filled with a world of fascinating shades of blue — unlike anything he'd ever seen. He smiled and slowly wandered out onto the warmth of his driveway, seeing his smiley neighbour, Mrs Emmerson, across the road, watering her plants. She took so much time and care with her garden and had the greenest grass the man had ever seen. She did it every weekend, it was almost a ritual. Her garden was square-shaped, with a border of exotic plants offering a magnitude of various colours that he couldn't describe — she'd told him some of the names but he never remembered, nor did he really care, because most of time he wasn't interested in her flowers, rather more so what she was wearing, as she tended to frequently flaunt her tanned, muscular legs.

He offered her a smile, then lowered his arm. An unwritten rule of living in such a classy area was being pleasant to others; it was expected. Due to the nature of some of his neighbours, not to mention the local book group he never seemed to be invited to, it was easier to get along. Save him being a part of their gossip, which he knew everyone was a victim to one way or another.

He pulled his phone from his red shorts, unlocked it, then re-read the message. He moved around his car, and lifted the bin lid carefully to peer inside. Regardless of the stench of food scraps and God knows whatever else jumping up and hitting his nose, he leaned in, picked up the book, then casually lowered the lid.

Across the road, Mrs Emmerson was in her own little world, quietly whistling a tune to herself. Bless her, he thought. It hadn't been long since her husband Nigel had passed.

'Good to see people doing well. Moving on with things,' he said quietly to himself before he pulled the roller door down, and the space around him darkened. Under the dim garage light, he opened the book and started reading, starting with the most recent pages in date order.

After he'd caught up, he felt a fit of rage and threw the book across the garage. It hit the roller door with a bang, then crashed to the floor.

'Everything okay in there?' a concerned voice asked from somewhere in the house.

He didn't know anyone was awake and it startled him for a moment. 'Yeah . . .'

He picked up the book again and turned back to read what had been written over the last few weeks.

'Shit, shit, shit,' he kept saying to himself over and over.

The words worried him. Had she told anyone about the things she'd written? Had she opened up to anyone about it? He seriously hoped not.

He put Amanda's diary on one of the shelves, carefully positioning it behind several large pots of paint so it was out of sight, then returned inside, still worrying if she had told anyone about what she knew.

CHAPTER 43

Tony had managed two hours of staggered sleep. He was sitting at the kitchen table, drinking his second coffee, when someone knocked at the door. He peered up at the clock and wondered who'd be knocking at this time.

'Morning,' his brother Michael said when he opened the door. There was a sympathetic smile on his face. He leaned forward to shake his hand. 'How you holding up?'

Tony smiled thinly, unsure what to say. If he was being honest, he didn't have a clue what to do with himself, constantly wandering around the house or walking the streets in search for his wife and daughter. Finding the car was something, but why was Amanda's passport in the glovebox?

'Sorry I haven't been to see you, Tony, I've been—'

'Busy?' Tony said, finishing his sentence.

'—really tied up with work stuff.' Michael's shoulders dipped a little. 'Sorry.'

Next to Michael was his other brother Peter.

They hadn't told Tony they were coming and he wondered why they were there.

'Got you some breakfast . . .' Michael said by way of a very small apology, holding up a brown bag filled with something and a white coffee cup with a lid on, steam rising through the small sip hole.

Tony smiled and moved aside to let them in. The divine smell of whatever was in the bag made his stomach rumble as he closed the door and followed them both through to the kitchen.

They took a seat around the table. Michael opened the bag and dug his hand in, pulling out something wrapped in white paper. 'This one's for you, Tony.'

'Thanks.'

They spent a few minutes eating, then squashed their empty wrappers up and put them in the bin.

Michael was wearing smart trousers, a white shirt, and brown shoes that cost more than Tony made in a week. He often worked from home, but liked to go for meetings and needed to look good for his clients. Even when he wasn't working, he still dressed immaculately.

'Working today, Michael?' Tony asked.

He nodded. 'Meeting someone later this morning.'

Tony looked at Peter, who was dressed in his casual clothes — T-shirt and jeans — which was a welcome change compared to the workwear he wore when he usually saw him.

'So,' Tony said, 'to what do I owe this pleasure? It's rare to see you both together.'

They both waited for the other to speak until the silence became deafening. Finally, Peter said softly, 'We're worried about you, Tony.' His words were genuine. It wasn't hard to see Tony was a shadow of his former self, even just in two days. His skin looked greyer; his hair appeared unwashed. The bags under his eyes had become noticeably darker.

'I'm fine . . .'

'Are you taking your tablets, mate?' pressed Peter.

He shot him a tired look. 'Yes.'

Peter wasn't convinced. 'Every day?'

His hesitation gave his brothers the answer.

'They'll help you, Tony, especially through times like this. It's important.'

Tony peeled his attention away from them, knowing his brother was right, and that their only intention was to help him.

'How's the lip?'

Tony touched it softly. 'Sore.'

A few moments of silence passed.

'Don't take this the wrong way, Tony, but . . .' Michael paused. Peter looked at him for a moment then settled on Tony. 'Is there anything you need to tell us? Anything you need help with?'

Tony frowned. 'I don't understand.'

'Anything you need to tell us about Amanda or Abigail.'

His frown deepened. 'What are you saying?'

Michael sighed a little, enough for Tony to notice. The question angered him — he wasn't sure the meaning but knew it wasn't good and felt it was more of an interrogation. He was about to reply when there was a quick knock at the door.

'Who's this?' Peter asked as he turned and peered down the hall.

'I'll check,' Tony said, happy to leave the situation for a moment. He pulled open the front door to DS Fisher and DS Phillips. Their blank faces didn't give any indication to why they were there.

'Mr Anderson, could we come in?'

'Sure.' He stepped aside. 'Have you found anything?'

Behind him, Peter and Michael appeared in the kitchen doorway.

'We need a sample of Abigail's DNA, please, Tony,' DS Fisher said matter-of-factly. 'We've found the body of a little girl in the river.'

CHAPTER 44

Martin Forlan, the man who attacked Tony Anderson on Thursday morning and stole his car with his daughter sitting in the back seat, picked up his phone, found the number, and pressed Call. He tapped his foot impatiently. The phone went to voicemail.

He had started to panic now.

The plan hadn't gone the way it was meant to.

'Come on,' he whispered as he tried again, rocking back and forth at the tiny circular table in his small, dark kitchen.

'Shit,' he said when the number went to voicemail again. He ended the call, sighed heavily, and placed the phone back on the table. Fourteen messages he'd left already — there'd be no point in leaving another one.

Something was seriously wrong.

It should have been easy. Take the car with Abigail inside, then call the number when he was in a safe place. He'd already tried, but the phone was never answered. He had to keep Abigail hidden in his flat, which had been a nightmare considering how close his neighbours were. She'd tried to scream and kick, but Martin was strong and calm enough to put a hand over her mouth, drowning out her desperation to escape.

Martin tried the number again, waited until it rang out, and threw the phone on the sofa, then stared down at his interlocked, sweaty fingers. He didn't know what to do now. All he needed to do was take the girl and hand her over. Everything was going to plan, it had worked like clockwork, even attacking Tony and taking the car.

Abigail, however, was quite sweet once Martin had given her a handful of jelly sweets to win her over, but, regardless of that, he had a two-year-old in his flat, and he didn't know what to do. He knew one thing: time was running out.

CHAPTER 45

'They told us not to go, Tony,' Peter said, relaying Fisher's words before she left.

'Let go of my arm, Peter.'

Peter knew by his tone if he had to ask again, then things may turn physical. And he didn't want that, not after everything that had happened. Peter let go of Tony's forearm and the three of them stood in his front garden, watching the detectives speed away in a white Volvo.

'The hell with it — it could be Abigail!' Tony attempted to step around him.

'Help me with him,' Peter said, angling back at Michael, who was standing a little further down the drive. Micheal nodded, stepped forward, and took hold of Tony's left arm.

'Tony, just stop. They said they would contact you if they found anything,' Michael tried to reassure him.

They tussled, and Tony attempted to outmuscle them but it proved pointless. An enactment of their childhood in a way — Tony was the weakest of the brothers, so there was no chance he'd get past the two of them.

'I need to see her . . .' Tears filled his eyes, then eventually ran down his red cheeks.

Fisher and Phillips had left after obtaining a hairbrush and a toothbrush belonging to Abigail. They told him they weren't sure it was Abigail, but the description of the small girl that had been found in the river certainly aroused enough suspicion.

'If it's her, I need to see her. I need to be with my baby.' Tony sighed and his body seemed to relax, so Peter loosened his grip on his brother again, watching him carefully in case he tried to bolt again.

'Listen to me, Tony,' Peter said. 'We'll stay with you until you hear back, okay? You don't have to be alone.'

Michael knew Peter was being hopeful, but, in reality, he knew there was a good chance the small body was Abigail's.

* * *

DS Fisher slowed the Volvo behind a line of marked police cars at the end of the terraced street, applied the handbrake, and turned off the engine. The street was narrow, lined with ageing 1930s houses on either side, their bricks dark and weathered. Both the path and road were cluttered with people, many of which were PCs trying to keep a lid on things and preventing people from getting into the cordoned-off area, which lead to an open gate and a small patch of grass, then, beyond it, the riverbank where the body was.

Fisher recognised the petite figure of Pamela Boone within the cordoned area, wearing her familiar white paper overalls and a face mask pulled down under her chin, standing with PC Baan and PC Jackson, who somehow had managed to get there before them.

Fisher and Phillips got out, closed their doors, and stared down the street, looking for a gap in the crowd to squeeze through. The PCs who stood at the tape, facing the rowdy crowd, were familiar to Fisher. They didn't work at the station, nor did she know them on a first-name basis, but she smiled and ducked under the tape.

'Hey, where on earth are they going?' a man shouted in a deep voice, scowling at Fisher and Phillips as they slithered through.

'Mind your business, please, sir,' replied the female PC who'd smiled and lifted the tape for the detectives to dip under.

They ambled across the grass and absorbed the scene around them. The sun had fallen behind a set of low hanging clouds, enveloping the world in a grey filter which, if anything, set the scene for what they were about to see.

'Hey, boss,' PC Baan said as she turned to her.

'Hey, Ash.' Fisher's eyes fell on the small figure a few feet from the water's edge and the forensic officers standing beside her. One of them was a tall male, who was crouched down beside the small girl. He seemed to be concentrating on something in particular. Pamela Boone was standing a few feet to his right, with an iPad in her hand, her attention on the screen.

'What have we got?' Phillips asked. 'Is it Abigail Anderson?'

Baan shrugged. 'We don't know yet. From the photos, it certainly resembles her. Come on, let's go see.'

The detectives followed Baan down the short bank and slowed on their approach, more so out of respect than anything. Fisher studied the scene, the way the little girl was positioned on her back, with some of her weight on her left hip, her legs bent at the knees, left arm down her side, and right arm awkwardly bent at the elbow with her small hand resting on her chest. She wore a red dress with black tights.

Fisher remembered what Tony said she was wearing. A red dress didn't come to mind, unless she was wrong.

She gazed up across the river. It was roughly twenty metres wide, the water in the centre moving noticeably quicker than at the edges, where it would be shallower. For a brief moment, she thought back to geography classes at school, vaguely remembering the formation of rivers and their dangers.

Across the river was another small, narrow bank of grass, leading up to a path, then beyond that, she wasn't sure. She looked right, then left, mentally collecting the space around her.

'What are you thinking, April?' DS Phillips said.

Fisher concentrated on Baan. 'How long do they think she's been here?'

'Not long, few hours at the most. Her body is still warm.'

'What are you thinking?' Phillips asked her again.

'A lot of things . . .'

'Well, start by the most relevant thing to this scene,' he replied, eager to know. Phillips knew Fisher was thinking about things twenty-four seven.

They heard the quiet footsteps of one of the forensics holding a camera nearby.

'Would you guys mind just moving away for a second?' the forensic tech requested.

They edged away from the body.

Fisher curled a few strands of loose hair behind her right ear and sighed lightly. The small body looked so innocent, so helpless; it almost made her scream with anger. She considered the possibilities — had the young girl fallen in somewhere upstream, drowned, then washed up?

'Who found her?'

PC Baan pointed to their left. 'She did.' A heavy-set woman sat on a low wooden railing about thirty metres away, holding a black lead that was clipped to the collar of a greyhound, sitting calmly and obediently on the floor beside her.

'Okay.'

Or was she killed beforehand and put here to make it look like she drowned? As far as they could see, there were no obvious signs of trauma, violence, or blood. Her body looked to be intact.

'She was walking along the river path, noticed her in the shallow water. She came over and pulled her onto the small stones,' Baan said.

Fisher dropped her head into her hands, battling against an incoming migraine.

'You okay, April?' DS Phillips placed a hand on her back, knowing Fisher wasn't quite on her game today.

Two nights ago she had got too hammered to know if she'd been raped by a man she couldn't remember. The following morning a woman and child went missing, and, so far, there'd been no sign of them. Then there was the ongoing investigation into the murder of Elaine Freeman, and the MO — the missing hands and missing eyes — which the media had suggested was a possible link between Ms Freeman's death and the unsolved murders of Kathy Walker and Joan Ellison.

It was a mess. It was hell.

Fisher, despite the fact she wanted to leave the scene, get back in her car, and drive as far away as she could, managed a gradual nod. 'I'm fine.'

'Take a break if you want, we can—'

'I said I'm fine, Matthew.'

Her stern words silenced Phillips, who knew her well enough to say nothing more. Fisher had been through a rough few days and needed his strength, not his pity.

They continued to look at the small body of the girl they believed could well be Abigail Anderson. A sample of her DNA would be taken and sent to the lab. The only person who would truly know if it was Abigail would be Tony Anderson, her father, but he was at home when they left.

'Let me through now!' they heard someone shout from up the hill.

'Sir, if you try and pass me, I'll arrest you — this is a crime scene,' a PC replied.

'What the hell's going on?' Phillips said, turning towards the commotion.

'Shit . . .' Fisher muttered.

He somehow had managed to get through the crowd and past the PCs at the tape. A furious Tony Anderson charged down towards them.

CHAPTER 46

DS Phillips watched Tony hurtling down the hill towards them, making a beeline for the small girl behind them by the water.

'Stop him, Matthew,' said DS Fisher, knowing she'd rather have Phillips standing in his way than herself.

'I've got him.'

'Is it her?' Tony shouted from a distance, pointing to the girl's body. 'Is it her?' His anger filled the silent air. Nearby, people stared at him, wondering who he was, and, more importantly, what role he had to play in this scene.

'Sure you have him?' Fisher said, frowning at Tony.

Phillips nodded and raised his palms. 'Listen, Tony. You need to calm down — this is a crime scene, for God's sake.'

Tony slowed and eventually stopped in front of Phillips.

'Is it her?' he whispered through gritted teeth, just loud enough for Phillips to hear him. It was clear he was almost at boiling point, no doubt millions of thoughts going through his head.

'We don't know.' Phillips kept his arms raised for a moment.

'Can I see her? I need to know.' Tony clasped his palms together, begging.

The detectives considered his request, then glanced at each other. Finally, Fisher nodded, then looked at Baan. 'Go with him . . .'

Baan followed Tony towards the body of the small girl. Pamela Boone, dressed in her white paper overalls standing a few feet from the body, scowled up from her iPad, immediately recognising who it was.

'Please, keep your distance, Mr Anderson.' Boone was firm but respectful, understanding the situation.

He nodded. He took a few hesitant steps and peered down at the girl's face. After a few moments, he let out a massive sigh, and his shoulders dipped.

'It's not her . . .' he said, just above a whisper.

'It's not your daughter?' PC Baan asked, now standing beside him.

He shook his head, then relief washed over his face. 'It's not her,' he repeated, this time quieter. 'She's still out there.'

Somewhere behind them, Fisher heard a woman screaming, her outburst disturbing the calm air. She couldn't make out what was said, but it was obvious she was distressed about something. The detectives, along with PC Baan, Tony, and the small team of forensic officers, glared over, wondering what was going on.

Had some kind of fight broken out between the onlookers?

The woman attempted to barge her way through two PCs, who were doing well to hold her off, until several of the nearby crowd joined in, shouting and shoving the PCs too. It was getting out of hand.

'We don't need this shit,' Fisher noted, who started up the bank to settle the situation down herself. Phillips and PC Jackson followed her. Baan decided to stay with Tony, who looked sad seeing the body of a small girl but relieved it wasn't Abigail.

The agitated woman was small and almost as round as she was tall. She wore a suit that barely fit her and her face was plastered in make-up.

'Please, miss, just calm down,' one of the PCs begged, his hands firmly on her wriggling shoulders.

'Move out of my fucking way,' the short, angry woman countered, extending her arms and shoving the young PC in the chest. By the expression on his face, she'd winded him, and he momentarily backed away.

DS Phillips wasn't necessarily strong, but his height gave him an advantage over most people. 'Miss, if you don't calm down, I'm arresting you.'

He wasn't in uniform, nor was he there to arrest people, but his words hit home and silenced her immediately.

'I just need to see,' she explained, pointing to the river.

'What do you need to see?'

'If it's her — my daughter Rosie.'

'Your daughter?'

'Yes, my fucking daughter. She's gone missing. I've just come home. My husband was looking after her. When I got home, he was asleep and I couldn't find her. The back door was open. I . . .' she trailed off, assuming the worst.

'What's your name?' Phillips asked.

'Mary Atkinson. My daughter is called Rosie Atkinson.'

Fisher considered her words.

Mary leaned forward and placed her palms on her knees for support, breathing deeply.

Phillips looked at Fisher, then gazed back at her, thinking before he spoke. 'This is a crime scene, okay? We need to keep our distance. Listen to the forensics.'

She nodded and followed Phillips down the short grass bank onto the small stones. On her approach, her eyes become teary, her hands coming up to her chest as she recognised the clothing on the small girl. Suddenly she darted forward past Phillips in the direction of the river, towards the girl, shouting and screaming, flaying her arms everywhere. The sound of her wailing panicked the forensics, who stared up in horror at the moving woman and began to move out of the way.

Phillips ran after her, surprised how quick she moved for her size, but managed to grab her shoulder and pull her back before she got too close and destroyed the crime scene. After a physical tussle, they both ended up on the ground.

'Let me go!' she screamed. 'My poor baby. My poor . . . baby!'

Phillips took a knock from the fall, his hip a little tender from the fall. He rolled over and stopped her from getting up. Fisher came to his side and lowered to the ground, taking hold of Mary's hand. 'Mary, please, calm down,' Fisher repeated.

Mary burst into tears.

CHAPTER 47

'Thanks for staying back, guys. I appreciate it.' DI James smiled briefly, then turned to the whiteboard. He pressed the small fob in his hand, revealing the next slide. 'As you know, we . . .' He trailed off and frowned.

'What's up, Thomas?' Fisher asked, watching him raise a hand to his temple.

'. . . we found the body of a small girl this morning, belonging to three-year-old Rosie Atkinson. For those of you who weren't there, we . . .' He paused again for a moment. 'I'm sorry, I have a headache.' He turned to Fisher and Phillips. 'Either of you mind taking over?'

Fisher stood immediately and went to the front of the room, taking the remote from him, and observed him wander to the nearest seat. 'You okay, Tom?'

He waved it away, indicating he'd be fine. 'Please, go on.'

Fisher had been to see James earlier and been through the case notes so was up to speed with what was happening and what the DI was intending to speak about.

All eyes were on her.

'So, we found the body of a small girl yesterday. We assume it's Rosie Atkinson; likely she walked out of the back door, over the road, and unfortunately went into the river and drowned. Her father, a Thomas Atkinson, admitted that while he was looking after her, he'd accidentally fallen asleep.'

She paused for a moment, filled with mixed feelings. One: how could a father do that — be so irresponsible? And two: the pain he'd be going through, knowing her death was down to him.

'We've interviewed both Mary and Thomas to find out what exactly happened. Also, PC Baan and PC Jackson spoke with neighbours to gather more information about them. As it stands, it's an ongoing inquiry.'

She took a breath and clicked the remote. The screen changed to a slide of two photos. One of Abigail Anderson, the other of her mother, Amanda.

She briefly looked over to DI James, who had lowered his hand and was sitting more comfortably, appearing more content. She went on. 'Amanda and Abigail are still missing. Do we have any leads that we're not all aware of?'

Her eyes searched the quiet room.

DS Phillips shook his head, knowing as much as Fisher, and PC Baan and PC Jackson remained silent. DC Arnold Peterson, who'd been out earlier on a different case, didn't have anything to say either.

DI James sniffed and ran a palm through his long blonde hair. 'Should we recap, April?'

Fisher nodded in agreement. James often liked to get one of them to recap the case to remind everyone what was going on and to ensure everyone was up to speed.

'Matthew?' said Fisher.

He smiled nervously. He wasn't one for public speaking, even in a small team. 'Okay, erm . . .' He frowned while he gathered his thoughts. 'Thursday morning Tony Anderson met a man he was planning to sell his car to. His daughter Abigail was in the car at the time. The man, who we know as Martin Forlan, attacked him, then stole his car with Abigail inside. Officers attended the scene where this happened and took Tony home to find an empty house. Blood was in the kitchen. We can only assume that something bad has happened to Amanda. We also found a collection of medication that Tony is on and have spoken to a doctor, who confirms that Tony has a series of psychological issues which stem from a car crash a few years ago. A neighbour has told us that she saw a white van pull up, then two men get out and knock on their house, then, moments later, they put Amanda in the van, then—'

'Any update on that particular van?' James interrupted him.

Fisher said, 'We went to the address the van was registered to — a Rory Appleby who lives in Little Bolton. His neighbour said he was away for the weekend, but doesn't have his number so can't reach him.'

James nodded. 'Okay, thanks, April.' He switched back to Phillips. 'Please carry on, Matthew.'

Phillips took another second to remember where he was. 'Yesterday we found a car in a lake belonging to Tony Anderson. We found her passport, but nothing else. Forensics are examining the vehicle now, so, hopefully, we'll hear something back shortly. Tony went home in the afternoon to find someone in his house. A male figure dressed in a hood. In his hand, according to Tony, was Amanda's diary. The man attacked him and escaped with the diary. It's still unclear if the male suspect had broken in or if the door was left unlocked. Or maybe the suspect had a key, as the locks were intact and were not damaged.' Phillips shrugged, offering no more on the matter.

'Very good, DS Phillips,' James said, nodding. 'Good recap. Thank you.'

Fisher nodded a thanks to him and gazed out the window. The sun beat down on the busy road below; there wasn't a cloud in the sky. Manchester United were playing at home, the traffic on the roads more congested than usual.

'What about Elaine Freeman — where are we on her?' James asked from his seated position.

A deafening silence moved through the room; no one had anything of value to add.

'The media have turned this shitstorm into a disaster. I have DCI Baker breathing down my neck every day. He said he wants to see me on Monday morning in his office. Now, I don't know what it's about but I have a feeling it won't be anything good.'

They all nodded at him in understanding.

'I need results. I need us, as a team, to piece this together. Why Elaine Freeman? Why do the victims all resemble each other? Why their eyes and hands? I know it's hard juggling ten things at once, but we all know it's a part of this job. It's what we all knowingly signed up to. And I can see it's taking its toll on you guys. I feel the same. Over the last week, I'd be confident saying I've averaged less than three hours a night.'

A tired-looking DC Peterson agreed with a smile and a nod.

'Find out everything you can on Tony and Amanda Anderson. Their social circles and social media accounts. Get me something I can take to Baker. I'll see you on Monday morning.'

He stood up and left the room without another word.

CHAPTER 48

Fisher, Phillips, and Baan spent much of their afternoon in the office, getting their heads together, trying to move things forward. It went without saying that Phillips was in the bad books at home, but he'd deal with the wrath later; he had to stay focused.

They needed to push this grim-looking case along.

They were all aware DI James shielded them from DCI Baker, taking much of the DCI's frustration on his own shoulders, and didn't allow it to filter down. Fisher knew from her experience shit normally rolled downhill, but respected DI James for his diligence.

Phillips sighed, glanced to his left, and noticed the paper on Fisher's desk. 'What have you got?'

'Well,' she said, picking it up, 'I have a list of five people who commonly appear either in her social media news feeds or some of her pictures. These five seem closest to her, but there's one name that crops up the most.'

Phillips waited.

'Jane Lamont.'

He nodded. 'Guess we need to reach out to her first, then.'

Fisher typed in her name on Facebook and was surprised when dozens of profiles came up, assuming it wouldn't be a very popular name. She looked at her phone to see the photos of Jane and Amanda for a few moments to match Jane's profile picture. Bingo.

Phillips continued looking at his computer while PC Baan sat behind them, using one of the spare computers. She was busy, clicking and typing. Although a weekend, she seemed to be in no rush getting home. Fisher enjoyed her time with Baan, they had built a solid friendship over the years, but she was beginning to tire of the overbearing concern Baan was showing, although only she knew she was just trying to be a caring friend.

'I have an address for Jane Lamont,' Fisher said, loud enough for them both to hear. 'Who's coming with me?'

'I would, but . . .' Phillips said, then smiled, not having to say how pissed off Jane would be if he didn't get home very soon. He had told her he was only popping in for an hour this morning to do a report. He'd already been out for two hours.

'I'll come along, April,' Baan said, and they shared a smile between them.

* * *

Jane Lamont lived in a decent-sized semi-detached house less than ten minutes from the station. Fisher slowed her Volvo and pulled in behind a brand-new Audi A7, the paintwork reflecting the bright afternoon sun like a mirror. They got out, closed the doors, and stopped side by side on the wide pavement.

The house was painted a light blue, a pleasant contrast to the others close by. The inclined driveway, as well as supporting a red Vauxhall Astra with pink fluffy dice hanging from the rear-view mirror, led to a wide gate. The lawn was to the right of the driveway and was trimmed short and neat, with a flower bed filled with a rainbow of plants that grew against the adjoining fence.

Fisher stepped up, knocked on the door, and dropped back near PC Baan. They waited a few seconds until the door opened to reveal a woman in her mid-thirties with short blonde hair swept across her forehead and stylish, small-framed glasses in front of little, attractive blue eyes.

'Can . . . can I help you?' she asked, holding a tea towel in her hand, a sign she was in the middle of something.

'Yes, sorry to bother you.' Fisher smiled and introduced herself and PC Baan. 'We're hoping we could grab a couple of minutes of your time?'

Jane Lamont's frown deepened. 'What's this regarding? I'm quite busy . . .'

'We apologise for interrupting you,' Fisher said, smelling something pleasant drifting along from the kitchen. 'It's about your friend, Amanda Anderson.'

Her eyes widened. 'Oh, I received a text message from her phone off Tony. What's happened?'

'She's still missing. We have information that leads us to believe that two men entered her house and took her. No one has seen her since Thursday morning.'

Jane's palm found her open mouth. 'Since Thursday? I . . .' she trailed off.

Fisher and Baan waited and watched her.

'Jesus,' she whispered, her words clogging her throat.

'I'm led to believe that you two are close friends?'

Lamont removed the hand from her mouth and nodded several times. 'Yeah, known her years.'

'Can we come in?'

'God, yes.' She stepped aside. 'Please, come in, we can talk in here.'

Fisher and Baan followed her through to the kitchen and both declined the offer of coffee as they sat down at the square table. The kitchen was rectangular, very clean, with top-of-the-range appliances that looked like they'd been installed the day before. It almost looked clinical, apart from the small area near the cooker that housed a chopping board and loose bits of prepared food.

'Sorry, I'm in the middle of cooking,' she confessed. She folded the tea towel and placed it on the worktop, then pulled out one of the chairs at the table. 'Please, tell me what's going on — I haven't spoken to Amanda since Wednesday night. I feel like a shit friend now . . . I should have known.'

'Do you two speak often?' Fisher asked.

She nodded. 'Mostly every day, to be honest. I've been busy with work and, you know, other things. Amanda is feeling pressure from her new job too. Her bosses are arseholes, apparently.' She raised a quick hand to her mouth. 'Oooh, sorry for the language.'

They both nodded and smiled thinly.

'How can I help?'

'We need some information on Amanda, anything that could help us identify the two men that went inside her home on Thursday morning. Does Amanda have any issues with anyone? Anyone that you know about?'

Jane thought hard, her tongue pushing on the inside of her cheek. 'Not that I know of. Not that she's told me, anyway.'

'You're sure?' asked PC Baan.

'She would have told me. I've known Amanda more than ten years. We're close, you know?'

'What's her relationship like with Tony?'

The question hung in the air long enough for Jane to look away. She then stood up, went over to the gas hobs, and turned them down a quarter turn, the flame below shrinking slightly.

Fisher observed her as she slowly returned to the table.

'Tony and Amanda haven't been great, to be honest.' Jane gave a sad smile. Fisher and Baan waited for her to elaborate. 'They . . .' She trailed off again.

'What is it, Jane?' pressed Fisher. 'Any additional information could lead to us finding her. Anything at all could help.'

'I shouldn't be telling you this.' She took a breath. 'I'm the only one who knows . . .'

'Go on,' said Fisher.

'Amanda had planned to get away from Tony. She told me things weren't good between them, that they hadn't been sleeping in the same bed. They constantly argued. She told me she had concerns about him.'

'Concerns?'

'She didn't say much, but she had a plan in place. She was going to leave him. Get away as far as she could. Start afresh somewhere else.'

'Was she planning on taking Abigail with her?'

Jane shrugged. 'I assume so. We didn't go into details about it. God, I wish I'd asked her more about it now.'

'Is it possible that Tony knew about her plans?'

Another shrug. 'She never planned on telling him. He would come home one day and she'd be gone — that's all I know.'

Fisher nodded with intrigue, then glanced curiously at Baan.

'I wish I could help you more,' she admitted. 'God, is there anything I can do?'

'Not really. Her phone goes straight to voicemail.'

'What about Abigail — where is she?'

'We're doing everything we can to find them both.' Fisher leaned forward, plucked out a card, then placed it down on the table in front of her. 'If you think of anything, please ring me. Or if she contacts you, please ring my number immediately. Day or night, it doesn't matter. I barely sleep anyway.'

Jane Lamont nodded several times. 'Yeah, sure. Absolutely. If I hear anything, I'll call straight away.'

Fisher and Baan stood, made their way to the front door, and shut it on their way out. They got back into the car, closed their doors, and settled into the soft leather seats.

'What do you think, April?'

'This just gets deeper and deeper.' She sighed, put the car into first gear, then, after checking for any oncoming traffic, pulled out. They sat in silence on their way back to the station.

Baan picked up on it. 'What are you thinking?'

'How do you know I'm thinking something?'

'Because you're always quiet when you're thinking about something, April.'

Fisher smiled, pulled out at the end of the road, and took a right, almost colliding with a car going a fraction too fast.

'I'm thinking this might have been Amanda's plan all along. The two men that came to her house, put her in the van. Maybe she counted on a neighbour seeing it and informing the police.'

'What about Abigail? What about the guy attacking Tony, stealing his car?'

'Maybe it's all a part of the plan.'

Their eyes met for a serious moment before Fisher looked back to the road. 'This could be deeper than we think.'

CHAPTER 49

Fisher had not long arrived home. She'd just hung her dark-blue suit jacket on a tall stand near the door when her phone rang. It was Kim Ashby, her best friend.

'Hey, Kim,' she answered tiredly.

Before Fisher had the chance to engage in conversation she was bombarded with the latest news of Kim's boyfriend issues. Fisher sighed in silence, tiredly shaking her head.

'Kim, would it be possible to phone you back soon?' interrupted Fisher. 'I've just got home.'

Taken aback, Kim replied, 'Yeah . . . okay. Ring me when you're free, then.'

'Will do.' Fisher ended the call and placed the phone back down on the table wasn't. She padded over to the sofa and dropped into it, feeling another headache coming on but knowing she'd need to be careful taking any more painkillers as it four hours from the last lot she took. She closed her eyes for a few moments in the hope it would soon pass. She recalled Kim had mentioned about going out tonight, so was probably ringing to make arrangements. Fisher couldn't be bothered with it.

She opened her eyes and studied the paperwork on the coffee table in the centre of the room. Not only did she dedicate time to her job while she was at work, she spent much of her time at home sifting through things and researching. Maybe it was sad, she didn't know. The simple fact was she didn't have much of a life outside of the police. Her circle of friends was small; she didn't have time for plastic, false friends who loved gossiping about others.

She sat up, leaned forward, and stared for a moment.

Deciding she needed a shower, she stood, stripped her clothes off, and placed them in the laundry basket. Afterwards, she dressed in a loose pair of jogging bottoms and a baggy T-shirt once she'd dried, then returned to the living room, picked up her phone, and checked her emails. Once finished, she decided to call Kim back.

Kim gossiped about her latest date, a six-foot-four rugby player who she'd met online. He had taken her out last night for a meal to a posh restaurant in the city, then had covered the bill as well as splashing out on a few drinks after.

'Did you two . . . you know . . .' Fisher smiled to herself.

'Of course not, April.' Both of them laughed. 'I'm a lady. It'll take more than a fancy meal and a few cocktails to get my knickers off.' Further laughter followed, as they both knew that wasn't true.

'Have you heard anything, Ape?'

'About what?'

'You know, with what happened the other night. The guy in the red shirt.'

'Oh, sorry, I should have said. The doctor called me. Said there were no signs of anything malicious.'

'How did you get the bruising, then?'

Fisher shrugged and smiled sadly to herself, looking down to her lap. 'I can't remember a thing.'

'You need to lay off the tequilas.'

Fisher smiled. 'I know.'

'I'm always here for you, no matter what it is. I've known you for a long time.'

'I know you have.' She paused. 'Thank you.'

'Not sure if you're still up for tonight? Remember we said we might go out?'

Fisher answered with silence.

'A few of the girls from work are going out, so it should be fun?'

More silence.

'Or, if you want, I could pop over yours? We could get a takeaway, have a few glasses of wine. Put the world to rights while we watch a shit film, then ask what happened when it finishes because we weren't watching it. We always do that.'

'I think I need to stay away from wine.'

'Fair enough, Ape. Just let me know what you want to do and we'll decide a little later. How're your parents?' asked Kim.

Fisher told her they were okay, but she hadn't spoken with them in a few days.

'Your sister?'

'Freya is good, you know. She's . . . just Freya,' added Fisher. Freya was six years younger than Fisher and still lived at home with their parents. It hadn't been long since she'd completed her four years at university studying to be a vet, but she'd so far been unsuccessful in finding an entry-level role anywhere, let alone a job worthy of a career. In her time studying it had become evident her heart wasn't in being a vet as much as her parents had hoped, and that maybe the tuition money had been wasted. Time would tell. Freya also worked in a bar several nights a week, lessening the load of asking her parents for money all the time — not that they declined when she did ask. It annoyed Fisher in a way. Why should she knuckle down, work hard, and support herself when her younger sister stayed at home, half-heartedly searching for a job she didn't even want, and getting financial support after wasting money on clothes she'd wear only once? She knew, as well as their parents, Freya was going nowhere.

During the call, Fisher was looking at the paperwork she was working on last night, positioned on the low coffee table in front of her, continually scanning the documents.

Jane went on. 'Did I tell you about—'

'I need to go, Kim. I'll ring you back.' She hung up the phone, placed her phone on the table, and picked up three pages, neatly positioning them in a row on the table. Each piece had information about a victim: the first about Kathy Walker, who was murdered two years ago; the second Joan Ellison, whose body was found a year ago; and the last with information on Elaine Freeman, the care worker who was found less than two weeks ago.

'Shit,' she whispered.

She grabbed her phone and dialled DI James. 'Pick up,' she said over and over.

It went straight to voicemail so she left him a message. 'Hey, Tom, I need to see you. I've found a link between the three victims. I'm coming over to your house right now.'

CHAPTER 50

DI James lived in a four-bedroom detached property in the west end of Manchester. It was a quiet estate, filled with neat green gardens, wide driveways, and homes made from old traditional-type bricks crafted by specialist builders.

Fisher stopped her Volvo outside of his house; compared to the other cars in the street, Fisher's looked out of place.

She opened the door, stepped down onto the pavement, and looked around at the surrounding houses and impressive selection of cars. She didn't know much about cars but spotted the Porsche next door.

The smell of a nearby BBQ hit her nose as she approached his door, along with the aroma of flowers coming from the extraordinary lawns on either side of the road. Each house was almost a mirror image of the next — a wide driveway leading to a double garage, the grey front door which looked to be inside of a dull titanium surround in the centre of the house, and a broad protruding bay window that poked out towards the road. Upstairs featured the same bay window, then three almost identical windows running left of the main bedroom, each window frame similar to the door, sleek and modern in its appearance and structure.

Fisher was impressed. DI James had never really spoken much about where he lived. She'd imagined him a penthouse suite somewhere closer to the city, where he could pick up girls and take them back whenever he wanted. Maybe he was more settled than she'd thought, perhaps waiting for that special woman to enter his life, someone to share the house with; the house certainly seemed too big for just him.

She knocked twice on his door, took a step back, and waited with a small sheath of papers tucked between her hand and right hip. A minute passed and Fisher was still standing at the unanswered door. Why wasn't he answering? His car was on the drive. Unless he'd gone for a run — did he run? She wasn't sure.

She leaned in and knocked again, before curiously taking a few steps to the right and peering through the bay window. The room was long and bright, running the length of the house, the end wall filled mostly with a set of French doors that showed off the size of the garden behind the property. A large sofa was up against the left wall, a low circular coffee table sat on expensive wooden flooring in front of it, and to the right, one of the biggest televisions she had ever seen, built into a protruding chimney breast, above the sort of luxurious-looking fireplace she'd only ever seen in magazines.

But there was no sign of him.

She studied the room and froze when she saw the broken glass near the fireplace.

'What the . . .' she whispered.

She knocked again at the door, this time harder, then pulled out her phone and rang him. Again, there was no answer.

Unsure what to do, she walked to the left side of the house, noticing a gate between the fence and the house. She felt she was invading his personal space but had no choice, so grabbed the handle and pushed the gate open.

'Thomas?' she shouted. No answer.

She reached the rear of the house, finding a neatly cut lawn that spanned from fence to fence, an extravagant

213

fountain tucked over in the right corner, the calming sound of water falling from it, and a set of table and chairs, filled with padded cushions under an overhanging parasol on a small square of patio stones near the French doors leading to the living room.

'DI James?' she said louder, making herself known so he wouldn't see someone in his garden and be startled.

Nothing. She tried his phone again but, again, no answer.

As she passed the kitchen window, she stopped to peer inside. The kitchen, much like the rest of the house, was of high spec; sharp white lighting shone down from under the top cupboards onto what looked like a marble worktop on the far side.

Her eyes suddenly widened when she saw the object on the white-tiled floor near the tall double fridge-freezer.

A knife with a small pool of blood under it.

'What the fuck is going on . . .'

She went over to the back door and snapped the handle down, but it was locked. She dashed across the patio to the French doors, but that too was locked. Pulling out her phone, she found DS Phillips's number and tapped the Call button. 'Pick up, Matthew. Please . . .'

It went to voicemail. 'For fuck's sake, come on!' She left him a message.

Then she picked up a loose boulder from the water feature and threw it through the French door.

CHAPTER 51

The sound of a lock turning startled Amanda into focus. She'd lain there in silence for days now, staring at nothing, feeling tired and hopeless. At first, when she woken, she'd tried screaming but that had proved pointless over time because no one came. She figured she was in some kind of basement, but was it a house, a commercial property, something in the middle of nowhere? She didn't know. The small window in the top corner of the room was so dirty, she couldn't see anything out of it.

She turned towards the noise, recognising it was the sound of the basement door opening at the top of the wooden staircase. The extra daylight was a small comfort to her, partially filling the space around her. Her breathing quickened as she stared up, wondering what he'd do to her this time. She briefly heard the sound of a television somewhere up the stairs, along with the clashing of pots and pans, telling her she wasn't alone in the house with him.

The man's bare feet came into view, then his hairy legs, then the rest of him.

He smiled widely at her, the shadows hiding his full face, making him appear not quite in human form.

'How are you doing?' he asked in a deep voice. If it wasn't for the tape binding her mouth shut, she'd have told him to piss off. The floor where she lay was cold, the concrete irritating her bare arms and feet the longer she was there. Ever since she'd arrived, she'd been in that position — her arms tied behind her back, her feet fixed together with rope, and knots strong enough to keep them there. She'd completely lost feeling in her body, now struggling to lift her head to see him properly.

'Jesus, what is that smell, Amanda?' He tipped his head back in quiet laughter.

Fuck off, she thought, feeling both vulnerable and angry.

He went to her right and pressed the switch on the wall, and the overhead strip light flashed a few times until it stayed on with a constant gentle hum. He stepped under it, his large body casting a shadow over her.

She watched him in fear and mumbled something under the tape.

It was the fourth day she had lain there. She was starving. Her stomach twisted in knots, desperate for food. So far, she'd had only water and smoothies fed through a straw to keep her alive. She had wet and shit herself several times until there was nothing left inside her body. The place reeked.

He took a few steps closer and looked down at her. 'Why did you have to do it, Amanda?' he asked her. 'All of this could have been avoided, couldn't it?'

She silently scowled up at him. He lowered slowly and reached for her face with his hand, causing her to shuffle back as far as she could and clamp her eyes closed.

'Steady . . .' he mused. He grabbed the duct tape and pulled it off quickly, the dried adhesive clinging to her skin.

She yelped in pain. 'Fuck you.' She grunted, but the sound was barely above a whisper.

'Don't be like that, Amanda . . .' He moved his hand to the top of her head and stroked her hair.

She jolted back and forth, attempting to free herself, but she hadn't moved her body for so long it was like she'd forgotten how to.

'Shhhh,' he whispered, his palm caressing her dry, matted hair.

She tried to scream but it was a pathetic effort.

'No one will hear you.' He smiled at her again. 'I read your diary. Interesting stuff.'

Her eyes widened, knowing exactly what he was talking about.

'How could you do that to him?' he asked, shaking his head at her. 'I can't believe you—'

The sound of glass smashing upstairs silenced him. He glared towards the wooden staircase.

'You don't go anywhere, Amanda. I'll be back soon.'

CHAPTER 52

Fisher carefully stepped through the broken French door onto the wooden floor in DI James's house. The glass had exploded into a million tiny cubes, now scattered all over the floor in the living room.

'Thomas?' She cautiously gazed around, then looked to the right, towards the stylish, modern kitchen.

No reply, and no sign of anyone.

She gingerly moved towards the knife on the tiled floor and the small pool of blood around it. A smell of bleach lingered somewhere, but there was no evidence of any cleaning products on the worktops on either side.

'DI James?' She was loud and clear with this, pausing a moment to hear for a response. 'It's DS April Fisher. Are you here?'

She was shaking now, her heart beating through her chest, the realisation of smashing one of his doors finally settling in.

'Thomas?'

Somewhere in the house, she heard a patter of frantic feet, coming from above.

She froze, staring left into the living room, then straight ahead into the kitchen, her head shifting side to side, trying to weigh up the direction of the sound.

'Shit,' she whispered. Her eyes darted for something to use to protect herself. Her first thought was to pick up the knife, but she didn't want to contaminate it, so she grabbed a tea towel from the worktop, wrapped the handle with the cloth, and picked it up. The blood seeped onto the tea towel and dripped on the tiles as she staggered back, lowering into a better position near the sink.

The footsteps were getting closer.

The knife was tight in her hand, the handle close to her stomach. She had no idea who was coming. Had something happened to DI James? Was this the person responsible?

The sounds pounded down the stairs, the reverberations shaking the house, until they reached the ground floor, then quickly approached the kitchen where she was. Clutching the knife, she moved to the opposite worktop, lowering slightly, her left hand steadying herself.

The figure quickly shot into view. A large man moving quickly, face red and full of anger. He came to a halt and stared at her, the sudden realisation of who she was sinking in.

'April?' He threw her a look of disbelief, then glared beyond her at the sea of tiny glass cubes at the end of the living room, and the unmissable gaping hole in his expensive door. 'April, what the fuck is going on?'

She let out a huge sigh of relief and dropped the knife and tea towel on the tiles. 'Jesus, Thomas . . .' She raised a hand to her chest to calm her breathing.

'Why on earth have you smashed my door?' He scowled at the mess as he moved towards it. 'April, what on earth?'

'I tried calling you,' she explained quickly. 'You didn't answer. When I saw the blood and the knife, I didn't . . . I didn't know what to think.' She took a few short, settling breaths and doubled over with her hand pressed against her chest.

'What are you doing here, April?'

'I've found something.' She noticed the white bloody tea towel wrapped around his hand. 'What happened to you?'

He glanced down. 'Cut it making dinner. Stupid, really. I was upstairs trying to clean it up, but it's a deep cut. Might need to see a doctor.'

The towel around his hand was redder than it was white. 'Show me.'

He walked to the sink and carefully unravelled it, wincing as he did so. She leaned in.

'Jesus. Yes, you need to go see someone.'

He smiled thinly. 'Yeah, I'll go.' He looked at the mess of the French door. 'Guess that's why people have insurance, I suppose . . .'

'I'm so sorry, Thomas.' She stood straighter. 'I thought the worst had happened, that's all.'

'You want a coffee?'

She shook her head. 'Forget the coffee, you need to see a doctor. Come on, I'll drive you.'

Reluctantly, he agreed. 'You can tell me what you've found on the way. I'll sort this mess out later.'

* * *

Fisher was heading to the hospital with DI James in the passenger seat. He'd grabbed another large towel to lessen the mess in her car on the way over. The cut hadn't stopped bleeding yet.

'You okay, boss?'

'It stings.'

She took her eyes off the road and noticed the cloth around his arm getting redder.

'So, what was so important you had to break my thousand-pound door for?'

'I broke your thousand-pound door because you didn't answer your phone and I saw blood.'

He made a 'fair-enough' face and looked out of the window at the passing traffic.

'All three victims worked at care homes,' she said, finally.

He frowned. 'Did they?'

She nodded. 'Yeah. We know Elaine Freeman was a carer at Sunnydale Care Home.'

'But Joan Ellison didn't work. She lived with her mum,' he countered.

'That's true, but she used to. Her mum was ill, I remember the case at the time. She'd taken time off to look after her — she couldn't cope alone.' Fisher slowed the car at the approaching lights, stopping behind a stationary plumber's van.

'Where did she work?'

'Aldach Care Home.' Fisher put the Volvo in first gear and pulled away. 'Although she hadn't worked for almost three months, she was still employed by them.'

He frowned. 'What about Kathy Walker? She worked in a supermarket, didn't she?'

'She did,' Fisher said, raising her eyebrows. 'But before that she worked at Barton Leach Care Home. She was fired from there a year before, was out of work for a while before starting at Aldi as a checkout operator.'

'Why didn't I know that?' he asked.

'You were there in the briefing, boss,' she replied softly, not wanting to embarrass him.

He looked straight through the front windscreen, thinking hard, mostly disappointed in himself for not making the connection. 'I think you should be the DI instead of me.'

They laughed.

'So, what does this mean, April?'

She shrugged. 'I don't know for sure. Maybe we need to look at the staff that used to work there. Or maybe an agency who provided the staff. Maybe there's a connection we've missed.'

He nodded. 'Shit, sorry!' He'd been distracted, not noticing the blood dripping on his clothes, down in between his legs onto her leather seat.

'Don't worry about it.'

He grinned at her, then inspected the blood on his lap. 'What a mess . . .'

'We're nearly there,' she said. 'Don't worry. That will clean.' She looked at his hand.

She slowed, flicked her indicator on, and waited for an oncoming car to pass before she took a right. 'You need me to stay with you?'

'No, you see what you can find out about the three care homes. There must be something. That's if you have no plans today.'

She replied with a sad smile.

'How you doing, April? You know, after . . .'

She clamped her eyes shut for a second, then glared at him with wide eyes.

'Okay. I get it — you're okay.'

'Here we are.' She stopped outside of the hospital and watched him struggle out. 'I'll ring you if I find anything.' After he closed the door, she checked her mirrors, then pulled away in the direction of home.

CHAPTER 53

Derek limped into the living room with two coffees and placed one down on the small table beside her.

'Thanks, love.'

'What's up?' he asked, seeing the worry on her face.

She frowned at him. 'Abigail — where on earth is she?'

'I know, I know.' With a pain in his leg that seemed worse today than it usually did, he made his way to the other side of the sofa, placing his mug on the side, and dropped into it with a heavy sigh. She angled over to him for a second, feeling sorry for him. The car accident happened years ago but the daily niggles and pain acted as a constant reminder of it. On bad days, he took painkillers prescribed by his doctor to lessen the aches but it was always there, threatening to worsen at any point. He knew one thing: he would always drive slow in the ice and snow — often painfully slow, but he didn't care. The crash had done enough harm.

'You finished in there?' she asked.

'Yeah, I'm done for today. I can't stop thinking about the car in the lake.'

'I know. I've been speaking with Debbie about it. I said I'd let her know when we hear anything.'

He'd been doing a small DIY project in the garage to keep his mind off current events. He'd tried driving the streets, looking for them, but each street he drove down made him more angry. Instead, he came home and continued working on his birdbox. Karen had seen one last week, but the price was extortionate in his opinion and he told her he could make one just as good, so she had challenged him to do just that. He had some spare pieces of wood and the tools at his disposal, and had spent the afternoon sawing and cutting, the noise drowned out by the closed door, so it didn't disturb her doing the cleaning, something she did tirelessly when trying ignore her real problems.

Karen was watching television — an ITV show, two guys presenting something. It looked promising, but Derek wasn't really into it; he'd spent much of his time doing DIY projects and keeping his hands busier.

It was approaching nine in the evening. The show had just finished and Derek sat, finishing the rest of his cold coffee while Karen flicked through the channels, mumbling about there being nothing on, although they had the choice of over five hundred channels.

'Just pick something.' He shook his head at how ridiculous she was being.

As she turned to say something to him, she was interrupted by a series of little knocks, almost inaudible.

'What's that knocking sound?' She gazed towards the hallway.

His brows furrowed as he concentrated on the sound. 'Is it the pipes?'

'The heating isn't on, Derek,' she said, stating the obvious fact it was nearly twenty degrees. 'I think it's the door. I'll go see.'

Derek glanced down at his watch as Karen slid off the sofa and wandered to the front door.

Through the small square of head-height glass, she couldn't see anyone on the other side of the door, which she thought was strange. She grabbed the keys from the hook on the wall, unlocked the door, and opened it.

'What is it?' Derek said from the sofa.

There was no answer from Karen.

'Karen, who's at the bloody door?'

After no response, he struggled up and made his way to the hallway, the pain in his knee aggravating him as he moved. There at the door was Karen kneeling down with her arms wrapped around something.

'Karen, what are you . . . Oh my God.'

His eyes widened as he dashed to the door, opened his arms, and pulled them both into him. 'Abigail, where on earth have you been?' he asked as tears streamed down his face.

CHAPTER 54

Tony's heart pounded as he jumped into his car and slammed the door shut, the sound echoing in the quiet cul-de-sac. Forgetting his seat belt, he turned on the engine of the courtesy car and set off quickly, the tyres kicking up hundreds of the little stones on his driveway towards his house.

He noticed Mary and Ronny Leatham standing on their doorstep as he flew past, watching him closely.

It had been three minutes since Derek had phoned him, telling him they'd found Abigail at the door. He couldn't explain why or how she had got there, just that she had been found, and, most importantly, appeared safe and unharmed.

It took Tony eight minutes to get to their house, breaking multiple laws and running two red lights. The annoyed drivers at both intersections used their car horns to show their frustration.

He stopped the car and dashed to the house, opening the front door and running inside. Abigail was seated on the sofa with Karen in the living room, her arms wrapped firmly around her. The joy on her face when she saw Tony made him go weak at the knees.

'Abigail,' he gasped as he ran over, dropping to his knees.

She jumped off the sofa and into his arms, hugging him so tight it hurt him, but he didn't care.

'Where on earth have you been?' he cried as he squeezed her back, tears streaming down his face onto her tiny shoulder.

'She doesn't know, Tony.' Karen had already asked the same question.

He pulled away for a brief moment, scanning her for any signs she was hurt or had sustained any injuries since she'd been missing.

'She seems perfectly fine, Tony.' Karen smiled.

'How did she get here?'

Derek appeared in the doorway of the living room and wiped his eyes with the back of his hand. Karen glanced over and gave him a sad smile before she looked back at her granddaughter and son embracing each other.

The sounds of sirens and cars approached from outside. Flashes of blue light shone through the living room window, hitting the back wall behind the sofa and highlighting Abigail's little face in a haze of blue innocence.

'I'm so happy you're okay, baby.' Tony pulled her close, squashing her for the umpteenth time.

Karen stood from the sofa and peered out the window, seeing DS Fisher step down from her Volvo and DS Phillips get out of the passenger seat. Behind the white four-by-four, a marked police car stopped, then uniformed officers got out either side. They all made their way to the house.

'I'll let them in,' said Derek, limping into the hallway.

Tony, still holding Abigail, looked up at Fisher and Phillips in the living room doorway.

'Abigail . . .' whispered Fisher, feeling her own throat clogging with emotions.

A moment of happy silence passed before Tony stood and put his arm around Abigail's shoulder.

Fisher stepped forward, lowered to her knees, and smiled widely at Abigail. 'Are you okay, Abigail?'

Shyly, she nodded but said nothing. Fisher stared into her blue eyes, now familiar from the photo she'd constantly studied. She stood and advised a paramedic who had just arrived on scene. Without knowing where exactly she'd been for four days, and not knowing exactly who she'd been with, they needed to confirm she was fine and no harm had come to her.

Tony knew what she was talking about.

* * *

After the paramedic had seen to Abigail, they sat at the kitchen table, speaking among themselves, nestling cups of coffee in their hands, thin smiles on their faces. DS Phillips stood behind Fisher, who was sitting in one of the four seats. Tony was opposite with Abigail on his knee. Karen and Derek were seated next to them. PC Baan and PC Jackson were currently in the hallway speaking to the paramedic. The small, plump woman in green confirmed that Abigail hadn't been touched in any malicious way and completed her report, asking Baan to sign it before she left.

Word must have got out about Abigail's appearance; a small news van was parked outside, a man in the driver's seat and a woman in her mid-twenties with blonde hair looking towards the house with searing eyes.

'So, Abigail,' Fisher said gently, 'can you remember where you went?'

They all knew it was pretty much pointless talking to her — the chances of getting anything useful out of a two-year-old were not good, but it didn't stop them trying. At the moment, they had nothing else to go on.

Abigail stared at her blankly then craned her neck to Tony; she didn't know what was going on.

'It's okay, baby.' He smiled at her reassuringly.

Fisher smiled then gazed across to Karen and Derek. 'So, she just turned up and knocked on the door?'

They both nodded. 'Pretty much.'

'Did you see anyone in the street?'

Karen thought about it. 'I may have heard a car, but I didn't look up. I just saw Abigail standing there on the step and hugged her.'

Fisher bobbed her head.

'We're just glad she's okay . . .' Karen turned, placing a hand on her small shoulder, and beamed at Tony.

DS Phillips frowned. 'I wonder how she got here.'

Derek offered only a shrug. Four long days had passed since Martin Forlan had attacked Tony and driven off in his car. The questions remained: who was the other man, and where the hell had they taken her? From word of the paramedic, it was safe to say Abi was in good health, so whoever these men were, they hadn't hurt her in any way. She didn't look thin or carry an unhealthy complexion. She'd been fed and watered. It was a strange scenario. Often, when a child went missing for four days after an act of violence, the child was either found dead or severely malnourished, not perfectly normal like Abigail seemed to be.

Fisher didn't say anything, obviously thinking about something. Then she said, 'Have you got a camera outside your house?'

Karen shook her head. 'I told him I wanted one installing a few months back — we had issues with the people opposite. Our car was scratched one day but no one owned up.'

Derek sighed and closed his eyes for a moment, another thing to have a moan about.

A frown found Karen's face. 'I think Gary does next door.'

'Who's Gary?' Phillips inquired.

'Gary Pullam. Lived there for years. He's quite high-tech. You know, into his gadgets.'

Derek bobbed his head. 'Yeah, he'll probably have cameras somewhere. Probably hidden, but he'll have them.'

* * *

229

Less than two minutes later, DS Fisher and DS Phillips were knocking on the green door of Gary Pullam's house. It was a similar size to Karen and Derek's — a four-bed detached, with a cube-like appearance, minimal kerb appeal but a generous double driveway where a sickly lime-green transporter van was parked.

The door was answered by a tall, thin, odd-looking guy with narrow-framed glasses and a goatee. He must have been six foot six, making even DS Phillips appear small.

'Mr Pullam?' Fisher gazed up at him, taken aback by his towering height.

The next-door neighbour tilted his head forward, observing her over the top of his glasses like a science teacher would a student. 'Er, yes?'

Fisher showed her credentials and introduced Phillips. Pullam eyed Phillips for a second too long, then focused back on Fisher. 'We were wondering if you have any cameras on this property, particularly any shots of the road?' She turned and pointed to the street.

'Can I ask why?' Pullam pulled himself up straight, appearing even taller, and folded his arms.

'Of course. We need to see footage of the street from an hour ago. A little girl turned up next door and we need to know where she came from.'

'Little girl — oh, is this Abigail? Has she been found?'

A nod from Phillips.

'Brilliant. Derek was telling me about her yesterday. What the hell happened?'

'That's what we're hoping to find out. And I think it would be a massive help if we could have a look at any CCTV you have?'

'Of course. Please,' he said, stepping aside, making room for them to enter. 'Please, mind the mess. I'm working on a project.'

Pullam led them down the simply decorated hallway, white paint covering the walls with very little ornaments or pictures fixed to them.

They followed him into the dining room, surprised how big the space was inside, the rear extension not visible from the front of the house. Phillips frowned walking across the floor, the wood under him creaking more than it should, then followed Pullam into a smaller room where his computer was.

'What's up with the floor in there?' Phillips asked, pointing to where they had just walked.

'Oh, it needs doing. A guy is coming next month to sort it. Been like that since I've been here. I'm looking at selling. A surveyor came over to have a look at the house and pointed it out straight away, saying it would need strengthening before I put it up for sale.'

'Why does it creak like that?'

'It's where the basement is. The floor beams were solid, but the surveyor thinks that damp has got in somewhere and the wood is starting to rot.'

Phillips said, 'Might want to get that sorted sooner rather than later. Don't want the floor to go through.'

Pullam sighed at the obvious. 'As I said, people are coming next month.'

Phillips watched him move strangely and couldn't describe it. Maybe it was his height, but he was almost mechanical. In the study where he had led them, two large screens sat atop an expensive-looking desk with multiple shelves and compartments in it. Neither Fisher nor Phillips had seen a setup like it, especially at someone's house.

Pullam took a seat on a black leather swivel chair, smoothly pulled himself close to the desk, and navigated to where he needed to be. 'You say an hour ago?'

'Yeah, around nine onwards.'

He double-clicked, opening up footage from a camera positioned somewhere above the door looking out onto the street. Fisher smiled to herself, remembering what Derek had said about him probably having a camera likely hidden from view.

'I didn't see any cameras. Where's that?' Phillips asked, pointing at the screen. 'Just above the door?'

'Yes. Just above the door,' he replied, not elaborating any more about it or taking his eyes off the screen. He was weird. 'Okay, here we go. This is from nine onwards. Each file runs for six hours. So the time now is twenty-two hundred and thirty-six minutes. We can view the whole time frame in this shot.'

Phillips offered Fisher a knowing look.

They watched the footage on double speed from nine o'clock. At three minutes passed nine, a red car went by very slowly as if it was coming to a stop. 'There,' Fisher said. 'Take that back, please.'

Pullam dragged the scroll bar back a few seconds and paused it when the red car was in view. There seemed to be a sign on the roof, which looked to be a taxi, although they couldn't be sure.

'It's a taxi,' Pullam confirmed. 'Hold on . . .' He let the video play in slow motion, trying the see the registration plate, but the angle didn't allow it. 'Can't get the plate, unfortunately. Oh, wait, hold on.' It was barely visible, but they all noticed it on the lower part of the rear passenger door. An All-United Taxis label.

'Can you see her?' DS Phillips said.

Pullam raised a finger to the screen. 'Just . . . there.'

They concentrated on the small object in the back of the taxi, the dark outline of a small head.

'It's Abigail,' Fisher said, turning to Phillips. 'We need to ring All-United Taxis to find out where she was picked up from.'

CHAPTER 55

Fisher and Phillips left the Volvo parked on the side of the road with the hazards on and went inside the small taxi office. The front of the shop was a narrow space, occupied by a door and a large rectangular window. Inside, a worn, flattened rug lay in the centre of the floor, an old and battered leather sofa with scratches and chunks missing from it sat to the right, and to the left, there was a small counter with a sheet of thick glass above it, revealing a woman in her late forties with scraggy hair, wrinkles around her mouth, and deep lines at the edges of her eyes. She wore a headset and spoke into the thin microphone by her cheek. Her bare arms were covered in tattoos. A smell of stale smoke still lingered in the space. Given the ban was introduced in July 2007, it made Fisher wonder if they still smoked behind the glass, but she didn't have time for that nor was she particularly bothered.

The tired-looking woman looked up at them through the glass. 'Where to?'

'We're not here for a taxi,' said Fisher.

'Then you've got the wrong place, love.' Her tone was flat.

Fisher wasted no time and pulled out her credentials, pushing them up against the glass. The expression on the blonde's face didn't change, she was obviously used to police coming and going. It was a central spot, no doubt seeing its fair share of trouble in the early hours of the morning, hence the need for the glass and the lack of rush to replace the tattered sofa behind them.

'We need some information, please.'

The woman waited, but said nothing.

Fisher told her that one of their taxis had dropped a small girl off at an address less than two hours ago. Who was the driver and where she was picked up?

The woman frowned. The fare was not familiar to her. 'Hold on.' She switched her attention to the screen in front of her. 'It was flagged down around eight fifty, according to driver's information, then dropped off just after nine. When drivers are on the rank or they're flagged down, the fare isn't booked, so they're required to fill it in on the dash computers.'

'Where was the fare picked up?'

She had a look. 'Wharfside Way, a hundred yards from the Old Trafford football stadium.'

'Okay.' Fisher nodded. 'Who was the driver?'

She had another look. 'Paddy McCormick. He's still working. Will be out till the early hours, I'd imagine.'

'Would it be possible to speak with him?'

The blonde sighed, not hiding the fact she had other things to do. 'I can call him, but he'll be busy.'

'Listen, I apologise for interrupting you while you're working, but this is important. Someone kidnapped a two-year-old and kept them for four days away from their home against their will. Her mother is still missing. Your cooperation here is very much appreciated.'

'Okay, I'll call him now.' Her demeanour seemed to change as she understood the gravity of the situation.

Fisher and Phillips both thanked her before stepping away from the glass for a moment, and stood at the large window overlooking the busy street. A modified Vauxhall Corsa whizzed by, filled with young teenagers, loud music blaring from the open windows.

'Those were the days . . .' muttered Phillips.

'Never pegged you for a boy racer, Matthew.'

'You have no idea,' he said, then laughed.

There was a knock on the glass behind them. 'He's coming back now. He's just around the corner,' the blonde said.

* * *

Paddy McCormick was barely five feet, and almost as wide as he was tall. An obvious gym-goer, he resembled an angry ball as he made his way through the door with an ID badge hanging from his neck. 'You guys wanna talk?'

They sat down on the sofa and Fisher asked him about the fare. 'Could you describe the person who put her inside the car?'

He pushed his bottom lip out in thought. 'Tall guy. Dressed in black. Short hair. To be honest, that's all I remember. He was stood with the little girl on the side of the road and put his arm out. When he opened the door, he leaned in, told me to take her to the address written down on the piece of paper in his hand. He gave me thirty quid and told me to knock on the door and leave her there.'

'And you just drove off, no questions asked?'

Paddy screwed his face up. 'He gave me thirty quid for a ten-pound fare. So yeah, that's exactly what I did.'

Phillips then asked, 'I hope you had a car seat for her. She's only small. It would be illegal to travel with someone so small without one.'

Paddy burst into laughter. 'What kind of a police officer are you? Taxis don't need child seats . . . are you sure you're fully trained in this job?'

Phillips knew that but wanted to throw it in there in case the driver didn't.

'Listen, we're not here for that.' Fisher momentarily gave Phillips a stare that suggested he should leave the talking to her. 'We just need information.'

Paddy nodded. 'As I said. A tall guy, thin. Short hair.'

'Any facial hair?'

'No, I think he was clean-shaven,' replied Paddy. He looked down at his watch. 'Are we done?'

They considered his question and nodded. 'Yeah, we're done,' Phillips said.

The taxi driver jumped up and left the shop, keen to get back out and make some more money. Fisher and Phillips thanked the blonde behind the glass, who ignored them as they left.

'Oh well,' Fisher said, sighing. 'No further forward with who the guy is.'

'At least Abigail's home now.' Phillips clicked in his belt and Fisher pulled away.

Fisher gave a thin smile. 'Just Amanda to find now.'

CHAPTER 56

Jack Mulberry smiled briefly as he made his way into the kitchen the following morning and flicked on the kettle. He was over the moon his granddaughter was back home safe. Derek, Tony's father, had phoned last night telling him that Abigail had turned up, so Rachel and Jack had gone round while the police were still there to see little Abigail, shedding tears along with the rest of the family when they saw her. Rachel had spent the majority of her night on the phone to friends telling them the good news, while Jack stayed downstairs drinking whiskey after whiskey in celebration.

He made two coffees and placed Rachel's on the side for now; she was sleeping, so could warm it up when she woke. He made his way into the hallway, but before he took a right into the living room to watch some television, he stopped. Something caught his eye near the front door.

'What . . .'

There was a white envelope on the mat. He bent down and picked it up. The words *Jack and Rachel* were written in black handwriting on the front.

'. . . the hell is this?'

He placed his coffee on the small windowsill to the left and carefully peeled the envelope open, then pulled out a piece of paper. Over the next two minutes, he read the letter three times, each time slower than the last, trying to make sure he understood its contents. He dialled DS Fisher immediately, telling her what it said.

She said she'd be straight over and told him not to do anything rash.

He ended the call, threw the letter on the floor, then screamed in anger.

On the floor, the unfolded letter read:

Jack and Rachel,

We have your daughter. Leave £50,000 inside a black bag that you will find on a seat at one of the tables in Costa Coffee at the Trafford Centre. Once the money is there, zip up the bag and put your hand in the air for three seconds. Do this by the end of the day. If you don't deliver the money, Amanda will die. If we see any sign of police there, she will die. The clock is ticking. If we get the money in time, your daughter will be delivered home first thing in the morning.

CHAPTER 57

'What do you make of this?' Fisher asked Jack and Rachel Mulberry.

They both looked up from the table, offering nothing but a shrug. Jack's face was nestled in cupped hands. Rachel was biting her elegant fingernails, something, judging by how neat they were, she only did in times of stress.

'Any idea who could have sent this?'

'None whatsoever,' Jack replied. 'But if I get my hands on them . . .'

DS Phillips had received the call from Fisher about the note, and left Janice and Dominic at home, after promising — for the umpteenth time — he'd spend the day with them. He apologised and told her that he would make it up to them, which was probably another empty promise in her eyes, he thought, as he drove away from their house less than twenty minutes ago. He wondered whether a career in the police had been a good call.

'What can we do?' Rachel said quietly, tapping the table with a finger, searching for an answer.

Fisher thought hard before speaking. 'Would you be willing to pay fifty thousand pounds for your daughter's safe return?'

'Of course,' she snapped, then looked at Jack, who nodded in agreement.

'Yeah, of course we would,' he added. 'But I'd rather find out who the son of a bitch is first.' He slammed a palm on the table. Fisher and Rachel jumped a little, but DS Phillips didn't flinch, watching him carefully in case his anger escalated and he needed to calm things down.

They understood his frustration. Ransoms were hard for anyone. Using people's loved ones in trade for money was a coward's trick, yet a very smart and effective one. Fisher hadn't been involved in many ransom demands in her career. They often happened over in the US or in films, usually involving mega-rich celebrities and professionals where families wait around a phone with a team of police near, and IT guys all hooked up with earphones and flashy computers and hard drives in an attempt to figure out the people behind the demands.

But this was different. There was no phone number to arrange anything, no room for negotiation. Just a note with a simple demand that, if not met, would, according to the note, result in the death of their daughter.

'They can't expect us to get fifty grand just like that!' protested Rachel. It was the first time Fisher or Phillips had seen frustration from her. She stood abruptly, the hind of her knees knocking the chair back across the tiles with a sharp screech, and went over to the sink to stare out the window. Her breathing was light and fast, her shoulders rising and falling quickly.

'It's ridiculous.' Jack glared down at the table in disbelief. 'Is there anything you can do?'

Fisher considered the question for a moment. 'Do you recognise the handwriting?'

He leaned over the note on the table. 'No, never seen it.'

'Excuse me for asking, but is fifty thousand a sum which you have access to, if needed?'

Jack stared at Fisher with narrowed eyes. 'We could get that sum if we needed to, yeah.'

Jack looked up at Rachel for a moment, pondering the consequences. She nodded in agreement.

'Does someone hold a grudge against you?' asked Fisher.

Jack pushed a ball of air from his closed lips. 'That list could potentially be endless.'

DS Phillips, based on what he knew of Jack Mulberry, could understood why.

'Listen,' Jack said, slapping the edge of the table with the side of his palm, 'if you guys did your job and found out what happened to her, we wouldn't be in this situation, would we?'

Fisher's eyebrows raised, but she said nothing. DS Phillips glared at him.

'And,' Jack went on, ignoring the heat of their glares, 'if we can get the money, Amanda will be safe. But how can we? The banks are closed.'

'Who do you bank with?'

'Halifax.'

'There could be a way . . .' countered Fisher.

Jack and Rachel listened.

The front door opened, stopping Fisher from continuing. They heard footsteps coming down the hallway. A voice shouted, 'Rachel? Jack?'

Jack sighed, recognising the voice. 'Here we go. The hero . . .'

Tony Anderson appeared at the kitchen doorway. 'Where's the letter? Let me see it.' He noticed it on the table and dashed over.

'What's he doing here?' Jack frowned.

Fisher had informed Tony about the note. After all, he was the husband and had a right to know.

Tony scowled and stared at Jack. 'Who sent this?'

'Do you think if we knew that, we'd be here talking about it?' Jack shook his head in disbelief. 'We'd be out there getting her back, wouldn't we?'

'We don't know, Mr Anderson,' DS Phillips said evenly, to prevent the likely argument. 'That's what we're trying to find out.'

Tony thought in silence for a moment. 'And they expect you to just drop it off by the end of the day?'

'Looks that way, Tony.'

'Tony,' Rachel said. She looked around the kitchen, then down the hallway. 'Where's Abigail?'

'She's with my mum and dad. I headed straight over here when Detective Fisher phoned me. I hope you didn't mind.'

'Right,' Jack said, clapping his hands. 'Let's get this money and get Amanda back.'

CHAPTER 58

The Trafford Centre was huge, with a multitude of shops over two floors, making it a popular spot with locals and tourists. Costa Coffee was located on the ground floor near the main entrance. Fisher had collected a team — including PC Ashleigh Baan — and informed DI James of the note and the plan she'd put in place.

'Are you ready?' Fisher said, half-turned, looking into the rear of her Volvo. Jack, with a film of sweat across his forehead and fifty thousand pounds tightly wrapped in a brown paper bag in his hand, gave her a nod.

'Good. When you approach Costa, check all the tables as you walk in. Hopefully you'll see the black bag mentioned in the letter. Once found, drop the money in, zip it up, and raise your hand for three seconds as instructed. Then leave. Walk out the way you walked in, back over to my car. Got it?'

He took a deep breath, then exhaled sharply.

'We have a team of four inside, dotted around in various positions. Once you leave, we'll watch the bag to see who collects it. Whatever you do, don't try to spot any of our people. Firstly, because you won't be able to — trust me, they'll be well disguised. And secondly, if the person who's set this thing up is watching you, and I'll bet my mortgage they will be, they may notice what you're doing, which will only arouse suspicion. Got it?'

He took another deep breath, opened the door, and stepped out into the hot sun. The car park was full, and cars slowly trailed around, searching for a free space or any sign that people were leaving.

Fisher breathed deeply herself. Phillips glanced at her. 'Think this'll work?'

'I bloody well hope so,' Tony Anderson said from the seat directly behind Fisher's.

They all watched Jack Mulberry, dressed in smart jeans, a thin black jacket, and smart black shoes, walk through the sliding double doors of the Trafford Centre.

It had been more than three years since Jack had been here. He remembered why as soon as he entered: a busy world of cheerful shoppers, many engaged in conversations, others laughing between themselves, young teenagers talking on phones, while others sat on benches in their small groups texting or whatever the kids do nowadays.

He hated people in general, let alone crowds of people.

Costa Coffee was on his left as he entered through the main doors. He resisted gazing around to spot the four people that Fisher had mentioned would be watching him. He didn't want to arouse any suspicion that he was being helped with this, remembering the words on the letter sent through his door.

The four discreetly positioned officers watched him. None of them, nor Jack Mulberry, had noticed the fifth person watching.

CHAPTER 59

The fifth man in the Trafford Centre pulled his phone from his pocket so subtly, you'd have missed it even if you were watching him. He quickly navigated to the number he needed, tapped Call, then raised it to his ear.

'Yeah?' answered a rough voice.

'He's in Costa now. The money will be inside the bag very soon.'

'Where are you?'

'Don't worry, I'm well hidden.'

'Are there other people there?' the voice asked. 'I have a feeling they went to the police first.'

'Not that I can see.' The man scanned the area. 'Can't see anyone. If anyone is watching, they are well hidden too.'

The man on the phone sighed. 'Okay, let me know when he raises his hand and leaves.'

* * *

Jack Mulberry got a few odd looks from the seated customers as he entered Costa. Not because of how he looked or what he was wearing, but the unfriendly, searching scowl on his face as he searched for the black bag.

'Got ya . . .' he muttered under his breath, seeing it on a chair at one of the tables near the back. He passed a pair of teenagers who were glued to their phones and an elderly couple sharing a pot of tea; the man tilted his head, looked at Jack through thick glasses, magnifying his huge blue eyes, and offered him a smile. Jack rudely ignored him and went to the table with the bag on the chair, gently picked it up off the seat, and sat down beside it. He placed the brown package carefully inside and slid the zip closed, then waited for a moment, unsure what to do. He knew he had to stand up, walk out, go back through the exit and back to Fisher's Volvo — that was the plan — but he wanted to stay to see who came to collect it, wanted to look into the eyes of the man or woman that was holding his daughter hostage. And, it was fifty thousand pounds. What if someone randomly picked it up before it was collected?

* * *

'What's happening?' Fisher said into the phone.

'He's sitting at the table, but he's not moving,' said the voice of a disguised PC watching him.

'Has he put the money in the bag?'

'Affirmative,' the PC said. The person speaking with Fisher was positioned in Pizza Hut, watching Jack Mulberry through the window with binoculars. He was so far away no one would suspect a thing, but in a good position to see what was going on.

'Okay, let me know what happens.'

The line cut off.

* * *

Jack inhaled a pocket of coffee-scented air, slid out, leaving the money in the bag, and stood. He raised his hand in the air and counted to three in his head, his cheeks warming as he caught a few strange glares from those around him. He

246

made his way to the front and took a right in the direction of the exit, worrying about the money in the bag.

He was so zoned out of everything else he didn't see the man walking towards him and they collided shoulders, which knocked Jack back a few steps. The man was of medium height, but muscular, wearing a tight-fitting T-shirt that showed the biceps he worked on several times a week at the gym.

'Watch where you're going, mister,' the muscle man said.

'Move out my way,' Jack replied, frowning at him. 'You walked into me.'

The man's eyes widened as he took a step forward. 'Wanna make something of this, old man?' He stepped closer, leaving a gap of only a foot between them.

'Please, I don't have time for this shit. Go and pick on someone your own age.' Jack tried to step around him but the younger man shuffled across to block his path. He was in his thirties, maybe younger. His face was of someone who had been through a lot — deep eyes and a menacing stare.

'Please, just let this go,' said Jack, shaking his head.

The man pushed Jack back with two quick shoves, causing Jack to stumble a little, and he was lucky not to lose his balance and fall. Several nearby people stopped to stare, a couple of them watching what was going on.

'Oh, come on,' Jack pleaded. 'It was an accident. Let me pass and we can go about our day like nothing's happened.'

Behind them, at the exit of the Trafford Centre — the same door that Jack had come through moments earlier — one of the glass panels smashed. Nearby people screamed and moved to get their children to safety. Everyone turned to see a teenager standing on the pavement outside with his hood up and giving everyone the Vs. He'd thrown a brick through the window, the rock now sitting among a sea of glass on the shiny floor near Costa. The boy ran away quickly when he saw a couple of thin security guards running towards him with walkie-talkies at their mouths.

The muscle man smiled and shook his head. 'I'll let you off this time, old man.' Then he walked around him like nothing had happened.

Jack decided to say nothing in reply and headed for the exit. He needed to get out of there.

* * *

'What the hell is going on?' Fisher said into the phone, hearing the glass smashing from a distance. 'Why's everyone rushing around?'

The man at Pizza Hut had seen the commotion and informed Fisher that a window had been smashed.

'Head over, see what's going on,' she told him.

'Roger.' With the phone to his ear, he lowered the binoculars and ran across the mall. He saw the brick on the floor along with the thousands of tiny cubes the cleaners were already sweeping up. A security guard stood by, speaking into a phone, looking around aimlessly.

The man saw the back of Jack as he walked through the exit. 'Jack is leaving now. Can you see him?'

Fisher spotted Jack leaving through the door and heading over to her car. 'Yeah, got him.'

'What was all that about?' the constable asked.

Fisher thought for a moment. 'Go check the bag, please. Do it now.' A sudden urgency filled her voice.

The man dashed into Costa, went to the table at the back, stared at the chair, and raised the phone to his head.

'Detective Fisher . . .' he said, panting a little.

'Go ahead.'

'The bag is gone.'

CHAPTER 60

'The money is gone?' Tony said, echoing the words Fisher had been told on the phone.

Fisher silently watched people gathering at the entrance door of the Trafford Centre, no doubt drawn to the commotion of the smashed window.

'Bastard!' DS Phillips slammed a hand on the dash just above the glovebox. Fisher gave him a cold stare. 'Sorry,' he added, realising it was his colleague's property and not his own.

Fisher typed a number into her phone, pressed Call, and put it to her ear. 'Did you see anyone?'

'Negative. I had my eye on Jack to make sure the guy wasn't going to beat him up.'

Fisher ended the call and tried another number belonging to a colleague watching nearby. 'Did you see the bag go?'

'No, I didn't,' the voice replied sheepishly. 'I was watching the window.'

Fisher sighed and ended the call. 'It was a setup. A distraction. How can we have four people watching one thing and that happens?' It was her turn to slam a hand on the dashboard. Phillips was going to say something, but thought better of it.

From the rear of the car, Tony said, 'Well, at least if they have the money, they'll return Amanda by the morning.'

Phillips rolled his eyes and watched Jack return to the car. 'Here's Jack.'

Fisher and Tony looked up.

Then Tony frowned at something. 'Eh?'

'What? What is it?' Phillips asked.

Tony pointed. 'There. Walking over there. It's my brother Michael.' Tony slid across, opened the door, and dropped to the ground. 'Wait here . . .'

'Tony, wait!'

Tony ignored Fisher's demand and broke into a run, weaving and bobbing through cars and distracted shoppers, focused on the man he believed to be his brother. The man was more than fifty metres ahead of him, walking away from the same exit that Jack Mulberry had just walked out of. Why was he there at that exact moment?

The closer he got, now less than twenty metres, the more confident he was that it was his brother Michael. He seemed to be carrying something.

'Michael?' he shouted, attracting a few glares from all directions.

Tony grabbed the man's shoulder and turned him around.

'Michael, what are you doing here?'

'God, you scared me there!' he declared, placing his free hand on his chest. 'Jeez.' A film of sweat lined his forehead, his eyes wide as if he'd seen a ghost.

'I saw you from over there — I thought you hated the Trafford Centre?'

Michael nodded twice. 'More than anything. Emma wanted some things for the kids. Ordered them online, wanted me to pick them up.' He turned to the exit he'd stepped through moments ago. 'Don't know what the hell is going on over there — someone smashed a window. There's glass all over. Security guards running up and down.'

Tony frowned at him and considered his words. He noticed the package he was holding. 'What's that?' It was small enough, wrapped in a carrier bag.

'Just a few games. It's Jaycie's birthday coming up soon. Emma had seen them online. Typically, she ordered them and couldn't be bothered to come and collect them. So, guess what? Muggins here had to do it.'

Tony's eyes narrowed. 'Show me . . .'

'Okay . . .'

Jack frowned as he unwrapped the bag and pulled out a box of Lego and a Barbie set, containing a hairbrush and fake hair. 'Happy? Hey, what are you doing here — wait, how's Abigail? Sorry, was going to come and visit but I've been so busy with work.'

'She's okay.'

'Good. Listen, I need to go, I have a meeting with a client and—'

'What's the client called?'

'Excuse me?'

'The client you have a meeting with?'

His frown deepened. 'What . . . what has that got to do with anything?'

'Please answer the question, Michael.'

'Why do I feel like I'm been interrogated? Ever since you came over, Tony, you've been acting weird. What's going on?'

'Have you spoken with Mum or Dad today?'

He shook his head. 'No. Why?'

'You sure?'

Michael screwed his face up. 'Course I'm fucking sure — I'd know if I'd have spoken to them. Tony, what the hell's going on? Why are you here?'

Tony filled him in about the note left with Amanda's parents, and about the drop-off in Costa, and finally about Amanda being let go if the money was paid by the end of the day.

'And it's gone — how? I don't get it. So, four police officers were watching and it's gone without anyone seeing it?'

Tony curled his lip, nodded.

'How on earth has that happened?'

Tony shrugged, wondering the same.

'Ahh, man, I wish I could help . . .' He checked his watch. 'Listen, I really need to go. I'll ring you later.' Michael turned, ran across the car park towards his car, jumped in, and drove off quickly.

CHAPTER 61

Fisher and Phillips had quickly stopped off at Subway to grab a bite before they returned to the station. They were starving and couldn't concentrate. DI James said he'd meet them there.

'How could four people miss it?' Phillips asked. He shook his head in disbelief and slapped his hand on the desk out of frustration. If he was going to give up his weekend time with his family to come and work, he wanted results.

'It's done now, so we need to move on.' Fisher focused back on her computer with determination, watching the security footage they'd collected from the security guards at the Trafford Centre. So far, nothing stood out.

'I thought Thomas was meeting us here?' said Phillips, gazing around the quiet office. There were a few PCs dotted around, unfortunate enough to be working the weekend shift.

'I'm here.'

DI James approached their desks, wearing tight-fitting jeans, brown boots, a shirt, with a brown suede jacket over the top. His hand was bandaged up.

'The hell happened to you?' Phillips frowned, looking at his hand.

'Did April not say?'

'No, I didn't,' Fisher replied, her eyes fixed on the screen. 'Thanks for coming in.'

With his good hand, James pulled out a chair and sat down. He carefully rested his wounded hand on his lap, and briefly informed Phillips about the incident with the knife.

'How is it?' Fisher asked, her attention still on the video footage.

'I'll survive. Anyway, where are we?'

Fisher filled him in on exactly what had happened.

'No one saw anything?' James shook his head in disbelief. 'How is that possible? Did we have all angles covered?'

A nod from Fisher. 'Absolutely. I set it up myself. The clever distraction did it.'

'What's that on your screen?'

'Footage from today.'

James pulled himself closer to Fisher's computer.

'Nothing stand out?'

Fisher shook her head and pressed her lips together. 'Unfortunately not. But we can watch it again.'

They all sat forward, their shoulders almost touching, and concentrated on her screen. The angle of the camera was better than James would have imagined, pointing directly down on Costa Coffee from roughly fifteen metres away, covering the opening, along with the first few rows of tables inside. Fisher scrolled the time to when Jack walked out empty-handed after leaving the money inside the bag on one of the chairs.

For DI James's benefit, she pointed at the screen, trailing Jack's movement. 'That's Amanda's dad, Jack. Keep your eyes peeled, Tom. You may see something we've missed.'

After Jack disappeared, Fisher told James about the man bumping into Jack, then the short argument. She checked the time in the bottom corner. At this time, the window at the exit went through, and they watched all the people on the screen freeze for a second, staring in the same direction.

'Have we got footage of the window being smashed?'

Fisher nodded at DI James. 'We do. But keep watching this screen. This is when the money must have been taken. Watch out for people going in and leaving.' Fisher glanced again at the time in the corner. 'This is when I was on the phone with PC Allen. I told him to check the money.' They all watched, seeing PC Allen, dressed in casual clothes, run into the shop. 'So, did you see anyone go in and come out in that time?'

James stared for a moment in silence. 'Literally no one.'

'Exactly.'

'What about cameras inside Costa?'

'There's only one. It's behind the counter, covering the front of the shop to around halfway. There's a blind spot. Strangely enough where the bag was left at the table.'

'Interesting,' he commented. 'Let's watch it again.'

Fisher rocked back on her chair after going through it a third time. 'Maybe it wasn't anyone who went in. Maybe the person who took the money was already in there. Is there an exit at the back?'

Phillips frowned. 'According to the staff, it isn't for the public.'

'Maybe we need to look at Costa employees, then. If no one came out with the money, then it must have gone somewhere. Maybe Costa was chosen because the person who planted it knew what the camera covered, knowing they could take the bag without being seen. They could have gone out of the back without a trace.'

James considered her words, then nodded. 'Good work, April.'

'I have a list of their employees,' Fisher informed him. 'Going to speak to them today.'

CHAPTER 62

Tony Anderson was in the living room, snuggled with Abigail and her little red lion on the sofa. Their attention was on the television in the corner, but he wasn't focused, his eyes glassy with emotion, in the hope he'd see Amanda tomorrow.

'Daddy needs to go to the kitchen,' he said softly, gently sliding himself out, leaving Abigail on the sofa. She was so glued to the screen she barely noticed him move.

He went to the kitchen, feeling frustrated and tired at the same time. He didn't know what to do with himself, let alone think how he'd get Amanda back. He leaned on the worktop, feeling useless. His boss had been on the phone less than an hour ago, asking how things were going, and if there'd been any sign of his family yet. After Tony had informed him what had happened, his manager told him to take as long as he needed before returning to work. Family always comes first, he said. 'Hope you see her tomorrow,' he added before ending the call.

His head swam with a million thoughts as he staggered over to the table, grabbed one of the chairs, and dropped into it.

He sighed, pressing a hand on his pounding head. It was the stress, no doubt. He waited for it to ease, then opened his eyes. He almost fell off his chair when he saw Abigail standing in front of him, red lion in her hand.

'Baby, you scared me . . .'

'Where's Mum?' she whispered. Her bottom lip curled.

'Come here.' He pulled her close. 'Mummy is coming back tomorrow. She's staying at her friend's house tonight. Okay?' He leaned back, smiling to reassure her.

She beamed lightly, embracing another hug.

'I'm so happy you're home, Abi.'

There were loud knocks at the door. Tony frowned and checked his watch; it was after half eight. It reminded him it was late for Abigail to still be awake, but it was a one-off situation and she had slept earlier, so she probably wasn't quite ready for bed just yet.

Abigail, after hearing the knocks, looked towards the door. 'Mummy?'

'Wait here,' he said, standing up off the chair, still feeling a little light-headed. He opened the door.

'Peter?'

His brother smiled at him. 'Just thought I'd stop by, see how you're doing. I was hoping to come earlier to see Abigail but got held back at a job.'

'She's still awake,' Tony said. 'Please, come in.'

Peter kicked his work trainers off and stepped into the hallway. 'Where is she?'

On cue, Abigail appeared at the kitchen door in her pink pyjamas, her curious eyes settling on their visitor.

'Hello, Abi.' Peter's voice filled the hallway and put a grin on Abi's face. She ran to him, arms out, and hugged him. Tony hadn't expected it; she was usually a quiet, reserved child, rarely showing love to anyone other than Amanda.

'Aww, bless her.' Peter's eyes were glazed as he hugged her back. He lowered to his knees and put a hand on her little shoulder. 'You looking after Daddy while Mummy is away?'

She nodded, glancing up at Tony briefly.

'Go on, Abi,' Tony said, 'go watch TV. I'm going to talk to Uncle Peter for a minute. I'll be in soon, okay . . . ?'

After she trotted off back to the living room, Peter followed his brother into the kitchen. They pulled out a chair each and sat down. 'How are you doing?'

A nod from Tony. 'Getting there.' He could imagine how rough and exhausted he looked.

'Can I make a coffee?' Peter asked. 'Ain't had one since lunchtime.' Tony said he could and observed him stand, pull two mugs from the cupboard, and drop a spoonful of coffee in each of them. When the kettle boiled, he made the drinks and brought them over to the table.

'Thanks.'

Peter took a sip, watching Tony curiously. 'You taking your pills?'

'Why do you ask?'

'Just curious.' Peter took another sip. 'I know what you're like when you're not taking them.'

Tony eyeballed his brother while had a sip of his own coffee, then he placed it down on the table. 'You're worried about me?'

'If I was being honest with you, I would say yes, I am.'

'Well, don't be.' Tony avoided his eye contact. 'I'm fine.'

'Tony, you don't look fine.' A long, awkward pause followed.

Tony stood abruptly, his legs knocking the chair back. He charged over to the worktop for a moment alone and stared into the garden, the sun just disappearing over the nearby houses, dark shadows spreading across the grass below.

Peter said nothing and watched him.

'Listen.' He turned to face his brother. 'I admit it's been hard. Jesus, I only got Abigail back last night. I thought she was gone for ever.' He realised he was speaking loudly, so toned it down a bit so Abi wouldn't hear. 'I just hope we both see Amanda tomorrow.' He let out a heavy sigh, tucked his chin into his chest, and started to cry.

Peter made his way over, putting his arms around Tony. 'I'm sorry. I know it's been tough. Of course it has. I don't have a wife and kid, but I'd go off the rails if it was me. I think you've done well, Tony.'

Tony smiled at him. 'Thanks.'

'So, let's concentrate on getting Amanda back. As long as she's back tomorrow, unharmed, let's forget what's happened. As long as everyone's safe.'

Tony smiled again, placing a hand on his shoulder. 'Yeah.' He then pulled his hand away to swipe at the remaining tears. To his left, they heard quiet footsteps and spotted Abi at the door to the hallway, her face blank and exhausted.

'You ready for bed, sweetheart?' Tony said to her.

'Mummy?'

'You'll see Mummy tomorrow, okay?' Then, to his brother, he said, 'I'm going to take her up to bed. Thanks for stopping by.' He padded over the tiled floor, bent over, and picked her up. He turned to Peter. 'Seriously though, don't worry about me. I'll be — *we'll* be fine.' He headed for the stairs. 'Right, let's get this monster to bed. We'll see Mummy in the morning.'

CHAPTER 63

Peter parked his van a few spaces down from his brother Michael's house. The street was busy. Most people were at home, settled for the night. He headed down the angled path towards their red door.

He knocked quietly, so it wasn't loud enough for Emma to come storming out and give him an earache; he knew what she could be like. Peter watched the outline of a figure approach the door through the vertical glass panes, then the door unlocked and was slowly pulled open.

'Peter?' said Michael, surprised to see him. 'What are you doing here?'

'I thought I'd pop by. I've been to see Tony and Abigail. I'm worried about him. Can I come in?'

For a moment, Michael just stared at him, then snapped out of what seemed like a daze. 'Yeah, sorry. Come in. Need to be quiet though, the kids are asleep.'

Peter walked in, gently closed the door behind him, and courteously removed his work boots.

'Through here.' Michael headed for the kitchen and Peter followed.

The smell of lavender came from a plug-in air freshener in the hallway. He entered the kitchen, where six dimmable spotlights were brightly reflecting on the grey-tiled floor. Brilliant-white bulbs shone down from the underside of white cupboards onto white marble worktops. Emma was sitting at the table looking down at her laptop over to the left, and peered up at him disapprovingly over the top of her glasses.

'Hi, Peter. What a nice surprise.' Her tone was laced with her usual unmissable sarcasm. 'What brings you here—' she glanced at her watch — 'at this time?'

'To tell Michael I've been to see Tony. I'm worried about him.'

She considered his words and stood with a smile. 'Can I get you a coffee?'

Peter nodded. 'Please.' He went over to the table and dropped into a seat beside the one Emma was sitting in.

'You've changed something in here.'

'We have,' Emma replied. 'It's been painted. We also have a new kettle and microwave.'

'You have a new cooker too,' added Peter, checking out the rest of the space around him. He spotted the wax melt on the window sill, the glow of the tealight candle bright against the darkness of the window behind it, the shadows of dusk settling in.

Emma's eyes widened. 'Mr Observant. I keep telling Michael he needs to be more observant about the things going on around him.'

Michael frowned her way but stayed silent; he couldn't be bothered with starting an argument. Instead, he sat in a chair near Peter.

'What's up with Tony?'

Peter pushed his lips together. 'Hard to say. Maybe it's just because of what's happened with Abi and Amanda. I don't know . . .'

'It's going to affect him. After four days of thinking they were both gone, he finally got Abi back.'

'Did he tell you about today at Costa?'

Emma looked over, eyebrows furrowing to the centre of her forehead.

'No, what happened?'

Peter filled them in about the note that was sent to Jack Mulberry and about the money being left at Costa.

'Four police were watching and it was taken without anyone seeing it?' Michael whistled, already knowing the story but hadn't informed Emma yet. 'That's crazy.'

Emma brought the coffees over, intrigued to find out more. 'So, what happens now?'

'We'll have to see if she turns up tomorrow. That's all the police know so far.'

Emma took a sip of hot coffee, then placed it down in front of her. 'Do they think they're linked?'

He shrugged. 'I'm not sure. I haven't spoken to them directly. They're looking for the guy who attacked Tony. A guy called Martin Forlan, but they don't know much about him. Probably a made-up name.'

Emma stood, closed her laptop, and picked it up.

'Don't move on my account,' said Peter, suddenly feeling like he was invading her space.

'No, don't be silly. I have a report to finish. I can do it upstairs.' Then, to Michael, she said, 'See you when you come up.'

'Okay.'

'Good night,' said Peter, watching her disappear into the hall, but got no reply. 'How're the kids doing?'

Michael pushed the air from his lips. 'You know, just kids. So, what do you mean, you're worried about him?'

'Not sure if he can manage Abigail on his own. Amanda did most of it anyway. If she doesn't come back in the morning, I . . . I don't know if he'll be able to do it.'

'Because of his mental state?'

'Maybe. I don't know what having kids is like, but you know what Tony is like . . . ever since the crash. And all that stuff with Layla McPherson.'

Michael nodded, understanding his point. 'He's been through a lot.' There was a pause. 'Is he taking his pills?'

'He said he was, yeah.' Peter then stood, went over to the sink, and looked out onto their garden through the window. 'You have a beautiful home, Mike .'

Michael didn't reply. Out of his siblings, he earned the most money and Emma had a great job too, so they were in a position very few people were in. Their kids got everything they asked for, and they bought whatever they desired.

'Have you spoken with Dad about all this?' asked Michael, still sitting at the table.

'Not yet.'

'Grandad isn't well, you know. Dad said about it a few days ago. They'd been in to see him. He'd attacked one of the residents, thinking he was someone from school and that he was in the schoolyard at dinner time. He even took his top off.'

Peter shook his head, but it came as no surprise. 'You're kidding?'

'Wish I was.'

'He's always been unwell. That's all I remember of him. We'd go see him and he'd just stare at you like he didn't know who you were. Tony goes to see him a lot, I think. More than I do anyway.' Peter dipped his head. 'I should make more of an effort. He won't be here for ever.' To the right of the sink, Peter noticed a few boxes piled up and a couple of packages. 'What's in them?'

'Just presents. It's Emma's birthday coming up soon. She sent me a list of the things she wanted.'

Peter turned and raised his eyebrows. 'Not sure how you cope with her sometimes.'

Michael got up, edged his chair in, and sauntered over to where Peter was so he could keep his voice low. 'She isn't that bad, mate. We're comfortable, you know. Sometimes it's easier just to agree and give her what she wants.'

Peter rolled his eyes, then noticed a small package wrapped in brown paper. He reached for it. 'What's this?'

Michael snapped his hand out, grabbing Peter's wrist. 'Don't touch it.'

Peter scowled at him, surprised by his sudden movement. 'Okay . . . I was only asking.'

CHAPTER 64

DS Fisher was standing at the front of the meeting room with the remote in her hand. It had almost become normal for her to lead the meetings in the past few weeks, due to her heavy involvement in recent cases.

DI James was happy for her to take charge and observe how she handled herself. There was, after a conversation with DCI Baker, a possibility of promotion coming up, so he wanted to test Fisher and see what she was made of.

All eyes were on her, waiting for her to begin. Pamela Boone, the senior forensic officer, was there too.

'Morning, everyone.' Her tone wasn't as upbeat as usual, and she appeared tired. She'd been up late last night, putting together a list of employees who worked at the three care homes she'd figured out each of the victims had worked at.

'We'll start with the good news,' Fisher began. 'Abigail Anderson is home safe, but the only name we have linked to her kidnapping is Martin Forlan. Have we located him yet?'

Phillips shook her head. 'No. We suspect it's a made-up name. The question is why he arranged the meeting. Was his only intention to take Abigail or was it to steal the car?'

'This the car found in the lake?' PC Jackson asked.

Fisher nodded. 'Yeah. But if he intended to keep her for four days, fed and unharmed, then return her to her grandparents, the question is why. Did he have a plan that didn't work?'

No one answered.

DI James chirped in. 'Do you have the list of employees at Costa?'

She nodded. 'I do.' She picked up a sheet of paper. 'There are six names. All working yesterday. I have their addresses and spoke to Carol Walker, the manager that was in yesterday, informing her I'll need to speak to them individually, which I'll do first thing this morning.'

'Good.' James gazed around the room. 'Does anyone have anything else other than what we already know on Tony Anderson?'

'I found an interesting article,' DS Phillips said.

Everyone turned to face him.

'A newspaper article dated back seventeen years ago when his girlfriend Layla McPherson went missing.'

'I remember that name,' James said.

A few nods around the room.

James turned back to Fisher. 'April, can you inform everyone what we were talking about earlier?'

She nodded. 'Looking into the victims — Elaine Freeman, Kathy Walker, and Joan Ellison — I noticed a similarity. They all worked in care.'

Several perplexed expressions appeared on faces around the room.

'Did they?' DS Phillips asked, looking as confused as everyone else.

She nodded. 'Yes. As we know, Elaine Freeman worked at Sunnydale Care Home when she was murdered. Joan Ellison was employed by Barton Leach Care Home but was taking time off. Kathy Walker worked in Aldach Care Home, but according to a source, she was sacked by the manager over a disagreement he didn't want to discuss.' They all absorbed her words, nodding as she went. 'So, all victims were found without eyes and missing hands. All victims looked similar in terms of appearance, height, and hair type. I've come up with a list of every employee that has worked in those places over the past three years to see if there's something unusual.' Everyone waited. 'The only link between these three homes is that they all used the same agency. Half of the employees work directly for the home, while the other half work for an agency. That way, the care home can dispose of them easier. No mess, no payouts, no holiday pay.'

'What's the agency?' James asked.

'Carry Care Limited. They're quite big, supplying carers all over Manchester. I'm heading down to their head office today to speak to one of the directors. Got a meeting with him at 3 p.m.'

'Good work, April,' James said. 'Well done. You need Matthew to join you?'

'He can if he wants.' She smiled at Phillips.

'What about the white van that took Amanda on Thursday morning?' PC Baan asked. 'Forensics were looking at it — have they found anything yet?'

Fisher nodded. 'That was next on my list, actually. Pam got back to me earlier today. They found strands of hair in the rear of the van that belong to Amanda Anderson, so we know she was definitely in the back of it.'

'What about the drivers?' James asked.

'Fingerprints were taken from the steering wheel, but so far there are no matches on the database.'

James nodded at Fisher approvingly.

'We'll go see the van owner today. According to his neighbour, he should be back today. If we can find out who's used his van, we'll be onto a winner.'

The door to Fisher's left opened. DCI Baker popped his bald head in and looked at her, then, when she wasn't the person he was looking for, he searched the room, locating DI James. 'Thomas. A word. My office.'

'Right now?'

'Right now,' said Baker before he disappeared, his quick footsteps slapping the hallway floor.

'Excuse me, folks. I won't be long. You have things to do today. I feel like this is moving forward. Stay positive. I'll catch up with you soon to see what progress we make.' DI James left the room.

Fisher stared at the open door for a few moments, then faced the room. 'Right, come on, we have work to do.'

CHAPTER 65

Michael Anderson had time to stop at his parents' house before meeting his client at 11 a.m.

He parked the car, walked up the path, and knocked on the door.

Derek was expecting him and opened it with a smile, wearing a pair of loose-fitting jogging bottoms and a grubby T-shirt. 'Nice to see you, Mike. Come on in.'

They made their way along the hallway and through to the kitchen.

'Is that the present, Son?' Karen asked him as he entered. She was sitting at the table, peering over a magazine. There was a half-full mug of coffee beside her.

'Yeah. Here you go.' He leaned over and kissed her check, then placed the package on the tabletop. Karen wasn't sure what to buy Emma for her birthday, so had asked Michael to order something from Amazon and bring it around so she could wrap it and give it to her personally.

'Thanks, Mike. You know how useless I am with all that internet stuff.'

Derek shook his head a little, knowingly. 'How've you been, Son?'

'Good. You know, busy,' he said, nodding. 'Busy with clients. Busy with the kids.'

Karen rolled her eyes.

'You spoken with Tony?' Derek asked him.

'Erm, funny you should say that. I bumped into him at the Trafford Centre yesterday, actually. He was acting weird.'

His father frowned. 'How?'

'Not sure if you've spoken to him, but Amanda's parents got a note through their door asking for fifty grand or Amanda will die.'

'Yeah, he told me about that. Is there any word yet? God, I should ring him to see what's happening.' Derek looked momentarily guilty.

'At least Abi is home safe though.'

'She is.' Derek sighed in relief. 'Now we just need Amanda home.'

Karen stood.

'Where you going?' asked Derek.

'My back is aching. I'm going to sit in the living room.'

They all took a seat on the sofas. Karen turned on the television, apparently uninterested in speaking with Michael. Ever since he'd started putting all his time into his family and his work, she'd seemed a little distant.

'So, how's Emma and the kids? Been a little while since we've seen them.'

Michael smiled at Derek. 'I know. Yeah, they're good thanks. You guys should come round to see them soon.'

Karen said nothing and maintained her focus on the television.

'That would be nice, wouldn't it, Karen?'

Karen turned to Derek. 'Huh?'

'To visit Emma and the kids. We haven't seen them in a while, have we?'

She shook her head. 'No, we haven't. We tend to see much more of Abigail really, don't we, Derek?'

Michael frowned, unsure if there was meaning behind her words, but decided not to pursue it.

'Can we get you a coffee?' offered Derek.

'Sure.'

Once Derek had left, he asked, 'How's Dad's leg? Looks bad today.'

'He has good and bad days. Today's one of the bad days.'

Yet he's the one making the coffees, Michael almost said, but decided better of it. He stared at the TV, and they sat in silence for a few moments. Michael felt a little uncomfortable, unsure if he'd done something wrong.

'Everything okay, Mum?'

'Yeah. Just tired, that's all, Son.'

Michael smiled thinly and looked around the room, letting the memories of his childhood flood back, remembering Christmastime, the tree positioned in the bay window, surrounded by presents. The unit near Karen, where she now put her coffee and magazines on, used to be closer to the tree, the place they'd leave Santa some milk and cookies. He smiled, thinking how shocked he was the next morning when the milk was gone and the cookie eaten, only crumbs left on the plate. He had a lot of great memories of this house. Playing in the back garden, playing up in the attic. Karen used to moan when they made a mess, but Michael understood her perspective better now. Looking after kids and keeping a house clean was like shovelling snow when it was snowing.

'Remember we used to play hide and seek?'

'I remember it like it was yesterday,' Karen replied. 'Remember when Dad thought you were in the attic, then went up looking for you for ages, and you and Tony were hiding in the basement?'

'Oh God, yeah, the basement. Do all these houses have them?'

'I think so. We have a young lad who often helps out with things who lives two doors down. Lad called Andy. They still use their basement for storage, I think. Your dad knows his dad from way back. He offers to do the shopping sometimes . . . which I think is nice.'

Michael nodded. 'That's kind of him.'

She pointed her finger. 'Just three doors down. He'll probably pass the window. Always taking his dog for a walk.'

She turned back to the television. A cookery show, two Italian bakers idly chatting, standing over a large island with multiple hobs, mixing bowls and plates in front of them.

Derek appeared in the doorway with a tray of three coffees and a small selection of treats. 'Got them biscuits you like, Mike,' he said, hobbling over to the coffee table in the centre of the room.

'I'll have mine here.' Karen pointed to the small table next to her.

'Dad, when did we brick up our basement? I must have been twelve or thirteen.'

Derek settled into the sofa and readjusted the position of his leg, the pain visible on his face. 'God, that's going back a while. Years ago. I don't remember, to be honest. I have a memory like a sieve nowadays.'

'Can I see it?' asked Michael, edging forward.

'See what?'

'The basement.'

'Your dad's turned it into something,' said Karen. 'Want to see?'

'Sure,' he said, standing.

Derek slid forward and struggled up.

'You alright?' asked Michael, stepping forward to aid him, but Derek held a hand up and proudly steadied himself. They left the room and walked down the hall. There was a door under the stairs, just before they reached the kitchen. Derek opened it.

'Have a look.' He turned the light switch on and moved aside.

Michael slid past his father, stepping into the small space. Derek shuffled back inside, pointing to the back of it. 'Remember the staircase was back there?'

Inside was a space around five feet wide and ten feet long. At the end of it, there used to be a door that led to a wooden staircase down into the basement.

'I remember how scary the basement was,' Michael said, smiling.

Now the space had shelving on both sides, filled with shoes and trainers, an umbrella, deck chairs, and various other items. The staircase had been blocked up more than twenty years ago and a sheet of plasterboard put in, no doubt to make it look tidier and a little warmer.

'Mum mentioned someone three doors down, guy called Andy. He still uses his?'

Derek nodded. 'For storage and various things, yeah.'

Michael glanced down at his watch. 'Right, I'll drink my coffee then I better get moving. Need to be back in time for a meeting.'

Derek switched off the light, closed the door, then followed Michael back to the living room.

'Have you spoken with your brother?' Karen said once Michael had sat and picked up his coffee.

'Yeah. I'm so glad Abigail's home.' Michael picked up his coffee, took a sip.

'We're happy about that too. . .'

Something in the way that Karen had said it was strange. She turned from the TV and stared at him.

Michael noticed it and offered a smile, but when she didn't return it, he asked, 'Everything okay, Mum?'

'We know . . .' she said.

He frowned. 'You . . . know?'

She nodded. 'About Abigail. We know about Abigail.'

'I-I don't understand.' He peered at Derek, who was also staring at him with a similar disappointment. 'You know what?'

'We know that Abigail's your child,' Karen said, matter-of-factly.

Michael was lost for words. 'I don't know what—'

'Don't bullshit me, boy.' Her voice was serious. 'We know Tony isn't Abigail's biological father. *You* are.'

CHAPTER 66

Michael sat silently in the leather chair, still as a stone. 'How do you know?'

'We got a DNA test done,' explained Derek.

'Wait — you did what?' Michael eyed them, wondering how that was possible. 'Why?'

'We've always wondered, you know,' said Karen. 'I saw similarities in Abigail as soon as she was here and told Derek about what I thought.'

'Why would you think that me and Amanda had, you know . . .' His cheeks flushed.

'I noticed the way you were together. You see, I'm very good at picking up on things. We had that party for Tony's birthday and you all stayed over. Do you remember?'

Michael did.

'We took a sample from Abigail's hairbrush and took your toothbrush.'

'You sneaky bastards.' His eyes widened.

'How could you, Son?' said Derek. 'How could you do that to your brother?'

Michael sighed. He didn't really have an answer. 'I can't explain. Emma and I . . . we went through a bad patch, I suppose.' Derek and Karen kept their eyes on him. 'The kids were hard work.'

'Kids *are* hard work!' Karen shouted. 'That's the point.' She looked away from him for a moment. 'As a parent, you need to get on with things. Kids being hard isn't a valid fucking excuse.'

Michael was taken aback by her language. It was the first time he'd ever heard her use foul language.

'Go on, then . . .' Karen persisted, scowling at him. 'Explain yourself, because your father and I would love to hear it.'

'I was out in town one night, I bumped into Amanda. She was out with her friends but sat by herself. She looked fed up. I went over, started talking. She told me that she wasn't happy with Tony, that she couldn't see a future with him. I told her that things would work out.'

He paused, feeling his cheeks warming.

'And then?'

'Then I offered to walk her home. All the taxi ranks were busy, so it was quicker to walk. We . . . we ended up kissing in a car park. Then—'

'You had sex with your brother's wife in a car park?' Derek this time.

A slow nod from Michael.

'You're disgusting. If it wasn't for my knee, I'd get up and belt you all over this Goddamn room, boy.'

His father's words hurt him the most. He looked down, ashamed, avoiding further heat from their glares.

'I suspected Abi was mine because of the dates. I spoke to Amanda about it. We were happy to forget about it and move on, pretending that everything was okay. Yes, we did something bad, but it didn't have to ruin things.'

He sheepishly looked back at them.

'But you did try and ruin things, didn't you?' Karen said.

'How do you mean?'

'Answer this one question, Mike, and then you can walk out that door. Be honest with us. Because, trust me, I'll know if you're lying to me. You've tried all your life.'

Michael nodded sheepishly at Karen, like a schoolboy in front of a headteacher. 'Okay.'

'Did you have anything to do with Abigail and Amanda's disappearances?'

The question hung in the air for what felt like an age.

'Not Amanda's . . .'

CHAPTER 67

Derek struggled up and staggered over to his son. He leaned on him, almost losing his balance, and repeatedly punched the side of his face as quickly as he could. Michael struggled under his angry father's weight, turning his head away from the blows and holding his forearms up in defence.

'Dad! Get off me!' he yelled.

Karen sat still, watching it with wide eyes, with no intention of intervening or telling Derek to stop. Michael deserved all he got.

'Dad, fucking get off me!' Michael bellowed, pulling away from his father's flying fists. He managed to restrain him for a second by grabbing his wrists, but it didn't stop Derek from headbutting the side of his face.

Michael cried out but the pain turned to anger as he overpowered his father and pushed him off, throwing him onto the floor, his head almost hitting the edge of the coffee table.

'Dad, calm the fuck down!' he shouted as he stood to his feet, stabbing a finger at him. He raised a hand to the side of his face. It was already tender; the swelling had already started. He turned to Karen. 'Don't try anything, Mum.'

She narrowed her eyes at him in disgust. 'Fucking tell me what you've done. Tell us, Michael!'

It was silent apart from Derek's huffing and puffing as he rolled onto his side and slowly got up. Exhausted, he dropped onto the sofa next to Karen, struggling to get his breath back. Michael remained on his feet to put some space between him and his parents.

'You alright?' Karen asked Derek.

'Come on, then,' said Derek. 'Let's fucking hear it.'

Michael took a breath and sat back down on the single chair. 'Amanda and I had started talking again. We both admitted we weren't happy at home. She said that her and Tony had been arguing a lot and, to be honest, as you guys know, Emma can be a nightmare. I wanted a fresh start. So did Amanda.' He breathed heavily, dropped his face into his hands, then looked up at them with tears in his eyes. 'When Tony put his car up for sale, I thought of a plan, a plan for someone to attack Tony and take Abigail, make it look like a kidnapping. This is someone I know, so I knew he wouldn't harm Abi.'

'Martin Forlan?' his father said, not quite believing what he was hearing.

Michael nodded. 'Although it isn't his real name. That's the name he made up. After he attacked Tony, he stole his car and took her back to his place.'

'Then what? What about Amanda?'

'When Tony was away on business in Darlington, she'd packed some things of hers and Abi's. When he went to meet Martin Forlan, she was going to finish packing and meet me somewhere. Then Abigail would be brought to us, and we'd drive away, start a new life together. But obviously she's missing now, so the plan didn't work.'

'I don't believe what I'm hearing.' The look on Karen's face was nothing like Michael had ever seen. 'How could you? What, so you'd leave Emma? Leave your own kids without a father?'

Michael didn't answer and looked away, embarrassed.

'You're pathetic. I can't believe you're my son!' blasted Derek, stabbing the air in his direction. 'What kind of man would do that?'

Again, Michael stayed silent, the heat of their glares prickling his skin.

'What about Amanda? Did she change her mind about leaving Tony and you got angry with her?'

'What?' Michael was confused. 'You think I've taken Amanda too. Why would I do that?'

'Why would you set up a kidnapping for your own daughter? It's clear to me that you're capable of anything.' Karen shook her head. 'Pathetic excuse for a man.'

'Once Martin had got Abi safe, and once Amanda had left with me, we'd contact him and arrange him dropping her off. But then something happened. And I swear to God I had nothing to do with Amanda going missing. I promise you. She was taken and didn't respond to Martin's calls. He didn't know what to do, so, after a few days, we decided to drive the car into the lake and scrap the whole idea. I told him to flag a taxi down and tell the driver to bring her here.'

They were both speechless.

'I'm sorry I put you through it all. I didn't know what else to do.'

'And I'm sorry you were ever my son,' said Derek. 'Now get the fuck out of my house.'

CHAPTER 68

At 3 p.m., Fisher and Phillips waited at a grubby-looking door that was in a need of a fresh coat of paint. The corners of the door were thin and flaky. The female voice on the intercom beside the door had told Fisher she'd be down soon to let them in.

They gazed around the small car park while they waited. The area seemed rough and run-down, possibly due to a lack of funding or maybe it was the people residing there, but they didn't want to speculate. The row of terraced properties, which looked more like they were used for businesses rather than personal use, needed renovating. Loose bricks rested in crevices on walls, guttering hung off overhead, drain pipes were detached, barely clinging to the walls.

'Nice place, eh?' Phillips said.

'Like the Ritz.'

The faded door opened, revealing a petite blonde woman caked in make-up. She was in her early twenties, assumed Fisher, judging by the absence of lines around her eyes and mouth. They stepped inside and followed her up a set of stairs. Moments later, they arrived at a door where they could smell something musty lingering in the air. The walls were filthy, the radiators were in desperate need of replacing, and the old rectangular strip lights above them hummed with electricity. The woman knocked on the door.

'Come in,' a croaky voice said from the other side of it.

She opened it and introduced Fisher and Phillips to the director of Carry Care Limited, a thin man in his late sixties who had whispery hair, brushed back over his tanned head. He wore a black suit that looked too big for him and wore glasses far too large for the size of his head. 'Hello, I'm Patrick Kelvin,' he said, extending a bony hand.

Fisher led first, followed by Phillips, then they both took a seat in the spare chairs at the desk.

'Can we ask a few questions?'

He nodded at Fisher. 'Yes. Please go on.'

Fisher mentioned the murder of Elaine Freeman, Kathy Walker, and Joan Ellison, then noticed the frown as if he was unsure what she was talking about.

'All three women worked for Carry Care Limited at some point, Mr Kelvin,' she said. 'All three resembled each other in some way.'

'I-I'm not sure why you're here,' he responded.

'I'd like to know if you noticed anything about them, anything that could be the link between these three women. All women were murdered and had at some point worked for this agency. A strange coincidence, wouldn't you say?'

'I would say that,' he agreed. 'I'd also say that two of the three names you've mentioned didn't work for the company at the time of their death. So, maybe not a coincidence at all.'

Fisher smiled briefly. It was clear Mr Kelvin had looked into why they were coming and what questions they were going to ask.

'Did you know them?'

'Who?'

'The three murdered women — did you speak to them?'

He smiled. 'No, none of them. To be honest, our agency employees are dealt with by other people, people that—'

'People lower down?' Phillips said, interrupting him.

He pressed his lips together. 'By other colleagues,' he corrected him. 'We have a large team here at Carry Care. You might look around this small office, and, to be honest, it's underwhelming, I admit. But we have several offices all over Manchester. This is the closest to my home so I named this the head office.'

'Hmmm,' Fisher said.

'So, if there's anything else I can help you with, I really must be getting on.'

Fisher stood, leaned forward, and shook his hand. Phillips didn't bother with the formalities. He followed Fisher out, down the rickety stairs, into the car park.

Back inside the Volvo, Phillips said, 'What do you think?'

'A strange guy. But maybe he's telling the truth. If they employ a large number of carers, chances are he's never met either Kathy, Elaine, or Joan.'

Phillips nodded, put his seat belt on. 'I could do with a coffee.'

* * *

Less than fifteen minutes later, they parked up at the Trafford Centre. Before they got out, Fisher phoned Tony Anderson to see if there were any signs of Amanda returning home yet. He said there hadn't been, but that he would let her know.

Phillips scowled as they made their way across the hectic car park. 'And this is why I don't come here. I can't be bothered with the queues.'

Fisher didn't comment as she manoeuvred around a stationary car driven by an elderly woman unable to decide where to park. As they drew near to the entrance they spotted the broken window, now boarded by a huge sheet of wood. It looked hideous, but better than a gaping hole. It certainly attracted the attention of shoppers going in and out, not knowing what had happened yesterday.

They angled left and entered Costa, immediately picking up the scent of strong coffee and sweet vanilla hanging in the air. Behind the colourful counter filled with muffins, cakes, and pastries, they were met with a smile from a young male whose name tag told them he was called Steve.

'Hello,' Fisher said, then introduced herself. 'Can we speak to the manager?'

He nodded and went out the back. A short woman with a bob came back out with him and smiled at both Fisher and Phillips. 'I wondered when you guys were coming.'

'Thanks for seeing us.'

The woman named Alison led them out the back, which, judging by the size of the café, took them both by surprise as they wandered down a wide corridor then took a right into another. The floors were covered with grey linoleum, the walls bright white and recently painted, lit by modern spotlights shining from above. A scent of bleach lingered somewhere as if it had been just cleaned. They stopped at the third door on the right, and Alison pushed down the handle and went inside. The room was square-shaped with a rectangular table in the middle, and a small worktop over to the left with a microwave, a kettle, and a sink. A small cupboard was fixed to the wall. Over to the right, there were tiny lockers you'd barely fit a pair of socks in, and a tall wooden hook, filled with hanging coats of Costa personnel.

'I heard what happened yesterday,' Alison said. 'Do you need to speak to the team members that were working yesterday?'

'If we can, yes please.'

'No problem. Five of them are here working and the other is just a phone call away. Probably get here within ten minutes if I ask him to come in, as he doesn't live far.'

One by one, Fisher and Phillips spoke to them. The first was the spotty teenager who they first saw when they came in. He nervously fiddled with his hands as he spoke, telling them he didn't know anything about the bag or the package. The next, a woman in her forties who'd worked there for eight years, also wasn't aware of any packages. At the time, she'd said, she'd been on a break, so couldn't help them. The third, a young university student who worked every Sunday and Monday, said she remembered Jack walking in and going to the back, then was too busy cleaning tables near the front to pay much attention to what he was doing. The fourth and fifth were both men in their twenties, again university students who worked outside of their studying hours. Neither recalled the event, and both apologised they couldn't be of any help.

The sixth one that came in was a thin male in his late twenties. He had bright-blue eyes, short hair, and was clean-shaven. For a moment, Fisher thought he looked familiar but couldn't place him anywhere that she may have seen him before.

'Sorry I'm late. Traffic was a nightmare,' he said, turning up nearly half an hour after Alison had phoned him.

'No worries,' Phillips started, smiling at him. 'So, you were working yesterday?'

The man nodded. 'I was. Interesting day, as it turned out.'

'How so?' Phillips tilted his head.

'You know . . . the smashed window and the bag.'

'What bag?' Fisher then asked.

The man frowned, switching his focus between them. 'The bag at the table.'

'How do you know there was a bag at the table? Did you see it?' Fisher said.

When he failed to reply, Phillips added, 'Did *you* take it? Funny how no one else knew about the bag.' Phillips turned to Fisher, raising his eyebrows.

'I know there was a bag there because my manager, Alison, said there was. She said that's the reason you called me in, to speak to me about it. Just to let you know, I know nothing about a bag. So if you want to continue to waste my time trying to trip me up, I'll just leave.'

Fisher was taken aback by his words, but, at the same time, impressed by his forthright attitude. 'Okay. So, when you took the bag, where did you take it?'

The man smiled at her. 'Come on, Detective Fisher . . .' He smiled widely. 'I didn't see a bag yesterday. I have no idea what it looks like. I didn't see anyone walk in or walk out with it. All I heard was the window being smashed and people shouting. Then, an hour later, I finished my shift, went home, and enjoyed my day. Just like any other.'

They both considered his words. Behind them, Alison walked in with an apologetic smile, filled a glass up at the sink, and left it on the side after drinking some.

Once they were alone again, Fisher said, 'Okay, well, thank you for coming in. Appreciate the time you've taken on your day off to see us.'

He stood. 'No worries, it was my absolute pleasure.'

CHAPTER 69

Peter was really worried about Tony and wanted to see what their parents thought about it. He knocked on the door, took a step back, and waited. He'd usually walk in, using his own key, but they'd changed the locks and hadn't given him a spare yet.

Derek opened the door. His bloodshot eyes sat above dark, puffy semicircles. He looked terrible. 'Hi, Peter. What brings you here?'

'Hi, Dad. You okay? You don't look too good.'

'I'm exhausted, Peter. Need to sleep.'

'I'm sorry I called. I can leave if you'd like?'

Derek smiled thinly. 'No, come in.'

They went into the living room where Karen was sitting in her usual place, watching the TV. 'We have a visitor.' She turned to him and her face lit up.

'Peter, what are you doing here?'

'I need to speak to you about Tony and Mike. I'm worried about them.'

She frowned at him and patted the seat beside her. 'Come and sit down.' He did as she asked. 'What's up, Peter?'

'I'll start with Tony.' Derek and Karen both leaned in to listen. 'I don't know if he can cope with Abigail on his own. I mean, there's no sign of Amanda yet. They have the money — I don't understand what's happening anymore.'

Karen rubbed his thigh. 'I know, Son, it's hard on all of us.'

'Amanda did most of the work with Abi. Tony's normally busy. He's . . . he's just not as capable as she is, that's all. And with his medication, and not being one hundred percent all the time . . . I worry for Abigail if Amanda doesn't come home.'

Derek sat on the other side of him and placed a caring hand on his back. 'We all do. It's been a hard week for all of us, Son.'

'Things will work out,' Karen reassured him, nodding. 'What about Mike? You said you were worried about him too.'

'Yeah, I went to see him last night. As usual, Emma was weird and went upstairs. But Mike didn't seem himself either. As if he was vacant, just kind of floating by.'

'It's hard having kids though,' said Derek. 'I know that myself from having you three.'

'There were these parcels in the kitchen,' Peter went on. 'I asked him what they were and went to grab one, then he acted weird, grabbing my wrist. I don't know why.'

'I must admit, Mike hasn't seemed himself recently.' Derek nodded. 'I might have to have a word with him about things, see how he's doing.'

'But apart from that, everything's okay?' Karen enquired.

'Yeah.' Peter smiled, and looked at the TV. 'Just wanted to see you, that's all.'

From somewhere outside, they heard someone shouting. They all frowned at each other.

'The hell's that?' Karen asked.

Derek stood and limped over to the bay window. Peter joined him, peering out onto the street.

The sound had stopped, the sound of the TV the only thing they could hear.

'See anything?' Karen was still on the sofa, watching them.

* * *

286

Peter finished his second coffee and stood. 'I really should be going, let you guys settle for the night. Thanks for the chat.'

Karen beamed at him and lovingly tapped his hand. 'You, Peter, are welcome any time.'

'I'll pop by in a few days to see how you're doing.'

'That'll be nice. Mind how you go,' said Karen, watching him leave.

Derek followed him out. 'Things alright with you, Son?'

Peter opened the door and turned to him. 'Yeah, all good, Dad. Just wish Tony and Mike were doing better.'

'I know, mate.'

They shared an emotional hug before Peter left and headed back to his car. He'd thought about seeing them more often. Working as much as he did was a good enough excuse not to, but they wouldn't be around for ever. What had happened to Amanda and Abigail over the past week had certainly taught him that life can be short and unpredictable.

Peter made his way to his work van as the darkness crept in. Before he reached the van, he heard the sound again, the same sound they heard in the living room. He stopped, frowned, and looked around, trying to find the source.

'What the fuck is that?' he whispered.

It sounded like someone shouting or moaning, but the street itself was empty — not a soul in sight. He waited in silence until he heard the sound again.

Was it coming from next door?

He walked back onto the path, slowly made his way up the driveway they shared with Gary Pullam, the guy who'd lived there for years and loved his computers and hidden cameras. Peter had never liked him, always thought there was something strange about him, something odd he couldn't quite put a finger on. Because it was shared, the driveway was wide, and ran from the path along to the rear of both properties, separating the two houses. Reaching for his phone, he turned on the torch, shone it down the driveway. When he was level with both houses, he stopped and listened, turning his head to the side.

The sound had vanished. He couldn't be sure, but it sounded like an animal, an injured dog or something. He smiled, shook his head, figuring it was a figment of his imagination, before he started back down the drive.

Then it happened again.

Moaning.

Shouting.

'What the hell is that?'

He turned back and it became clear the sound was coming from the right. From his parents' house. Was there an animal stuck down the side of the house? He went back up the drive with wide eyes, searching, his torch shining brightly on the ground as he moved cautiously. The last thing he wanted was a wild animal suddenly scurrying near his feet. He checked the side of the house. Nothing.

'What the hell is it?'

His eyes fell on the small basement window he used to look out from when he was a child. Playing hide and seek with his brothers, he remembered standing on a chair in the basement and watching them through the glass, laughing at them as they ran up and down on the driveway desperately looking for him. He knelt on the hard ground, cleaned the dirty glass with the back of his hand, and shone his light through the window, down into the basement.

Then he saw her, tied up as she lay on her front. He recognised the side of her face immediately. She opened her eyes and glared up at the dazzling light.

'Amanda . . .' he whispered.

'I really wish you hadn't seen that,' a voice said from behind him.

CHAPTER 70

Tony had been awake for ages when his phone rang early the next morning. It was DS Fisher.

'Morning, Tony. Are you at home?'

Tony said he was and wasn't planning on going anywhere in case Amanda returned. The note that was sent to Jack said she would be delivered yesterday, but so far there was no sign of her.

'I need to see you. I have some news . . .'

'Is it Amanda? Has she been found?' There was hope in his voice, something he hadn't felt for days.

'I'd rather speak to you in person. I won't be long.'

* * *

Half an hour later DS Fisher and DS Phillips pulled up. Fisher noticed Tony watching them from his living-room window. They got out and closed their doors, then went up to the house, clearly not looking forward to breaking the news to him.

'Is it Amanda?' Tony asked as he opened the door.

Fisher gave him a sad smile. 'Can we come in?'

Tony sighed heavily. 'Oh God, what's happened?'

'Please, Tony. We need to come in,' Fisher persisted. Tony stepped aside, allowing them space to enter, and motioned them into the living room, where Abi was playing with her toys; she looked up and smiled widely. It almost broke Fisher's heart.

'Please,' Tony said, 'sit down.'

They did.

'So . . .' Tony leaned forward with his hands together. 'What news?'

'I'm afraid it's bad news.' Fisher pressed her lips together. Tony waited, staring at her with glassy eyes. She went on. 'I'm sorry to tell you it's about your brother Peter. Earlier this morning his body was found in a back alley not far from here.'

'God . . . Peter?' Tony's eyes widened. 'What . . . what the hell happened?'

'I can't officially say until a post-mortem has been carried out.'

'Please . . . what happened to him?' Tony begged.

Fisher sighed. 'He was stabbed.'

CHAPTER 71

A while after Fisher and Phillips had gone, Tony sat silently in the living room with his hands covering his face, digesting what he'd been told.

Abigail was playing with her toys and occasionally glanced up at him, oblivious to the news her father had just been given. Fisher informed him their parents knew about Tony as they'd been to see Karen and Derek before calling to see him. He needed to be with them, for the comfort only they would give. He grabbed Abi's trainers and coat, wrestled them on her, and headed for the door. 'Let's go see Grandma and Grandad, okay?'

He carried her, holding on to her little red lion, out to the courtesy car, and they set off towards Karen and Derek's house.

* * *

Derek answered the door. It was obvious he'd been crying and wasn't bothered about hiding it. 'Tony.' His voice was flat, tired. 'Come in, Son.'

Tony stepped in with Abi in her arms. 'Where's Mum?'
'In there.'

In the living room, Karen sat in silence, rocking back and forth almost mechanically, tears streaming from her red, puffy eyes. She angled herself towards the door. Upon seeing Tony and Abi, she cried harder, then stood up, and padded over to him. She hugged him, then took hold of Abigail and carried her back to the sofa; Abi watched her crying but was too young to understand why.

'I don't believe it.' Tony took a seat on the single leather chair. 'I just . . . I just don't understand. The police said he'd been attacked, someone had used something hard, hit him in the head.'

Derek hobbled in and sat down next to Karen and Abi. 'Yeah, that's what that Detective Fisher said. A blow to the head.'

'Why?' Tony asked, his hands out in front of him, as if searching for an answer.

They sat in emotional silence for a minute. Then Derek said, 'Peter came here last night, you know.'

'He did?'

'Yeah. He told me he was worried about you. About the medication, looking after Abi.'

Tony frowned. 'Why was he worried about me?'

'Before he left, he said he might pop over to yours to see how you're doing.'

Tony picked up on something. 'Okay . . .'

'Did he?'

'Did he what?'

'Come over to see you?'

'He saw me on Sunday. Came to my house.'

'But not last night?'

'No, not last night. Like I said, Sunday was the last day I saw him.'

Derek pushed his lips out.

'Detective Fisher said his body was found in a back alley near your house.'

Tony rocked his head back and scowled. 'Hang on a minute, Dad. What is this?' He looked at Karen. 'Mum, what's he talking about?'

292

Karen, instead of replying, held onto Abi. 'I think it's a good idea if Abi stays with us from now on, Tony. I think Peter was right. With you being on your medication, you might not be able to loo—'

'Now hold on a fucking second here!' Tony jumped to his feet.

'See . . .' Derek pointed at him. 'He's angry, loses his rag too easy.' He looked at Karen with his hands out wide in front of him. 'This is what I was talking about. He's not well.'

'Dad, what the hell are you on about?' He felt himself starting to boil inside.

Derek peered up at him from the sofa. 'Why don't you start being honest with people. The police, for starters.'

Tony was gobsmacked, unable to comprehend his own father's words, and stared at them with so much rage, he felt like he was going to explode. 'I don't believe what I'm hearing. Are you saying that you think Peter came to my house last night and I lost my rag with him because he suggested he wasn't sure if I could look after my daughter. So then what? I hit him? Killed him?'

Derek shrugged. 'Your words, not mine, Son.'

'Are you fucking joking?' Tony snapped and gritted his teeth at his father. Abigail, who was still in Karen's arm, looked afraid of him and started to cry.

'See, Tony, you're scaring her now. Look at her.' Derek stabbed the air in Abigail's direction.

Tony lost his rag and lunged forward, pulling his arm back and swinging his fist as hard as he could at his father's face. The impact of the blow knocked him flat to the sofa with a thud.

Karen screamed and slid to the side, almost dropping Abi headfirst onto the carpet.

Tony mounted his father and hit him repeatedly in the face until his fists were numb and his father's face was covered in blood. Crimson liquid spilled onto the leather sofa beneath his swollen face, coming from his nose and cut lips.

Karen screamed, 'Stop it! Please . . .' then started to sob uncontrollably. She still held on to Abi.

Once Tony realised what he had done, he jumped off and took a few steps back, throwing his hands up to his head in despair. His father was semi-conscious, now doubled over on the sofa, moaning and groaning, blood spilling from various parts of his face. Abi tightly held on to Karen as they both watched him in fear.

'Give her to me!' he shouted at Karen.

She shook her head. 'You're a monster. She's staying with us.'

'Give her to me!' he bellowed again, his anger making them both jump. When she failed to comply, he stormed over and ripped Abi from her grasp, hurting his daughter in the process. Then he pushed Karen onto the sofa as she whimpered in terror.

He stormed out the front door with a shaken Abi in his arms, leaving Karen crying on the floor in the living room and his father with the worst beating he'd ever had.

CHAPTER 72

DS Fisher and DS Phillips were standing at Karen and Derek's door. They'd already been to see them earlier to inform them about their son Peter, but they had another question they needed to ask. While they waited, Fisher looked around the street at the old traditional semi-detached houses with long, shared driveways. The house, she guessed, must have been built in the nineteen thirties. It had aged well, each house the same as the next. Up the road, she watched a blue car slow down, pull over to the side of the road, and come to a halt. A man wearing a cap and a hoody climbed out, closed his door, and glanced over as he made his way towards his house. Fisher thought he looked familiar, but it was hard to say for definite with him wearing the cap.

'Do you recognise him?' she asked Phillips.

He turned and looked over, but by the time he did, the man had disappeared down the drive and into his house.

The front door opened, revealing Derek Anderson, his face swollen and bloody, his eye half closed. Fisher frowned. 'What on earth happened to you?'

'It was Tony,' he explained. 'He did this.'

Phillips leaned closer to inspect the damage. 'You may want to go to the hospital to get that checked. It looks bad.'

'Trust me, it feels worse.' Derek winced in pain.

'Why did Tony attack you?'

Derek shrugged. 'Tony isn't well, to be honest. He sometimes has these fits of rage that he can't control. It was the same when he was younger. I always thought the medication would settle it and calm him down.' Derek shook his head.

'Can we come in?' Fisher asked. 'There're a few things we'd like to ask you both.'

Once seated in the living room, Karen appeared at the door, offering coffee or tea. Both detectives declined. Derek's chair was covered in blood.

'You sure you don't want to go to hospital, Derek?' Fisher asked, concerned about the swelling.

'He'll be fine,' Karen said, waving it away. 'Nothing a few painkillers and some rest won't sort out. Why are you here? Is there news on Amanda?'

'Nothing yet.' Fisher gave a slight shake of the head. 'Firstly though, I'd like to speak about what happened between you and Tony. He doesn't seem the kind of guy who'd be capable of such violence. What happened?'

'I'm sure in your line of work you know that people are capable of anything, Detective.' Karen shrugged.

'Why did he do it?' Fisher pressed, eager to know.

'We argued,' explained Derek, but neither Phillips nor Fisher said anything, baiting him to explain further. 'I suggested he wasn't capable of looking after Abigail on his own.'

'You think that upset him?'

Derek nodded and smiled, stating the obvious. 'The thing with Tony is, ever since the crash, he's been different. He's quicker to anger than usual and he gets stressed easier. It used to be Peter and Michael that were always fighting with each other, and Tony would be sat in the corner smiling at them and minding his business. He was always so patient.'

'But not now?'

'No.' Derek glanced at Karen, who smiled thinly at him. 'As long as he takes his medication, he's usually fine. But with everything that's happened . . . it's a lot for anyone. The

296

thing is, I love him with all my heart, but could he look after Abigail all by himself?' He pondered his own question with some thought. 'I can't answer that.'

Fisher looked at Karen. 'What are your thoughts on that?'

'Hard to say, Detective. All I know is that he has a good heart.'

Phillips and Fisher both considered their words, and fell silent for a moment. Then Phillips asked, 'I'm not suggesting you should, but do you want to press charges against your son?'

Derek thought about it for a second, mentally calculating the consequences. 'No. If he gets in trouble and if Amanda for whatever reason doesn't return home, then there'll be no one to look after Abigail.'

'We could always look after her,' suggested Karen.

'No, I won't do that to him. I understand he's frustrated and angry. I'd be the same. So, no, I do not want to press charges against him. Have you heard anything on Amanda yet?'

Phillips said they hadn't then paused. 'Is the name Layla McPherson familiar to either of you?'

Both Karen and Derek nodded.

'Yes, she dated Tony back when he was seventeen,' Karen informed them. 'She went missing the same time they were going out together. It crushed Tony when that happened. She just disappeared. How . . . how come you're asking?'

Fisher leaned forward. 'Her name came up in our enquiries. Some of the team remember the case. Others, well, some of them weren't in the force then, me included. I was hoping you guys could add something that we didn't already know. Not sure if you're aware, but the case is still open. They never found her body.'

The room went silent for what felt like an age.

Karen and Derek exchanged a noticeable glance, then Derek said to Fisher, 'She was a lovely girl. Tony was smitten. They both were . . .'

Fisher pressed her lips together. 'So, when it happened, what were your immediate thoughts at the time?'

'God . . . it was so long ago.' Derek rocked back. 'Well, firstly, I felt bad for Tony. Losing someone at any age is bad enough, but before you're twenty, it's hard to take.'

'How long had they been together for?'

'Let me think,' Karen said as she tapped her chin. 'Not very long. Two years, maybe. I remember he cried and cried up in his room.' She pointed above her head. 'Tony's room was the one above here. We used to sit down here and could hear him — it was awful.'

Fisher bobbed her head in understanding, imagining hearing the pain of your own child's suffering.

Derek scowled at her. 'I feel like there's more to your questions than you're letting on. What is it you're trying to say? Just be upfront about it.'

'Okay, then. Do you think Tony had anything to do with Layla McPherson going missing?'

Karen's eyes widened. 'How do you mean?'

'I believe that you should never judge a book by its cover, Derek, and I also believe that people are capable of anything. From what I've seen so far — the kidnapping of Abigail, the disappearance of Amanda, the ransom demand, the death of Peter — all these things are happening around him.'

Derek stood and stabbed a finger at her. 'Are you suggesting Tony has something to do with this?'

'That's what we're trying to get to the bottom of, Mr Anderson.'

Derek turned away. 'Listen . . .' He swivelled back to them. 'I think he's going through a tough time. But is he capable of anything like that?' Pressing his lips together, he broke their eye contact for a moment. 'I'm not sure what to believe anymore . . .'

CHAPTER 73

The night before

'I really wish you hadn't seen that,' the voice said behind Peter after he'd seen Amanda down in his parents' basement. The sound startled him and he craned his neck quickly, seeing a man in his late twenties staring down at him with wide eyes. He was wearing dark clothing. The cap, along with the darkness around them, shielded much of the stranger's face.

Peter jumped to his feet. 'Who the hell are you?'

The figure stared at him. Peter could see his wide-set, dark-brown eyes, but not much else, so he angled the phone's torch up to his face. As he did, the man moved quickly and grabbed the phone with one hand, throwing a punch with the other, the man's fist colliding with the side of Peter's chin. The powerful blow rattled him, sending him crashing back to the floor near the small window he'd been looking through moments earlier.

'What the fuck?' he shouted, wriggling around on the tarmac in pain. The phone had been knocked from his hand on impact, but he could see its light somewhere near him. The figure moved closer.

'What do you want?' demanded Peter.

The man didn't answer.

Peter could hear him breathing as he bent over. In. Out. In. Out. Their faces were a few feet apart.

'I really wish you hadn't seen that,' the man repeated, this time quieter, almost a whisper, the words fading in the night around them.

Peter shuffled back a few feet to create some distance between them, and managed to climb to his feet, focusing on the stranger as he did so. A throbbing pulse pounded through his chin from the attack.

The man just stared at him silently. Unnervingly.

'Who the fuck are you?' Peter persisted.

Yet again, the man didn't answer him.

'Who the fuck are you?' Peter shouted this time, and stepped forward, finding a new lease of courage.

Peter was far from a fighter, and he'd been rattled by the man's punch, but he knew he could deliver a decent right hook if he needed too. His younger years in karate and boxing would see to that.

With his attacker still silent, Peter considered the possibility of the man not being fully aware of what was going on, perhaps being under the influence of alcohol, high on drugs, or something else. Loads of people around Manchester had those sorts of problems, so it wouldn't surprise him.

'Listen,' Peter said, 'I don't know who you are, but I'm ringing the police. You'll be done for assault.'

The man didn't move.

'I'm going to move around you now . . .' Peter shuffled to the side of the figure, making sure to leave enough room in case he went for him. As Peter moved, the man didn't shift, but his eyes did, trailing his slow, cautious movements. Peter bent over, watching him as he did so, and slowly picked up his phone from the ground, then stood, pushing it down into his pocket in case he needed both hands to deal with whatever happened next.

The man darted towards him with his right arm held high. Peter, using the muscle memory from his teenage boxing years, raised both arms and dodged the attempted attack. When the man's momentum carried him around, Peter slipped his right arm around his neck and up into his chin, then pulled him close and gripped his hands together, forming a messy but effective chokehold. After five seconds, the man's body became limp, and Peter let go, letting him slide to the ground.

'What the fuck is going on?' a voice said from Peter's right,

He looked up to see Derek, staring wide-eyed, his face full of shock. 'Jesus, is that you, Peter?'

'Dad,' he said, gasping for air. 'He attacked me.'

Derek limped over and squinted in the darkness. 'Who is it?'

'I don't know.' He pulled his phone from his jeans. 'I have a torch — hold on.' He turned on the app function, shone it down onto the attacker.

'It's Andy from a few doors down,' explained Derek. 'Wait, he hit you? Andy is the most caring lad I know. He wouldn't hurt a fly.'

'Well, he punched me in the chin, knocked me on my arse, Dad.' Peter managed to get his breath back, and suddenly remembered what he'd seen moments before he was attacked. 'Dad?'

Derek looked up. 'What?'

'Why is Amanda in your basement?'

He frowned at him. 'What? Amanda? What on earth are you talking about, Son?'

'I've just seen her in your basement — she's tied up, her arms pinned behind her back. Why is she down there?'

His scowl deepened. 'Peter, my basement has been blocked up for years. I have no idea what you mean . . .'

'Here, look!' Peter shouted, going to the small window at ground level. 'Look — she's in there . . .' Peter lowered to the ground, holding the phone's light through the window. He could see the bright glare reflecting against Amanda's weak, pale face. 'See for yourself, Dad.'

Derek left Andy on the floor unconscious, and limped over to Peter.

'Get down, have a look.'

Derek stayed standing, instead just stared down at Peter. 'I don't need to look. I know she's there.'

Peter didn't see Derek's boot hit him in the face before it was too late, and his world went black.

* * *

Peter's eyes opened slowly. The first thing he realised was a dim light coming from the other side of wherever he was, followed by the realisation that when he tried to open his mouth he couldn't; his lips were held shut by tape that was wrapped around his head. He attempted to get up from the sitting position he was in but realised his feet were tied, his arms were pinned behind him, and his wrists were tied together.

The floor below him was hard and cold. Concrete, he realised.

The space in front of him looked familiar, a space he hadn't seen for nearly twenty years. His parent's basement. He craned his neck. He could feel the throbbing of the stranger's punch and his father's kick to the face. To his right he saw his sister-in-law Amanda, tied up as she lay on her side, facing him, watching him in the dim lighting. The basement smelled horrific. Urine and faeces. He wondered how long she'd been trapped down here.

He mumbled something, but the tape bound to his mouth ensured it wasn't audible.

They were both helpless.

They heard the sounds of footsteps gradually growing louder, until a figure came into view, then another one. It was Derek and Andy coming down the old wooden stairs. His father went to the right, flicked a switch, and the cold, damp space erupted in light.

'Peter . . .' said Derek, sighing. 'Why didn't you just go home?'

Peter stared at him in amazement, wondering what on earth was going on. Why was he tied up? Why had his father attacked him? Why was Amanda there? Nothing made any sense.

Derek limped over to Peter and dropped slowly to his knees, the simple act causing a little discomfort. Andy stayed back and took a seat on the wooden stairs, cupping his chin with his hand, watching them. 'I bet you have so many questions.'

Peter frowned at his father.

'Okay,' Derek said as he leaned forward. He took hold of the tape attached to his son's face and pulled it away just enough so his mouth was free. 'Fire away . . .'

'What the fuck is going on, Dad?'

Derek simply smiled. 'It's complicated, Son. I'm sorry you were mixed up in it.'

'Whatever it is, I'm sure we can sort it out. I'm sure we can fix it,' Peter told him. 'We can fix whatever it is. Tell me.'

Derek wasted no time shaking his head. 'It's too late for that now. The damage is already done.'

'Why is Amanda here, Dad? Why is she tied up?'

'Amanda is a nosey bitch that should have kept her thoughts to herself.'

Peter glanced at her in pity. 'What did she do?' He looked at his father again. 'Tell me . . .'

'She's done plenty she should be ashamed of. Sleeping with your brother Mike for one.'

Peter scowled. 'Mike?'

Derek nodded. 'Did you know that Abigail isn't even Tony's? They had sex in a fucking car park. Can you believe it? Then, nine months later, little Abigail arrives.'

Peter's mouth opened, but nothing came out. He wasn't often lost for words.

'Unreal, isn't it? Yeah, we got a DNA test done. We'd thought it all along. Used to notice the way she looked at him. Plain as day, really, when you think about it.'

'No, I don't believe that for one second,' whispered Peter. 'Michael wouldn't do that . . . God, Amanda wouldn't do that.'

'Well . . .' His father glared at Amanda and pointed her way. 'She *did* do that. That's exactly what she *did* do.'

'So you locked her down here for four days? Took her away from Tony and Abigail? God, did you have something to do with Abigail going missing too?'

Derek appeared shocked and pointed to his own chest. 'Peter, how could you suggest such an awful thing.' He smiled. 'No . . . However, Amanda did have plans of her own.' He glared at Amanda. 'Didn't you?'

'What plans?' Peter's eyes danced between them. 'Tell me.'

'She was going to get Abi out of there, run off with Michael, start a new life somewhere. Leave Tony behind. Michael was going to leave Emma and the kids behind. Just sail off into the distance.'

'So Abi's kidnapping was . . . fake?'

'You got it, boy! It's romantic, if you stop to think about it.'

Peter's colour had drained from his face. 'I honestly don't believe what I'm hearing.'

'Every word is true, Son.'

'So you kidnapped Amanda because she slept with Mike and had a baby, or because she planned to run away with him?'

He shook his head. 'I took her because of her threats. She can't threaten me and get away with it.'

Peter frowned, briefly glancing to Amanda, then back to his father. 'Threatened you with what?'

'With what she thinks she knows.'

'And what's that, Dad? What does she think you've done? Obviously, whatever it is, it's the truth, because you've gone to this extreme.' Silence filled the basement. 'What did you do? God, what the fuck have you done, Dad?'

'The less people know, the better, so I'm going to keep it that way.'

'So now what? You're going to keep me locked up down here too? Wait, does Mum know about all this — about us being here?'

304

A smile ran across his face. 'As far as your mother is concerned, this basement is blocked up. But as you can see, it isn't . . .'

'But I remember we bricked it up twenty years ago. We helped you do it.' Peter screwed his face up, not understanding what was going on.

'You did. But one day, I decided to knock it back down. You boys were out. Your mother was working, back when she actually contributed something to this house. I knocked it down, hid the bricks down here, and built a door instead. From the outside it looks like plasterboard. Your mother asked me why I'd put plasterboard over the brick, but I said it was to make it look better. She didn't ask any questions.'

'Where is she now?'

'She's upstairs in bed, asleep. I made us a cup of coffee, put something in it to knock her out. She thinks I'm in the garage doing my DIY project. Don't worry, she'll sleep like a baby. A fucking birdbox she has me making, although wondering why it's taking so long, I'm sure.'

'Dad, why did you knock the wall down?'

'That, my boy, is something I'm going to keep close to my chest at this time.'

'So, are going to let us go? Let us both walk out and go free, let us carry on living our lives as normal?'

Derek considered his son's question for a moment, then looked at Amanda. 'Unfortunately, I can't let either of you go. You know too much.'

Peter stared at Derek. 'Please, Dad . . . don't do anything stupid here. I'm your son, for God's sake.'

'I kept Amanda alive for her father's money. I'm sure you've heard about the drop-off at the Trafford Centre?' Peter nodded. 'Well . . .' He turned slightly and pointed to Andy, who was still sitting on the wooden stairs across the basement. 'He works at Costa. We paid someone to start a fight with Jack and the other guy to break the window, giving young Andy over there enough distraction to wander out behind the counter and take it. No one saw him. No cameras were there. He put the money in his work bag, then, an hour later, walked out like any other shift. When it was safe, he came over with it.'

'Mum isn't involved in this shit, is she?'

'Your mother has no clue. I pretend like I'm living a happy little life up there with her, making her cups of tea and coffee, running around after her while she's watching her daft fucking programmes on the TV.'

'So, you have the money — now what?'

He shrugged and smiled sadly.

Amanda, over to Peter's right, started to sob, her body vibrating on the concrete.

'She would already be dead if it wasn't for your mother. Every night she watches the TV, so I can't get down here. As far as she knows, it's blocked up. Last thing I want her knowing is that it's not. It's the last thing I want anyone to know. Tonight I decided this would be the day. I got hold of some pills, dropped one in her coffee just before she went to bed. I told her I was going to finish her daft birdbox. But tonight is the night that Amanda dies. Unfortunately, you got yourself mixed up in this too . . .'

Peter looked beyond his father around the dark space, trying to think of a way out of this. To his right, past Amanda, was a worktop against the brick wall. Underneath it, an array of old cupboards and drawers, the wood so old and worn it looked like they'd fall apart at any time. To the left of that, there was a large chest freezer at least twenty years old. Peter had never seen it before but heard it gently humming in the corner.

Derek, for a moment, edged forward, almost losing his balance. 'Huh?' he said, then raised a hand to his temple, and looked confused about something. His eyes started to flutter.

'What's the matter, Dad? Someone get the coffees mixed up?' Peter laughed.

'Get the knife,' muttered Derek, his body half-turned to Andy. 'Da knife . . . gee dee naa . . .' Moments later, he passed out, his body falling forward very close to Peter, who stared in amazement.

Andy stood, went over to one of the drawers, pulled it open, and put his hand deep inside the drawer. In his hand was a long-bladed butcher's knife.

'Please, mate,' Peter begged. 'Don't do this. You don't have to do this.'

Near him, Amanda started to groan loudly, then her jeans darkened with more urine, and the space on the floor around her.

'I'm begging you, don't do this,' pleaded Peter.

Andy stepped over the unconscious Derek and drew closer.

Peter tipped his head back and screamed, 'Hel—'

Andy lunged forward and shoved the knife into Peter's chest. The blade pierced his skin like a hot knife through butter. Amanda shrieked in horror as Peter rocked back against the wall with wide eyes. Blood filled his mouth, then fell down his chin. Andy removed the knife, brought his arm back and stabbed him again, over and over and over. The sound of the blade stabbing the skin was sickening.

Amanda physically jolted as she retched, clamping her eyes shut, trying to block out the horrendous events happening a few feet from her.

Once satisfied, Andy stood, watching Peter slide down the wall onto his side. He smiled at the blood as it filled the floor around him. 'Another one bites the dust,' he said. He took a few steps back, his focus now on Amanda. 'You don't go anywhere. I'm going to take him somewhere for the police to find and come back for you. You just wait there, okay?'

Andy bent down, picked up Peter like a rag doll, and threw him over his shoulder like he weighed as much as a bag of sugar. He strode across to the wooden stairs and turned the light out.

CHAPTER 74

Derek opened his eyes. For a moment, he didn't know where he was. His head hurt: constant waves of pain running across the front of his forehead. His memory was blurred, but there was a slim recollection of crushing sleeping tablets and putting them in Karen's coffee. Maybe he got them mixed up — he couldn't remember.

He sat up in the darkness, and recognised the feel of the cold floor under him.

The basement.

'Peter . . .' he whispered, remembering he told Andy to get the knife. He looked to his left and noticed Amanda. She was still, maybe asleep, maybe not. He climbed to his feet, knee in agony as he did so, and shuffled over to the light switch on the wooden post near the foot of the stairs.

Amanda opened her eyes and stared up at him. To her right, there was a huge pool of blood and a trail to the stairs.

'Jesus, what happened?' he demanded.

There was no sign of Peter or Andy. 'Where the hell are they?'

He turned and slowly climbed the wooden stairs as quick as his knee allowed him to, frowning when he noticed the doorway to the basement stairs was closed. He gently pushed it open, stepped out into the small cupboard, turned, and edged the door closed again, making it appear untouched.

Downstairs was in total darkness.

He entered the kitchen to the left, turned on the light, and the clock on the wall told him it was 2.30 a.m.

'God . . .' he muttered. He quickly pulled out his phone, worried about Andy, Peter, and, of course, Karen upstairs. There was a missed call and a message from Andy:

Dumped the body. Coming back for Amanda.

Followed by another message:

Car has broken down. Won't make it back. You'll have to deal with Amanda.

'Shit,' he whispered, then stared into the dark hallway. He assumed Karen was asleep, but, before doing anything rash, he needed to check she really was. He tip-toed down the hall and when he reached the bottom of the stairs, a bright light came on.

'Derek?' said Karen, rubbing her eyes. 'What are you doing? It's half two in the morning. Come to bed.'

He sighed lightly in relief and shook his tired head. 'I-I must have fallen asleep. Sorry. I'm coming up now.'

He turned off the lights and made his way upstairs. After he undressed, he climbed into bed. Karen snuggled into him and fell asleep in his arms. Derek didn't sleep a wink and knew he'd have to deal with Amanda tomorrow.

CHAPTER 75

The present day

Fisher drained her coffee, put the cup on her desk, and sighed.

'That bad, eh?'

She turned to Phillips. 'I just don't get it. I can't see anything here.'

He understood her frustration. Having drawn a blank at Carry Care Limited they'd gone back to the drawing board in the Hand-Eye Killer case. Less than an hour earlier, DI James had been in to see them. He'd looked shattered, his hair messy, bags under his eyes, skin dull and dry. The worst Fisher had ever seen him.

He'd said about a recent meeting with DCI Andrew Baker, that Baker had gone through him with a tonne of bricks, demanding more from not only him, but the team as a whole. They needed results and needed them yesterday. He told James to figure out who killed Elaine Freeman, Kathy Walker, and Joan Ellison. And to quote his exact words: 'Find fucking Amanda Anderson and whoever the fuck killed Peter Anderson. The city is fucked.'

'We need results, Matthew.'

There was a buzz around her, the idle conservations of other colleagues, the tapping of keyboards, clicking of computer mice. She couldn't concentrate properly. The windows over to the left were all open, warm air drifting in and making her feel hot and sweaty. The AC units had stopped working mid-morning, which added to the exasperation of everyone, but the show had to go on.

'Hold on a sec . . .' she said, thinking.

'What is it?' Phillips asked, peeling his eyes from his own monitor.

'I have an idea.' She opened a new word document and picked up her phone, typing a number in.

'What are you doing?'

'Just wait. I'll let you know if I find anything.'

* * *

Almost an hour later, after Fisher had been on the phone to nearly a dozen people, she had a document on the screen, filled with hundreds of names, separated into three separate lists. Phillips slid over on his desk chair, and narrowed his eyes at the screen.

'What are you doing?'

She didn't reply. Instead, she scrolled down the list slowly, then, with a twinkle in her eye, said, 'There . . .'

'What is it, April?'

'You see, when I figured out our victims were carers, my first thought was finding a list of employees across all three care homes. Sunnydale, Aldach, and Barton Leach. Then we figured Carry Care was the link. But—' she raised a finger — 'maybe it had nothing to do with the agency, maybe it was something else.'

'What?' He frowned at her.

'Something to do with the patients. Is there a patient that has been in each care home?'

He tilted his head at the possibility. 'Is there?'

She pointed to the screen. 'Have a look.'

'George Anderson.' He scowled. 'Who's that?'

She opened up a profile of George Anderson. 'Look . . .'

He leaned closer to the screen, his eyes narrowing in concentration. 'Father of Derek Anderson. Derek Anderson, as in Tony Anderson's father?'

Fisher nodded twice. 'Seems so.' She picked up her phone and rang DI James.

CHAPTER 76

Fisher gathered a small team to go to the Andersons' house once they realised that George Anderson was a potential link to the three murder victims. DS Phillips went with Fisher in her Volvo. PC Baan and PC Jackson were in a marked Astra behind. Before they reached the turn into their street, her phone rang, the number coming through on her dashboard. It had the police switchboard number.

'Hello?'

'Hello, is this Detective April Fisher?'

'Yes, speaking. Who's calling?'

'My name is Rory Appleby. My neighbour told me you were at my house asking questions about my van a few days back. It seems someone has taken it? I've spoken to your operator, who's told me it's been involved in some kind of criminal activity. What's going on?'

'Yes. We believe your van has been involved in a kidnapping so we towed it to be forensically examined.'

'. . .'

'Mr Appleby?'

'And you're allowed to do that, are you? Just take whatever you want?'

'Yes, sir, we have the right to seize any vehicles that we believe have been involved in a criminal offence.'

'. . .'

'Mr Appleby?'

'When can I have it back?'

'Very soon. We're almost finished with it. In the meantime,' Fisher said, 'your neighbour mentioned that you allow others to borrow it for various things, such as moving house.'

'That's right, Detective,' he said. 'Better than it sitting on the driveway collecting dust. I really should get rid of it.'

'Can you tell me who's used it over the last two weeks?' Fisher flicked the indicator on and took a right, powering through the gears up to thirty. In her wing mirror, she noticed PC Baan following them.

'Are they in some kind of trouble?'

'If you could just name the people who've used the van, that would be a great help.'

'Okay, erm, let me think.' He fell silent for a few seconds. 'My mate Jeff had it for a few days, then he dropped it straight round Hopey's house. Just last week, Ando had it.'

'Who's Ando?'

'My mate Derek. Derek Anderson.'

'Thank you, Rory. Appreciate that.'

'Is Derek in some kind of trouble?'

'Time will tell, Mr Appleby. Thanks for calling back.'

'When can I have the—'

Fisher hung up and glanced at Phillips. 'We need to speak to Derek Anderson immediately.'

They took a left, pulled into their street, and stopped halfway down on the left. The house looked quiet — no one at the windows, no car in the driveway.

'Looks like there's no one home.' DS Phillips unbuckled his seat belt and they both got out, made their way over the small area of grass to the door.

Behind, Baan stopped their car and got out. Fisher banged on the door several times, stood back, then peered in the windows while they waited. Phillips and Jackson went around the side of the house while PC Baan came beside Fisher.

The double driveway led to a garage, and, to the right, there was a brown gate fixed to the rear of the house, preventing them access around the back.

Phillips tried to open the gate, but it was locked. He sized it up, weighing the chances of climbing it. Jackson stood back and looked down the side of the house. He spotted a small window, just above ground level. He went over to it, lowered himself, and peered in.

Phillips peered over the gate into the garden and saw no one. He took a step back and noticed Jackson leaning against the house. 'What's that, Adam?'

Jackson didn't answer.

'Adam, what is it?'

'It's a window . . .'

'See anything?'

'Oh God . . . look.' He leaned closer to the glass. 'There's someone down there . . .'

Phillips dashed over and dropped to his knees beside him. 'Let me see.' Through the glass, he saw the pool of blood and a woman tied up. He turned his head to the front of the house. 'April, we found something!'

CHAPTER 77

Tony turned the corner into his parents' street and saw the police cars. He was shaking. He couldn't grasp what Fisher had told him: Amanda had been found at his parents' address. It didn't make sense. But nothing in the last five days had made much sense.

Up ahead, an ambulance, a white Volvo, and three police cars were parked at the side of the road. Tony came to a sudden halt behind one of the marked cars and jumped out, went to the back, and pulled Abi out. She didn't have a clue what was going on.

There were people in the street watching in small groups from both sides of the road, obviously keen to know why the influx of emergency response vehicles were parked up. The two PCs were doing a great job of keeping them back behind the cordon.

Tony stared at the house, the police, and the ambulance with the rear doors open. Inside the ambulance, a female paramedic sat beside someone on a stretcher wrapped in a silver foil sheet. Another paramedic sat to the right, filling in some paperwork.

'Amanda!' shouted Tony on his approach, his wide eyes on the back of the ambulance.

Fisher heard the shout and looked down the street, spotting Tony and Abigail approaching.

'Stay here,' Fisher said to DI James, leaving him on the front door step. 'I'll deal with this.'

James grabbed the attention of DS Phillips, who was speaking to Forensics, and pointed in Tony's direction, indicating she might need help. He nodded, and walked over the grass to the approaching Tony.

'Where is she?' Tony shouted. He was frantic, moving quickly with Abi in one arm. 'Is that her?'

Fisher smiled thinly. 'Yes, Tony. She'll be okay. The paramedics are taking care of her. She'll have to go to the hospital for further assessment. She's not in a good way.'

'Move. Let me see her.' He tried to get closer.

She raised a hand to stop him, but he swatted it away.

'Tony, we need to let them help her. She's severely dehydrated and desperately needs fluids. Just please allow them to do their job.' She noticed Phillips in the corner of her eye, charging across, and shook her head at him, suggesting he should stand down. She looked back to Tony. 'Give them space, okay? You can see her, but please stay back.' Tony ran to the rear of the ambulance and the detectives slowly trailed him.

'Amanda — hey, love, it's Tony,' he said quietly, standing at the rear of the ambulance with Abi still in his arms. 'It's me. You're okay now.'

The male paramedic who was seated to the right of Amanda looked at him, offered a sad smile, then looked past him, seeing Fisher and Phillips. Fisher nodded at him, implying Tony wasn't a random lunatic and that he shouldn't be alarmed.

'Is she okay?'

The other paramedic continued aiding Amanda, inserting a needle into her wrist and setting up IV fluids. The male paramedic told him that she was stable but severely dehydrated, that she would have to go to the hospital and be treated by a doctor. He absorbed his words with tears and kissed Abigail on the forehead, who seemingly didn't recognise her mother on the trolley a few feet away.

'Tony?' Fisher said.

Tony turned, wiping his eyes. 'What the hell happened?'

'We're trying to find that out — could we go over there, give the paramedics some room to work? We need to have a chat for a moment.'

He nodded at Fisher, then followed her and Phillips a few metres over to the path. Tony stared at her and waited.

'We came here to speak with your father. When we arrived, we found Amanda tied up in the basement. There was a lot of blood near her, but she has no injuries bad enough to warrant that volume of blood. Your parents' house is currently a crime scene. We have reason to believe the blood belongs to someone else.'

'Where . . . where's my mum and dad?'

'There's no sign of them.' Fisher shrugged. 'I've tried calling a few times but it goes straight to voicemail.'

'I could try calling them?' Fisher nodded at his suggestion, and Tony plucked Amanda's phone from his jeans with trembling hands to call his dad's number. He sighed heavily and pulled it away from his ear. 'Straight to voicemail. Why was she in the basement? Tied up . . . I don't understand. Where are my mum and dad?'

'We're trying to put the pieces together, Tony. But we'll need to speak to your parents immediately. Any idea where they could be?'

He thought for a moment, and eventually shook his head. 'No.' He turned back to the ambulance. 'What happened to Amanda?'

'She was tied up and gagged, on the floor in the basement. Whether she's been there for the whole time she's been missing, we don't know. She's not well enough to talk. Once she gets looked over at the hospital, and she's better, we'll speak to her and find out what's gone on.'

Tears fell down Tony's face, and he raised a hand to wipe them away. In his arms, Abi stared up at him and raised a little hand to his damp cheek. 'Mummy,' she said.

'Mummy will be okay, baby.'

Phillips and Fisher exchanged looks and smiled thinly. At least she and Abi were now safe, away from danger.

'Why did you need to speak to my father?'

'There was something we found out,' she explained. 'I need to understand it.'

'What is it?'

'I need to speak to Derek first, then I'll tell you, okay?'

He kissed Abi's head. 'Just glad she's okay.'

Fisher looked past him to the ambulance. The female paramedic nodded, pointing at Tony. She said to Tony, 'Amanda is being taken to the hospital now. You and Abi can follow, so you can be with her.' She took a few steps towards the house where Baan was standing and waved her over. 'Would you mind going to the hospital with Tony and Abigail? Make sure things are okay?'

Baan bobbed her head. 'Yeah, certainly. Mr Anderson, you and Abi can come with me if you like, save you driving?'

He thanked her and followed her over to one of the marked cars. He was in no fit shape to drive anyway.

'Keep me updated, please, Detective,' he shouted back to Fisher, who smiled at him. Baan helped them both into the back of the police car.

Once the car disappeared, Pamela Boone, dressed in white paper coveralls and a mask pulled down under her chin, walked over to Fisher and DI James. She addressed James. 'Tom, we've found a substantial amount of blood in the basement. Judging from what the paramedics have said and lack of physical injuries to her, I'm confident it belongs to someone else.'

'Is the blood fresh?'

'Relatively, yes.'

Absorbing her words, he nodded. 'Okay.'

'We've taken a sample to be tested at the lab immediately,' she informed them.

'Good work, Pam,' he said. 'Anything else in there?'

'Yes. You two really need to come in and see for yourself. Get some overshoes on and a face mask, please. I think we'll be here for a while.'

CHAPTER 78

After putting on overshoes and collecting masks, Fisher and James anxiously followed Pamela Boone down the hall and took a left into what seemed to be nothing but a small cupboard under the stairs. Inside, at the end of the tiny space, an open doorway led to a set of wooden stairs. They could see moving torch beams and hear light conversations below, no doubt the remaining forensic team.

'What have you found, Pam?' James asked, delicately trailing her down the steps, unsure of the strength of the wood under his feet.

'Let me show you.'

When they reached the bottom, Fisher saw a pool of blood in front of them, close to the wall opposite. The crimson liquid had started to clot and change colour. The space around them was bigger than they expected, but there wasn't much there. Much of it was covered in spider webs, and there was a scent of neglect in the stagnant air. One of the forensic team — a tall, thin male who Fisher knew went by the name of Pete — was carefully rifling through a pile of cardboard boxes over to the right.

'Watch where you step.' Boone pointed at the pool of blood in front of them.

Fisher and James glared down for a few moments, their minds running wild with the awful possibilities. They pulled their attention away and observed Boone go over to the left. There was a collection of cupboards and drawers, with an old worktop that reached the wall to the right. Above that was the small window that PC Jackson had looked through to see Amanda. A thin sliver of sunlight poked in, illuminating Fisher's foot.

'Come here,' Boone said, waving them over with a gloved hand.

One of the forensics, a small woman in her mid-thirties by the name of Alex, peered into what looked like a chest freezer. They went over to join them.

'Look inside,' Boone said quietly.

Fisher leaned over, snapping her neck back immediately. 'Jesus Christ . . .'

DI James did the same. 'What on earth?' he shouted, and raised a quick hand to cover his mouth. He edged back in disgust.

Boone and Alex both remained at the freezer, looking inside.

'Who the fuck is that?' Fisher spluttered, hanging back for a moment. She plucked up the courage to go back. James gingerly did the same.

A small, frozen female body sat inside the freezer. She had a thin face and her eyes were closed. Her blonde hair had formed into long, rigid icicles, appearing to be stuck to her head. She was curled up in a sitting position, her knees almost touching her face, and her arms were tucked into her body, as if she was hiding from someone.

'What's that?' Alex said, frowning. She spotted something by the frozen feet and leaned in, the upper half of her body disappearing for a moment in the chill of the fridge. They all watched her with wide eyes, wondering what, other than the frozen body, she had seen. She slowly pulled out a small white bag; it was clear to see there was something inside of it. She meticulously curled back the rigid sides, and pulled out the item.

'Good God . . .' Fisher glared at it.

It was a frozen hand, severed at the wrist.

'Hold it for a moment,' Boone said, and went over to her forensics kit and pulled out a plastic sheet, which she carefully positioned on the floor nearby with the Fisher's help.

'I'll take it now. Thank you.' Boone told hold of the wrist and placed it down on the plastic sheeting.

Alex pointed inside. 'There's something else in here.' James moved to his left so he could have a closer look.

'I can see it,' James said weakly, unsure if he was able to stop the bile rising in his throat. He took a step back, and thought about anything else to distract him.

Alex placed her petite hand inside, grabbed the small item with her thumb and forefinger, and pulled it free of the plastic bag. She gagged, doing well not to throw up. DI James, however, didn't have his strong stomach with him today; he stumbled over to the right and vomited on the floor.

Fisher scowled his way and wondered what was in Alex's hand. 'What is it?'

Alex turned and presented the frozen eyeball. Boone stood, left the hand resting on the plastic sheet, and put her gloved hand out. Alex placed it on Boone's flat palm then watched her position it next to the amputated hand on the plastic sheet.

'Just be mindful of the objects on this sheet, please, guys,' Boone said loudly, making everyone aware.

'What the fuck is going on here?' James wearily wiped his mouth.

Fisher went back to the freezer to look at the rigid body again. To the left, near where the forensic had seen the bag, she noticed more plastic. She bent down, avoiding the frozen body as much as possible, pinching the highest point with her forefinger and thumb. In her grasp, there were two bags, very similar to what Alex had found moments earlier.

She didn't need to be a detective to work out what was in them. Another hand and eyeball.

Fisher, James, and the forensics stood back as Boone meticulously placed the items beside each other on the sheet. Six hands and six eyes.

'Looks like we found our Hand-Eye Killer, Tom,' Fisher said, looking his way. 'DCI Baker will be thrilled, I'm sure.'

'We'll get them back to the lab. Thaw them out and get some DNA,' said Boone.

Fisher thanked her. James dropped his head, and it appeared the weight of the world had slipped from his shoulders.

'We need to speak to Derek Anderson immediately,' said Fisher. 'I'll chase it up on the radio, see if we have a location on him yet.'

James gazed over to the freezer. 'We do. We also need to find out who that is. Because if the hands and eyes belong to our three victims, then who the hell is that?'

CHAPTER 79

DS Fisher contacted the town hall control room to see if there was a trace on Derek and Karen Anderson, but so far nothing had been highlighted through road traffic. In the meantime, she made her way to the hospital. Baan had informed her Amanda was in a room by herself, away from other patients, and that a doctor had set up the necessary medication.

When she arrived and explained to the receptionist who she was and who she was there to see, she went up and spoke to Dr Farrah, who informed PC Baan that Amanda was severely dehydrated with open, infected sores on her buttocks and legs from where she'd soiled herself over the time she'd been held captive. The doctor had also pointed out that she was very close to dying, and might not have lasted another day.

Before Fisher went in, Baan had informed her that Jack and Rachel Mulberry had turned up. Jack had come in raging, demanding to know what had happened to her. Tony didn't have all the answers, which led to an argument everyone on that floor could hear.

Everyone looked Fisher's way as she entered the small room. PC Baan smiled. Tony was seated next to Baan in an uncomfortable-looking chair, with Abigail on his knee. Jack and Rachel were seated on the opposite side of the bed, Jack shooting daggers at Tony.

'Hi, Detective,' Tony said, as he readjusted Abigail on his lap.

'Hey, everyone,' said Fisher, arriving at the foot of the bed. Things seemed to have calmed down.

'Hello, Detective,' Jack replied, his tone dull and flat.

Fisher studied Amanda. 'How's she doing?'

Before Tony could reply, Jack said, 'She's on the mend.' He pointed to the equipment and various wires connected to her. 'Medicated drips. She'll be okay soon.'

'Good,' replied Fisher with a firm nod.

'I *was* asking Tony but clearly he doesn't have a clue.' Jack glanced his way disapprovingly before focusing back on Fisher. 'Do we know why *our* daughter was found in *his* parents' basement?'

Fisher considered the question. It was hard to miss the anger inside Tony, so before he had the chance to retaliate, she said, 'Not yet. Their house is being searched. The whereabouts of both of Tony's parents are unknown. We have teams looking for them.'

'I just can't believe your parents would do that to her,' Rachel whispered, scowling at him as if it was his fault.

'Listen!' shouted Tony, raising a finger in their direction. 'We've been over this — I didn't know. Do . . . do you think I wanted this to happen to Amanda?'

Jack stood, puffed his chest out, and glared at him. Tony shook his head, waved it away, not reacting to him.

A nurse appeared at the door a moment later. 'For the second time, I'm going to have to ask you to keep the noise down. You're disturbing other patients on this ward. If this continues, then you'll all have to leave. You understand that?'

Fisher smiled at her. 'I'll make sure it doesn't happen again. Sorry.'

The nurse smiled thinly and backed out, disappearing along the corridor.

'As the nurse mentioned, guys,' said Fisher, 'if we could keep this to a civilised conversation, we'll be able to talk and not get thrown out of here.'

They all dipped their heads.

'Tony, can I have a word in private?' Fisher asked.

Tony nodded, stood, and handed Abigail to Jack and Rachel, then left the room. Fisher pulled the door closed so they could speak without being heard.

'Tony, we really need to speak to your parents. We've found something else down there.'

'What?'

'We found a lot of blood, but we don't think it belongs to Amanda. We've taken samples which are being analysed as we speak.'

He frowned. 'Whose blood is it?'

'We'll soon know when the results come back.'

He nodded. 'I don't understand all this — I was looking at the small room he'd converted under the stairs. It's bricked up. Or it was . . .'

'I can assure you it's well and truly open. And no doubt been used over the years. Did you definitely brick it up?'

He nodded in confidence. 'Yes. *We* did it. I remember because there was a mess. Brick mortar stained the kitchen floor. I remember Mum going crazy about it. We used to get it on our feet and trail it through the house.'

Fisher smiled thinly. 'We found something else down there . . .'

Tony's frown deepened. 'What?'

'Did you ever see a freezer in the basement?'

'A freezer?'

'Yeah.'

'I didn't even know he used the basement, never mind the freezer. He used to have a freezer in the garage years ago. An old thing, low and wide.'

'Was it grey?'

Tony nodded. 'He said he'd got rid of it because he didn't use it. Mum was so glad it had gone — she said it wasted space.'

Fisher didn't reply.

'What did you find?'

'We found a female body, three severed hands, and three eyeballs, all bagged up, the smaller items in their own individual plastic bags. Forensics have taken them to be tested at the lab.'

'Jesus . . .' He put a hand to his mouth. 'This must be a mistake, surely.'

'As you can imagine, we need to find Derek and Karen immediately.'

He sighed heavily. 'I don't believe this . . .' He trailed off, shaking his head.

'I wouldn't have either if I hadn't seen it with my own eyes.'

Before Tony had the chance to reply, Fisher's phone rang. She plucked it out and answered it. 'Hi, Matthew. What do you have?'

'We found something in the bottom of his wardrobe. We've bagged it and taken it to the station. You need to see it.'

'Can it wait? I'm at the hospital.'

'No, I'd come now. It's important, April.'

'Be there soon,' she said as she ended the call. 'I have to go,' she told Tony, whose face looked like it had been slapped.

'What is it? Have you found my parents?'

'No, but we've found something else . . .' She paused when a nurse walked by, smiling at them as she passed. 'You stay here. I'll ask PC Baan to stay and get in touch when Amanda wakes up, which hopefully won't be too long.'

She turned, briskly walked out of the hospital and back to her car, knowing whatever DS Phillips had found, it was crucial to the case.

CHAPTER 80

Fisher pulled into the station's car park, excited and nervous about what Phillips had found. For him not to tell her on the phone meant it was very important.

She walked briskly across to the rear of the building and went through the sliding doors, smiling briefly at the tired-looking receptionist who looked up from behind the desk to the left.

The office was less busy than usual; people were out and about and no doubt seeing to other things. She saw DI James standing with his arms folded near her desk, and DS Phillips sat facing him with papers in his hand — a mixture of newspaper articles and notes.

'Hey, April,' James said, turning to her. 'We found something interesting at the house.'

'Do tell.' She pulled out a spare chair, dropped next to Phillips, and eyed the papers on his lap.

Phillips handed her one of the newspapers. 'Here, have a look.'

Fisher scanned an article about Kathy Walker, how her body had been found without hands and eyes.

'Here, look at this one . . .' Phillips said, handing her another.

She set the first one down on her lap and read the next one. It was an article written on Joan Ellison, about her body being found in the same condition.

'And, as you can guess, here's another one . . .' he said.

She gazed over to see the third article on Elaine Freeman. 'Very likely our victims, then. But we'll wait for DNA to come back to confirm it.'

'Absolutely,' DI James agreed. 'But there's something else . . .'

Fisher exchanged glances between both of them. 'What?'

Phillips collected the three articles into a small pile, swivelled, and placed them down on the desk, then picked up another. It was pale in colour and so old it almost fell apart.

'When the hell is this from?' Fisher said as Phillips carefully placed it in her hand. She read it carefully, her eyes widening when she saw the name. 'Layla McPherson?'

'The body in the freezer, April.'

'Wow.'

'Exactly. The lab results will come back soon, so we'll see if they match with what we have on record.'

'Was her sample taken from twenty years ago?'

Phillips nodded. 'It was. A toothbrush and hairbrush samples were collected and stored, according to the files.'

'Jesus . . .' Fisher dipped her head, finding it hard to comprehend. 'She's been down there this whole time?'

DI James shrugged. 'Looks that way.'

Fisher tipped her head back in thought . . . could Derek and Karen Anderson be responsible for all their deaths? And whose blood was in the basement?

So many questions. So far, not enough answers.

'We urgently need—'

Fisher was interrupted by her phone ringing. She pulled it out and frowned. 'It's the switchboard.' She answered it. 'Hello?'

'Detective April Fisher?' It was a woman's voice, just above a whisper, barely audible.

'Yes, this is DS April Fisher. Who's calling?' she replied, her eyes narrowing as she focused on the sound.

'It's . . . it's Karen Anderson. I need your help.'

CHAPTER 81

'All units, all units, please tell me your availability,' PC Jackson said into the radio as he climbed into his car. He was joined by another PC, a young male in his early twenties, looking excited yet nervous about his first week on the job.

A cluster of replies let him know who was available.

'Head to the Premier Inn in Prestwich, northbound. Postcode is Mike-two-five-three-Alpha-Juliet. We have a kidnapping situation. Get there quick, but keep the sirens off. We don't want to alert anyone. Stay in touch, let everyone know your location over the next ten, fifteen minutes.'

'Roger,' someone replied.

DS Phillips and DI James joined Fisher her Volvo, hearing Jackson's message across the radio as they clipped their seat belts in.

'Come on, let's get this son of a bitch.' DI James lightly slapped her dashboard with his palm, his other hand still bandaged from when he'd cut it a few days back.

Karen had told Fisher that when they returned to the house and saw the crime-scene tape and police cars parked outside, Derek had panicked and drove away immediately. She'd said maybe it was news about Amanda, but he didn't want to hear it and sped off, driving straight to the Premier Inn in silence.

She'd asked him what the hell was going on, but he'd just said he needed to get away for a night, to think about things. He'd turned off his phone and told Karen to do the same.

'Where is he now?' Fisher had asked while Phillips and James watched her closely.

'He's gone to a shop. He took my phone though, said his battery had died or something. I'm using a phone from the lady in the room next door. I don't know what's happening, but he's scaring me.'

'What room are you in?'

Karen told her. 'Please come quick. I've never seen Derek like this before. He could be back any minute.'

Fisher pulled slowly into the car park almost twenty minutes later and spotted a police car to the right with two uniforms inside. Over to the left was another car, the reg familiar. It was PC Jackson with the new PC.

Fisher parked in what appeared to be the last remaining space and sat for a moment. 'We know the room number,' she said. 'But we don't know where Derek is. So we'll wait here, make sure he goes inside before we make our move.'

James and Phillips nodded. They were ready to go.

* * *

Derek, carrying a bag of shopping, took a right after the reception, walked down the corridor, and stopped near the end. He lowered the bag and pulled out his key card. There was a woman standing outside the room next door just further down, looking through the contents of her bag. She looked up and smiled at him, but he ignored her and went inside.

Once their door had closed, the woman pulled her phone out and texted the number that Fisher had given Karen when she'd used it minutes earlier. *He's back in room.*

'Right,' Fisher said, seeing the message come through, 'let's go.' She got out, followed by Phillips and James. They closed their doors and looked at the building. From what Karen had said, the window to their room backed onto the road out the front, so there'd be no way to see anyone approaching from the car park. PC Jackson and the new PC got out and walked over to Fisher.

'What's the plan, boss?'

She told them. They all followed Fisher inside, apart from the other two PCs, who Fisher asked to stay in the car park in case Derek somehow slipped past them. At reception, a bald man looked up from behind a high desk.

'Can I help you?'

'You can,' she said, showing him her ID. 'We need the key card for room 125, please. A matter of urgency.'

Frowning, he looked at the screen in front of him. 'We have people in that room. I'm sorry, it's taken.'

'We're not here to stay the night. We're here for the people in that room. A matter of police urgency.'

He considered it, unsure what to do. He obviously wasn't used to dealing with the police.

'We're wasting time here, sir,' pressed Fisher.

He grabbed a key card from a small pile to his right, then, after pressing a few buttons on the screen, swiped it through the card reader. 'There you go — is there anything you need me to do?'

'Just act normal, as if it's any other day.'

He told her the direction of the room.

Fisher thanked him and they quietly made their way down the corridor, eyeing the numbers as they went. Down on the left, a man stepped out, closed his door, and froze, staring at them. Fisher pulled out her ID and put a finger to her mouth. The man nodded several times and timidly passed them.

At room 125, Fisher came to a halt and took a deep breath, readying herself. Phillips and PC Jackson were by her side. DI James had positioned himself further down, know-ing he'd be useless with only one hand if anything physical happened.

She placed the key card in the slot and shouted, 'Housekeeping!' Then she opened the door quickly.

Inside, she heard a rush of feet and saw Derek pointing towards the door. 'Not now, thank you!'

PC Jackson went in first with a baton raised high, followed by Fisher. 'Police, police!' Jackson shouted.

Derek glared at Jackson and Fisher, frozen to the carpet, unsure how they'd been found.

'How . . . ?' he muttered. He then turned and scowled at Karen behind him. '*You?*'

'No, it-it wasn't me . . .'

Derek charged in her direction. 'You fucking bitch, you set me up.'

She started screaming, throwing her arms to her face, but before he reached her, PC Jackson bolted after him and threw his arm around his neck, got him in a chokehold, and pulled him back near the bed, capably dragging him to the floor.

'Get the fuck off me!' Derek squealed, trying to pull Jackson's tight grip off his throat. Jackson held on, squeezing until Derek's body went limp, then DS Phillips helped roll his hefty weight off Jackson so he could clamber to his feet.

'Good work, Adam,' Phillips said as he helped him up.

Karen sat on the chair by the window with tears streaming down her face. Fisher came over and placed a sympathetic hand on her right shoulder. 'You're safe now. You're safe.'

PC Jackson cuffed Derek, and, together with DS Phillips, hauled him to his feet as he came to.

'Karen!' he screamed as he was manhandled out of the room and down the hall.

DI James smiled at Fisher. 'Good job, April. Finally nailed him.'

She nodded. 'Let's see what he has to say back at the station.'

CHAPTER 82

Fisher pressed the button on the recording device to her right. 'My name is Detective Sergeant April Fisher. I'm sitting here with Detective Sergeant Matthew Phillips. We're interviewing Derek Anderson on the grounds of kidnapping and multiple accounts of first-degree murder. The time is 19.03 and the date is the fourteenth of August 2021. Mr Anderson had decided not to seek any representation for this interview.'

The interview room was square-shaped. A desk was positioned in the centre of it. Fisher and Phillips sat on one side; Derek Anderson, wearing a scowl, sat opposite.

There was a window of one-way glass to the right of the detectives, where DI James and PC Baan were watching.

'Mr Anderson . . .' Fisher began. 'As you are no doubt aware, we have been to your house and found some disturbing things. The forensics team have taken samples of all the items in your basement and we should be getting those results back very soon. Would you mind, for the purpose of this interview and for the recording, offering us an explanation of what we found in your basement?'

Derek said nothing. Instead, he smiled from ear to ear.

'We're ready when you are,' Fisher said, maintaining control of the anger building inside of her.

His smile faded. 'It's a long story.'

'Don't worry, Mr Anderson. We have all the time in the world.'

He took a deep breath. 'Where do I start?'

'Why don't you start with Amanda?'

'Okay . . .' He inhaled a lungful of warm air. 'Amanda found something she thought was important.'

'What did she find?'

'For whatever reason, she was in my bedroom, looking through my wardrobe. She found newspaper articles. They were about—'

'We've seen them,' Fisher interrupted, smiling. 'So, then what happened?'

'Well, she texted me, saying she knew I'd done something very wrong. I played dumb, unaware she'd seen the clippings. But when she mentioned them, I knew I had to do something. She threatened to tell Tony and the police. You see, Amanda and I have an okay relationship, but we've never been best friends.' He paused. 'I went round there to see her on Thursday morning.'

'Yes,' Fisher said, nodding. 'You went there with someone else, didn't you?'

'I did, but I'm not getting into that right now.' He stared at both of them for what felt like an age. 'So we went to see her and asked if she'd mentioned anything to Tony or anyone else. She said she hadn't, but I didn't believe her. We wrestled with her in the kitchen and she grabbed a knife.' He smiled. 'She actually went for me with it, catching my forearm with it, the silly little bitch. Then she ended up knocking her head off the counter. I think there was blood on the floor and the worktop, I'm not sure.' He scowled in thought. 'Anyway, then we put her in the van. I didn't know what else to do.'

'What happened to the knife?'

'I panicked, so put it in one of the drawers.'

'Then?'

'Then we took her home. I waited until Karen was out and we put her in the basement, out of sight.'

'The basement which you blocked up years ago?'

He nodded. 'We did block it up, yes.'

'But it's not blocked up anymore?'

He didn't answer.

There was a knock at the door. 'Come in.' Fisher turned towards it.

It edged open and PC Jackson entered with paperwork in his hand. He smiled and placed it down on the desk in front of them. Derek eyed it suspiciously, but the detectives knew exactly what it was. In silence, Fisher picked it up, opened the first page, and started reading. Less than two minutes later, she inhaled deeply and placed it face down on the table. She craned her neck to Phillips, who was watching her, and nodded at him, which told him everything he wanted to know.

'So, why isn't the basement blocked up anymore?'

'Something happened,' he explained.

'What happened, Derek?'

His eyes fell to the table. He opened his mouth but nothing came out.

'You need to tell us, Derek. We have everything on this report. Everything we need we have right here. So have some dignity and tell us what happened.'

'Layla McPherson happened.'

Fisher nodded. 'Go on . . . tell us about Layla.'

'She was seeing Tony at the time. Been seeing him for a little while. I don't know, maybe a year or two — I can't remember.' They waited, watching him. 'I was driving home after work, passed her in the street. She was walking, so I stopped to offer her a lift. It was raining at the time. Her face and hair were wet. I remember her taking her jacket off. We set off and, I don't know . . . I pulled over, went down an alley. She asked what I was doing. I explained to her that Karen and I weren't happy, that we hadn't been having sex. She told me she wasn't interested in what I was saying and tried to get out. I grabbed her, put a hand over her mouth. I-I couldn't help myself. She reminded me of an ex. Slim, big boobs. I got excited. Once I'd committed to it, I couldn't stop. I got her pants off, got on top of her, and we had sex.'

'You mean you raped her?' Fisher somehow managed to keep her voice even.

Derek winced, then shrugged as if it was nothing, which boiled DS Phillips inside.

PC Baan and DI James were both shaking their heads at him through the one-way mirror.

'Then what did you do?' asked Fisher as she tilted her head, absorbing the disgusting story.

'When I got off, she was shaking. I told her that I was sorry and didn't know what had happened. I asked her not to tell anyone, especially Tony or Karen. She said she promised she wouldn't, but there was a look in her eye which made me doubt her. And I certainly couldn't risk it. So I asked her for a cuddle, but I held on, pulling her close to me so she suffocated. Once she was dead, I didn't know what to do. I was on autopilot. I went home. By that time, it was dark. I went into the house. Karen was having a bath and said she was going up to bed. I knew she was at work the next day, so I went back outside, dragged Layla from the front seat, and put her in the boot of the car until she went to work the next day, then I knocked the wall down we'd blocked up years earlier. I parked my car near the back gate and took Layla through the back door and down into the basement. I didn't want the body to smell, so I dragged the freezer down there — I nearly fucking killed myself doing it.'

Wouldn't have been a bad thing, thought Fisher.

'So I put her body in there. Luckily, I hadn't disconnected the power.'

'Why did you block it up in the first place?'

'We didn't use it for anything other than the kids playing games and hide and seek. One time, Tony went down, twisted his ankle on the stairs, so we decided to not use it.' He paused. 'So, to hide the fact that I'd knocked it down, I built a stud wall on hinges and told Karen that I'd put plasterboard up to make it look better. She didn't have a clue.'

Fisher looked down for a moment, unable to look at his face; she was appalled. 'What about the other items we found in the freezer?'

'What other items?' he replied, frowning.

'Derek, I think you know . . .'

'If you've read the newspaper clippings and have the DNA tests back, you know that's a wasted question.'

'I'd like you to tell me, Derek.'

He frowned. 'Kathy Walker, Joan Ellison, and Elaine Freeman?'

'Why them?' Fisher scowled. 'This something to do with your dad, George?'

He raised his eyebrows. 'You've done your homework, Detective Fisher.'

'I have . . .'

'Yes, they worked in the same care homes that my father went to. The kills were simply impulses I had. I couldn't help it.'

Fisher pushed her lips out. 'Please explain . . .'

'The first was Kathy Walker. She worked in Aldach Care Home. I used to see her when I went in to see my dad. She was lovely. She was beautiful. Reminded me of another ex.'

'What was your ex called?'

'Denise.'

'Okay,' Fisher went on, 'so, what happened next?'

'Well, I thought she was being a little flirty with me. I enjoyed it. I used to go there even when I knew my dad was sleeping just to see her. But then she told me I was making her feel uncomfortable, and, before I knew it, she'd left. A few months later, I saw her in a shop somewhere. Her face was a picture when she saw me. So, I waited till she'd finished her shift and followed her home. I wanted her. She reminded me so much of Denise.'

'What did you do?'

'I knocked on her door, asked her if I could come in. Of course, she wouldn't let me, so I pushed my way in, ended up raping her too.'

'So why cut off her hand and take one of her eyes?'

The question seemed to make Derek think for a while. 'When I was with Denise years ago, I thought everything was going really well and all of a sudden, she decided that she didn't want me and left. I was heartbroken. So, because Kathy Walker resembled her so much, I couldn't help taking my anger out on her. I cut off her hands with a hacksaw so she couldn't touch anyone else and cut out her eyes so she'd only have eyes for me.'

'You're quite the sick individual, aren't you, Mr Anderson?' Fisher grimaced at him.

'Then I dumped the body.' He finished with a nod, as if ready to move on with the next chapter in the horrific story. 'I had to hide it, get away from what I'd done, so I moved my dad to a different care home. Barton Leach, it was called. And there was Joan Ellison. She looked even more like Denise than Kathy Walker did. Jesus, it could have been her double. I got to know her, this time with no intentions of raping her, but to kill her. The high I'd felt from killing Layla and Kathy was indescribable, a feeling like nothing else. I watched the way Joan was with other men, members of patients' families, how they had a twinkle in her eye when she was around. I'm not going to lie, it made me strangely jealous.'

'Why were you jealous?' Fisher asked.

'It's crazy, isn't it? But I couldn't help it. This one time, I went there to see Joan, but heard one of the carers say she'd taken time off to look after her mum, who'd fallen ill. A few months went by and I thought nothing of it. But this one time, I went in, and in one of the halls, there were photographs of the employees. I saw her face smiling back at me. It brought all the anger back. I had to find her, but the other carers wouldn't tell me where she lived. Anyway, a few days later, funnily enough I bumped into her at the petrol station. I had a spare afternoon, so I followed her to her house, waited until it was dark, went around the back of the house, and broke in. She confronted me in the kitchen. Things got a little heated, and I stabbed her in the chest. I removed her hands and used a screwdriver to dig her eyes out. I wrapped her body in some plastic I found in her garage. I then cleaned the kitchen like nothing ever happened. I dumped the body, went home, and put the hands and the eyes in with Layla's body.'

For a moment, neither Fisher nor Phillips couldn't speak. They remained in a sickened silence. A small smile found Derek's mouth; Phillips did extremely well not to dive over the table and pound his head in with his fist, although nothing would have pleased him more.

'Elaine Freeman?' pressed Fisher, suddenly finding words, desperate to get to the end of these inhumane acts.

'I had to move my dad again. I told Karen that he'd been violent to the other residents. He was fine, but it was a good excuse and they all believed it. So I put him in Sunnydale Care Home. It wasn't long before I saw Elaine Freeman. Her personality reminded me of Denise more so than her looks, but she did resemble her in many ways. This one time, we disagreed on something, and I had to get my own back. I waited for her to finish one night and asked her to come sit in the car so I could apologise and explain myself. She got in, willing to sort it out. Before she had the chance to speak, I put a knife in her throat. Blood went everywhere. Once the coast was clear, I dumped her body and cleaned the car the best I could, but I had to get rid of it. I sold it and bought the piece of shit we have now. You think I like driving around in that?'

Neither Fisher nor Phillips said a word.

'So, after dumping her body near the river, I put her hands and her eyes in a bag, put it in the freezer with the others. Believe me, I'm not a bad guy. I just have these urges I can't control.'

'There are words we use to describe people like that, Mr Anderson. Words like psychopath.'

'Bit harsh,' he replied, smiling thinly. 'What happens now?'

'Well, I'd like you to tell me who the blood in the basement belongs to.'

'Blood?'

She nodded. 'The blood next to Amanda — it doesn't belong to her, does it?'

'You have your results there.' He pointed a finger to the papers on the table. 'You tell me.'

'As you wish . . .' Fisher smiled. 'The blood belongs to your son, Peter Anderson. Did you murder him, too?'

'Actually, I never,' he said. 'I can promise you I never.'

'Who did?'

'I can't say,' he said, leaning back. 'I can almost promise you one thing though . . .'

'What's that?'

'That if you hadn't found me, I'd have carried on killing, every year till I died.'

'Well, it's a good job we did, then, isn't it?' replied Fisher. 'Tell me one thing though . . . why didn't you kill Amanda?'

'I kept her alive to get the money from her parents. They're loaded, they wouldn't miss fifty grand. Shit, I should have asked for more.'

'Why keep her alive at all?'

'Insurance, I suppose. If Jack wanted to see a picture of her or something, I could get one. I wanted to kill her as soon as I got the money, but Karen's always there, getting in my fucking way.'

'Why do you need money?'

'All the savings are gone. My dad's costing me a fortune. There's nothing left. Plus, I need a new car — the radio doesn't even work in that piece of shit.' He paused for a breath. 'Are we done?'

'We are. Enjoy your time in prison, Mr Anderson.' She stood and leaned over. 'Interview terminated at 19.41.' She pressed the stop button, smiled at Derek, and left the room.

CHAPTER 83

Fisher was emotionally drained after speaking with Derek Anderson, and focused on her next task. She parked her Volvo in one of the few remaining spots at the hospital and, for a few minutes, sat in silence with her eyes closed.

'What a day . . .' she whispered, resting the back of her head against the leather headrest.

She was soon in Amanda's room. The IV lines and drips were still hooked up to her, rehydrating her body so it returned to normal. Fisher was surprised how well she looked compared to when she'd last seen her; her cheeks had more colour, although she still looked exhausted.

'Hello, Amanda.' Fisher beamed at her. 'How are you doing?'

'I'm . . . I'm okay . . .' She looked at Fisher as if trying to recall whether they'd met.

'That's good.' Fisher stopped at the foot of her bed. 'It's great to hear, Amanda.' Fisher looked to the right of the bed where Tony was sitting with Abigail on his knee. It was obvious he'd been crying, his eyes still wet and red. 'How are you doing, Tony?'

'I'm good.' He nodded, but Fisher didn't believe him. It was no surprise considering what he'd been through.

'Are you okay giving a small statement, Amanda? I can write it up officially later. Just notes for now, if you can manage it?'

She pondered the question for a while.

'It's okay if you need rest. I know you've been through hell these past few days.'

'No, no, it's fine. I'd like to get it out of the way sooner rather than later.' She sat herself up and readied herself for the conversation. Fisher smiled and took a seat next to Tony, then pulled out a small notepad and pen from inside her jacket pocket.

'Ready when you are,' she said softly.

Amanda recalled the story about Derek and another man knocking on the door and barging their way in. She sort of recognised the other man but couldn't be sure where she'd seen him before. She said Derek was angry with her, then she began to get upset, telling DS Fisher about the newspaper clippings in the bottom of his wardrobe.

'Why were you looking in his wardrobe?'

Tony gazed her way, interested too.

'I went round there with Abigail when Tony was away. Derek was at work. I mentioned getting some shoes for Tony for an upcoming wedding, so Karen said to have a look upstairs, that Derek had plenty, so I checked the wardrobe.'

Fisher nodded.

'I told Derek about how I thought he may have been involved in the murders. They grabbed me, took me back to his house, tied me up, left me in the basement. It was horrible. He let me shit and piss myself and barely fed me. Scraps of bread, drops of water. Just enough to keep me alive.'

Fisher pressed her lips together, knowing from speaking with the doctor that her body had almost given up. Another day would have done it, Fisher recalled the doctor saying.

Tony leaned over to her, grabbed her hand, and squeezed it, disgusted at his father's actions.

'Amanda, I'm so sorry,' he told her.

She offered him a sad smile. 'It's not your fault, Tony.'

Amanda then told her about Peter. 'I didn't know why he was there in the basement with me, but he turned up. They tied him up like they did with me.'

This was all news to Tony, who glared at her with an open mouth, lost for words.

'Then Derek passed out. I heard them say something about him drugging Karen's coffee, but he must have got them mixed up. He fainted near Peter. Then . . .' She fell silent, gradually raising a palm to her mouth.

'It's okay, Amanda, take your time.'

'It . . . it sounded like Karen knew nothing about it. She didn't even know that I was down there, I'm sure about that.' A long pause. She looked away from Fisher down to the bed for a moment. Tears welled up in her eyes. 'Peter . . . he . . . oh God, it was horrible.'

'What? What happened?' Tony asked, leaning forward with a scowl.

'When your dad passed out, the other guy picked up a knife and stabbed Peter in the chest. Oh God, the sound, Tony. It . . . it . . . there was blood all over.' She covered her mouth to soften her sobs. 'Tony, it was awful. I'm so, so sorry about Peter.'

'Then what happened?' Tears filled Tony's eyes too.

'The man picked him up and left. Before he went, he said he was coming back for me. But he never did.' She broke off into tears again.

Tony clamped his eyes shut, fighting against the rage he felt for his father right now. When he calmed a little, he took a huge breath and opened his glassy, bloodshot eyes. He needed to be strong for Amanda and Abigail. After all, they'd been through so much.

'Can I have a word with you in private?' Fisher said to Tony.

Tony nodded, then asked Amanda if Abigail could stay with her. She said it was okay, so Tony put her on the chair and left the room with Fisher. Fisher informed Tony about his father out in the corridor and told him what he'd done over the years: Layla McPherson, the hands and eyeballs in the freezer. And that he'd admitted to it all. Tony broke down in tears and fell to his knees, attracting the attention of nearby nurses. Before he knew it, Abigail had wandered out of the room and was hugging him hard.

'No cry, Daddy,' she said quietly. He cried more, rubbing her small back gently. Fisher found herself teary and wiped it away, staying professional and keeping her emotions in check.

'What will happen to him?' he asked, peering up at Fisher.

'He'll go away for life. He won't see another day outside of prison, I can assure you.'

Although angry and upset, Tony was pleased to hear that. 'I honestly didn't think he was capable of such evil.'

'I know — it's hard to digest.' Fisher rubbed his shoulder. 'I'm happy for you that Amanda and Abigail are safe. I'll let you get back in there with her. I'll give you some time and I'll be in touch.'

Fisher turned slowly from him and waved at Abigail, before heading off down the corridor.

* * *

Tony watched DS Fisher go until the dark jeans and dark-blue jacket disappeared from view. He wiped his eyes and picked up Abi, then he went inside the room again.

Amanda smiled at him when he entered. She'd heard the majority of the conversation between him and DS Fisher.

'Hey,' he said as he sat down beside her. They both cried and held each other's hand for a few minutes.

'Tony, I need to be honest and tell you something.' She sniffed and wiped her eyes again.

He looked up at her. 'What is it?'

She told him how she hadn't been happy with him, about how Abigail wasn't his and was his brother Mike's. She told him that Abigail being kidnapped was a set-up and that she and Mike were going to move away, to start a new life.

Tony exploded into uncontrollable tears, letting Abi fall to the floor beside him. Devastated, he stood up and dashed around the room with his face in his hands, then he leaned on the window, breathing hard, glaring out into the darkness of Manchester with rage.

'Everything okay in here?' a nurse said, peering in from the doorway.

Amanda nodded, but Tony stared vacantly out the window, his shoulders rising and falling quickly.

Tony turned to her. 'How could you, Amanda?' He padded over. 'How could you do that to us? To fucking Abigail?'

'Tony, don't use that language around—'

'Don't you dare tell me what to do!' He pointed at her. Spittle dribbled from his mouth. 'You are a disgrace.'

'Tony . . .' She welled up again and started to sob.

'Don't you dare play the victim here.' He grunted in anger. Abigail gaped at him. 'I honestly don't know what to say.'

'Please, Tony. I made a mistake. I-I . . .'

'You *what*?'

She fell silent and didn't reply, instead hung her head and kept her eyes on the bed.

He shook his head, picked up Abigail, and walked towards the door.

'Tony? Tony, where are you going?'

'I don't want to see you right now.'

He left Amanda and took Abigail home.

CHAPTER 84

DS Fisher went to Meadow Close to visit the Andersons the following day, to make sure they were okay.

'How you guys holding up?' Fisher asked when she was settled on the sofa in his living room. She watched Abi playing with a selection of toys and her little red lion.

Tony smiled sadly. 'Amanda stayed at her parents last night. I didn't want to see her. Not after what she'd told me. It's too much to take in at the moment.'

Fisher nodded in understanding. Although she was invested in the Andersons, whether they'd try to work things out was out of her hands. She needed to drop her own feelings towards the case and focus on the next. Her sole purpose of the visit was to make sure they were safe.

'I need to see my dad,' explained Tony. 'I want an explanation. I need to look him in the eye.' He paused for a moment. 'Is that something you can arrange?'

She nodded. 'I'll arrange it.'

'Here you go . . .' Karen said from the doorway, slowly padding in with two coffees in her hand. She placed one down near Fisher. 'There you go, Detective.'

'Please, call me April,' she replied, gratefully taking the mug from her.

'Nice name, that,' Karen said. She handed Tony his coffee, before she dropped into the seat beside him.

'I'm going to see Dad,' Tony told her. 'I need an explanation.'

'Finding out your father is a monster is hard to take in. You go see him and let him know how you feel.'

Abi had lined up a row of cars, then, one at a time, moved them around the flat rug, parking them up as if using an invisible map only she could see in her head.

'I'm so glad she's safe,' muttered Karen. She took a sip of hot coffee and beamed. She reached over and squeezed Tony's hand. It was a nice moment, Fisher thought, observing them.

* * *

Two days later, Fisher picked Tony up from his house and escorted him to the prison where his father was being held. He was nervous, angry, and bitter all at the same time, but knew he had to face him.

Tony was escorted by a prison guard into a small, narrow, rectangular room, where there were three individual glass panels side by side, each panel with a seat in front of it and a telephone fixed to the left of the glass.

'Sit at the end panel please, Mr Anderson. Your father will be here soon.'

Tony thanked the prison officer and sheepishly made his way along the linoleum floor, pulled out the chair, and dropped into it. He rubbed his sweating hands and waited nervously.

The sound of a door opened somewhere, then, a moment later, Derek was escorted to the seat, his limp appearing worse than usual, hands out in front of him. He looked tired. He also had a black eye and his cheek was bruised. Tony smiled inside.

For what felt like an age, they stared at each other until Derek picked up the phone. Tony did the same.

'Hello, Son,' Derek started.

348

'Don't you ever call me that again. You are *not* my father. *You* are a pathetic waste of space and I'm happy that you'll rot in here for the rest of your life.'

Derek absorbed his son's frustration and nodded. 'I can understand that, Tony. I see you're upset. I would be too.'

'How could you — all those girls? Amanda? Your own son? Good God. You're a monster.' Tony slapped the glass to vent his anger, but it wasn't long before the prison officer warned him if he did it again, he would have to leave. He apologised and took a deep breath.

'I have nothing to say to you,' his father told him.

'How could you kill Peter?'

'I didn't kill him.'

'But you were going to, weren't you?'

Derek didn't answer, only stared vacuously at him.

'Don't you even feel bad for it — your own son?'

Derek shrugged. 'Guess I'm not the man you thought I was.'

'You're less than half the man I thought you were. And I tell you what — I hope you suffer in here every day. Once they all know what you did to those girls, you'll wish you hadn't. Hope that stupid leg causes you agony too. Seen you limping in. Has someone spotted a weakness already?'

'The only weakness I'd ever had in my life was you, Tony.'

Tony scowled at him and pointed to his own chest. 'Me? Fucking me?' He was going to bang the glass again, but thought better of it.

'Do you actually know how you crashed the car all those years ago?' his father said. 'The real reason why you have to take pills to control that broken brain of yours?'

'Yeah, I skidded off the road and went into a wall.'

Derek smiled at him.

Tony didn't like it, knowing there was something he didn't know.

'What?' Tony asked, his brows furrowed. 'Go on then, fucking tell me . . .'

349

Derek readjusted his position on the seat. 'When you came to our house that day and argued with Mum, it made me so angry. I remember you leaving. Your mum stood in the kitchen and cried, so I went after you. The roads were icy, it was too dangerous — I should have known better really.' He paused. 'So, when I managed to catch you up, I felt this fit of rage inside me. You slowed at a junction, and I slammed into the back of you. Your car went off the road and you passed out. Unconscious for three days. I hurt my damn knee and have limped ever since because of it.'

'You crashed into *me*?'

Derek nodded, almost as if he was proud of it. 'It was me. And I won't lie, I wanted to hurt you, just like you did Mum. But instead, I shattered my own knee. Then when you woke, we lied to you, saying I'd done it elsewhere the day after. We paid for your car and sorted your insurance out for you. You didn't have a clue.'

Tony was gobsmacked.

'The truth hurts sometimes, doesn't it, Son?'

Tony slowly raised from the seat and stared at his father. 'It was nice knowing you, Derek Anderson. Enjoy the rest of your life in here.' Tony glanced around like he was sarcastically admiring the place. 'You'll have fun, I'm sure. Plenty more black eyes like that, I'm sure.'

Without another word Tony lifted his head, turned, and walked away with his head high, knowing it would be the last time he would ever see his father. But before he went home, he had to go see someone first.

CHAPTER 85

Martin Forlan worked a regular job. He'd known Mike Anderson from way back; they went to school together. They'd been best friends at one point, but things changed; people moved on.

He lived in a smart, modern two-bedroomed apartment in a well-respected neighbourhood. It seemed like a nice place filled with nice people, but Tony knew that to be a lie. What went on behind closed doors often told a different story.

Tony sat in the car and waited patiently, watching the entrance to the apartment building. He glanced down at his watch; it was almost time. Almost time for Martin to come home, except it wouldn't be Martin coming home. It would be Liam Palmer. Martin Forlan never existed; it was the name Liam had used when he met Tony last week.

He drove a silver 3-series BMW, and turned into the street right on time. Tony observed the Beemer in the rear-view mirror as it approached from behind. Once it passed, it slowed and pulled into the parking space with the number seven painted on it.

The sun behind the building was just fading, the street now settling into a dusky existence.

Tony watched Liam with narrowed eyes as he got out, closed his car door, and locked it. Then, like any other day, he stepped up, placed his key in the entrance door, and opened it. Tony got out of the car and dashed over, catching the door before it closed. Liam turned, but, before realising who it was, Tony punched him in the face, knocking him back into the hallway of the building. He fell back onto the carpet and glared up in horror with a bloody, broken nose.

'Jesus . . .' Liam whispered, recognising him immediately.

Tony entered the hallway, not caring who else was there or who was watching from outside, and pounded the man's face with his fists, over and over, until they went numb.

Once Liam was unresponsive, Tony stood up, his hands aching and bloody, and stared down at him.

'I'm not usually an angry man, but if you come near my family ever again, I'll fucking kill you.'

Tony Anderson turned, closed the door on his way out, and dashed back to his car. Life was going to be different, that's for sure. He still had Abigail and his mother Karen. And that's all he'd ever need.

CHAPTER 86

After a long but rewarding day, DS Fisher and DS Phillips waved at each other before they climbed into their own cars and pulled out of the station just after 8 p.m. They'd finished their daily reports, shut down their PCs, and walked out together, glad the day was over. Fisher mentioned grabbing a bottle of wine on her way home to celebrate.

Earlier that afternoon, DCI Baker had asked DI James to bring them along to his office to speak to them about recent events, primarily finding the so-called Hand-Eye Killer and, of course, their tenacious efforts which led to the discovery of Layla McPherson's missing body.

'I'm so proud of this team,' Baker told them, giving nods of approval. He addressed James, who stood beside them. 'Thomas, you've served your department well. You too should be proud of yourself and the team.'

Fisher and Phillips smiled at Baker, appreciating the hard-earned recognition.

'Thank you, sir,' replied James, visibly inflating.

'Keep up the good work, April and Matthew. I see a very bright future for you two.'

Once Fisher had pulled up in front of her house, she tipped her head back against the headrest and stared at the end of the street; the sun was setting over Manchester, the sky around it clear and calm, just how she felt inside. It had been months since she'd felt that way.

Once she'd stripped and showered, she put on a dressing-gown, went down to the kitchen, and poured herself a glass of wine. Taking a big gulp, she tasted the quality of the smooth, rich, opulent liquid in her throat, before she carried the glass over to the back door and stepped outside onto the decking. It was still warm. She remembered the bin still needed taking out, so she left the wine on the table and opened the back gate, then dragged the bin out into the back lane.

'April?' a voice came from behind her.

'Jesus.' She jumped and threw a hand to her chest.

Marcus, a guy in his late forties who lived opposite, was also putting the bin out. 'Sorry I scared you there.'

She waved it away, smiling. 'Don't worry about it.'

As she turned back to her open gate, he said, 'I'm sorry to ask you this, but are things . . .' He fell silent for a moment. 'Are things okay?'

She frowned. 'Yes. Erm, things are . . . fine. Why do you ask?'

She didn't know Marcus very well. They'd seen each other a few times in passing, mainly when putting the bins out each week, but she could count on her hand how many times they'd interacted.

'You know, the other night?'

Her frown deepened. 'I'm sorry?'

'When you . . .' He pointed to the gate. 'When you were trying to get in.'

'I'm sorry, when was this?'

He smiled nervously, feeling a little awkward. 'I was in my kitchen and heard something. I came out and saw you banging on your gate over and over. It's no problem, but you woke our baby up. The missus wasn't too pleased. But I asked you if you were okay, and you weren't making much sense. Being honest, I was worried about you — had you been drinking? You were slurring your words a lot.'

She looked down at the cobbles in thought, wondering what night it was, then realised it must have been the same night she went out after work and met the guy in the red shirt.

'I'm so sorry I was loud, I . . . I don't remember much.' Pressing her lips together, she felt her cheeks warming.

'It's okay. Honestly. We're all entitled to a good time.' He smiled. 'You said you were locked out and had lost your keys. I offered to ring someone, but you said it was fine, then you tried climbing your fence but fell hard. I helped you up, you could barely stand, but you'd hurt your wrists.'

She couldn't remember a thing. This is why she didn't drink much anymore. 'Then what happened?'

'You asked for help to climb the fence, so . . .' He winced. 'I did. Not sure if that was the brightest move, but you weren't giving up on the idea. When you climbed it I think you hurt your legs or *somewhere else* before dropping to the other side.' He pointed down briefly between his thighs but didn't want to make her feel uncomfortable.

The bruises she found on her wrists and thighs the following morning made more sense now. She must have been dropped off at home by the taxi, lost her keys in the gravel, and decided, in her wasted state, it would be a grand idea to get over the back gate into the garden, knowing she'd left a key out there just in case.

'I'm sorry,' she confessed. 'I don't make a habit of that . . . usually.'

He grinned. 'Like I said, we're all entitled to have a good time. Was just checking you were okay after your fall.'

She smiled and thanked him before she went back inside, closing the gate behind her. From the table she picked up her wine, carried it back inside and poured it down the sink.

'No more drinking for me.'

CHAPTER 87

A few days after Tony had been to see Derek, Karen plucked up the courage to do the same. After being searched for drugs or weapons, she stepped into the visiting room feeling nervous and angry, her stomach in knots just thinking about seeing his face again.

The PO, a small guy not much taller than five feet, pointed to the last remaining chair and told her that Mr Anderson would arrive soon. She thanked him and gingerly made her way past several people sitting at the other booths, talking to inmates on the opposite side of the glass.

Derek was soon accompanied to the chair opposite and took a seat. He looked tired; his eyes were sunken and dark. One of his eyes was closed a little and slightly purple. There was a mark on his left cheek too.

She held her breath for a moment as they made eye contact.

Karen felt her heart pounding in her chest at the very sight of him but managed to grab a breath and pick up the phone to her left with a trembling hand. Derek, not breaking eye contact, leisurely reached for his phone and put it to his ear.

'Hello, Karen.'

'Hello, Derek,' she whispered.

'How've you been, dear?'

Her words clogged in her throat. 'Okay, I guess . . .'

'Bet it's good on that side of the glass.'

She nodded twice, but said nothing.

'I was disappointed what you did to me, Karen.' He pressed his lips together and looked down to the small wooden desk in front of him. 'It hurt me, you know.'

'What you did to Layla McPherson hurt me,' she replied, tears welling in the corners of her eyes.

'I know. And that's why I told you about it at the time. I wanted to be honest with you. When I married you, I told you I would be, no matter what happened. I thought we'd be able to have each other's backs on this one.'

She nodded at his words. 'Why did you do it?'

'Do what?' he asked, frowning.

'Take the fall for it?'

He smiled. 'Why should both of us be in here? We have two sons and three grandchildren out in the world. There's no point in denying them both of us.'

'Thank you, Derek.' She shuffled in her seat, making herself more comfortable. 'I'm sorry I did what I did,' she confessed. 'I couldn't help myself. You know what I get like when I feel jealous.'

'Nothing happened though, Karen.' He sighed. 'You didn't have to kill them.'

She pointed at him. 'I saw the way they looked at you when you visited your dad. And they reminded me of Denise so much I thought we were going through all of that again.'

'They were nearly half my age, Karen, for God's sake. Elaine, Kathy, and Joan did nothing wrong.'

Derek was involved in a relationship with Denise behind Karen's back in their late teens. When she found out, she nearly beat her to a pulp, forcing Denise to move away from Manchester. She was petrified of Karen.

'I couldn't risk it, Derek,' she explained with a shrug. 'I just couldn't take that risk.'

'So you thought you'd kill them to make sure?' He shook his head.

She smiled. 'Listen, we've been through all this. There's no need to reminisce about it all.'

After Derek had moved the freezer into the basement and put Layla's body inside it all those years ago, it was less than three days before he confessed. He promised to always be truthful with her no matter how hard it would be for Karen to hear. As well as giving him a black eye, she promised if he ever did it again or looked at a woman that way, she'd chop his penis off and shove it down his throat. Even to this day, he wouldn't put it past her.

He took a deep breath and absorbed her words. 'How long have you known about the basement door?'

Smiling, she shook her head in disbelief. 'You must think I was born yesterday. I've always known about the door, Derek. I heard you one time when I was upstairs and went down the following day when you were working. Let's just say I was surprised to find Layla down there, all tucked up cosy in the freezer. I'm sure you said you'd got rid of the body, but maybe you were keeping her as a trophy?'

'Same way you were keeping the hands and eyes? Why did you have to do that?'

She grinned at him. 'Sorry about that. If they don't have hands, they can't touch you. If they don't have eyes, they can't see you. I wanted to take that power away from them, Derek.'

'You told me what you did to them, but you said you got rid of the hands and eyes?' he said.

'I panicked, Derek,' she confessed. 'I thought having their body parts in the freezer with Layla was the safest option.'

'I intended to move Layla, but was scared I'd get caught,' he explained. 'The longer I left it, the worse my fear became.'

She sat in silence for a few moments.

'Why Amanda?' she asked. 'I had no idea she was down there, even though I heard you going down more often. I assumed you were checking on Layla. I was waiting for you to mention the hands and eyes but you mustn't have seen them?'

'I haven't opened that freezer in over ten years, Karen. The police telling me what they'd found came just as much of a shock to me as when you first told me you'd killed them.'

'So, why Amanda?' she persisted.

'Well, she'd found the clippings in the wardrobe of Layla. And I must say, I was amused to hear about the articles you'd added to the collection.'

'I like my trophies, as do you,' she admitted, half smiling. 'Then what?'

'Amanda messaged me, telling me she knew what I'd done, threatening to tell Tony or go to the police about it. I panicked, Karen, so me and Andy went round and grabbed her. I thought I'd get some money from her parents. You know how much we're struggling right now.'

She nodded. 'What about Peter? What did he do? You know, I'd feel sorry for you sitting there if it wasn't for him. Our own flesh and blood, Derek?'

He peeled his focus away from her and looked down, unsure what to say. 'I . . .'

'Spit it out!'

'I didn't know if I could trust him not to say anything. Amanda was there. She was obviously going to blab to the police about it. I'd taken her hostage. I didn't . . . to be honest, I wasn't going to kill him. He's our son, for God's sake. I was only trying to scare him. It was Andy who did that, not me.'

'Okay.'

'You better tell the police that Andy did it, because if I ever had the chance to get my hands on him, he'll be in the freezer too.' He was deadly serious.

A few moments of silence passed.

'Why did you tell Tony about the accident — that you crashed into him? I thought we were never going to tell him.'

'I don't know, I shouldn't have. I'm sorry.'

She didn't respond.

'As a way of apology about Peter, I took the fall for everything, Karen. I won't say a word about what you did to Joan, Kathy, and Elaine. Go and live a happy life.'

'That's exactly what I intend to do.' She placed the phone back on the receiver and stood up, knocking her chair back.

Watching her turn, he shouted, 'Karen!'

She stopped and swivelled his way. He pointed to the phone on the wall, so she leaned in and picked it up. 'What, Derek?'

'I need you to promise me something before you go.'

She nodded and waited.

'Be good from now on. Be there for Tony and Mike, and their kids.'

'I'll try.' She placed the phone back on the wall, and, after blowing him a slow kiss, she turned and disappeared through the door, smiling to herself.

EPILOGUE

A week after Amanda was home, Tony went to see his brother Michael. When he sheepishly opened the door, Tony asked him to step outside, so his wife and children couldn't hear the conversation they were going to have. Tony gave Michael time to explain himself, then punched him straight in the face. With that, he told him he never wanted to see him again and walked away. Whether Michael ever told Emma about what had happened, he didn't care.

Tony decided it wasn't going to work between him and Amanda and filed for divorce. He couldn't forgive her for what she'd done and for her plans to run away with his brother. She begged and begged him, but he was better than that.

They agreed to sell the house and, in the meantime, Tony moved out into a one-bedroom flat. He couldn't stand the sight of Amanda, but went there several times a week to pick up Abigail and take her out.

Amanda saw her parents more frequently now Tony was out of the way. Even if Amanda and Tony had made it work, they'd be on his case more than ever as they blamed him for what his father did to her, although it had nothing to do with him.

Tony visited Peter's grave several times a week and told him he loved him and missed him very much. He told him about the electrical work he wanted doing and said he'd do anything for him to be able to come over and do it.

It wasn't long before Karen sold her and Derek's house as there were too many bad memories. She bought a smaller, more manageable place and asked Tony if he wanted to move in for a while, give him chance to save up some money and find his feet. That way, she'd see Abigail more.

Karen told the police about Andy, that he was likely the man helping Derek with the murders and Amanda's abduction, but when they searched his house there was no sign of him.

Tony never saw his father again. Less than a year later, Derek was killed in an altercation with another prisoner. After hearing the news via a letter sent from the prison, Tony folded it up and put it in the bin. A month after that, he received a phone call from Sunnydale Care Home to inform him his grandfather had passed away peacefully in his sleep.

DS April Fisher and DS Matthew Phillips were commended for their efforts on the Hand-Eye Killer case by both DI James and DCI Baker. They told them both to keep working hard and striving, as the department had been given extra funds and there'd be promotions coming very soon.

DS Fisher continued giving her best, staying back later to work on her cases, but PC Baan decided to help her set up an online dating account to get herself a man. DI James also told her she needed to take time for herself, to unwind and take a break from the office. She agreed, knowing she'd still give the police her everything, but she decided it was time she went out, enjoyed herself, and started making the most of her life. She needed to see her friends more and make time for her family. If there was one thing she'd learned over the past few weeks, it was you never knew what was around the corner.

THE END

THE JOFFE BOOKS STORY

We began in 2014 when Jasper agreed to publish his mum's much-rejected romance novel and it became a bestseller.

Since then we've grown into the largest independent publisher in the UK. We're extremely proud to publish some of the very best writers in the world, including Joy Ellis, Faith Martin, Caro Ramsay, Helen Forrester, Simon Brett and Robert Goddard. Everyone at Joffe Books loves reading and we never forget that it all begins with the magic of an author telling a story.

We are proud to publish talented first-time authors, as well as established writers whose books we love introducing to a new generation of readers.

We have been shortlisted for Independent Publisher of the Year at the British Book Awards three times, in 2020, 2021 and 2022, and for the Diversity and Inclusivity Award at the Independent Publishing Awards in 2022.

We built this company with your help, and we love to hear from you, so please email us about absolutely anything bookish at feedback@joffebooks.com

If you want to receive free books every Friday and hear about all our new releases, join our mailing list: www.joffebooks.com/contact

And when you tell your friends about us, just remember: it's pronounced Joffe as in coffee or toffee!

ALSO BY C.J. GRAYSON

TANZY & BYRD THRILLERS
Book 1: THE TEES VALLEY KILLINGS
Book 2: THE DENES PARK KILLINGS
Book 3: THE LINGFIELD POINT KILLINGS

DETECTIVE APRIL FISHER THRILLERS
Book 1: TAKEN WHILE SHE SLEPT

Milton Keynes UK
Ingram Content Group UK Ltd.
UKHW010721311023
431661UK00004B/219